CRITICAL ACCLAIM FOR
BEVAN FRANK'S DEBUT NOVEL
THE MIND OF GOD

Winner
2018 Indie Reader Discovery Award for Popular Fiction

Winner
Judge's Choice Award
Killer Nashville Silver Falchion Awards

Finalist
Best thriller
Best Fiction First Novel
Killer Nashville Silver Falchion Awards

"Frank does an amazing job."
—*San Diego Book Review*

"A cocktail of Deon Meyer and *The Bourne Identity* mixed with a dash of James Bond."
—*CapeTownMagazine.com*

"Unlike any book you've ever read... if you've read Dan Brown's *The Lost Symbol*, you're already aware of Noetic Science. Frank's approach covers fresh ground."
—*BestThrillers.com*

"Robert Ludlum knew how to get you wrapped around his finger—Frank has the capabilities to do the same... Bevan Frank definitely could be the next 'big name' in international thrillers."
—*Brian's Book Blog*

"A great compelling mystery... a fast-paced adventure full of intrigue and political suspense that keeps you guessing until the last page."
—*Readers' Favorite*

"Moves along at break neck pace... a bit mystery, a little bit suspense and a whole lot of action. It reminds me a bit of Robert B. Parker's works, and also Lee Childs, James Rollins or Tom Clancy... For a first novel the writing is very tight."
—*Steven R. McEvoy, Amazon Hall of Fame and Top 100 Reviewer*

THE MIND
OF GOD

Dear Mary,
Happy reading!
Best wishes
Bevan Frank

Elm Park Publishing

BEVAN FRANK

ELM PARK PUBLISHING

The Mind of God

Bevan Frank

Copyright © 2015 Bevan Frank

All Rights Reserved

ISBN: 978-0-9933592-1-7

www.bevanfrank.com

Published in the United Kingdom by *Elm Park Publishing*

To Dana

"Someday, after mastering the winds, the waves, the tides and gravity, we shall harness the energies of love, and then, for a second time in the history of the world, man will have discovered fire."

—Pierre Teilhard de Chardin,
French philosopher and Jesuit priest (1881 – 1955)

PROLOGUE

For the first time in many years, Bob Maggins had spent the night awake. He normally enjoyed at least seven hours of sleep despite the stresses of his work. This night had been different, though.

A nauseating feeling gripped him as he stumbled around his cluttered New York City apartment. As he paced the worn Persian carpet he had inherited from his mother, he was not sure what to do next. He felt his stomach churn.

Maggins yanked open his faded brown curtains. Although it was already six am there was still no hint of sun, and he peered into the darkness below. A few streetlights flickered, while a stray cat rummaged through someone's spilled garbage.

Maggins shuffled to his kitchen and flicked on his kettle. While waiting for the water to boil, he glanced at the rickety antique table in the middle of the room. On the table was a small black object hardly noticeable next to the bunch of overly ripe bananas beside it. The object resembled a box, almost the size of two cigarette packs sandwiched together.

"What the hell?" Maggins muttered as his eyes remained transfixed on the black box. He blinked, and looked at it again. Was he dreaming? He could have sworn the box had just moved slightly. A little shake.

Impossible, he thought. Perhaps he was just exhausted and his imagination was running wild. But then again, he knew a day like this would eventually come, that something would happen. It was as inevitable as taxes and death. His stomach continued to churn. Maggins had learned over time to obey his instinct. This morning, 11 September 2001, his instinct told him something was wrong.

He shifted to the table to take a closer look at the tiny machine on the table. It seemed still.

"Am I seeing things?" he whispered.

He switched on his small Sony television, one of the few possessions his ex-wife had not grabbed after the divorce. He picked one of the sports channels and

1

turned the volume down a little. Perhaps watching golf might calm him; it usually did. There was always something peaceful about watching the sport, whether it was the soporific commentary or the tranquil green settings. But that feeling was still in his gut. He located a teabag and began to pour the boiling water.

A noise began to emanate from the machine. The noise was a low murmur, like the hissing of a snake, but it was loud enough to transcend the golf commentary.

Maggins's mouth fell open. He was oblivious of the NYU mug slipping out of his palms and crashing to the floor. He stood frozen, his gaze fixed on the contents on the kitchen table. The noise was definitely getting louder.

Maggins walked towards the tiny machine.

"It can't be... it just can't be," he tried to convince himself.

But he knew the machine was accurate. Deadly accurate. He had been working on this secret project for long enough to know that the findings of the black box were always right.

Trembling, Maggins leaned forward and stared at the black box that was now vibrating and moving around frantically on the table.

"I've got to let Macmanus know," he said. Maggins fumbled for his phone.

"Must tell Macmanus." He stumbled as sweat dripped from his forehead. "Must warn him."

He picked up his grey cordless telephone and punched in some numbers. It was a phone number he knew by heart. And he knew Macmanus wouldn't mind being woken at this hour, given what he was about to tell him.

"You've reached the phone of Eric Macmanus," a cheerful voice announced. "I am unable to take your call at the moment. Please leave a message at the tone."

"Shit." Maggins paled as the machine started to vibrate with even more intensity. "Macmanus, it... the black box... strong indication that..."

But no matter how much Maggins tried to speak, the words remained in his throat. Maggins stood there gaping at the machine.

Still holding the phone, Maggins let out a heavy groan and collapsed onto the hard tiled floor, unconscious.

CHAPTER 1

Cape Town, Present Day

Moses Noxo felt a chill as he shuffled out of his claustrophobic but warm booth. At two forty-five am, it was time for him to do his regular foot patrol around the science faculty. He zipped up his puffer jacket that clung tightly to his bulging stomach. The jacket had been a gift from the faculty staff ten years before, and remained one of his prized possessions. While Moses's stomach had continued to grow over the past decade, the jacket could only be stretched so far. Moses clasped his basic walkie-talkie onto his belt, grabbed his baton and torch, and stepped into the darkness.

He grumbled to himself as he began trudging along University Avenue. With three weeks to go until his seventieth birthday, he decided he had had enough of spending his nights as a security guard. Despite having a wife and several grandchildren to support, he believed he was getting too old to face countless cold nights at his assigned observation post.

Gone were the days when Moses, once a regional karate champion, was so nimble he could adequately protect everything in his realm. Yet, everyday at five thirty pm, he put on his faded blue uniform complete with a shiny gold Campus Control badge, and reported in for his twelve-hour shift. He was not one to give up, and although he was perhaps not as dedicated or alert as he had been in his youth, Moses grudgingly stuck to his routine in the knowledge that one day he would walk into his employer's office and give in his badge. As a general tiredness had begun to creep into his being in recent weeks, he knew that day would be coming soon.

It was not as if the science faculty at the University of Cape Town needed any security anyway. There was generally no cause for alarm at the science faculty at night, with the exception of the occasional drunk student wandering from the student residences down the road. But the university insisted on having the science faculty guarded in addition to the other parts of the campus that outsourced a private security company to which Moses didn't belong.

Moses considered himself blessed to have six grandchildren. The second oldest one, Prudence, was pregnant, the baby due in two months. Moses would soon be a great grandfather, and it was this thought that had recently helped him through the long winter nights in his security hut.

Moses reached into his pocket and took out a small magnetic frame. In the frame was a photograph of him with his family. Everybody was smiling and pointing to Prudence, who at the time when the photograph had been taken, had just announced she was pregnant.

He smiled and put the frame back into his pocket, continuing to walk his usual route. The glow of the city and surrounding views beyond the campus flickered in the distance. Other than the last of the die-hard partygoers, most people of Cape Town were in dreamland, whether sleeping in their mansions in Camps Bay, or their tin shacks in Gugulethu.

The outside of the science faculty building was in need of a facelift. The walls were facebrick but the exterior parts, not covered in ivy, had faded as the decades rolled out. After patrolling the full perimeter of the lengthy science faculty, he reached for the bunch of keys on the rusty key ring hanging on a chain around his neck, and unlocked the main door of the building.

Moses allowed the door to creak closed behind him, turning around to lock it again, but the pain from his arthritis stabbed through his throbbing hands. The less he moved them the better. Leaving the door unlocked, he headed towards the elevator. He began his rounds in the building by taking the elevator on the ground floor down to the basement area.

The basement area of the science faculty was not really frequented by students or academic staff, but was more of a storage area and used as a gathering place for the cleaners during the day. Moses switched on the lights. He scanned the area, enjoying the silence he had become used to during his shifts. Work had made him a creature of habit and Moses followed the same procedure every night. He took out his family photo again and placed it on the table, smiling as he stared at it. He was so blessed.

After coming to the conclusion that everything was in order in the basement area, Moses took the elevator to the top of the building, where he would then make his way down, floor by floor.

———

Rafik Jaffer's instructions had been clear: "Get in, get it, and get out. And if you have to shoot anyone, don't hesitate."

This assignment was no different from the other escapades he had carried out over the years. Easy money. Rafik's reputation preceded him and he was well known in various circles for his excellent work. Yet, with the recession, even his line of business had felt an impact. His savings account was becoming rapidly depleted. He knew he would soon have to start considering other options.

Rafik treaded down the long passage in the basement area of UCT's science department. He turned left down another corridor and halted. But it was just a broken mirror hanging on the wall, which had reflected his flashlight. Rafik stared at himself. He ran his fingers over the knife scar that stretched across his left cheek. The scar was courtesy of a fight he had been in when he had just entered his teens and had catapulted him into instant adulthood. Despite the scar, he looked like he was in pretty good shape. No wrinkles or anything. Just some other small pockmarks and of course his one white eyebrow. He couldn't change that.

A few minutes later, Rafik arrived at a steel door marked "Fire Exit". It had two double-barrel Yale deadlocks on it and in fact was no fire exit door. Those who did frequent the basement never went to the end of the passage anyway, and those who did didn't take much notice of a locked steel door.

Not many people knew of what lurked behind this particular steel door, but the perception of a staircase leading outside ensured that no one's curiosity was aroused. In fact, what really lay behind the door was another short passage and then another steel door.

Rafik wedged his flashlight between his teeth when he felt something brush against his foot. He leapt back, grabbed the flashlight and shone it downwards. He breathed a sigh when he saw a rat scurry off into the corridor. Somehow the darkness always made things seem worse. He had realized that early on when the nightmares had violently shaken his childhood.

Rafik stared down the cold corridor just to make sure he was not being followed. Satisfied he was alone, he hauled out a small cluster of hand-grenades welded together with brown masking tape. He stuck his self-made explosive device in between the Yale locks on the door. Seconds later, after a muffled explosion, Rafik covered his eyes and coughed as an avalanche of smoke swept through the air. He climbed through the gaping hole in the door and tried to ignore his watering eyes and ringing ears.

Soon he was at the second door. It was a plain solid steel door with no markings, not even a lock or keyhole. Mounted on the wall next to the door was a small keypad lit up by a red light. Only a few people knew the ten-digit code that would allow the steel door to swing open. Rafik Jaffer was one of them.

He paused, glanced behind him, and then focused on the keypad. His adrenalin had taken over now. He made sure his gloves were on tightly. Slowly and methodically, he pressed the digits on the keypad. The exact sequence he had memorized. After the final digit was pushed, a soft long beep went off and the red light above the keypad turned to green.

Still coughing from the smoke, Rafik pushed the door open and strolled in. *Like I thought, piece of cake!*

———

After completing his walkabout of all the floors in the science faculty, Moses headed into the elevator and made his way to the lobby. He glanced around the entrance area before leaving the building and locking the front doors.

He was almost at the hut when he put his hands in his pocket. He instinctively reached for his beloved photograph only to discover that his pockets were empty.

"Damn!" he said out loud and stopped walking. He looked towards his hut in the distance. All was quiet. No one was in sight. Moses decided to go back inside the science faculty to retrieve his prized possession. It would just take another few minutes. Soon he would be back in the hut sipping his hot Rooibos.

———

The room Rafik entered was about the size of a single garage. It was a very neat room with no windows. The walls were plastered with various charts and graphs in a myriad of colors that were of no interest to Rafik. Two simple bulbs dangling from the ceiling provided sufficient light, although there were large reading lamps on all three desks, which were situated behind each other in classroom fashion.

A large flat screen LCD monitor was perched on each of the three tables. Rafik headed straight for the middle table. Like your average computer, the monitor was linked to a solid hard drive and printer.

But this monitor was linked to something else too. Attached to a wire linked to the monitor was a small black box, almost the size of two cigarette packs sandwiched side by side. Rafik removed a blanket from his backpack, unplugged the wire, and grabbed the box. He wrapped the blanket around the box and put it back into his bag. Then, as per his instructions, Rafik lifted the large hard drive fixed under the table and placed it in the same bag.

He ignored the other computer screens that were sitting on the desks and began his exit. He had gotten what he came for and now it was time to get the hell out of there. Rafik exited the room, proceeded down the passage and went through the gap that had been created by the silent explosion of the first steel door. He coughed again as a cloud of smoke wafted past his face.

———

Moses was about to push the down button on the elevator when the throttling noise of the already-moving elevator shattered the silence he had become accustomed to on his shifts.

He stared at the changing orange light on top of the elevator; the elevator was moving up towards his floor. But he hadn't pushed the button yet. Moses scratched his head. In all the years he had been doing these shifts he had never actually encountered anyone in the building outside daytime hours. He wasn't sure what to make of it.

Perhaps it was just a faculty member catching up on some research? But surely nobody in his right mind would come in to do extra work at this time of the night? And Moses would have seen someone come into the building. But he had not seen anyone. He remembered that he had not locked the main doors earlier. Small pockets of sweat formed above his eyebrows. One pocket dripped onto his eyelid and momentarily blurred his vision. He blinked it away and ran to hide behind a stack of chairs next to a cabinet.

His breathing became heavy as he waited for the elevator doors to open. *I wonder if I should call Campus Control?* He felt for his walkie-talkie as he moved towards the wall behind the chairs and tried to lean as upright as he could so as not to be seen by anyone walking out of the elevator. He could always call Campus Control once he got a hold on the situation. *It's probably nothing. I'm sure there's a simple explanation.* He was in a spot that was out of view from someone exiting the elevator, but he would need to move forward slightly if he wanted to see what was happening. Or he could just sit still, wait a few minutes, and then hopefully the intruder would have gone. But what if it was a thief? How would it look? It was his shift. He was ultimately responsible.

Moses edged forward to try and get a view. The elevator doors hissed open and a man in dark clothing strode into the lobby. Moses stared in horror at the gun in the man's hands. He moved back to hide further, knocking into the pile of chairs that swayed before thumping to the floor. His eyes widened as the fear engulfed him like an unstoppable tidal wave. The man who had just walked out of the elevator clearly got a fright too and took a step back before eying his victim who was now exposed.

Moses didn't hesitate and rolled over to get out of the firing line. He managed to hold onto the side of one of the fallen chairs and lifted himself back onto his feet. He didn't wait to see if the intruder was going to pursue him or flee. He charged back down the corridor and then turned left down another one. At least he knew the building as if it were his own home. He reached for his walkie-talkie. Hopefully Campus Control would be there fast. But there was nothing clasped to his belt. *Dammit!* It must have fallen off when he fell over the chairs. Moses stared ahead. He was in a small canteen and student area.

He raced towards another door at the end of the area and soon found himself in another passage. He stopped to catch his breath. He was wheezing now and held his arm over his mouth. Underneath his jacket his shirt was drenched. He couldn't remember when he had last sweated so much. He turned to look behind him but there was no one there. Other than his breathing and the shrill of a cricket, there was silence. Maybe he'd lost him?

Moses's movements were becoming slower. He headed towards some glass doors ahead of him. They would lead to a little garden. He arrived at the glass doors but was almost in tears when he realized that it was not only his walkie-talkie he had lost, but his bunch of keys too. *This can't be happening to me.*

A distant echo of footsteps became louder as someone marched towards the canteen area. Moses paled as he heard his assailant and sprinted toward the serving counter that bordered the canteen. He crouched behind it and prayed the intruder would not hear the thumping of his heart.

"I know you're in here," the man said. "You can run but you can't hide."

Moses tried to crouch even lower. He heard the footsteps head towards him. They were almost upon him when the assailant stopped.

"Come out now." The words were slow but firm.

Moses bit his lip. The sweat was rushing down his face but he dared not wipe it away. He dared not move. The footsteps seemed to head away from the counter. Moses heard the sound of the glass doors being pushed.

"These doors are locked so you're obviously in here somewhere."

If the intruder was near the glass doors, it meant that he was at least two hundred meters from the counter. Moses had to do something quickly. *It's now or never.* He leaned towards the edge of the counter and peered out sideways. His assailant was dressed in black but his beanie had been removed. His back was turned away from Moses.

Moses took a deep breath and ran towards the door he had moments ago come through.

"Stop!" The man charged towards the door. But before he could fire his pistol Moses had disappeared down the corridor.

Moses hadn't known he was capable of running so fast. He had to get back to his walkie-talkie so he could call for backup. Soon he was huffing near the area where he had fallen. If he could just grab the walkie-talkie and carry on running, there was another passage he could take refuge in. But the walkie-talkie was nowhere to be seen. Moses kicked some of the scattered chairs into the path of his attacker, hoping they would block his path. He jumped behind the cabinet near where he had originally fallen and waited.

Seconds later the man appeared. He stopped just short of some of the chairs. He stood there looking around in the darkness.

"I've had enough of this!" the intruder shouted. "You've wasted my time. I'm outta here."

Moses listened to the footsteps head towards the elevator. He heard the doors open as the area momentarily lit up. Then the doors closed again and darkness ensued once more. Moses sighed. He could hear the soft throttling of the elevator as it began to move upwards. Soon there was silence. Moses stepped out from behind the cabinet and headed towards the light switch that was on the opposite wall. He needed to find that walkie-talkie. The intruder needed to be apprehended before he left campus.

Moses flicked on the lights and turned to see if the walkie-talkie was lying under one of the fallen chairs. *It has to be here!*

"Looking for this?" Moses stared up at his attacker waving the walkie-talkie in one hand and aiming his weapon with the other.

The last face Moses Noxo saw was the cold grimace of his assailant pulling the trigger of his automatic pistol, complete with silencer. The man fired twice. Once in Moses's chest, and once in his forehead. The security officer fell to the ground instantly, his final flash of thought that he would never see his family again.

CHAPTER 2

Professor Greene stared at the computer screen and shouted with delight. After many months of observations and further research, he had made a breakthrough in his scientific project, the one that he had been aiming for.

Eyes still on the screen, he reached for his cup of chamomile tea and sipped it, not even registering that the water he had boiled over an hour ago was now cold.

It was late in the night but Professor Greene was oblivious of the time. Sitting in his private study in the comfort of his suburban Rondebosch home, the professor leaned forward on his stool, accidentally knocking off the small pillow he used to support his back. The room was littered with piles of paper and several graphs in various colors had been puttied onto the walls. A large calendar depicting a pack of African wild dogs basking in the sun broke the statistical monotony of the décor. Professor Greene wiped some of the tea dripping off his short grey beard and moved his reading glasses closer to the top of his nose.

After this moment of brief euphoria, the professor stared again at the screen to make doubly sure there had been no error; that his calculations had been made based on the correct assumptions and data.

He quickly scanned through the key ingredients and rationalizations that had changed the very dynamics of his project.

Again his results matched the previous ones. He couldn't have stopped smiling even if he tried. The fact that the result was the same again could only mean one thing. He tugged his beard and pondered what was once unthinkable.

He was certain of his accuracy and the scientific advancements made. He was also certain of something else: The world would never be the same again. The professor pushed away a clump of daily newspapers that had been growing steadily on his desk over the last few weeks. He reached for his antiquated ring-dial phone that he still insisted on using. Several minutes later

Professor Greene found the number he was looking for scrawled on a piece of paper he had torn out of some complementary magazine catalogue depicting the new men's summer clothing range.

"Hello." The voice on the line was crisp and the tone was curt.

"It's happening," said the professor.

"When?"

"Within the last few hours."

"Are you sure?"

"Yes."

There was a pause of a few seconds.

"Is there a chance you might be mistaken?" the voice was now less curt and more strained.

"I don't think so."

"I need a definite answer."

"What I mean," said Professor Greene, "is that there is no chance I am mistaken. I've re-tested at least three times, and each time the results are the same. It certainly is no coincidence."

There was another pause while the professor waited for the response. He could hear fingers drumming on what was probably a table nearby.

"We've been waiting for this moment for such a long time and now that it's here is frankly, well, it's frankly quite daunting, that's what it is."

"Daunting indeed," said Professor Greene. He could barely contain himself and wondered if the person on the other end of the phone could hear his erratic breathing.

"I can't believe this point in time is here already. I know we've been working towards it and wanting it to happen but now that it is, well, I must say I seem to have been caught unaware."

"It still hasn't quite sunk in," said Professor Greene.

There was another pause on the phone and the professor started to bite on his fingernails, something he hadn't done since the day he got married.

"Well, we better get moving then. Are you going to make the necessary arrangements?"

"Yes, I've already started. Just as we originally planned."

"And everything is in place?"

"Almost."

"Make sure it's all done. We can't afford for anything to go wrong now."

"I know," said the professor. "I'm on top of it."

"We need the plan to implemented as soon as possible. There's not a moment to lose."

"It will be. Very soon."

"If something goes wrong or if any outsiders get involved, well, you know that the consequences would be disastrous."

"It won't come to that."

"Not only disastrous for us," said the voice, "but for humanity as we know it."

Professor Greene swallowed, hoping that the sound couldn't be heard.

"I won't let anyone down."

"Let me know when it's all done."

"I will."

"Oh and, Harry?"

"Yes?"

"Be careful!"

Professor Greene clutched his phone for a moment after the call ended, pondering this discussion—the most important phone call he had ever made. He was about to replace the receiver when there was another click. Professor Green's smile fell. Someone else had just hung up too. Someone else had been listening to their conversation.

CHAPTER 3

There was no one in sight outside the science faculty as Rafik strode to his car and departed from the campus. He sped along the highway, momentarily glancing at the bulging backpack on the seat next to him.

He wondered what was so special about the subject of his latest theft, but didn't dwell on it too much. Whatever it was or whatever it was needed for was of no concern to him. He was getting paid a decent price for this job, and he needed to ensure he completed his mission successfully, and thus maintain his solid reputation. The mission wasn't complete yet. It could still go either way.

The Fox had been clear as to what Rafik had to do after he left the university. As per his instructions, Rafik drove along De Waal Drive to a small deserted clearing just off the highway en route to his apartment. There was a small unofficial parking lot situated next to the entrance of a shooting range. Most people driving past during the day would not even notice the shooting range behind the rocky surrounds. Rafik reversed his car into the lot and parked at the back of the clearing that overlooked the lit-up city and its surrounds.

He took out his cellphone and sent off a text message to the number he had been told to contact. He doubted it was to a specific phone; the Fox was not stupid enough to give away a phone number that could be traced easily. The message was probably being sent to a web address on the Internet. The message contained just one word: "Successful".

Rafik climbed out the car, hiding in the shadows behind a cluster of nearby rocks. He couldn't take the chance of just waiting in the car. One never knew which shady characters were out in the middle of the night in Cape Town. And Rafik didn't know which would be worse—to get accosted by some homeless vagrant, gangster or drug lord, or to let the Fox down.

Rafik settled behind the rocks, his one hand clutching the strap of his backpack. His other hand gripped the pistol. A few minutes later a black Audi appeared on the highway. It had no number plates and the windows were tinted. The Audi slowed down as it drove into Rafik's view, and entered the clearing where it pulled up alongside the Mazda.

Just as he had been told, the driver of the Audi flashed his lights three times. There was a pause and the driver then flashed a further three times. Rafik lowered his pistol and moved toward the Audi. As he approached the car, the front window slid open, revealing the driver. He was also dressed in black and wore leather gloves and a balaclava, his face completely hidden.

The man nodded his head towards the back seat and motioned for Rafik to open the back door. Rafik lifted up the backpack and placed it in the car. The man handed Rafik an envelope but no words were exchanged. They nodded at each other as the window began to slide up again. Rafik watched the Audi leave the clearing and head off on De Waal Drive in the direction of the city. Rafik opened the envelope and, seeing the wads of cash, grinned and got back into his car.

CHAPTER 4

Professor Greene had a sick feeling in his stomach. He had had it before and over the years had realized he had to trust his instincts. Something was wrong. There had definitely been someone listening in on the phone conversation. This could only mean one thing: If they were listening to his calls, they were watching his every move too.

He was pacing through his house, trying to catch up with his thoughts that were frantically taking on a life force of their own.

"Time for nuts!" a shrill voice sounded from across the room. Professor Greene jumped and then breathed in relief as he stared at his African Grey parrot. The parrot had been given to his father thirty years ago as a gift from a Chinese businessman who had been grateful to the professor's father for helping catapult his clothing business to success. After his father's death, Professor Greene could not part with the parrot that had become part of the furniture.

"Time for nuts, time for nuts!" the parrot shrieked.

"Sure, Alex." He grabbed a handful of sunflower seeds from the porcelain bowl on the faded black kitchen counter top.

He had to start organizing an alternative. If they were indeed watching him they might strike soon. And he couldn't take any chances. He needed to implement his Plan B. Just in case the unthinkable happened. He hoped it wouldn't but he was a man who always planned for the future. At least he hoped he was. He had to do something and he had to do it fast.

He slouched into his prized reclining armchair and stroked his beard, something he always did when he was deep in thought. Various contingency plans had often crossed his mind, but he had never come up with any serious alternatives. Not yet, anyway. Maybe he was being paranoid and it was just a normal phone click. Maybe too many late nights were finally taking their toll? But what if it wasn't paranoia?

He sat staring at nothing in particular. Other than the sound of Alex shuffling and munching on his seeds, the room was quiet. The parrot finished pecking at the sunflower seeds and then the professor heard it: the beeping. He leapt up and cast his eyes towards the end of the room. There was a blinking red glow coming through his jacket, accompanying the beeping sound which was growing louder and louder.

Please don't tell me that it is what I think it is. He reached for the small light-blue beeper that had been dormant in his jacket for so long. He had almost forgotten it was there. He flicked a tiny switch underneath the beeper and the sounds immediately dissipated. The red flashes were also halted. His beeper was operated by automatic remote control. It was telling him that someone had broken into his secret laboratory at UCT. The silent alarm had been triggered for the first time. The black box had been lifted from its secure spot.

Professor Greene chucked the beeper to the floor as he grabbed his jacket and charged out of the house.

CHAPTER 5

Wahied Madat checked the anonymous text on his cellphone to make doubly sure he had the correct address. Satisfied that it was, he drove down the long dirt road for several minutes until he arrived at a large wrought-iron gate.

———

It had been another agonizingly hot summer day on the coast of KwaZulu Natal. At the top of a steep sandy road just outside the popular tourist village of Umhlanga lay a small plantation owned by the Madat family. Having been there for several generations, the small green estate had a pristine view of most of Umhlanga and its luxurious coastline.

The location of the Madat plantation was one of the reasons why their business had been so successful for many decades, and it was one of the reasons why the family had constantly turned down offers from real estate agents who saw the potential of this magnificent property, and who were desperate to snatch it up so another hotel in the area could be built. Top international names had been turned away as the Madats insisted that they would never sell.

Although the Madats were delighted with their view and geographical position, their main asset was the natural waterfall and river that ploughed its way through the west side of the property. Not only was this abundant river and spectacular water flow a beautiful sight, but it was the primary source of their livelihood, an asset for the family to embrace. For generations the Madats had built up a worthy reputation as one of the best bottled-water suppliers in the country. Madat Water was constantly sought after, as it became a leading brand.

In front of the Madats' six-bedroom home at the top of the estate were the showroom and a little shop. Adjacent to these was a small office complex where the Madats had their own offices to pursue all the administration and duties that came with the nature of their award-winning business.

All orders were processed at the offices. Whether it was to local shops or major retail outlets and hotels, every order was always accounted for. All orders were recorded in special logbooks. Even months after a shipment of bottled water had left the premises, its order was stored in the archives. The Madats could go back years and see orders that took place fifteen years previously if they so desired.

The efficient paperwork and meticulous administration were part of the Madats' business success strategy, and ensured that things ran smoothly.

Dressed in just a faded pair of jeans, Wahied Madat's back sizzled as the sun's rays pounded down on him while he walked around making sure that proceedings at the plantation went smoothly. His dark mop of hair fell neatly on his head and his boyish face almost succeeded in hiding an emerging crop of stubble.

"What's the schedule like for today?" Wahied asked Venecia, the Madats' receptionist who occupied a suede swing chair behind a large walnut desk at the corner of the showroom.

Venecia glanced at the open diary on the desk. "Your schedule is pretty open today," she said.

"And there's nothing else happening here where you need me specifically?"

"Nope. It's all clear."

"Great!" Wahied grinned. "Might actually take some time off."

Wahied knew exactly how his schedule had looked. He had made sure he had not booked any client meetings or appointments for that day. In fact, several weeks back, Venecia had scheduled a meeting between Wahied and a potential buyer for that very day. Wahied had phoned the buyer and moved the meeting date, rewriting it in the diary.

Nobody was any the wiser, including Venecia.

"Should I tell callers to try you on your cellphone?" she asked.

"No," he said. "Just take a message. I'll get back to them during the week."

Definitely no unnecessary calls today, Wahied thought. He couldn't have any distractions. Not today. This day was far too important. And the next day too. Wahied rubbed his hands together as he headed into the luscious garden that formed a few acres of the Madat estate.

Below a grassy slope away from the other buildings on the plantation lay a small warehouse where Wahied spent time conducting some of his business affairs, both for the company and privately. He reached into the tight pocket of his jeans, pulled out a rusty key, and entered the garage. There were several brown boxes stacked on top of each other, forming a type of makeshift pillar reaching towards just under the high ceiling.

Wahied pushed open the double sliding door at the end of the warehouse to reveal a small yellow tractor complete with forklift. He clambered onto the tractor and turned the ignition. As the machine began to throttle he steered towards the boxes and began to stretch the forklift towards the pile. After three attempts he managed to move the pile onto the forklift.

He slowly turned the vehicle around and headed towards the sliding doors and outside to his parked truck. The truck itself was regarded as a small size but it had a large container attached to its back, no different to the other container trucks the Madats used. Wahied had left the doors to the container open, and he maneuvered the forklift to place the boxes inside it. Sweating, he then reversed the tractor and parked it where it had been originally.

Wahied slammed the doors on the container shut and looked around. Some birds fluttered overhead but there was no one else around. He got into his truck and drove towards the exit.

He waved to the security guard at the entrance, who opened the boom allowing Wahied's vehicle to pass through. Normally members of staff driving off the premises were searched by security personnel. This was a result of an incident a few years back when the recipe for a special flavored carbonated soda water had been smuggled out by one of the long-standing employees. The staff member had sold the recipe to one of the Madats' competitors, and after a protracted legal battle the recipe was officially deemed a Madat creation.

The security officer waved Wahied through and proceeded to close the boom. Wahied waved back, gave a broad grin, and headed on to the road that would soon take him to the highway. Wahied glanced in his rear-view mirror a few minutes later as the Madat estate became a spec on the horizon. He tried to hold the steering wheel firmly, but he noticed that his hands were trembling.

CHAPTER 6

Professor Greene slammed on his brakes on University Avenue just meters away from the science faculty building. He left his car on a yellow line, dashing towards the unlocked glass entrance to the faculty.

University Avenue was illuminated by the streetlights scattered all the way along it. Professor Greene was relieved that there were no other cars visible, nor signs of any die-hard partying students, the only ones who might be awake at that hour.

As the professor approached the entrance he noted that the security hut nearby was vacant. There should have been someone there—why the hell wasn't someone guarding the place? He suspected he might have the answer to that question very soon. Goose bumps spread across his arms as he entered the lobby and stormed down the stairs to the basement.

Once at the bottom he reached for the light switch on the side of the wall. "Holy shit!" he said as he almost tripped over the body sprawled by his feet. He stared at the security guard lying in a pool of blood, then fell back. He doubled over and found himself vomiting. Several seconds later, he stood up and brushed his sleeve across his mouth.

He walked around the body, avoiding looking at it properly. He quickly made his way towards the doors leading to his research laboratory. The door was open. The second door beyond it had a huge hole. He ignored the faint smell of smoke as he rushed into the room. His fort had been infiltrated.

Professor Greene advanced straight to the middle desk. Sure enough, the black box, along with its hard drive, no longer occupied its usual place. The professor stared at his frowning reflection on the bare desk. He tugged on his beard and surveyed the room. All the graphs were still stuck on the wall. The other computers seemed to be intact, although the data would be useless without the black box. The thief had known exactly what he was looking for. This was no random break in.

"Damn!" Professor Greene punched his hand into the air. "Damn, damn,

damn!" He knew he had to immediately formulate his Plan B. He had to soldier on.

He looked around his small workstation one last time and then headed through the doors again. He couldn't do anything about the battered main door, but the first door with the broken lock was undamaged. An outsider wouldn't even notice that the Yale had been picked. Professor Greene pulled the door closed behind him.

When the door looked like it was firmly closed, the professor proceeded to one of the several stacks of chairs near where he was standing. He dragged a stack in front of the door. He did the same thing with a second stack and then a third. He walked a few steps forward and then turned to look at the door again. Confident that no one would think anything of the so-called fire exit door behind the chairs, he walked to a tiny storeroom in the next passage.

Professor Greene smiled gratefully as he noticed that the storeroom door was unlocked. He had hoped this would be the case. He swung it open and peered inside. The light from the passage streamed in and he scanned the contents of the room. The storeroom was used by the cleaners and consisted of various dusters, detergents and buckets. It also contained mops, and this is what the professor had come for.

He reached for the largest mop and filled a tattered yellow bucket with water from the stained basin propped up in the corner of the storeroom. He almost vomited again as he saw the man sprawled across the floor. He looked at his watch. It was getting close to four am. It would still be dark outside. He had time but he had better move fast. It wasn't unheard of for joggers to begin their day in Cape Town around five-ish.

Professor Greene dragged the corpse towards the elevator. The doors slid open and the professor heaved the security guard into the elevator, leaving a trail of blood on the floor behind him. The guard's legs were dangling out of the elevator and formed a wedge between the doors, preventing them from closing and the elevator going up to the lobby.

The professor stepped over the body and mopped up the red pool on the tiles. Time was of the essence, but he had to sort out this mess before he could attend to his other plan. And he had to make sure that not a trace of blood remained in the basement.

When Professor Greene was satisfied that the floors were clean, he kicked the corpse's legs into the elevator and, still clutching his mop and bucket, pushed the "G" button. The elevator chugged up to the main floor and the professor once again pulled the body out so that it formed a wedge between the doors. He went through the same cleaning routine again until he was happy there was no evidence in the elevator.

The professor dragged the body to the glass doors at the entrance and, before leaving, cleaned the bloody path that had been created from his exit from the elevator. He was almost at the security hut when he let go of the body onto the tar. This would be sufficient. He left the security guard slumped just next to the pavement and mopped up the bloody trail behind him.

Taking a deep breath, the professor reached into the security guard's jacket

THE MIND OF GOD

pocket. He retrieved a black wallet. There were two twenty-rand notes inside it and an identity card. *Moses Noxo. Poor bugger.* Professor Greene took out the two twenty-rand notes and stuffed them into his own pocket, making a mental note to give the money to charity at a later stage. He threw the wallet onto the ground next to the corpse.

When the body was discovered, it would seem that Moses Noxo was a victim of a random robbery. Murders occurred every day in South Africa and the police did not have time to devote all their attention to every single crime. The murder here would be described as opportunistic. A random robbery might not receive a detailed investigation. Sure, there would be a huge outcry that a murder could take place on one of South Africa's finest higher education institutions. There would be the usual calls for more vigilance on campus and for more crime control in the country generally. But to the public it would seem that Noxo was shot outside his hut. No one would think to go down to the basement and inspect for blood there or for any other evidence pertaining to the crime. It had taken up a lot of his time when he should have been sorting out his contingency plan, but the professor was confident he had compressed the crime scene into an area of a few meters on University Avenue.

Professor Greene couldn't afford prying eyes and ears meddling with his research. Not now, especially with the black box in the wrong hands.

The professor grabbed the bucket and walked to the side of the building towards a drain. He emptied the bucket's contents and watched as they swept down the drain. He walked back to the body, grabbed the mop that he had leaned against a green rubbish bin, and headed for his car. He threw the mop and bucket into his boot.

He looked one last time at the body and then jumped into his car. He had to get off campus.

CHAPTER 7

Tucked away in the luxury of his private study, the Fox marveled at his new acquisition. He smiled confidently as he reached into the backpack that now lay on the table next to him.

He beamed at the black box lovingly like a father looking at his newborn child. His eyes glinted as he basked in the knowledge that this prized possession was now his.

"I didn't realize just how small you were," he said, chuckling as he placed it back onto his desk. "And who says that size counts?"

A few minutes passed by as the Fox just gazed at it, almost entranced by this powerful object that now graced his study.

"I know you won't let me down," he whispered. "It's almost time."

The Fox took a small metal wire from the back of the black box and attached it to another wire linking it to the flat LED widescreen monitor on the main shelf of his ornate bookcase.

He flicked a switch and sank back into his comfortable lounge chair, his eyes focused on the black box.

And then he began to wait.

CHAPTER 8

Mike Bonnington could not remember when he had last had a decent night's sleep. He had spent most of his waking hours in Cape Town working day and night. Now, at this late hour of the night or this early hour of the morning, he was wishing he could just catch up on some sleep. But first he needed to eat.

Thank goodness for twenty-four-hour fast food. He switched off his engine and leaned towards the passenger seat to retrieve his double cheeseburger complete with supersized fries. He had parked his hired car on one of the top roads on UCT's main campus. The view of Cape Town mesmerized him every time he stared at it. It could be the middle of a cold night or of a bright sunny day—no matter how many times he saw it, its effect lingered afterwards like the taste of a long passionate kiss between two lovers, and he could not put it out of his mind. He also enjoyed the fact that he was on a university campus and on some level the atmosphere, even if the students were currently asleep, still catapulted him back to his student years, a time when life had seemed relatively simple.

A mosquito hurried through the open window and buzzed as it descended on Mike's cheek. He waved it away, but the mosquito was not intimidated by Mike's bulging biceps and seconds later landed on Mike's thick black curls on the top of his head. He shook it off. *Damn mosquito.*

Mike munched his burger as his stomach moaned gratefully. It had been his third UCT meal at this hour in the last four days! A drop of tomato sauce weaseled its way out of his carton of fries, edged past his tight white T-shirt, and splashed onto his favorite faded blue jeans. The city lights flickered in the distance. Soon the city that had been chosen as one of the most desired holiday destinations in the world would be waking up to face the trials and tribulations of another day.

Mike took another bite and turned his gaze from the lights. He glanced towards University Avenue directly below him. Something aroused his curiosity. A quick movement in the shadows. He blinked.

After realizing that his eyes were not playing tricks on him, Mike almost choked on his double cheeseburger. *That guy is dragging a body?* He rubbed his face as the figure, now in full view of a streetlight, threw something onto the ground next to the body.

"What the hell is this?" Mike gasped, as he watched the man chuck a mop and bucket into his boot and then drive off.

Mike switched on his engine and drove along the top road, keeping a clear view of the fleeing vehicle. He stayed far back and allowed just enough space between the cars not to attract any attention. A few minutes passed and both cars were on the highway.

Mike kept his distance as the car he was tailing eventually entered the residential area of Rondebosch. Driving slowly, he was able to keep sight of the vehicle steering in and out of a maze of roads.

A few minutes later the car came to a halt. The man parked in the road and entered his house, slamming the door behind him.

Mike stopped his car a few houses down and switched the engine off. The street was lined with towering oak trees, plush lawns, and neatly painted walls and fences. The area remained deserted as its inhabitants clung onto the last moments of their slumber. A squirrel darted across the lawn near where Mike had brought his car to a halt. Mike reached towards his ankle, lifted up his jeans, and removed a gun in a small holster tied to his leg. He examined his weapon, made sure it was loaded, and moved to open the car door.

CHAPTER 9

The Fox leaned back in his chair, his eyes transfixed on the screen. The screen remained blank. He drummed his fingers on the table. *Come on, come on!* He waited a few more minutes, but the screen remained lifeless, so he reached for the power switch and switched it off. *Damn computers!* He waited for several more seconds and then pushed the switch on again.

The screen continued to be in darkness. It was not supposed to be like this. Something was wrong. *But what?* He gave it another minute. Nothing.

Cursing, he lifted the black box and examined it. It seemed that everything was in place, but on closer scrutiny the Fox noticed that the bottom left corner was loose.

He ran his fingers along the side and removed the tiny panel. Staring at the hollow corner that revealed an empty space, a space that should have been filled with a little microchip, he gasped.

The Fox slammed his hand on the desk. He was fuming. The black box would not function without the missing microchip. It was a vital cog in the wheel. He had to get that chip and he needed to get it fast. He wasn't prepared to let everything just go to waste. All that time and effort to get to this point. All that money. There was too much at stake.

He flicked the switch one more time in the foolish hope the box would start functioning despite the missing part. But again he was met with no success.

Shaking his head, the Fox reached for a shiny silver tin inside the top drawer of his desk. He flipped open its lid to reveal a pile of cellphone sim cards that had been stolen for him. This was how he conducted his communication. If the authorities were trying to track down the relevant numbers, they would come across the details of the original sim card owners, not him. And just in case there was some detective out there one step ahead of the pack, the Fox only used each sim card once before throwing it out. No repeat messages! He randomly picked a sim card from the pile and inserted the new sim card in a black cell phone. It was time to contact Rafik Jaffer.

CHAPTER 10

Professor Greene rushed into his house and down the passage to his living area. Shaking from everything that had happened that night, he poured himself a much-needed scotch.

Drink in hand, he walked to the lounge and collapsed onto the couch. He welcomed the cold swirl of the whiskey around his mouth. All those months and years of hard work and to now suddenly be in a situation like this. It was earth shattering. Earth shattering and dangerous. He had been so meticulous that it was hard to believe someone had known exactly where the black box had been kept, and had managed to penetrate the security system. It confirmed for him that someone had been following his movements and listening to his conversations. But for how long? How deep did this go?

What a night.

The black box is gone. The black box is gone.

Now it was just a matter of time. The professor shivered as he thought of what still lay ahead. There were things he had to attend to as a matter of urgency. His thoughts immediately turned to Liz. He needed her help. He trusted her; he knew he could rely on her. She was, after all, his only child. Even if they hadn't spoken for months. Perhaps he should speak to her directly? Meet up with her and tell her everything? He finished the whiskey but still held the glass. She was his family. There was no excuse for severing ties.

He stood up and headed for another ring-dial phone that he often used, this one next to the serviette holder at the end of the kitchen counter top. It was early but his daughter had always been an early bird. She had even been born early! At the sound of ringing, the professor was seized by a momentary panic and put the phone down. *What am I doing? I can't speak to her over the phone.* He turned away.

CHAPTER 11

Elizabeth Greene had just made her morning fix of coffee in the form of a large mug of Alta Rica, no sugar, and just a drop of milk. Her new silk pajamas clung to her slender legs as she leaned forward on her bed to sip her coffee. She moved a clump of her blonde hair hanging over her blue eyes. She was huddled with her laptop and scanned her Facebook page, catching up on who in her network had been eating where and doing what. This morning fix had become as essential as her coffee. She didn't even bother with the news any more. It was usually all negative stuff. She had no inclination anyway to read about gun control in America or whether Iran would finish building a nuclear bomb in the near future.

She was about to "like" a picture when her landline began to ring. She glanced at the clock on her bedside table. Who would be phoning so early? The phone rang twice and then stopped. Liz walked towards the living area of her one-bedroom Claremont apartment. She pressed a button on the phone to see the ID call function. It was not a number that she had expected at all. *Wonder what he wanted? Maybe he phoned me by mistake?*

Liz sighed. She had been thinking of making contact with her father but each time decided that no contact was for the better. And now he had called her. She stood wrestling with her emotions once more. In the end she reached her usual conclusion: She was going to ignore the fact that he had phoned.

She went back to Facebook. She kept thinking of the phone call. *Why did he only let it ring twice? Surely he remembers I have ID call and I would be able to see he phoned? And why didn't he just leave a message if he really wanted to talk to me? Or call me on my cellphone?* She stared at the computer screen and noticed that her battery was running low. She had meant to charge it the night before but had forgotten. Now she wouldn't be able to take her laptop with her today. Why did she always forget to charge it when she needed to? She grabbed the charger, hooked it into the laptop and plugged it into the wall. A few minutes later Liz climbed into her blue boyfriend-style jeans and grey turtleneck sweater. She grabbed a jersey and left the apartment.

CHAPTER 12

Wahied brought his vehicle to a stop outside the wrought-iron gate. It had been many hours of non-stop driving since he had left the family estate in Durban the day before and it was time for the next part of his journey, as well as having a much-needed nap.

He picked up a small remote control and pressed the green button in the corner. The gate creaked open and Wahied steered his vehicle to the single garage door that lay ahead. After pressing the red button on the remote, the garage door began to slide up and Wahied drove inside.

The small farmhouse Wahied entered from the garage was simply furnished and spotless. The open-plan area consisted of a compact kitchen in the corner and a long black leather couch in the living area. A wooden table sat next to it, with an orange and silver mosaic bowl of fruit perched in the middle. Off the living area was a bedroom and en-suite bathroom. At the end of the lounge area a sliding door led on to a stone patio. Wahied slid the door open and stepped outside. He stared at the endless hills and green fields becoming visible in the dawn light. The neighboring plots were some distance away.

Wahied might as well have been in the middle of nowhere. The farmhouse was indeed the perfect pit stop for him to spend a few hours and get some necessary rest. He needed the isolation. There was also the certain task he had to complete before he could continue with his journey later that morning.

After microwaving a macaroni and cheese meal that had been waiting for him in the freezer, Wahied ate his food, and then went into the bedroom. He knelt next to the bed and stared under it. As had been previously instructed to him, he saw a brown case that would have remained hidden had he not known about it. He stretched his arm to reach for the case and slowly dragged it towards him.

Wahied carried the case to the living area and swung it onto the table. He sat down and clicked the case open. His eyes gleamed as he looked inside.

The day ahead was going to be a big one.

CHAPTER 13

Mike Bonnington had loaded his gun and was about to leave his vehicle and confront the man he had seen dragging a body on the UCT campus. He jumped as loud trumpet sounds permeated his vehicle. It was in fact the sound of his cellphone ringing.

"Whew!" he murmured as he reached for his phone lying beneath the folder next to him. "Mark, this is a great surprise!"

"How are you, Dad?" The voice on the phone was faint, but Mike could hear him despite the poor signal exacerbated by the fact that it was an overseas call.

"I'm great!" said Mike. "Exhausted actually, but what can you do! How's everything at home?"

"It's real good!" said Mark. "Went to a Lady Gaga concert last night."

"How was it?"

"Totally awesome. When you coming back?"

"Hopefully soon, son."

"How's your asthma been?"

"Ups and downs," said Mike. "The weather here can sometimes aggravate my chest but generally I've been okay. Nothing your strong dad can't handle!"

There was a chuckle on the other end of the line.

As Mike spoke, he started to feel more relaxed. He listened to his son's tales of local gossip, and became momentarily distracted from watching the man's house.

Standing in Professor Greene's garden, Rafik took out a small bottle of chloroform. The tried-and-tested formula had been Rafik's savior in many of his jobs in the past where murder had not been a specific instruction. Rafik poured the entire contents over a checked hanky that he then stuffed back into his jacket pocket.

He tugged on the glass terrace doors but they were locked from the inside. Rafik lifted up the open window next to the doors and within a few seconds he had maneuvered his body through the opening and landed silently on the blue carpet spread across the tiled floor. Years of physical endurance and steadfast martial arts training had allowed Rafik to become nimble and flexible, hard and dangerous.

Rafik took a step forward, feeling for his pistol stuck into his waistband—just in case—while his other hand gripped the handkerchief. With one silent foot in front of the other one, he crept toward the kitchen part of the open-plan living area.

"Are you okay?" a shrill voice pitched through the air and Rafik froze. "Eddie?"

It took Rafik a few seconds to register that these words were coming from a parrot dangling in a cage in the corner of the room.

The man he had come for was hunched over the counter top in the kitchen area, sipping from a tumbler, oblivious of the parrot and the intruder. He seemed about to take another sip when Rafik's arm swung before his eyes.

"What the hell?" Professor Greene tried to move away and the crystal tumbler dropped out of his hands, shattering on the floor.

Rafik was taken by surprise. He was not accustomed to resistance and he certainly had not been expecting it from this old man. He pushed the professor against the counter top but the man was able to kick one of the metallic barstools. The stool swayed and then fell over, knocking into Rafik, almost causing him to drop the bottle of chloroform.

"You bastard!" Professor Greene yelled. "You'll never get what you are looking for! Never!"

Rafik was losing his grip on the professor, who was writhing. The professor broke the grip and tried to make his way to the terrace doors. But Rafik grabbed the professor's foot and clung to it like a pit bull. He dropped the chloroform bottle and it fell onto the carpet, spilling its contents. The professor had fallen and Rafik jumped on him, kneeing him in the stomach.

Rafik forced the handkerchief over the professor's mouth. Seconds later, he was unconscious.

"And how's Lois?" Mike asked, yawning as he leaned back in his seat.

"She's good. She says hi and that she hopes your trip goes well."

"Isn't it almost your anniversary?"

"Yip, next week it's going to be two years since we met."

"Marry her already!"

There was another chuckle. "Patience, Dad, patience."

"I would like to have grandchildren, you know," said Mike, laughing.

"How's the accommodation there?" Mark was always good at changing the subject.

"It's okay. Not that bad, I suppose. Not that I've had much sleep or much time to relax."

Mike glanced at the man's house, but the front lawn was deserted. *Maybe he's not going anywhere for now,* Mike thought.

"Dad, do you have a fax number I can reach you on?"

"A fax number?"

"Yeah, I want to get your opinion about some of my sketches for my engineering project."

"Um, there is a fax but I'm not sure of the number. Can't you just scan them and email me?"

"It will just take too long. They're really large sketches and I'll have to reduce all the sizes. Would be quicker to fax."

Mike looked around the street as he spoke. No movement anywhere. He glanced at the passenger seat beside him, on which he noticed some pamphlets and papers.

"Oh hang on, I've got some documents here with me," said Mike. "The fax number might be on one of these."

———

Rafik Jaffer slipped out of Professor Greene's house, dragging the professor behind him. Noticing a car in the distance, Rafik crouched lower as he moved the professor through the rose bushes outside the house and around the corner to where Rafik had parked his car.

With one quick movement, Rafik shoved the professor into the mustiness of the boot. He reversed the car into a neighbor's driveway so he could turn around and head in a different direction. He had no intention of driving past the vehicle he had seen parked down the road. He was sure, in the quick glance he had cast in that direction, there was someone sitting inside.

———

"I look forward to checking it out!" said Mike as he sat up and put the papers back on the seat.

"Thanks a lot."

"Anyway, son, I'll be in touch again soon. Love to everyone at home."

"Bye, Dad."

Mike pushed the red button to end the call. He sighed as he looked around the street. It was deserted, but the man's car remained parked in the driveway.

CHAPTER 14

"I almost forgot you were coming!" Liz confessed.

"Yeah right!" said Tim as he climbed into the front passenger seat of the car.

Elizabeth's face broke into a big grin. She shifted the gearstick and the vehicle was thrust forward with a jolt.

"Whoa, easy!" Tim narrowly avoided knocking his head against the door.

"Welcome to Cape Town!"

"I hope the rest of Cape Town doesn't drive like you do!"

"Well, I'm sure you'll soon find out." Liz revved the engine and immediately brought the car to a halt as traffic lights in front of them turned red. Tim's hotel was ten minutes from Liz's apartment, and he had been standing outside on the pavement as arranged.

Liz glanced at him and, seeing he was looking at her too, she quickly averted her gaze. He was wearing brown corduroy pants and a striped shirt that was mostly covered by a worn black leather jacket. His short brown hair remained smooth as the open window brought in a galloping breeze. She wondered whether it had been a good idea for him to come to Cape Town like this. There was still so much she didn't know about him. *What do we have to lose,* she had told herself. He had been taken aback when she had given him a list of hotels and guesthouses in the area but that was the only way she was prepared to do things.

"How was your flight?"

"Lousy and long."

———

Indeed it had been one of the longest flights Tim had remembered. He rubbed his eyes, oblivious of the passing scenery as his thoughts were cast back to the night before.

"Another drink, sir?"

Timothy Fletcher yawned as he stared in half vision at a blurred brunette speaking behind a tight uniform. For a moment he thought he was in a strip club. But the clothes on the smiling airhostess remained on her as Tim gathered his thoughts and realized just where he was.

"Sure, I'll have another Coke," he said.

The airhostess smiled sweetly as she poured the contents of a can into a half-sized plastic cup.

"Only a few more hours to go, and we're almost there, sir," she assured him before turning to the seats behind him.

Tim yawned again as he stared at his watch. Not a fan of flying in the first place, Tim had braved hour-long queues at JFK airport. After the rigorous routine security checks he had boarded the plane and silently cursed when the captain had announced that there would be a delay before takeoff—some old lady had knocked her leg against the corner of someone's small suitcase and was bleeding profusely. All the passengers had to wait for her to be removed from the plane, for the wound to be attended to, and for her to be helped back on board and to her seat.

After having finally fallen asleep for a few hours, Tim awoke with the comforting thought that the flight was almost over.

"Airplanes. Gotta love them," said the stranger next to Tim, as the onboard lights signaled it was soon time for breakfast.

Tim nodded.

"And they call this a meal," said the stranger, pointing to the stale roll and tiny fruit bowl on the tray in front of him.

"I've learned never to expect much more on these airlines," Tim said and grinned.

"Well, I at least had some hope there would be something decent to satisfy my stomach," said the stranger. "Especially after such a long flight."

The man speaking to Tim was not American. Tim could not decipher the accent but did not press any further. His many years as a journalist had often allowed him to form impressions of people that were usually accurate. More often than not, Tim was able to figure out someone straight away. Though there were times when he had been wrong, Tim decided to trust his instincts and did not venture to ask the man any questions.

Tim reached into his manbag that his mates at work had humorously given him for his last birthday. He had kept it between his feet for the duration of the flight, as he didn't enjoy standing up the whole time and rummaging through the overhead lockers whenever he needed something. He fished out two yoghurt muesli bars.

"I like to come prepared," he explained to the stranger and offered him one of the bars. "This should hold you in good stead until you get something decent to eat in Cape Town."

The stranger smiled, revealing some missing front teeth. "You are very kind."

They ate in silence while Tim stared at his watch. Soon he would be seeing Liz again.

"Ladies and gentlemen, we will be landing shortly," the captain announced.

After a turbulent descent the plane finally landed and the passengers began to stand up, collecting their hand luggage from the storage compartments above their seats.

The stranger took his small suitcase and turned to face Tim. He hesitated and then spoke.

"I wish you a good time in South Africa," he told Tim. Then he lowered his voice. "But you must listen carefully—it is better that you do not go near the centers for business activities."

"What?" Tim asked. "What do you mean?"

"Stick to the tourist sites. It is better for you not to go the main places of business activities."

Before Tim could say anything more, the stranger winked at him, gave him a farewell pat on the shoulder, and headed off, camera bag over his shoulder.

Puzzled, Tim pondered these words as he disembarked and headed for the conveyor belts where he could collect his luggage. The stranger seemed to have vanished.

Now, his thoughts returned to that warning as Liz's car raced over the highway. Tim found himself having to hold the edge of his seat so he wouldn't get flung around again.

"This is almost as bad as the plane," he said, looking at her.

"Sorry, but we're almost there."

"Have you been crying?" said Tim.

"Why?"

"It just looks like it, that's all."

Elizabeth remained silent and kept her gaze on the road ahead.

CHAPTER 15

At seven am Sindy began her day like she did on any other—she went for a jog along the paved path of the popular beachfront in Sea Point. It was a fine Cape Town morning as the thick mist started to lift. Sindy jogged along the promenade while the waves splashed against the rocks beneath the walkway, spraying cold drops onto her toned body.

Several other people were already engaged in their morning exercise. Some fellow joggers smiled as they jogged past her. In the distance two elderly folk were taking a leisurely walk and behind them a mother was pushing her pram.

Although Sindy was a fitness fanatic who adhered to her routine, this morning, like the three previous mornings, would include an extra stop. A rendezvous that she had been waiting for.

She checked her watch to make sure she was still in time and continued her stride. Her long dark hair swayed against her lower back in the soft breeze. After months of careful preparation, she knew it was just a matter of time before her goals would be achieved. Like a runner who has an air of triumph as he or she edges closer to the end of a marathon, Sindy's big brown eyes dazzled with a smile indicating success was just around the corner.

She continued to jog along the beachfront and slowed down as she approached a lamppost in the distance. Next to the lamppost was a bench overlooking the sea. Directly behind the bench on the other side of the road was a small parking lot for a popular eatery that would have just opened for another busy day. At this hour there would not be too many people there and, all going well, Sindy would miss the breakfast rush by at least half an hour or so.

Amidst the sound of the ever-present waves and shrieks of the seagulls hovering above, Sindy took in a deep breath of fresh sea air before looking around one last time and stepping inside the restaurant. The week she had been anticipating for so long had finally arrived. And now there wasn't a moment to lose.

CHAPTER 16

Liz had one stop to make before she could even begin to think about what sights to show Tim. She steered the car into the Rondebosch suburb that was also home to her father. The route she used inevitably meant she would have to drive down his road. This was not something she really wanted to do but she had no choice if she was to get to her destination.

She soon found herself on the dewy street she tended to avoid. Edging up a hilly slope and then down again, she drove past a car parked a few meters away from her father's house.

Liz stared straight ahead of her, determined not to look in the direction of her father's house, yet she found herself glancing towards it. Her father's car was parked in the driveway, but the front door was wide open and there was no one in sight. Liz slowed down and continued to stare at the house.

"Why you slowing down?" Tim said. "Is this where you wanted to stop?"

"Not exactly," said Liz. "It's just that... oh, nothing." But it was strange that the door was wide open like that. He would never normally leave it open.

As the car passed the house, Liz noticed that the side gate leading into the back garden was also open. From what she remembered, her father never usually used that gate. *And he definitely called my phone earlier.*

Liz tried to keep driving but a few more meters down the road she screeched the car to a standstill and then reversed it. She parked right outside the front lawn.

"What are you doing?" asked Tim.

Liz sighed. "Looks like we've got an extra stop." She climbed out the car and walked across the front lawn towards the open front door. *I'm going to see him, give him a piece of my mind, and then I'm leaving.*

"Wait, I'm coming with you," Tim said as he followed her into the house.

"Whoa, what have we here?" Mike had ended the phone call with his son and was still holding his phone when he saw the car drive past him down the road, reverse, and then park outside the house.

He remained seated as the two occupants, a young blonde woman and a male of lean build, left the car and went inside the house. Mike used his phone to take some photos of the new arrivals. He zoomed in and snapped a few close-ups: first the girl, then the guy, and then some pictures of both of them.

He decided it would be better to wait until these people departed before he could go in and confront the body dragger. He placed his gun next to him, then leaned back into his seat again, wishing he had a cup of coffee.

The house was quiet—eerily so—as Liz and Tim navigated their way through the passage and different rooms.

"Hello?" Liz ventured. "Are you here?"

It felt as though the silence had wrapped itself around Tim as they headed to the lounge and living area.

"Whom exactly are we wanting to see?" said Tim.

"My father."

Liz glared at Tim as she answered his question. He knew that look. He had seen it on another woman before. A look of anger and frustration tightly mixed with a hint of sadness.

"Look, the glass door's open!" Liz said. "What is it with all these open doors?"

"Maybe it was just the wind."

"It would never normally be that wide."

"And how do you explain this?" Liz asked, as they turned towards the kitchen. There were barstools lying on the floor. Tim could see her fingers begin to tremble.

As he walked towards Liz, Tim felt a loud crunch underneath his shoe— there was broken glass lying on the floor, some liquid pooled in the curve of one of the fragments. Tim kneeled down and picked up the piece of glass. He moved it toward his nose.

"Does your dad drink whiskey?"

Liz turned around. "Yes. Why?"

"I think you should look at this."

Liz walked to the couch and her face went white when she saw the broken glass on the carpet.

"Jesus!"

"Let's not panic," said Tim.

"What do you mean, don't panic? My father is supposed to be home and he's not. All the doors are wide open, chairs are lying on the floor, and a broken glass of whiskey is lying next to the couch."

"Yes, but that doesn't necessarily mean anything is wrong. Maybe your dad dropped the glass and has now gone off to get cleaning detergent or something."

"His car is parked outside," she said softly.

"Time for nuts. Time for nuts." The shrill of a loud voice permeated the room. They jumped and turned to see Professor Greene's parrot comfortably perched in his cage hanging from the ceiling in the corner.

"Alex," Liz said; she sounded on the verge of tears. "Sweet old Alex."

"Time for nuts. Time for nuts."

"I know, Alex, I know."

Liz collapsed onto the couch as a tear trickled down her cheek.

"I don't know what we're going to do."

Although Tim had no idea what to say, he was impressed she had used the word "we". He sat down beside her, deliberating whether to put his arm around her or not. He rested his arm on one of the beaded orange scatter cushions instead.

"Maybe we should call the police?" he said.

"No." Liz shook her head.

"Liz, if his car's here and he's not here, it sounds quite sinister. As you said, what with the doors, the fallen barstools, and the broken glass of whiskey?"

"No police." Liz was adamant.

"It could have been a robbery or something. This is Cape Town. Didn't you tell me there is a huge crime rate here?"

Liz nodded.

"Then why not call the police?" said Tim. "They can get to the bottom of it. Probably put the right people on the right trails."

Liz looked into Tim's eyes, wiping the tears off her face with the back of her jersey sleeve. "It's complicated," she said.

CHAPTER 17

Professor Greene woke up to find himself with his hands tied, his eyes blindfolded, and his mouth gagged. He was scrunched up in what seemed like the boot of a car. He could barely breathe in the stale air. He groaned as his body rolled back and forth amidst the motion of a vehicle that was speeding down hills and bumping over potholes. The professor tried to free his hands and winced as the rope cut sharply into his skin. The last thing he remembered was leaning over the kitchen counter drinking.

His mind went over the events of the morning. He did not know where he was now, who had taken him, or where he was going, but one thing was for sure—whatever was happening now was linked to the theft of the black box. Professor Greene was certain about that.

His thoughts shifted to Liz. He hoped she was okay. It had been so long since the incident, he didn't remember when they had last spoken.

The car came to a halt and the professor was flung against the back of the boot, knocking the side of his head. He could hear the opening of a door and then footsteps that became louder, and suddenly the boot was opened as sunlight came flooding in.

"Let's get you outta here," a voice said as he was lifted onto the ground. "I'm going to untie you. You make one attempt to run and I'll shoot you. You understand me?"

The professor nodded.

They must be near the ocean. He could smell its salty scent and heard the soft roar in the distance.

The professor could feel his hands being untied, and they walked on level ground for a few meters until the sound of the sea became much louder.

"Stop here," said the man, pushing the end of his pistol into the professor's back as a reminder that he meant business. He could hear the waves crashing now and, although he was still gagged and blindfolded, he took in a deep breath through his nose, inhaling the fresh scent of the ocean breeze.

"Lift your leg up and take a step in front of you," ordered his abductor.

Professor Greene stepped on to what seemed like an uneven surface and as the surface beneath him trembled, he realized he was no longer on the ground. It must have been a boat. They were now on water and the moored boat rocked gently while the professor was pushed out to a seat.

He heard a lot of fumbling. His abductor was indeed busy starting the motor of the small speedboat. A few minutes later, amidst the throttle of the engine, the boat sped off. The professor clutched his seat. He wondered if he would ever set foot on land again.

CHAPTER 18

Liz opened her mouth to say something when she suddenly closed it again.

"What were you going to say?" said Tim.

"Shhh!" Liz said as she placed her finger on her lips.

They remained quiet. A door creaked.

"Did you hear that?" Liz whispered.

Tim nodded and jumped off the couch. He grabbed a tall purple vase holding several white daffodils that was placed on the coffee table, and hid behind the lounge door.

There was the sound of a soft footstep and then another one slowly getting louder. The footsteps were slow but clearly heading in their direction. Liz couldn't move, remaining frozen on the couch.

"It's okay," Tim mouthed to her. "I've got this under control."

Another footstep got closer and then another one. She looked at the door, waiting for the intruder to enter. The footsteps stopped, and a terrifying silence fell across the room.

And then they started again, the footfalls getting louder. The intruder was almost at the lounge.

"Hello?" a croaky voice enquired as the figure of a small frail woman appeared. She was dressed in dark pants and an oversized jersey, her shoulders hunched over and her grey hair netted in a bun.

"Tim, wait!" Liz said as Tim began to smash the vase downwards. "It's okay, I know her."

The vase was already in motion, but Liz watched as he tried to avoid the old lady's head and narrowly missed. Glass shattered on the floor.

"Liz?"

"Miss Havisham!"

"What on earth is going on?"

"Sorry about that," Tim mumbled.

"What do you think you are up to, young man? You could have smashed my head to bits!"

"We thought you were someone else," said Liz.

"I'm really sorry," said Tim.

"Good grief. Why would you want to hit anyone with a vase?"

Tim shrugged.

"Why didn't you just ring the doorbell?" Liz asked.

"I rang for a few seconds but there was no sound," said Miss Havisham. "It seems to be broken."

Liz remembered that even months ago the doorbell hadn't been working. Her father had planned to fix it but it clearly wasn't high up on his list of priorities.

"That's right," Liz said and nodded.

"Anyway, I thought I recognized you outside. So I came in! You ought not to leave the front door unlocked, you know."

"I know, Miss Havisham." Liz sighed. "Anyway, my father isn't here."

"I know that," said Miss Havisham.

"You know? What do you mean?"

"Well, I don't see him. So I assume he is not here!"

"Do you know where he is?"

"I don't. But it's you I came to see."

"Me? Why?"

Liz and everyone else in the neighborhood called this old woman Miss Havisham because she had never recovered from a failed relationship when she was much younger. Now in her early eighties, Miss Havisham was a familiar figure to residents on Everitt Drive. When neighbors went away on holiday or left their homes for business trips, it was Miss Havisham whom they chose to water their plants and feed their pets in their absence. She was even liked by the patrol officials in the private security company hut several houses down, to whom she would often take slices of her renowned home-made cheesecake. Owing to her familiarity with her neighbors, Miss Havisham generally knew the comings and goings of mostly everyone in the vicinity.

Miss Havisham glared at Tim as she edged past him and sat down on the couch. "Mind if I sit down?" she asked.

"Miss Havisham, what's going on? Why did you want to see me?"

"How fortuitous that you are in the neighborhood now," said Miss Havisham.

"Your father knocked on my door late last night. He was speaking very fast. Told me that I needed to do something for him and that he didn't have time to explain."

"What did he ask you to do?"

"Your father was very specific."

"About what?"

"He wanted me to give you something if you were in the neighborhood. I don't know why he just didn't give it to you himself."

Liz frowned at Miss Havisham and shrugged her shoulders as her eyes briefly met Tim's.

Miss Havisham reached into the pocket of her drooping white jersey, taking out a crumpled sealed envelope and handing it to Liz.

"Your father wanted me to give you this envelope."

"I wonder what's going on?" Liz looked at her name scrawled across the envelope. It was her father's handwriting.

"Oh, Liz, it's obvious!" Miss Havisham's eyes were twinkling. "Happy birthday!"

"Happy birthday?"

"She's always been so modest." Miss Havisham smiled at Tim. "Your father said I was to give this to you if you came by. And here you are. It's a birthday card from him."

"You didn't tell me it's your birthday!" said Tim.

"It's not my birthday," she said. "Not for another five months."

CHAPTER 19

His abductor yanked off the professor's blindfold and chucked it in the water. The icy waves splashed over the sides of the speedboat onto the deck. The professor was blinded momentarily by the glare of the sunlight, and he shivered as the engine came to a halt. The sudden silence gave way to the piercing shriek of some seagulls flying by. They might as well have been in the middle of nowhere. Surrounded by endless sea, nothing else was in sight. No one else was in sight. *No one to hear me cry for help,* thought the professor.

"Where is it?" the man said.

"I told you already," said the professor, not taking his eyes off the revolver that was now pointed straight at his face. "It was in my lab at UCT."

"I'm talking about the microchip," he snapped. "Don't play dumb with me."

"You took the black box yourself. It's not my problem that you don't know how to work something you stole."

"That's where you're wrong." The man was speaking slowly while his arm remained up in the air, the revolver still pointing at Professor Greene. "It's totally your problem."

"As I've said, the black box was working last time I checked it. There's no reason why it shouldn't be working now, provided of course it is set up correctly."

"Something is missing from it."

"I don't know what you're talking about. You won't get away with this."

Professor Greene stared at the waves crashing against the boat. Is this how it was going to end for him? He looked at the pistol pointing at him and then at the vast stretch of ocean that engulfed them. For the first time in his life, he felt helpless and trapped. There was nowhere to run. There was nowhere to hide.

It is said that when one's life is about to come to an end, various moments of experiences and loved ones flash before one's eyes in a split second that marks the transition from life to death. As the professor stared death in the face, his thoughts focused on the light in his life, his daughter Liz.

From the moment she had come into this world, she had brought him an endless flow of joy and happiness. Throughout all the trials and tribulations that he had endured, Liz had always been there for him. And when Susan had died, causing the professor suddenly to inherit the role of single parent, it was Liz who had helped her father get through the grieving process, never mind she had just lost her mother.

"So, what's it going to be?" His abductor was sniggering now. "You going to tell me what I need to know, or am I going to feed you to the sharks?"

"You already have the box," said Professor Greene. "How many more times must I tell you this?"

"Give me the damn microchip. Give it to me now. This is your last chance."

The breeze momentarily died down and the waves striking against the sides of the boat subsided, allowing for an uneasy silence between the professor and the callous soul pointing a gun at him.

He wondered where Liz was now. He hoped she was safe; that she would be able to do what was necessary. He sighed. He had no doubt that Liz would sort out the black box situation, and that the final outcome would be a positive one.

There was nothing more he could now do. The black box had been taken from him and he was powerless to protect himself or Liz. All he could do was hope that Liz would not meet the same fate that he was about to meet. But if they could get to him they could definitely get to her.

He had spent the last few years working almost entirely on developing the black box. Now it was in the wrong hands, and there was only one person who could not let all the years of hard work and progress go to waste. That person was his daughter, someone—he knew as he continued to stare down the barrel of a gun—he would probably never ever see again.

The boat rocked. His mind continued to hover over Liz. He couldn't leave her like this. He still needed to tell her how much he loved her. Why didn't he leave a message when he had called her earlier?

Liz had been right. He had been too involved with his work and since the death of his dear wife all those years ago the professor had begun to neglect Liz and a wall had grown between them. The more in-depth his experiment became the more he had forgotten his only daughter.

To leave this world now would be to leave with much unanswered. He couldn't have Liz carry this burden of their conflict. She would have to bear it for the rest of her life and that was the last thing he would ever wish for her. He cursed himself for not having spoken to Liz already. Although they were estranged, there had been several opportunities where he could have met with her and made peace. Now there was the chance he would never see her again and he would be taking his emotions and apologies with him. The truth would be buried with him.

"Please don't shoot me," he pleaded.

"Where is the damn microchip?" the man yelled.

"I told you, I don't have it."

He remembered the day Liz was born. He was the proud father who had offered all the nurses cigars after he first held Liz. It had been raining that day and after his wife's water broke they had been lucky enough to get to the hospital in time without navigating through any major traffic. There were no problems during labor, and Liz had come into this world a happy and healthy baby. She had had an uncomplicated childhood. An only child, she was spoilt by both her parents; nothing was too good for their child.

But then his wife was diagnosed with liver cancer. And his world as he knew it changed forever. Treatment after treatment, chemo after chemo, and his wife was reduced to an unrecognizable heap of bones, a state he wouldn't wish on anyone. The doctors had given her two months after that but, being the stubborn fighter she was, the stubborn fighter whom Liz took after, she lasted an extra seven months. And from that day onward, the professor built a wall around himself, cutting himself off emotionally from the rest of the world, including the person who needed his love and support the most, his baby girl.

"I'm not going to sit here all day."

"Please, turn this boat around. I told you what I know."

Professor Greene was afraid of losing the only other love of his life. Yet by engrossing himself in his science he had isolated himself in the fortress of his work. He had become so entrenched in it, he had lost Liz even though she was alive. But his experiments became more promising and with each breakthrough, he used it as an excuse to further detach himself from Liz. He would spend all his days in his laboratory at UCT, or in his study at home, and sometimes all his nights too.

He reflected on those moments where he could have attempted to rebuild his relationship with Liz. He should have made more effort; looking back, he had hardly tried. She was as stubborn as her mother; he would have had to go the extra mile in order to win her back. But he had not bothered. His halfhearted attempts were of no use and he was now faced with the possibility that he would never have the chance to speak to her again.

"I'm counting to three," the man said. "What's it going to be, old man?"

"Please," the professor said. "It's not going to help to shoot me."

"You're of no use to me if you aren't going to give me the microchip. If you haven't told me where it is before I get to three, I will pull the trigger."

"Please let me live," Professor Greene whispered, almost if he were in the middle of the most important prayer of his life.

"Get onto the edge of the boat."

The professor lifted one foot onto the outer perimeter and then the other. He stood and faced his assailant. He kept his mind on Liz and all the good times they had celebrated. The wind had picked up again and began to howl as it circled the boat's two occupants.

"One."

The professor just stared back at him blankly.

"Two."

The professor continued with his silence. He might have been standing in front of this assassin who was about to take his life, but mentally he remained with Liz. He could see her smile and he could hear her laughter. He would always be very proud of her.

"Three!"

As the man pulled the trigger, a strong wave crashed against the boat, causing it to rock, and knocked Professor Greene into the water a split second before the first bullet.

As the professor was plunged into the depths of the icy sea, Rafik ran to the edge of the boat and fired several more shots into the water. There was no chance he would survive that barrage of bullets. Besides, even if the man were only wounded, he wouldn't last long. The ocean would take no prisoners and the violently strong currents would ensure he drowned. Even Rafik doubted he could have handled those tides.

Rafik looked down into the sea but there was no sign of the professor. Rafik roared the engine back to life. As the boat started moving again, he thought he noticed something moving in the waves. He looked again carefully as the boat edged past a shimmering object. It was the first time Rafik Jaffer had smiled in a very long time. Heading to where the boat had stopped was a huge shark.

CHAPTER 20

"I'll have an orange juice, and quite a bit of ice."

The young barman nodded as Sindy pulled out a chair and perched herself at the long counter in the eatery. She was still wiping sweat off her face from her beachfront jog.

"Ah, what a nice healthy drink." An overweight man with greasy hair and a stained shirt stared at her from two seats down.

Sindy gave him a polite smile, then turned her back on him, glancing around the room. There were already more people here than she thought there would be.

The bartender reappeared and placed her drink, complete with a mini paper umbrella pierced through a bright red cherry, on the countertop. "Extra ice." The bartender slid another glass towards her.

"Thank you."

She took a sip. Most of the customers had hot drinks in their hands while some were eating omelets and croissants. In the background, the sound of U2 filtered through the speakers in the ceiling corners. There was no sign yet of the person she would be meeting.

"Waiting for someone?" The greasy man had shifted a seat down and his bulging waistline was now almost touching Sindy.

"No," Sindy said curtly, hoping he would just leave her alone.

"Want another one?" he pointed to her glass.

"I'm fine," she said and turned her back to face the other side of the room. A large mirror on the wall next to the bar allowed her to still view the room and get a view of the man next to her. If he tried anything funny she would be onto him. Fast.

The glass door at the entrance swung open and a group of busty, long-legged girls entered the room. At least half of the male customers stared as the girls, loving all the attention but feigning ignorance, marched to a reserved table in the corner.

She looked at her watch and then took another sip of her orange juice.

"Are you sure I can't get you another drink?" In the mirror she saw the greasy guy lean in slightly towards her.

She had been as polite as she could but was now starting to get irritated.

The front door swung open again and this time an elderly gentleman hobbled in. The eatery was very busy, but still no sign of the person she was supposed to meet.

"I said, do you want another drink?" This time the greasy man reached his arm out and touched her on the shoulder. Sindy spun around and glared at him.

"Just fuck off," she said.

"I like it when you talk dirty," the man said.

She turned away. She wondered if her meeting would even happen that morning. Maybe he was stuck in traffic? She would give it a few more minutes; five minutes and she would be out of there. And would have to try again tomorrow.

She stared into the mirror. The greasy man had edged even closer. She could smell the gin bouncing off his breath. *Who the hell drinks like this so bloody early in the morning?*

"I know you want a drink," the greasy man sang. "You're obviously the shy type."

She stood up.

"Where's the bathroom?" she asked a passing waiter.

Sindy walked around the bar and then took a narrow corridor the waiter had pointed to, which led to the toilets. She walked slowly and deliberately and, as she correctly predicted, it was soon not only her footsteps she heard on the dirty tiles. She didn't have to breathe in to know that the pungent gin odor was following her.

She stopped at an oak door that had the word "Ladies" carved into it. She listened for the footsteps behind her. She could feel him creeping closer. She waited a few more seconds and then pushed the bathroom door open and went inside.

The bathroom was deserted. A mirror adorned the wall overlooking three basins submerged in black granite. She decided to stand behind the door. She glanced at her watch again. This had better be quick. She couldn't afford to miss her appointment if he did show up.

Seconds later, she heard a cough from just outside the bathroom. The door opened slightly. The greasy man paused and then the door swung open fully. He took a step forward and then swayed inside, the gin smell enshrouding him like a dirty cape. He barely had time to utter another sleazy pick-up line when her leg appeared against his cheek. A roundhouse kick to the jaw and he stumbled forward in a daze.

Sindy leapt into the air and before the greasy man had time to react he was the recipient of another powerful roundhouse kick to the other side of his face. As he doubled over, he was met with a knee in his chin. He stumbled. Whatever thoughts were floating around his bewildered mind, they were lost as Sindy lifted her arm, clenched a tight fist, and rammed it into his face. He slumped to the floor, unconscious.

She dragged the heavy lump into the far-end cubicle and slammed the door shut behind her.

Staring into the mirror, she pulled back some strands of her hair that had fallen across her face and left the bathroom. She walked down the corridor back to the bar. She leaned against the counter and gave one final glance around the room. Her meeting was a no-show. She was about to head for the main door when a man wearing a white bowler hat and dark sunglasses spoke. She hadn't noticed him earlier. He had obviously just come in.

"Good morning!" said the man.

"Morning," said Sindy. The man's face was virtually hidden by his hat.

"It really is a wonderful Cape morning," said the man.

Sindy felt a cold shiver run through her. Those were the words she had been waiting to hear.

"It sure is," she said as she turned to face the counter properly. "As beautiful as a red robin singing in the trees."

The man nodded at her and stood up. Without another word, he walked away and strolled through the main doors. Sindy stared at the counter top. Next to an empty glass where the man had been sitting was a small brown unmarked envelope. Sindy glanced around. Everyone else was so engrossed in their conversations, nobody was watching. She picked up the envelope and stuffed it in the pocket of her running shorts.

CHAPTER 21

Michelle Sloane opened her curtains as the sun peered in. She flicked on her antique clock radio and the room was filled with the soothing sounds of Enya's *Orinoco Flow*. It momentarily took her back to a happy place. Yet, the calm music did not affect the butterflies still gathering in her stomach.

Today is the day of reckoning. Michelle took a deep breath. She generally never got flustered, but today was different. The HIV orphanage meant everything to her and she had invested so much time and energy into it—she couldn't just let it fail.

Four hours until her meeting with Eric Simms. Four hours until one of the most important meetings of her life. It was going to be such a long four hours.

She decided to get dressed first and then head downstairs to prepare the coffee. She could survive the next few hours on caffeine, and cave in that afternoon.

She checked her cellphone and plugged it into the charger behind the cushioned headboard of her double bed. No messages yet.

Michelle climbed over the other side of the bed and opened her cupboard door. As she did so, she glanced through the window at the oak tree in the center of the garden down below. Behind the tree, next to the rabbit enclosure, the empty swings moved in the breeze. The jungle gym remained damp from the heavy dew. The garden was unusually quiet for this time of the morning; the children had gone on an overnight educational excursion and would return only later in the day. It had been planned that way—Michelle couldn't afford to have any interruptions. She had to remain steadfast and focused. It was to be a very important day.

She concentrated again on the blouses hanging up in front of her. Did she want to come across as smart, or smart and sexy? Did she want him to get lost looking at her tits, or did she want him to focus on the issues?

She held some of the clothes to the light, still undecided. The song on the radio had come to an end. "Hope you are having a fabulous morning here in the Mother City," the DJ said brightly. "And remember that traffic routes might be varied today owing to certain road closures because of the visit by United States President Rafferty. Stay tuned for our next traffic bulletin in ten minutes' time."

Michelle had forgotten that the American president was going to be in Cape Town. *Of all the days to meet Eric Simms, he chooses the same day as a presidential trip!* She clenched her fists tightly like she did on the few occasions she was on edge.

Her thoughts were interrupted by the landline telephone ringing downstairs. Michelle almost jumped at the sound of the first ring, and raced out of her bedroom to get to the staircase. She thought the call was probably about her meeting.

Michelle hadn't noticed that a sock had fallen onto the second step when she had hauled her basket of clean laundry up the stairs the night before. In her rush she stepped on the sock, and found herself in midair as she slipped and then tumbled down, step by step, crashing onto the landing below.

The telephone continued to ring.

———

Eric Simms had been looking forward to his trip to Cape Town. He had heard so much about this beautiful city enveloped by mountain and sea that he wanted to experience it for himself. Cape Town had been on his to-do list for a long time and like many other successful businessmen, Eric Simms always enjoyed crossing something off his list.

Even though it was going to be a very short visit, he had made sure he would at least have time to fit in one or two of the main attractions. He had been advised that a day and a half in Cape Town was not nearly enough, as there was so much to see and do. But being the busy businessman he was, he rationalized that a day and a half was better than none. And so he had booked in advance a ticket to catch the ferry to Robben Island so he could see the jail cell in which Nelson Mandela had spent so many years. He also booked an open bus tour of the city. He knew he could not come to Cape Town without going to the top of Table Mountain, one of the seven modern wonders of the world. So he booked a ticket for the cable car too.

Eric Simms reckoned he would be able to fit all this in as well as his meeting with Michelle Sloane. His schedule was planned methodically and there was no chance he would deviate from his plans. Eric Simms liked order and precision, and that was part of the reason why he was so successful. The other reason was his hard work ethic and his aggressive, sometimes cutthroat way of doing business. Over the years he had built up his own financial empire and had garnished a fierce reputation. When Eric Simms said jump, you jumped. When he said sit, you sat, and when he said here's my money, you said thank you!

The Texan arrived in Cape Town and, after dropping off his luggage at his plush five-star hotel where he freshened up, he was driven straight to the Clock Tower at Cape Town's popular Waterfront area. Then he made his way to the pier where he would catch his ferry to Robben Island.

Eric handed his pre-booked ticket to an official and climbed on to the ferry. He stared in awe at the breathtaking views around him. He had a few hours and he was determined to enjoy every single minute. Then it would be time to meet Michelle and to get down to business. After all, that was the main reason for his visit.

CHAPTER 22

Liz and Tim said goodbye to Miss Havisham, who hobbled off to go feed her cats. Liz closed the door behind her and returned to the living area to join Tim.

"Strange old lady!" Tim laughed.

"You got that right! But not as strange as what's going on here." Liz ripped open the envelope and pulled out a card. On the cover there was a picture of a Labrador and inside the printed words said: "Happy Birthday. Hope you have a Doggone Day!"

"What does it say?"

"It's my dad's handwriting all right," said Liz. "It says, 'Darling Liz, you are my favorite birthday book and you don't look a day younger than thirty-five! All my love, Dad.'"

"That's it?"

"That seems to be it," said Liz.

"What does it mean, you are his favorite birthday book?"

"I don't have a clue." Liz's voice was high with irritation. "I don't know what the purpose of this card is. I don't know why Miss Havisham gave it to me. I don't understand what it means. I don't know what's going on." Liz closed her eyes and put her hand on her head. She could hardly think clearly with all the thumping going on inside it.

"Does your dad often communicate with you like that?"

"You mean via birthday cards?"

"No, I mean is he sometimes cryptic with you?"

"He can be."

"So maybe there's a hidden message in there or something."

"I was thinking that," said Liz. "But why couldn't he just be direct or a bit more explanatory?"

"I'm sure you'll figure it out," said Tim.

Liz drummed her fingers on the couch. "He reads a lot of books and I do too, but I don't have a favorite one that stands out above the rest."

"And the dog?"

The picture of the Labrador looked familiar. Liz knew she had seen this exact image before but she could not place it. It reminded her of the Labrador they had when she was a little girl but this picture evoked more recent memories. There was something about this Labrador's expression, something in the gleam of its eyes that mesmerized Liz. She had definitely seen it before, and the image had mesmerized her then as it did now.

Liz continued to stare at the card. And then it dawned on her. *Of course I know this image. And he knows I know it.*

Liz leapt up and headed for the ceiling-high bookcase at the side of the room. She quickly scanned several of the shelves and then reached for a book in the corner of the third shelf.

"What book is that?" Tim asked.

"It's a glossy coffee table book about various dog breeds. I gave it to my father for his birthday a few years ago."

"So he likes dogs?"

"Yes, but he loves Labradors. We had one when I was growing up. My dad absolutely loved it. It looked just like the one on the cover of this book."

"And it seems to be the same one as the one on the card," said Tim.

"So maybe you are more perceptive than I thought," Liz said.

"Indeed! But even if your father wanted you to look at this book now, how do you know what exactly it is you're looking for?"

"Well, I'm assuming it's got something to do with the fact that he uses the number 'thirty-five'."

"Your age."

"Well, not exactly my age but that seems to be the general idea."

Liz placed the book on the kitchen counter top and pulled out a barstool and sat down. "I have a hunch," she said.

She flicked through the pages until she got to page thirty-five. The page only had one small photo on it and was otherwise filled with text. There were various paragraphs dealing with the ideal eating routines for Labradors.

"Found what you're looking for?" Tim walked to where Liz was sitting.

"I'm not quite sure what I'm looking for, but this page is crowded with text so there must be some type of meaningful words or phrases here he knew I would understand."

Liz scanned the page. She couldn't see anything. She began again and tried to go slowly through each line. And then she saw it. She had almost missed it again, but blinked her eyes and leaned forward to examine her discovery.

In between the eighth and ninth paragraphs towards the end of the page a sentence in tiny letters had been scribbled with a faint black pen. The color of the ink blended in with the color of the ink of the book's text so anyone reading the paragraphs with an unsuspecting eye would have missed the sentence.

"Bingo!"

"What is it? What can you see?" Tim was leaning over Liz's shoulder trying to catch a glimpse of the pages in front of her.

"There's a sentence here: IN THE CLUTCHES OF THE STRONG LION A WAFER WILL QUENCH YOUR THIRST."

"What does that mean?" asked Tim.

"Your guess is as good as mine," Liz sighed.

"Wow, but at least you found something. You solved your father's clue in the birthday card so quickly and now there's something else for us to work out."

"Us?"

"Well, two heads are better than one."

"We'll just have to see," said Liz. "Anyway, I have a feeling this sentence will be a lot more difficult to decipher."

"Why? I reckon you'll crack it in no time!"

"It's not as easy as it seems," said Liz. "My father wanted me to know something but he didn't want anyone else to know. Even though he made the birthday card trick fairly easy for me, this sentence here is more complicated. He wouldn't have wanted anyone else to decipher it. It might not be as easy as you think."

Liz sighed and leaned back against the back of the barstool. It was cold and the shiny bars jutted into her back.

"I have faith in you, Liz." Tim moved the book towards him so he could scrutinize the words. "Judging by what I can see, it seems your dad likes lions?"

"I suppose," said Liz. "I mean, he likes all wildlife. He's never really overtly expressed a penchant for lions. But it's clearly something we have to focus on."

"And the other words?"

"I don't know." Liz shrugged. "If something seems obvious, it's probably not. My father deliberately hid this message. He wouldn't have just blatantly told me what he wanted if he didn't want anyone else to know what I would decipher."

"Why?"

Liz paused. Could she be open with Tim? Did she know him well enough to confide in him? "Before we continue I just need to tell you that by helping me with this, our lives might be in danger."

"Liz, what's going on? What do you mean?" Tim's eyes were wide. She couldn't tell if it was with fear or interest.

"My father was involved in some groundbreaking research."

"Yes?"

"Well, he had made some vital discoveries that could have a significant impact on mankind."

"What type of discoveries?"

Liz shook her head. "I don't actually know all the details. It has something to do with global consciousness."

"Global consciousness?"

"It's probably best you don't get involved."

"But, Liz, I'm here with you. I'm already involved."

"Yes, but the less you know the better. I don't want to put you in harm's way."

"So you think your father's disappearance has something to do his research?"

Liz tried to suppress her tears. She couldn't believe she was in her father's house and that something might have happened to him. She cleared her throat. "I don't know. All I know is that I somehow have to decipher this message. It will lead us to what he has wanted me to find."

Tim's voice was quieter now. "But I don't understand why our lives would be endangered?"

"It's possible that those pursuing my father—if my father is even being pursued—will go after us in the belief we can provide them with whatever has to do with what my father was doing. For now, I just need to work out what is meant by this sentence."

"Okay, well let me try help too."

"Tim, it's not too late for you to just get out of here. Go see some of the sights or something."

"I'm not going anywhere," said Tim.

Sindy walked across the parking lot from the eatery and found an empty bench overlooking the sea. The bench had been sprayed by a large wave but Sindy did not notice. She wiped some more sweat off her forehead and stared at the envelope in her trembling hands. She had almost missed the rendezvous. Thank goodness she had gotten there when she did. All the planning. All the preparation. And she was about to find out how soon it would all come together.

She stuck her finger through the top of the envelope and glided it along to force it open. Inside she saw a small single piece of paper that was neatly folded up. She opened the paper and stared at the two words that were boldly emblazoned on the page. The words had been formed with letters and numbers cut out from a newspaper.

She nodded as she stared at the page, her mind racing with the permutations and consequences this simple message had brought. Now she had more clarity.

She smiled as the realization began to sink in. The moment had finally arrived. She looked down at the piece of paper again just to make sure. The cutout words stared back at her—"13h00 today".

Several months before Liz found herself trying to decipher her father's cryptic message, she had gone to visit her father at his home. They were sitting in his study while he had been marveling at something on his home computer. Liz had accused him of being so engrossed in his research that he had neglected her—that he'd cast her aside. He denied it and told Liz that he would never abandon his daughter.

Liz had stormed out of the house, ignoring Professor Greene's pleas for her to come back so that they could resolve their issues. Liz had sped off in a rage. She hadn't returned any of her father's subsequent phone calls. And he had made several.

Now, as she tried to work out what it was he had entrusted her with, she felt her stomach tighten at the thought it was her fault how things had ended the way they had. *Please God, let him be okay.*

She remembered that day so clearly. When she had walked in to the study, he had beamed at her, saying he would only be a few minutes and then they could chat.

"What are you doing?" Liz had asked.

"I'm in the middle of something that could be a game-changer for humanity."

"Is this linked to your other research, the stuff with that black box?"

"It most certainly is."

"What is that you're holding?"

"It's linked to my experiments. I can't go into it now but it's a vital piece of data."

"It looks so small for something so groundbreaking."

"It's a powerful wafer of silicone," Professor Greene had said.

Liz shuddered as she recalled the conversation. She had asked her father what he had meant by a wafer of silicone. He had chuckled and explained that a wafer of silicone was merely a microchip.

"I think we need to retrieve my father's microchip," said Liz.

"A microchip?" Tim echoed.

"It has to do with his science experiment and research. I don't know why but it seems this clue indicates we should get the microchip. Maybe there will be a message with it about why we need it."

"So where do you propose we go looking for it?"

"I'm thinking that the lion is also an important part of the clue," said Liz. "The hidden microchip must have something to do with a lion."

"What do you think it refers to?"

"I'm not sure. I do have a hunch though. I know that if it's something valuable my father would have kept it somewhere safe. And I don't think it has anything to do with real lions. I'm thinking something symbolic or an emblem of some sort." Liz began thinking aloud. "If you wanted to keep something of value and you didn't want anybody to lay their hands on it, where would you consider keeping it?"

Tim was silent for a few moments. "I don't know. Maybe a bank?"

"Exactly. That's what I was thinking. A bank."

"So you have a bank called Lion Bank?"

"No, there is no such bank that I know of. I'm thinking of Vuyisana Bank. It's the bank our family has used for years."

"What does that have to do with a lion?"

"The bank has a lion's face as their emblem. Their marketing involves treating customers like kings."

"Kings?"

"Yes," said Liz. "And the lion is known universally as the king of the jungle. More than this, the bank has a division for elite clients which includes safety deposit boxes."

Liz had already stood up. She ruffled in her pants pocket and jingled her car keys. "You coming?"

CHAPTER 23

Still craving a cup of coffee, Mike Bonnington shifted in the driver's seat. His legs ached and he was beginning to feel claustrophobic. He wondered how long the girl and her male friend would be in that house for. He had seen the old lady go back to her place next door but the car belonging to the two visitors was still parked outside the house, as was the car he had followed from UCT.

Mike decided to stretch his legs. He eyed his gun on the pile of papers on the passenger seat and then swung his door open. The air outside was crisp and fresh. *So much greenery.* The feel of suburbia catapulted Mike back to his own suburban street in his neighborhood back home. The wave of nostalgia swept through him, causing him to miss his family even more. The sooner he was home the better. And what better way to show his employers it was time for him to go home than solve a murder? No more paper pushing. No more mundane assignments to flatten his ego further. He could be home in no time doing what he did best. And with the Red Sox hopefully making the World Series final in a few weeks, Mike was presented with a double incentive.

Mike's thoughts were interrupted by the roaring engine of a large yellow rubbish removal truck chugging along the road in his direction. He jumped back into his car and closed the door as the truck edged past. The truck's shrill beeps got louder as the vehicle slowed down. It stopped a few meters from where Mike was parked, blocking the view of the house Mike was watching. A few men dressed in blue overalls were clinging to the back of the truck and jumped off when the vehicle came to a standstill.

Mike observed them collect the large refuse bins that stood at the bottom of the driveways and then empty the contents into the back of the truck. The stench of the rubbish rushed towards him. Mike turned away in disgust as he wound up the car window. He tapped his fingers on the steering wheel and began to fiddle with the radio.

The Fox was pacing in his private study when his phone beeped. He opened the text message: "Please Call Me". It was from Rafik Jaffer. The Fox frowned. His orders were always very clear and his rules were always obeyed. That was how the system worked. That was how results were achieved. Rafik Jaffer knew the rules very well. One of the main rules never to be broken was: Don't ever try and get in touch with the Fox. If the Fox requested you to contact him, that was different. But if you tried to initiate contact with the Fox, that was not welcome. Not welcome at all.

The Fox thought about it for a minute. The message could only mean something had not gone according to plan. And, if that was the case, could the situation be resolved?

Knowing Rafik and his caliber, the Fox realized something had gone horribly wrong and the repercussions could be ominous, not only for Rafik but for the Fox himself.

The Fox cursed. It was always risky speaking to an accomplice on the phone. One never knew just who could be listening in or which conversation could be monitored or intercepted. A few minutes later, the Fox connected his electronic voice changer device to his cellphone. He would never risk any of his employees hearing his real voice. It was safer that way. Against his better judgement, the Fox made a call to the number he used for Rafik.

Mike Bonnington continued to anxiously tap his fingers on the steering wheel of his parked rental.

Five minutes later, the men in blue overalls hopped on to their little ledge at the back of the truck and the truck meandered into the distance. Mike's view of the house was clear again. The lady and her male companion must have already left; their car was no longer there. Bonnington was relieved, however, to see that the professor's car was still parked in the driveway.

Finally! Mike grabbed his gun and rushed out the vehicle towards the front lawn. He instinctively glanced around him, but the rest of the road remained deserted. Mike crept up to the front door. He hesitated. He could ring the doorbell and risk the man inside fleeing or he could enter the premises and take his target by surprise. He decided the surprise element was the better approach. He was sick of having to always follow procedure and kowtow to criminals. If he wanted this catch, then he would do what he needed to do to reel him in.

Mike turned the door handle and was surprised that the door had been left unlocked. Gripping his gun, he stepped inside the house. The entrance was stuffy. Mike turned left and found himself in a bedroom. There was a single bed that showed no signs of it having been slept in. A small empty wooden desk stood against the wall. Other than that the room was empty.

Mike entered another bedroom next to it. The bedroom boasted a double bed and the sheets and duvet were crumpled across the bed. Some used tissues stuck out of a brown wicker bin next to a pedestal. The lamp on the pedestal remained on, yet there was no sign of anyone in the room. Mike tiptoed into the en-suite but all he saw was his reflection in the mirror that stretched over the double basins.

Mike walked out of the bedroom and past another door, presumably a study. The room was large and filled with papers scattered over a desk. A computer screen was partially visible through the piles of clutter. Mike carried on towards the other end of the house.

He pointed his gun as he entered the open-plan living area.

"Time for nuts! Time for nuts!"

The hairs on Mike's arms and back rose as he spun around and aimed his gun in the direction where the sounds had come from.

"Nuts, nuts, nuts!"

"Mother-fucking parrot!" Mike let out a deep breath. He walked forward and heard the crunch beneath his feet. There was glass all over the floor.

"What the fuck?"

He leaned down and picked up a piece, studying it. He had learned over the years that often the smallest detail carried the heaviest weight. And he liked to think he was still very thorough. Thorough enough that he could smell the distinct scent of whiskey. And chloroform. An empty house and traces of chloroform.

The person he had followed from UCT was no longer in his house. It was as if his ticket back home had been snatched out of his hands and shredded.

"Those bastards must have taken the guy with him." Mike shook his head in disdain. How could he have let this happen? He had to sort this out. No one was going to stand in the way of him going home. No one.

CHAPTER 24

After navigating the busy early morning streets of Claremont, Liz took a sharp left off the main road into a narrow side street. They were in the heart of Claremont's business and shopping district. At the top of the street was an impressive building that housed the bank. As Liz and Tim approached the entrance to the parking garage, they were faced by a closed thick boom and two burly security officials. One of the officials approached Liz's side of the car and she opened her window.

"We're coming to the bank." Liz pointed ahead.

The guard nodded and handed her a clipboard. Liz filled out her car registration number, her name, and contact number on the form. She gave the clipboard back to the guard and drove into the parking lot, steering the car into a bay marked "visitors".

"I'm quite surprised by all the visible security I've seen since I arrived," Tim remarked as they climbed out of the vehicle.

"Don't you have security like this in the States?"

"Not on a scale like this."

"I guess we're just used to it," said Liz. "But there are some major banks in this building so I would assume they would be more vigilant here than, say, a department store."

They made their way down a short flight of stairs that led to a small lit-up lobby where they waited for the elevator to arrive on their floor. Liz thought she heard some heavy footsteps getting nearer, and looked to the staircase where they had just walked from.

"Did you hear that?"

"Hear what?"

"I thought I heard footsteps."

Tim looked around. "Doesn't seem to be anyone else here."

Now Liz could hear only the faint passing sound of a car revving its engine in the parking lot above them. "It doesn't matter," she said as the elevator doors moved open and they both stepped in.

Tim and Liz exited the elevator into a lavish foyer with marble floors and large stone pillars interspersed throughout the area.

"How I can I help you today?" A man in a dark black suit at reception smiled. An emblem of a large lion's face was emblazoned across the front of the counter.

"I need to access my family's private account," said Liz.

"What are the account details?"

"I'm not exactly sure of the actual account number but the surname is Greene."

The man looked down at Liz through the glasses on the end of his nose. "Madam, we need an account number."

"I unfortunately don't know it."

"Do you have any identification with you?"

Liz rummaged in her bag and pulled out a green identity booklet. Under South African law, all citizens had to carry such a booklet when they had to present someone with formal identification. Some places were happy to just see a driver's license but many places still insisted on the green booklets.

The man in the suit scrutinized the ID and punched some numbers into a computer. He waited a few seconds for some information to appear on the screen.

"And you say it's your account?"

"Well, actually it's a family account. But it would be in the name of my father, Harry Greene."

"I'm not seeing anything on the system," the man said. "And you don't have any bank cards or statements on you that can help identify the account?"

"No." Liz felt a heavy weight in her stomach.

"The computer is having trouble verifying you," the man said. "It's not recognizing your ID number."

"But you can see I'm the person in the ID picture," Liz said.

"Yes, but that doesn't prove you're linked to any account here. I'm afraid I am unable to help you."

"You've got to help me," Liz begged. "Please. It's very urgent."

"I'm sure it is, Madam, but there is nothing I can do unless you provide me with the account details."

"I already said I don't have that information on me," Liz raised her voice.

"Well, then there is nothing more that I can do."

"Please, just keep looking."

"Madam, I am going to have to ask you to leave."

"I'm not going anywhere until you sort this out, dammit. We have an account here and I demand access to it right away."

"Madam, unfortunately I have to ask you to leave. This is the second time I am asking you."

"And I said I'm not going anywhere." Liz was on the verge of screaming.

"Surely there's something you can do?" said Tim.

"I'm afraid there isn't, sir. Please leave now."

"No!" Liz yelled.

CHAPTER 25

Sindy made her way back home and took a long hot shower, something she did every morning after her jog. She then put on a tight grey skirt and a striped red and white blouse, grabbing a muesli yoghurt bar as she headed back to her car. It did not take long before she found herself in the midst of the regular heavy morning traffic.

Sindy, like most people in Cape Town, did not take kindly to sitting in traffic jams. Instead of the usual sigh of exasperation and symptoms of road rage, Sindy remained calm and stayed unusually focused; today she had far more important things on her mind. Important really didn't even do the feeling justice.

Some individuals go through their lives totally committed to a certain cause. Whether it is the quest to reduce greenhouse gases, or building shelters for the homeless, some people are extremely passionate about achieving certain goals and will do their utmost to uphold their beliefs and visions.

Sindy knew herself to be this type of person. Determined and ambitious, Sindy believed in acting on her convictions and standing up for her beliefs. She took pride in her value system and in her work. Not only was Sindy smart and sophisticated, but she was sexy and beautiful too. A lethal combination.

Sindy's qualities did not go unnoticed by certain individuals in a certain network and she was soon recruited by the Fox. She had joined the current project fifteen months before, and could not believe that its culmination was imminent.

Sindy steered her vehicle in and out of the traffic, oblivious of all the other suits in the surrounding vehicles. Her vision was perfectly clear. She stared out of the window, the sea beckoning in the distance. Her heart was pounding.

The day of reckoning had arrived.

CHAPTER 26

Tom Marron had been Manager of the elite Executive Client Division portfolio at Vuyisana Bank for twelve years. He had built up a small but substantial client base and had come to know his clients and their needs very well. As the portfolio was an exclusive one and not for ordinary bankers, Tom had become accustomed to dealing with his elite clients and building up solid relationships with them.

Some of his clients included wealthy businessmen, award-winning sportsmen and women, yacht owners and other high flyers. Not all of his clients were majorly wealthy but had sufficient money to keep their accounts discrete to protect their assets and whatever else they wanted protected. Not all of his clients wanted to keep luxurious watches and jewelry protected in safety deposit boxes. There were those who valued other things to store such as contracts, photographs, computer equipment and other technological advancements.

Marron prided himself on providing the best service he could for his customers, all of whom were given his private cellphone number in case a client needed him after hours. No problem was too small for Marron.

Marron had just ended a phone call with an irate journalist who had discovered some irregularities in the bank's code of conduct. He didn't know how she had gotten his contact details or why she had called him. He repeated several times during that it was not his division that she was referring to, and that she needed to take her grievances up with the manager of their main banking arm, as it was that section which dealt with ordinary banking and the public. When the journalist finally got the message and put the phone down in a huff, an exasperated Marron was about to pour his coffee. And then a red light above his desk started flashing.

It could only mean one thing: Trouble. As if his morning couldn't get any worse.

He stood up and shuffled over to a set of closed circuit television screens in the corner of the room. He reached for a nearby remote control and turned up the volume. On the main screen he had a clear view of the front reception desk.

"I demand some decent service here!" The woman who was talking had her back to the hidden camera.

"Madam, I've already said there's nothing more I can do."

"This is ridiculous," said the man standing next to the woman. He turned around, perhaps hoping to see some other bank officials. "Is there no one else around here who can help?"

As the man turned, Marron was able to examine him closely on the screen. He scratched his head, not recognizing him. *Is that an American accent?* Tom had several clients who were Americans and he would have recognized every one of them. This man was completely unfamiliar.

"Sir, I've got security on the way. This is your last chance to take this lady out of these premises before you make a big scene."

"I'll give you a scene!" shouted the woman. At that moment, three burly security officials arrived at the front desk.

"Please escort this lady and gentleman outside." The man at reception had lost his smile.

"Please, I just need to sort this out. My family has an account here." The woman turned to plead with the security official and as she did so Marron was able to view her face. He stared at the close-up of the shouting woman.

No, it can't be! Surely that isn't her?

He fumbled for his keys and then headed for the elevator for special private staff that could take him speedily to any floor of the bank. As the elevator moved upwards, he took out a stained white handkerchief from his jacket and wiped the sweat from his forehead.

Luckily for Rafik, the dire situation he had caused the Fox resolved itself quicker than he had anticipated. A few minutes after the Fox had slammed down the phone in disgust at the news Rafik had shot Professor Greene, the Fox had sent Rafik an urgent text message instructing him to apprehend the targets when they left Vuyisana Bank. The Fox had bugged Professor Greene's house and received this new information by eavesdropping on a conversation that took place there. The Fox had made it clear he did not want to hear from Rafik until he was able to tell him he had the microchip.

Now, standing at the side of the foyer in Vuyisana Bank, Rafik watched Professor Greene's daughter and her friend argue with the bank official at the reception desk. Soon he would be holding the microchip himself. Whatever it took.

"What's the problem here?" Marron approached the front desk.

"Just someone trying to gain access inside," one of the security officials began to explain.

"No verification or proper ID," the other guard added.

"This is ridiculous," said the woman. "And you have the cheek to say you treat your customers like kings!"

She turned to look at Marron to plead her case. He stared back at her, trying to keep an official facade. *My word, it is Elizabeth Greene.*

"Do you have any form of ID on you?" Marron asked her.

"As I've already explained to all these people, I have shown them my ID book and my driver's license, and this should be enough to prove to someone who I am." It sounded as if she were about to cry.

"May I see it, please?"

The guards let go of her while she reached for her ID book.

"I've never known a bank to treat people like this," said the American.

Marron ignored the comment and examined the woman's ID book and then looked up at her face before examining the ID book again. *It's her, all right!*

"I'll take it from here," Marron said to the guards, who hesitated. "I'm your superior and I'm instructing you to leave these people with me and to return to your surveillance unit downstairs immediately."

The guards looked at each other and then at the man behind the reception desk. The man nodded and the guards proceeded down the hallway and were soon out of sight.

"Come with me, please." Marron gestured to Elizabeth and the American, and they all walked in the direction of the elevator Marron had just used.

"What is going on here? What type of a bank treats customers like this?" Elizabeth demanded.

"Let's not talk out here," Marron said quietly. "Wait until we get to my office."

CHAPTER 27

"Have a seat please," Marron pointed to the black leather couch in his office. Marron had introduced himself to Elizabeth and the American, who said his name was Tim, and now he wheeled the big cushioned chair out from behind his desk to where they sat.

"I urgently need to access my father's account," said Liz.

"We generally only allow family of our account holders to access an account when they are accompanied by specific documentation authorizing them to access such an account," Marron explained.

"I am aware of that, but this is an urgent situation."

"Why?"

"I believe my father has left something for me in his safety deposit box."

"Well, then you need to get a letter or something from him explaining that he has given you permission to access it."

"That's part of the problem. My dad has disappeared."

"What do you mean he has disappeared?" Marron felt his body go cold.

"Exactly that. He's vanished into thin air. Not even answering his cellphone."

"And he wasn't planning on going away or anything."

"No, not that I know of. But even if he has gone away, I'm sure he would have let me know, and even if he didn't let me know he would still answer his phone or phone me back as soon as he could."

Good grief, what is going on? Professor Greene has disappeared?

Marron tried to contain himself, hoping that Liz and Tim didn't see him trying to suppress a gulp.

"Maybe it's nothing sinister," Marron said. "I'm sure he'll show up soon."

"I think there's more to it than meets the eye," said Tim.

Tim and Liz relayed to him the sudden events of the morning.

If what they're telling me is true, it could be a calamity.

"Please can you help me?" said Liz.

"I wish I could help you," Marron cleared his throat. "But without any letter of authorization or permission by your father himself, there's nothing much I can do."

"Just make an exception this once," said Tim.

"And lose my job? I have a wife and three-month-old baby to support."

"It could be a matter of life and death," said Liz.

Marron stared at them. He wondered what the right approach would be. A heavy decision was now resting on his shoulders. Two weeks ago, the professor had come into the bank and requested to see his safety deposit box. Marron had left him alone in a private cubicle, as was part of the bank's service. The professor had not examined the contents of his box for five minutes before he rung the little bell on his desk to summon Marron to collect the box.

Marron had been at the bank for many years and had come to know the professor quite well. When the professor had come in for his most recent visit, Marron couldn't help notice that the professor had looked unusually flustered. Now, Marron scratched his head as he stared at the professor's daughter and deliberated how much information he should reveal.

"Please, I think my father has left me something or is trying to tell me something that might help us work out why he has disappeared and where he might be." Some tears began to slide down Liz's cheeks.

"It's all very bizarre," said Tim.

The professor had never mentioned anything to him about Liz coming to the bank's vault section with a friend. He hoped the old bugger was all right. If his daughter was telling the truth, then he had a moral obligation to help her.

Marron sighed. He was glad he wasn't a judge and that he didn't have to make such critical decisions on a daily basis. His heart sank as the thought of a lawsuit briefly swept through his mind.

"Are you going to help us?" said Liz. "Please, I don't know where else to turn right now."

Marron looked at her and tried to remain expressionless. *Should I tell her that her father was here?*

"Please help me," said Liz. "If you know my father you would know that under these circumstances he would want you to allow me access to the safety deposit box."

Marron stood up and walked to his desk. He picked up a brown receiver that looked like those old telephones one doesn't see any more. He handed the phone to Liz. "Here."

"Why are you giving me a phone?"

"I want you to phone your father."

"But I already told you I couldn't get hold of him," Liz raised her voice.

"I need you to dial whatever number you use to get hold of your father," Marron spoke slowly. "After that I will call him on the number he has given us in our records."

"And what if we still can't get hold of him?" Tim asked.

Marron didn't answer and kept his eyes fixed on Liz.

"Fine," said Liz. "But I'm telling you now this is a pointless exercise."

She dialed Professor Greene's number. It didn't even ring and went straight to voicemail.

"Listen." Liz gave the phone to Marron. He pressed it against his ear. *"You've reached the number of Harry Greene. I'm unable to take your call at the moment. Please leave your details and I will try my best to get back to you shortly."*

Marron hung up and sat down behind the desk. He punched some letters on his keyboard. A few seconds later the bank's contact number for Professor Greene appeared in front of him. He dialed the number for the professor's cellphone and clenched his teeth when the phone went straight to the same voicemail message.

"Well?" asked Tim.

If the bank directors got wind of him allowing someone access to a premium elite safety deposit box account and they weren't the account holder and had no written authorization, he would be fired on the spot. No further questions asked.

Marron did not know what he would do if he lost his job. He shuddered at the thought of not being able to support his family financially. He glanced at Liz and how sad she looked and how helpless her situation seemed to be.

It was highly unlikely the professor would ever complain to the bank or report Marron to the higher authorities. And if something had happened to the old guy, then nobody would be able to point a finger at Marron anyway.

He had to make a decision.

CHAPTER 28

At approximately eleven thirty, Sindy left her desk on the fifth floor of the office section at the Cape Town Convention Centre and took the stairs down to the second floor. She walked down a long corridor in the direction of the men's bathroom at the far end. A janitor was standing outside with a small green bucket in one hand and a mop in the other. He was leaning against a large trolley that had an array of cleaning liquids and toilet rolls on it.

"My husband came to visit me earlier and he lost his wedding band," said Sindy. "Can you believe it?"

"That is most unfortunate," said the janitor.

"So anyway, I am going everywhere he went while he was here just in case it's still lying around."

The janitor nodded, placed the mop and bucket onto the trolley, and began to push it away.

"Do you mind if I go look in there?" Sindy pointed to the men's bathroom. "Have you finished cleaning?"

"I'm finished in there," said the janitor. "It's all clean now, but I didn't see any ring lying around. But hey, go ahead!"

"Thanks." Sindy smiled. She knew the bathroom had been cleaned already. She had been observing the janitor's routine for a few weeks.

She looked around to make sure no one else was approaching, and then she opened the door to the men's bathroom and went inside. Entering one of the cubicles, she locked the door behind her and reached into her pocket, pulling out two cards, each the size of a credit card. The cards were laminated and each was attached to a small silver peg. She wrapped the cards in toilet paper until they weren't visible.

Checking to make sure the men's bathroom had remained empty, Sindy then walked to the large dustbin in the corner underneath the paper towel section. She placed the wrapped up cards at the bottom of the bin, put the lid back onto it, and proceeded out the door. There was no one in the passage as

Sindy made her way to the elevators.

———

Approximately half an hour later, two men dressed casually in jeans and faded t-shirts strolled into the Convention Centre. They had to walk through a metal detector but there was no security problem, as they were not armed.

They made their way, as instructed, to the men's bathroom at the far end of the second floor. The one went inside while the other leaned against the outside wall on the lookout.

The man who went into the bathroom did the standard check to make sure it was indeed empty. When he had ascertained that it was, he reached in to the dustbin, taking out the two plastic cards that had been wrapped in toilet paper.

He went back into the cubicle and opened his tog bag. He took out various items of clothing and changed into black pants and a blue long-sleeve button-down shirt, and then used the silver peg to attach the plastic card to his outer pocket. It was an identity card and the photograph on it was an identical match to his face.

He walked out of the bathroom where his colleague was still waiting. He handed him the other identity card and the man went into the bathroom to change. Soon they were both smartly dressed and suitably ready. They headed down the passage and into the elevator.

CHAPTER 29

"I'll help you," Marron said to Liz, "but we've got to be discreet."

Liz wiped her eyes. "Thank you."

Marron unlocked his door and they exited his office. "Come this way," he whispered. He led them down another corridor and into another elevator, and they disembarked onto a luxurious carpet on a level deep under the building.

"Welcome to our lounge for premium account holders."

They were standing in a large room that was decorated with some African fine art. A painting of an open-mouthed leopard that had just completed its kill graced the far wall, while the walls on either sides were filled with enormous framed canvasses of a variety of animals gathering at the foot of a hill.

"So this is where my dad would have come?" said Liz.

"Yes, this is our private vault section of the bank. It's reserved for an elite few who have access to the safety deposit box section. Once our clients go through the necessary authorization upstairs they get escorted down to this lounge."

"So are you just going to access my father's safety deposit box?" Liz asked.

"We'll go through to that section now."

They walked down a ramp through another passage and into a small foyer.

"I must ask you to have a seat here," Marron said to Tim. "I can only let Miss Greene through here."

Tim looked at Liz and she nodded her approval.

"We'll be back soon," said Liz.

"There's a cappuccino machine in the corner if you're thirsty." Marron showed Tim and then prompted Liz to follow him through the foyer door. They found themselves in another carpeted area with three private cubicles in front of them.

"What happens now?" asked Liz.

"You must go into the middle cubicle. Your father's safety deposit box will be waiting for you inside it."

"Are you coming too?"

"No, I am not allowed to enter the cubicle. Our clients have the utmost discretion and privacy, and that is why we have built up such a solid reputation over the years. To many of our clients we are known unofficially as the Swiss Bank of Africa."

Liz was about to walk to the cubicle when Marron started speaking again.

"There's one other thing... I'm assuming you are aware of our extra security system?"

"Extra security? More than what I've already gone through in the past hour?"

"Well, yes. You knew from the start about the rigorous security at this institution. That's obviously why your father trusted us enough to store his valuables here. Well then, if your father wanted you to access his account here, he would know that you would have to have the right ingredients to open the safety deposit box?"

"The right ingredients?"

"All of our safety deposit boxes can only be accessed by the relevant person concerned. In other words no member of our staff, no matter how high up they are in the bank's structure, can open these boxes. That is part of our excellent security."

"So, you are saying that the box is not unlocked for me?"

"That is correct."

"But then how am I going to open it?"

CHAPTER 30

Wahied Madat continued his journey through the hills and valleys as he drove along the N2 highway heading in the direction of Cape Town. It had been a long ride.

Caught up in his expectations for what lay ahead, Wahied did not seem to notice that the speed zone for the area he was now in had just been lowered to sixty kilometers, nor did he notice the traffic officer sitting on a deck chair obscured by a large bush at the bottom of a hill, waiting to lure in passing motorists, like a fisherman casting out his rod and eagerly hauling in his catch.

Wahied's vehicle screeched to a halt as the officer waved him down.

"Damn!" he muttered and switched off the engine while the burly officer ambled towards the car. Wahied looked at his watch. He couldn't afford to lose any time; it was vital he stuck to his schedule.

"In a rush, are we?" said the officer.

"Sorry, I didn't realize the speed limit had changed," said Wahied.

"Step out of the vehicle please."

"What?"

"I said step out of the vehicle."

Wahied silently cursed and clambered out of the truck, scratching his head.

"Driver's license, please."

Wahied fumbled in his pockets and brought out a small tattered black credit card holder. After sorting through several cards, some of which he no longer even used, he found his driver's license and handed it over to the man in the uniform.

The officer stared at the license and looked up at Wahied again to make sure the face was the same as the photograph. It was. Handing back the card to Wahied, the officer peered into the driver area and scrutinized the front seats. Nothing of particular interest. An empty tomato-flavor chip bag, half a packet of sugar-free peppermints, and an almost-full small plastic bottle of water.

"Hmm, I need you to take a breathalyzer test."

"Why? I'm not drunk!" Wahied was indignant. "You can see that I am sober."

"It's standard procedure," said the officer. "We're on a strict campaign to clamp down on drunk driving."

There was a rustle from the bush behind which the officer had been sitting. Another officer emerged from the greenery.

"Everything okay, Albert?" he asked the other officer.

"Yes, everything is fine," said Albert. "Just wanting this young gentleman to take a breathalyzer test.'

"How long is this going to be?" asked Wahied.

"Just a few minutes. Obviously the longer you take before the test, the longer you will have to wait for the result."

"Okay, okay," said Wahied. "Let's just do it. I can't stand here all day."

While Albert organized the breathalyzer, the other officer walked up to Wahied's vehicle and peered inside. The officer proceeded to the back of the truck and looked at the locked doors, frowning.

"We need to look inside here," he said, tapping his fingers on the metal of the container doors. If he had been looking carefully at Wahied, he would have seen Wahied flinch.

CHAPTER 31

Liz was waving her hands around madly as she spoke. "How am I going to access this safety deposit box if it is locked? Don't you as the bank lock them and unlock them for your clients?"

"We actually don't," said Marron. "That's part of the appeal. If someone had to break in—and it is highly unlikely that someone would be able to penetrate this secure basement perimeter anyway—but if someone broke in they wouldn't be able to open the deposit box."

"Well, they could probably run off with it and smash it into pieces somewhere else."

"They couldn't. The boxes slide out on a special railing linked to the main vault. They cannot be ripped off from the motherboard, so to speak. Also, they are made with such strong materials that they can't be smashed."

"So you're saying that if I want to open my father's safety deposit box then I need a key to open it?"

Marron shook his head. "A key won't help you here."

"It won't?"

"You need the correct password."

"A password?"

"Well, to be accurate, three passwords."

"Three passwords? I can't even remember one password for my own internet banking, let alone all the other damn passwords society expects me to remember these days."

"I'm sorry." Marron shrugged. "Three passwords. And the first and last passwords have to be a minimum of eight characters to be exact."

"But I don't have three passwords." Liz could have pulled her hair out.

"Well, take your time and think about it."

"I don't have time, that's my worry. Can't you override it or something?"

"I'm afraid even if I did want to override the system for you, I wouldn't be able to. There is no way around this system. It's completely foolproof."

"I can't believe this." That familiar lump was rising in Liz's throat again.

"Just think about what your father might have used for his passwords," said Marron. "What was something that had meaning for him?"

"I don't know," said Liz. "My mind's gone blank. I can't think of anything."

"Take your time," said Marron. "I'll leave you for a few minutes. If you need me again just ring that small bell over there."

"What if I can't work out the right passwords?"

"I'm afraid there's nothing I will be able to do. I've done everything I possibly could in a situation like this. I brought you to your father's safety deposit box."

"I know. And don't get me wrong, I'm extremely grateful for your help. But I can't believe there is nothing the bank can do in a situation like this."

Before Marron walked off he cleared his throat. "I don't know if you are aware but you only have three attempts."

"Three attempts? To crack the passwords? But what happens if I can't get the correct passwords?"

"If your third attempt is still incorrect then the system itself will automatically go into what we call a protection overdrive. In simple terms it will shut down. I'm sure your father would have formulated them into something that makes sense to you. Otherwise you wouldn't be here now, would you?"

He waited for a response but Liz was silent as she stared wide-eyed at the various buttons on the safety deposit box in front of her.

"I must also add that even if you do come up with the right passwords, you need to punch them in in the right sequence."

"The right sequence?" Liz's words were barely audible now.

"If you type the right words but in the wrong order, the computer system will still not recognize it as being correct."

Liz wanted to get up from her seat and smash the tiny hand bell over Marron's fat head. But she refrained herself. "Okay..."

"I didn't devise the system," said Marron, reading the expression on her face. "I just work in it."

CHAPTER 32

Tim helped himself to a cappuccino and sprawled himself across the dark leather couch, careful not to spill. The soothing sound of African music and marimba drums echoed through the speakers that were placed in the ceiling corners.

He swung his feet onto the long wooden table that stretched across a bright red carpet. It had been such a rush since his arrival in Cape Town that he hadn't realized just how tired he was. It always took him a while to catch up with a new time zone when he traveled out of the USA. Not that he traveled much, but he knew his body always took long to adjust. Since he'd gotten here, he barely had had a moment to relax and really appreciate where he was.

He took a sip from one of the official bank lion-emblem mugs and let the hot liquid warm his chest as he continued to admire the artwork on the walls around him. He glanced at his watch, wondering how long Liz would need.

As he finished his drink, he reached into his jacket pocket and took out his cellphone. There were no new messages. He moved it from one hand to the other, contemplating whether to make a call or not. *She might walk in any minute. How long can it take to access a safety deposit box?* He decided against making the call and put the phone back into his pocket.

A sweet scent filled the air. Although he could not see it, an incense burner must have been nearby. The lighting in the room was dim, adding to the peaceful ambience. It was clear that whoever was sitting in these couches was supposed to feel comfortable and relaxed, away from the stresses of the fast-paced life lurking on the other side of the wall on the busy streets.

A flat screen was set on the wall immediately in front of him. The volume was off but the visuals were of a sports game that was played in South Africa. He wasn't sure what it was. It looked like a football the players were running with but he knew for sure that it wasn't NFL!

The walls seemed to be made of a variety of brown stones cemented in and placed next to each other. On the one wall an impressive array of African tribal masks surrounded an unlit fireplace. Next to the masks was a real spear that looked very sharp. On the far wall to his left he saw several framed prints of Zulus dancing with Kingsley Holgate.

But what caught his attention was on the far wall to his right—by far the most impressive original artwork he had seen in a long time. He gasped at the original acrylic-on-canvas paintings. The main one depicted three lions leaning down into a watering hole. Their eyes gleamed; their expressions had been painted to the last immaculate detail.

"It's a David Bucklow original."

Tim looked around to see that Marron had entered the room.

"It's an amazing piece of art," said Tim.

"It sure is. All these Bucklow paintings are highly sought after. David Bucklow actually lives here in Cape Town."

"I like his style. Such attention to detail, and what fine use of the colors."

"Years ago he gave up his day job to pursue a career in art. Quite a risk given the fickle art market and notwithstanding the fact that he has a wife and three kids to support," said Marron. "He had no formal training. True natural talent. Now his paintings are wanted all over the world."

"I can see why. This one is so lifelike," said Tim. "Almost like I can reach out and touch the lions."

"Anyway, Miss Greene will still be a while," said Marron after a moment of silence.

Tim thanked him for letting him know and Marron walked off into the distance. As soon as he was out of sight, Tim waited another minute and took out his phone.

He looked around the area to make sure there was no one else within earshot. Then he began to dial a number.

CHAPTER 33

"When you are finished with your breathalyzer, you can open the back of the truck," the nosy officer told Wahied.

Wahied nodded and cursed again silently. He was hoping the officer would have changed his mind about opening the doors. He stared at his watch. He had better get moving soon.

"All clear," said the officer conducting the test. "No trace of alcohol in this fellow!"

"I told you!" said Wahied.

"Just open the truck doors for us now and then you can be on your way," said the other officer.

Wahied shook his head as he marched to the back of the truck and unlocked the doors. A stream of sweat that had been gathering around Wahied's neck finally made its way down his back.

The officer peered into the open container and climbed in. He stared at the various boxes and crates that were stacked up in piles across the vehicle floor. They were all sealed.

"May I?" he asked, looking at Wahied over his shoulder.

"I've got nothing to hide," said Wahied angrily.

The officer pulled out his standard pocket police penknife and cut along the sealed strip at the top of the box. There were several six-packs of small bottles of mineral water. Nothing sinister at all. The officer took out a bottle, held it to the light, stared at it closely, and put it back in the box.

"Are they all the same?" Wilfred asked, pointing to the rest of the crates and boxes.

"Yes, they are all the same," Wahied swallowed hard and spoke slowly and clearly. "What exactly were you expecting?"

They officer climbed off the truck.

"You are free to go," he told Wahied. "Just watch those speed limits."

Wahied nodded and slammed the doors shut, putting the lock in place once more. He walked around to the driver's side and jumped in, switched on the engine, gave it a thumping rev, and drove off.

CHAPTER 34

Liz ground her teeth as she stared at the safety deposit box in front of her. She needed to open it and she knew that she needed to open it fast. Her mind went over the cryptic message her father had scribbled for her in the dog breed book. *In the clutches of the strong lion a wafer will quench your thirst.* She had worked out "lion" and "wafer", and those parts of the clue had led her to this bank. But how did "quench your thirst" relate to possible passwords? She didn't have any idea.

Liz sighed. *Three passwords? What on Earth could they possibly be?*

Her father would not have just used random passwords. He wasn't like that. Liz knew the passwords would have to be in some particular sequence, something that was logical and made sense. If he had wanted her to open up the safety deposit box he would have devised the passwords in such a way that Liz would be able to work it out. And it dawned on her that maybe the passwords had nothing to do with the original clue that had led her here. Maybe she was supposed to figure out these passwords on her own. So it would have to be something she would know easily, something close to her that her father would have known she could work out.

Liz could barely remember the passwords she used on her own computer on an almost daily basis. There were so many websites and systems for which she had various passwords that she had resorted to sticking a small piece of paper on the corner of her computer screen. On the paper she had scrawled seven of her main passwords and used this as a regular reference point. But now she needed to work out passwords herself. And there was no piece of paper with passwords to help her now. This time it wasn't just about entering into one of her websites. This time it could be a matter of life and death.

Liz reflected on the word games she used to play with her father when she was a child. When Liz was twelve years old, her father had given her a super-sized Scrabble set for her birthday. It was an especially large board, much larger than the average Scrabble board, and it became one of Liz's prized possessions. Professor Greene had taught his daughter the art of playing the game well and Liz, being the girl she was, grasped the concept very quickly, and soon became a deep strategist and a worthy opponent for her father. It wasn't long before she had started to beat the professor at his own game and this resulted in a healthy competitive relationship.

It was not only the formulating of words that Liz took to, but a desire to understand complicated meanings too. This led her to the world of riddles and her fascination and determination in solving them. It was clear that she showed deep academic potential, which was not surprising for the daughter of an esteemed academic and researcher.

So Professor Greene encouraged Liz to use her word-deciphering skills at every chance he could get. He would often hide things in the house and garden, and then write out various clues for Liz to follow. She loved the challenge and inevitably would solve the clues and find whatever it was the professor had hidden. It became their favorite weekend activity, and there was seldom a time when Liz didn't decipher the professor's cryptic clues.

Things were so simple back then, Liz thought. *What I would give to have my childhood back.*

But like all chapters in life, there was no turning back and, as Liz's childhood seemed further and further away, her adult life seemed to have taken on more serious dimensions. She was now faced with the possibility of losing her father and all his research. This was something she had never even considered, and it terrified her.

Liz looked at the big white and gold clock on the far wall above the cubicles. She had been there for just over fifteen minutes and still she had no idea as to what the passwords could be.

It's got to be something easy for me, something obvious.

She bit her fingernails on her left hand as her other hand glided over the cold surface of the safety deposit box.

Her father had given her the clue to get to this point, so he obviously had the confidence that she would be able to handle the passwords. *But three passwords that had to be in the right order? What was he thinking!*

Marron had said that the first word had to be a minimum of eight characters. Liz pondered some of the significant personal details her father might have considered in formulating the passwords. She thought about the name of his first dog, B-U-G-S-Y, his high school, P-R-I-D-E, and his favorite holiday spot, V-E-N-I-C-E. They were all less than eight characters.

She wondered if the three passwords were linked to each other, or if they were totally unrelated. Knowing her father, she concluded they must be linked to each other. He believed everything was connected! So she had to figure out three words that went together, three words she would be supposed to know.

What else is important to him?

The silence was broken as Liz became aware of the harsh ticks of the clock. Each tick seemed to get louder and louder as if the clock was saying hurry up already. Marron didn't tell her how long she had but she was sure he wouldn't rush her. Not at a crucial time like this.

Another ten minutes passed while Liz continued to stare dismally at the safety deposit box. She had to come up with something soon. She felt a cold shiver as she contemplated not coming up with the right passwords and combination.

No, she told herself. *Defeat is not an option. I just need to work it out. Something obvious.*

But she knew that, although it had to be something obvious, there was the chance her father might have been subtle in his choice of words.

But it has to be something I know. Otherwise why would he have sent me here if he knew I would never be able to crack the passwords?

Something that I know. What could that be?

Liz thought of the names of her first dolls, of the neighbor's cat that used to jump over the fence of their house while she was growing up, and even the ingredients for her mom's famous recipe of her favorite chocolate chip cookies. But although she came close to the number of characters, it wasn't enough and it certainly didn't fit into the combinations.

That's it! Maybe he used his full names. That's obvious enough.

Liz was about to punch in Professor Greene's full name, middle name and surname when she hesitated again. She went over it in her mind to make sure the numbers of characters for each word would fit the combination puzzle. But the letters did not fit.

Dammit! Liz slammed her hands against the table. She was running out of options.

CHAPTER 35

Sitting in the heart of Vuyisana Bank's vault section, Liz thought she had exhausted all possible password combinations. She sat glumly as she tried to work out what to do next. And then Liz had a thought that brought a big smile across her face.

"Of course," she whispered. *This has to be it.*

She counted the letters in her mind and each word sure enough corresponded with the correct amount of characters. She repeated the process just to make sure.

If I'm right then the words are actually very obvious! Liz couldn't believe that she hadn't worked out the combination earlier. *How could I be so stupid?*

Liz's fingers were trembling as she began to punch in the numbers on the digital code pad at the top of the safety deposit box.

E-L-I-Z-A-B-E-T-H.

The screen did not react negatively after she typed the first word. *If it were wrong, I'm sure it would have flashed red or something.* She took a deep breath and punched in the second word.

A-N-N-E

Liz clenched her fists as she stared at the screen waiting for the computer system to reject her password. But just like the first word there was no technical reaction. *So obvious now that I know it!* And with that Liz typed in the last word in the password sequence.

G-R-E-E-N-E

The digital pad whirred slightly and there was a click as the words "Welcome, Professor Greene" flashed across the screen.

"Yes!" Liz exclaimed. "Yes, yes, yes!"

She flicked the lid of the box open and stared inside, knowing she was about to see her father's prized possessions. She had to blink a few times as she looked inside the safety deposit box. Her smile faded as a grim realization took hold, causing a sick feeling in her stomach.

"It can't be empty!" Liz screamed. "It can't be!"

As she stared in disgust at the empty safety deposit box she heard the sound of running footsteps heading towards her. Marron had obviously heard her screams and rushed into the cubicle, his face red and puffy.

"What's wrong?" he asked, trying to catch his breath.

"There's nothing in here!"

"What do you mean?"

"It's empty."

"Oh?"

"How can this be?"

"Sometimes our clients do remove their secure items yet they still keep their accounts going," Marron tried to explain.

"But it doesn't make any sense. Why would my father remove whatever he kept in here and then tell me to come here to retrieve it?"

Marron shrugged. "Well, my understanding is that he didn't actually tell you directly."

"I'm sorry?"

"I mean," Marron wiped the sweat off his brow, "you worked out that you had to be here based on some cryptic clue or message that your father left for you. Are you sure you are in the right place?"

"There's another part of the bank with safety deposit boxes?"

"No, I'm saying that maybe you've been on a wild goose chase. Maybe your father never intended you to come to the bank at all."

Liz's bottom lip started to tremble. "But it made sense that this was the place."

"Maybe there is another place that makes sense too." Marron spoke softly. "Something you have completely overlooked?"

"I don't know." Liz sighed. She took a crumpled tissue out of her pocket and rubbed it across her eyes.

"He didn't have to be cryptic to send you here. Our security system is tight enough, especially with the password combinations. He could have just mentioned the bank by name."

"I suppose…" Liz wasn't convinced. "But I wouldn't know where else it could be."

"Perhaps you do and you just don't realize it."

Liz glided her hands along the bottom of the safety deposit box.

"There are no hidden compartments in these things if that's what you are looking for," he said politely.

"And there's nothing else here in the bank where my father might have stored something?"

"I'm afraid not." Marron shook his head.

Liz stood up. Her head was spinning and she needed an aspirin badly. "Take me back to Tim," she said.

CHAPTER 36

In 1971, a United States Navy Captain, Edgar Mitchell, went into space as part of the NASA crew of Apollo 14. He became the sixth person in the history of humankind to walk on the moon. On the return flight to Earth while viewing our planet from space, Mitchell had a trance-like experience where he consciously felt the awe and universal connectedness of our planet. It was a significant moment that caused Mitchell to believe life is more intricate and mysterious than what traditional science has taught us to believe. Mitchell believed that a deep understanding of consciousness could lead to a new and expanded view of reality.

As a result of this epiphany, Mitchell founded the Institute of Noetic Sciences. *Noetic*, from the Greek word *noetikos*, means "inner/intuitive knowing". Today, the institute continues to explore the basic powers and potential of consciousness by utilizing the tools of basic science. Based in Petaluma, California, the institute believes it is contributing to an ongoing paradigm shift that recognizes the vital role consciousness plays in our human evolution.

The institute boasts an extensive global network that continues to grow as more people around the world begin to explore the mysteries and interconnectedness of consciousness through the merging of science and spirit.

Tucked away on the edge of the institute's luscious two hundred-acre estate in Petaluma, California, the occupants of the Macmanus residence were deep in dreamland under a starry sky.

Professor Macmanus, one of the most senior fellows at the institute, sat up in shock when the phone rang. He stared at his private phone ringing on his pedestal. It took a few seconds to register that he was now awake from a heavy sleep. He switched on his bedside light and reached for the phone.

Who the bloody hell is ringing me at one in the morning?

"Hello?" he croaked as he glanced next to him to see if his wife had been woken up too. She was still fast asleep.

Macmanus climbed off the bed, phone still pressed against his ear, and headed out the room, down the passage and into his airy study that overlooked the garden.

"Professor Macmanus?"

"Who is this?"

"I... er..." There was a pause. "I'm looking for Professor Macmanus."

"Who is this and how did you get my private mobile number?"

"I'm phoning from South Africa. I was given your number a while ago by a colleague of yours, Professor Harry Greene."

"Professor Greene?"

"Yes, he gave me your number and said I was to call you immediately if I ever needed to."

Professor Macmanus's mind was now waking up very fast, like a runner on the inside lane about to sprint into the lead. He tried to make sense of what the caller was saying. "So the fact you are ringing me at this ridiculous hour means there are problems?"

"Yes, sir. I... I... I'm not sure how secure this line is?"

"For goodness's sake, just tell me what's going on? Where is Professor Greene and what exactly is the problem that has warranted you disturbing me from a much-needed night's sleep, and from risking the wrath of waking my wife?"

"Professor Greene has disappeared."

"What?"

"He's vanished. I think there might be some foul play involved."

"Vanished? Foul play?" Macmanus slumped into the suede chair in which he had spent so many hours at his desk. He stared out the window. The garden lamps revealed a frosty and quiet landscape.

"I think it has to do with a microchip."

At the mention of "microchip", Macmanus leapt up.

"What about the microchip?"

"I think it has gone missing."

"So you think maybe the professor has the microchip and is perhaps hiding somewhere for reasons unbeknown to us?"

"Er, I don't think so, Sir. I... I... well—"

"Speak for heaven's sake!" Macmanus roared into the receiver. He was pacing the room now.

"His daughter was just here to collect something."

Elizabeth? He had met the daughter at least fifteen years back when the professor had brought her with on a business trip. She had been an inquisitive girl.

"Collect something from where? Who did you say you are?"

"Tom Marron, sir. I belong to the same division as the professor, if you know what I mean?"

"Carry on," Macmanus said curtly. *That would explain why Greene would have given him my number.*

"I work at the bank where the professor keeps a safety deposit box. The girl and a friend of hers were just here."

"And so?"

"She was successful in cracking the clues that her father had apparently left for her but after opening his safety deposit box nothing was inside."

"And you think it was the microchip she was searching for?"

"She mentioned it by name."

"And the professor?"

"I made her call him and I tried calling him too after they left. But no luck with any of the numbers we have for him."

"Maybe he's just out somewhere, or doesn't want to be disturbed?"

Marron explained what Liz had said about the broken glass and traces of chloroform in the professor's house. Professor Macmanus stopped pacing. He was sure his blood pressure levels had just tripled. Greene had been at the forefront of their black box experiments and the microchip contained all the data and crucial breakthroughs of recent times. Macmanus shuddered. He didn't even want to contemplate the possibility that something had happened to his colleague and the unique microchip.

He walked over to the desk and picked up another phone while Marron relayed the details of Liz's visit. He found "Harry Greene" under his contacts and pushed the "call" button. Sure enough the phone went to voicemail.

"So what do you suggest?" Marron asked.

Macmanus paused while he allowed his thoughts to take over. He could be parked at the Petaluma Municipal Airport in half an hour. The institute had a private plane there. There didn't seem to be much choice in the matter.

"Sit tight. I'm coming to Cape Town. If you hear anything let me know."

There wasn't a second to lose. This was a crisis indeed. And it had the potential to get much worse.

CHAPTER 37

Liz tried her father's mobile number again as she and Tim exited the elevator and walked back into the parking garage towards her car.

"Still on voicemail," she said.

"I really think we should report this to the police, Liz."

"I don't want the police involved. My father wouldn't want any publicity about his research."

"But you don't have to say anything about his research," said Tim. "We can just tell them he's gone missing. Just alert them to the signs of forced entry and the broken glass."

Liz remained silent as they climbed into the car. She still couldn't believe the safety deposit box had been empty. She needed to think about what her father was trying to tell her.

"Liz?"

"I don't know." They drove out of the building as the exit boom swung open.

"If something has happened to him, you have to let the police know."

Tim was right; Liz knew that. The truth was, she was scared of finding out she had already lost her father. Without police involvement there was still the possibility in her mind that her father was alive and being kept prisoner—or something. With police involvement there might be no more hope left to cling to if they discovered the worst. And Liz wasn't ready to handle that type of finality. Why hadn't she just called her father months ago? Why did it have to end like this?

"Liz? We've got to go to the police."

"Okay," Liz said as she swung a left turn on to the bustling main road. "We'll go to the police but strictly no mentioning of the microchip."

Tim nodded. "Just tell them about the disappearance."

Several minutes later they arrived at one of the nearby police stations. Despite the dingy atmosphere they found themselves in, it brought a welcome relief to the uneasiness and hint of danger that seemed to be lurking outside.

Rafik had seen Liz and her companion head back towards the parking lot at Vuyisana Bank. He had no doubt that by now the girl had the microchip. He had almost intercepted them as they reached Liz's car but a security guard doing a regular patrol had interrupted his mission.

"Can I help you?"

Rafik whirled around to see a uniformed guard frowning at him. He was used to this: the scar on his face gave him a menacing look and it often automatically aroused hostility wherever he went.

"Looking for my car," said Rafik. "I think I'm on the wrong level."

"No worries," said the guard and ambled off.

Damn, Rafik thought. *I've lost the opportunity. Now I'll have to follow them.*

He had sprinted to his car and was just in time to see the girl and her friend drive out of the building.

Rafik now stared in alarm as his targets parked right outside the police station. Rafik had an aversion to police stations. They made him feel sick immediately, just like mushrooms did, catapulting him to unpleasant depths in his memory banks.

Rafik had only been eleven when he was abandoned by his abusive father who skipped the country mired in debt. Rafik and his two younger brothers were left to fend for themselves on the streets. Eventually, social services stepped in and the boys were placed in foster homes. Rafik was separated from his brothers. The other two were placed together in the home of a wealthy musician, a spinster, who lived in a smart triple-story house. The deal was that the boys would never see their brother again, and in time would forget about Rafik.

Rafik was placed in a small family home in Athlone. The parents, a seemingly humble religious couple, only had one child, a daughter. They were unable to conceive again and warmly took in Rafik as one of their own. Yet the happy, harmonious family they seemed to be in the beginning began to change as time went on. Every weekend the couple would notice several items disappearing from their house, including an abundance of clothing and vegetables. They couldn't understand it, and blamed Rafik.

The father would confront Rafik about the disappearance of the items and Rafik would vehemently deny any wrongdoing. He would then get a beating from his foster father and the more he protested the harder the hits became. One day in a fit of rage the father grabbed a steak knife that was resting on the kitchen table and slashed it across Rafik's cheek.

This time Rafik hit the foster father back, a thumping punch that sent the man flying. His foster father could hardly stand up and when he did, Rafik hit him again. All he could picture was the face of his real father and the pummeling became even more violent.

The family reported Rafik to the police and to social services, who promptly removed Rafik from that family's care. Rafik had been telling the truth—it wasn't him stealing from his foster family, but he soon realized the truth held little sway in this world.

As he now waited for Liz and her friend to come out of the police station, Rafik tried to remain as levelheaded as possible. *What the hell are they doing there?* There was no way Rafik would set even one foot outside his car while in this vicinity. He swallowed hard and desperately hoped they would be back outside soon. He shuffled in his seat as three policemen walked past his car chatting to each other. Rafik breathed a sigh of relief, as the policemen didn't even so much as give him a passing glance. The claustrophobia was torturing him and he rolled down his window slightly. As the cool air rushed in, he stared at the entrance across the street and waited.

———

Liz and Tim were standing in a dimly lit face-brick foyer that had a number of doors and passages leading off it. In front of them was a high desk counter that stretched across most of the back wall, serving as a buffer between members of the public and the police officials. The counter was marked with dirt.

"Luckily there's no one else waiting," said Liz as they walked to the counter.

A sullen policewoman stood behind it. She looked up and saw Tim and Liz standing there, and then instantly looked down at her papers again to continue with what she had been reading. She was wearing a standard SAPS blue jersey over her uniform. The strong aroma of coffee found its way to Liz and Tim while the policewoman sipped from a white polystyrene cup.

Tim cleared his throat. There was no response; he looked at Liz and shrugged. The policewoman looked up and caught his glance.

"I'll be with you shortly," she mumbled.

This is bloody ridiculous. "Sure," said Tim, giving Liz another glance.

They stood in disbelief as the policewoman continued to drink her coffee and focus on the papers in front of her.

"Must be something important," Liz said.

A few policemen walked out of one of the adjoining offices. They were talking and laughing amongst one another, then disappeared down a corridor.

More minutes passed until Tim cleared his throat again. The policewoman looked up and took another sip of coffee.

"How can I help you?" she finally said.

Before Liz could answer her, a mobile phone rang.

"Just a second," the policewoman said as she fished out a small silver cellphone from her pants pocket. Liz and Tim stared at her as she continued to have a conversation with the caller in a language Tim didn't understand.

"Can you believe this?" It was Liz's turn to fume.

"Why aren't there more staffers at this reception desk?" said Tim.

The large clock on the wall behind them continued to tick. Another ten minutes passed and the policewoman finally ended her call.

"You were saying?" She looked at Liz, ignoring Tim's icy glare.

"I'm here to report a missing person," said Liz.

"How long has the person been missing for?" The policewoman reached for a pen.

Liz's answer was drowned out by the sound of several more police officers entering the room. Two more policewomen made their way behind the counter while a few others disappeared down another passage.

"Could you help these people?" the original policewoman asked her colleagues. "I'm about to go on tea break."

Her colleagues nodded and the policewoman headed through a door at the far end of the room. Tim was about to shout something at her but Liz quickly started speaking to the new officials now standing opposite them from behind the counter.

"What's the problem, ma'am?"

"I need you to send out a search party," Liz said. "My father is missing."

The policewoman pulled out a tattered notepad and flicked her ballpoint pen lid onto the counter top.

"When did you last see your father?"

"A few months ago." Liz could feel the lump swell in her throat.

"Was that the last time you had any contact with him?"

"Yes."

"So you think he has been missing since then?"

"Oh, no," said Liz. "I got a missed call from him early this morning."

The policewoman placed her pen on the counter top and looked at Liz. "I'm afraid there's nothing we can do right now."

"What?" Tim saw Liz's eyes widen.

"Her father's gone awol. What do you mean there's nothing you can do right now?" Tim's voice started to get louder.

"If he called her this morning, then technically he isn't missing."

"But he's definitely missing," Liz said. "His phone goes straight to voicemail and he hasn't made any contact with me again."

"Does he usually stay in touch with you?" asked the policewoman. "You just said you last spoke to him a few months ago."

"We haven't spoken for a while." Liz sighed. "But this time it feels different. My gut is telling me something is wrong."

"Ma'am, we cannot file a missing person report based just on a gut feeling." The policewoman had now closed her notepad. "As it is, the SA Police Services are swamped with cases and we have to prioritize them."

"But there was broken glass at his home," Tim said. He was desperate to help Liz. "And the door was wide open…"

"Sir, there is nothing we can do right now."

"What if he's been attacked or kidnapped or something?"

"Do you have any evidence to indicate that? Any ransom note or anything like that?"

Tim and Liz both shook their heads.

"Well, until you have something concrete for us to work with there is nothing we can do for you right now."

"I don't know what to do." Tim could hear Liz was about to cry.

"Just sit tight for a while. Maybe there's a logical reason you haven't heard from your father." The policewoman offered a warm smile. "Maybe he's gone on a sudden holiday or something?"

"He's not the sudden-holiday type. He's a big planner and usually does everything in advance. If he were traveling somewhere he would definitely have told me."

"Let me go to the back office to get a folder for you so we can open up a housebreaking case, at least." They policewoman went through one of the inter-leading doors.

A group of policemen entered through the front entrance. They were escorting a young man whose hands were handcuffed and whose feet were clasped together by a short metal chain.

"Hello, my darling!" The prisoner mouthed a kiss to Liz. "Come visit me any time, *ne*?"

The policemen ignored the prisoner's comments as they hoisted him towards a passage entrance before they disappeared.

"Hey, did you see that prisoner had a large American flag sewn onto the back of his jacket?" said Tim.

"He's probably a member of one of the criminal gangs that are plentiful in the Cape," said Liz. "Probably 'The Americans'."

"Gangs? The Americans?"

"There are many gangs in this province. They are part of the reason why the crime stats for Cape Town are so high. Violence, drugs, murders, turf wars. These gangs make the Cosa Nostra look tame by comparison!"

The entrance area fell silent. With the policewoman in one of the back offices still getting a new folder, there were no other staffers in sight. A low ringing noise began to hum from the side of the counter. Liz and Tim glanced towards where the hum was coming from. On the end of the counter was a large black scanner, copier, and fax machine. A fax was coming through.

"Always delays when there's red tape." Tim waved his hands in the air in frustration. "Happens back home too."

Liz nodded, but Tim could see she was distracted by the fax. Tim glanced at it. The page was filled with what looked like three photographs and some large writing. The hum came to a halt as the page flicked out of the machine and glided on to the counter top.

"Look!" Liz grabbed Tim's arm as she stared in horror at the page. "Look at this!"

For an instant, Tim thought he was caught up in a bad dream. On the page was a photograph of Professor Greene. The other two photos were of Tim and Liz.

"What the hell is going on?" Liz whispered, her eyes transfixed on the fax.

"Let's get out of here." Tim was already pulling Liz towards the front doors. "Now!"

Written in harsh bold letters at the bottom of the page: "WANTED IN CONNECTION WITH MURDER".

———

Liz and Tim charged out of the police station and dashed to their car.

"What the hell is going on?" Tim's voice was high-pitched in panic. "How did my picture come to be on a 'Wanted for Murder' poster?"

"I don't know what's happening." Liz started the engine.

"How did someone get my picture anyway?" said Tim. "I've barely been in this country."

Liz turned the steering wheel. Her whole body was shaking. She didn't know what was going on but she believed it all had to do with her father's disappearance and with the microchip.

"We need to find that microchip." Liz stared at the road in front of her.

"Murder?" Tim didn't hear her. "I've never even harmed a spider."

"Well, we certainly can't involve the police now," said Liz. "That at least is clear."

"So what exactly do you suggest?"

"I'm not sure."

Liz was so deep in thought she did not realize she had moved the car slightly over into the next lane for oncoming traffic. A flower delivery truck whizzed past and she almost collided with it.

"Liz, watch out!" Tim yelled as he was thrust forward in his seat.

The vigorous hooting from the flower truck driver brought Liz back to reality and she swerved to avoid it.

"Sorry," Liz muttered.

Tim looked at her, shook his head and leaned back again. She could see his body was trembling now too.

"Did you see what type of truck that was?" Liz asked as she indicated to turn right.

"No," said Tim. "A big one that could have crushed us?"

"It was a truck delivering flowers."

"So?"

"So seeing flowers suddenly triggered something in my memory."

"Okay?"

"Something from my past." Liz was smiling now. "Have you heard of Kirstenbosch?"

"Nope."

"It's the famous botanical gardens and it's only a few minutes away from here."

"Liz, is this really a time to go wandering around the botanical gardens when there are posters out there saying that we are murder suspects?"

"When I was younger my father and I often would go to Kirstenbosch." Liz ignored Tim's sarcasm. "They also have permanent exhibitions there."

"So?"

"Various exhibitions of art and sculptures. But more importantly, we used to go to what became one of my favorite exhibitions."

"Which is?"

"A gathering of special hand-crafted statues," said Liz and glanced at Tim to see his reaction. "A gathering of lions."

Tim was smiling again.

CHAPTER 38

Kirstenbosch National Botanical Gardens sits in the Cape Floristic Region, a region also known as the Cape Floral Kingdom on the eastern slopes of Table Mountain. It is easily accessible via Cape Town's southern suburbs. The famous lush gardens that border the Table Mountain National Park are popular among locals and tourists alike. Top musicians and artists from all over the world have played open air concerts there, and the garden's various paths and trails allow one to escape the travails of the city and delve into a world of serenity and immerse oneself in nature's majestic splendor. The gardens even have a braille trail for the blind.

Kirstenbosch has an abundant variety of plant life unique to the Cape Flora, commonly known as *fynbos*, as well as many plants from southern Africa's other regions. It was the first botanical garden in the world to be dedicated to a country's indigenous flora. It was also the first botanical garden in the world to be included within a natural World Heritage Site. The gardens boast more than seven thousand species and are part of a five hundred and twenty-eight-hectare estate containing protected mountainside supporting natural forest and *fynbos*, along with a diverse range of animals and birds.

Liz and Tim parked at the bottom entrance and made their way across the quad to the ticket office. The morning air was crisp, and the fresh smell of dew wafted towards them as they entered the gardens. Despite the early time of day, the gardens were surprisingly busy.

"Come up this way," Liz beckoned Tim up the path. "This route will take us to the area of lawn where they have the lion statue exhibition."

A few minutes later, they stopped in a quiet area near a bench that was in front of a clump of green bushes sprouting yellow and white flowers.

"Don't move, or I'll blow your brains out."

Liz and Tim stared in horror at the man with the huge scar across his cheek. He was pointing a gun at straight at them.

"Please don't hurt us," said Liz.

"We'll give you our money," said Tim, reaching for his pocket.

"Keep your hands where I can see them," the man whispered. "I don't care about your money."

"What do you want?" Liz could barely muster the strength to speak.

"The microchip."

"What?"

"The microchip. Give it to me."

"How do you know about the microchip?"

"That's none of your concern," the man said impatiently. "Now hand it over if you value your lives."

"We don't have the microchip!" Liz cried.

"I know you have it. I was at the bank too."

"But we don't have it," said Tim.

"Quit playing games," he hissed. "Do you think I'm an idiot?"

Liz noticed that the man was standing just in front of a large puddle of mud at the end of the slope. She hesitated and stepped forward very slowly. The man instinctively took a step backwards and lost his foothold as his shoe spluttered into the grime. He began to roll down the hill.

"This way," Liz grabbed Tim's arm and yanked him back in the direction they had come.

They dashed down the path and Liz took another path to their right. She glanced behind them but there was no sign of the gun-wielding attacker. It would take him at least a few minutes to make his way up to where they had been standing. *Kirstenbosch is the perfect place to get lost in*, Liz thought.

"Down this way." Liz pointed. "We can go under those large trees. It will be difficult for him to spot us from above."

"Shit, he's seen us!" Tim yelled, as a muffled gunshot sounded.

"Okay, let's go down that other path down there."

Liz took a gravel path that led to higher ground again.

A few minutes later they got to another clearing and the edge of another slope.

"I think we've lost him," said Tim.

"I hope so."

Before either of them could say anything else, another bullet whizzed past Liz, missing her by centimeters and landing in the tree next to her.

Liz looked over the slope. "We need to jump off here," she said.

"What? All the way down?"

They were very high up in a deserted part of the gardens. "We don't have much choice," she said.

CHAPTER 39

"You must be mad!" Tim shouted. "I'm not jumping off here."

"Look, either you jump or that thug will get us. And you better decide soon."

Tim stared down at the steep rolling hill before them.

"Hurry!" Liz urged.

"But there must be another way down."

"We really don't have time to take that chance. Do you want to be shot?"

"No."

"Me neither. Being shot at three times in one day is my absolute limit."

Liz turned again and gazed behind them at the path they had just been running on. Tim followed her gaze. Their attacker was gaining momentum.

"Look," Liz pointed. "Can you see that?"

"He's almost here." Tim cursed.

"Let's do this," said Liz.

Tim hesitated and stared again down the slope. For a moment he felt paralyzed, fear consuming every muscle of his body. He tried to move but he couldn't. He stared at his body and then looked at Liz. *We're so high up here.*

A shot rang out and the figure of the madman rushing towards them became clearer.

"Let's do this," Liz said.

Another shot landed in the tree. Tim nodded.

"You'll be fine," said Liz and moved herself to the edge. Tim edged forward too. And then Liz jumped off. Tim closed his eyes and jumped too.

He found himself rolling down the hill and landed on the sandy bottom with a thump. Liz landed right on top of Tim, their eyes locking momentarily before she rolled off and clambered to her feet.

They raced to the nearby forest that overlooked the clearing.

"I'm not as fit as I used to be," Tim huffed.

"I've never been fit!" Liz said.

They made their way along a pebbled path winding through the trees. They didn't look back. Ten grueling minutes later they finally stopped to catch their breath.

Tim looked around. No one else was in sight. The soft chirps of birds perched high on the branches above them permeated the forest as the cool breeze continued to gently nudge a myriad of brown and orange leaves onto the ground.

"I think we've lost him," he said.

"I'm not so sure."

"What are we going to do now?"

"Well, we can't tell the park authorities," said Liz. "They'll ask us all sorts of questions and who knows if they're linked to the police."

"Let's just get to the car."

"We need to see if the chip is here."

"At the risk of getting shot or whatever else that guy wants to do?"

"We've got no choice. We have to find that chip."

"Well, we better do it quickly then." Tim peered around the tree but the path behind them was still clear.

"I think if we follow this route through the forest we land up in one of the Protea gardens which then leads us to the main gardens." Liz pointed ahead of her.

"But if that guy knows these gardens, he's probably waiting for us on the other side."

"And if he doesn't know the set up, then he might not be. He might still be somewhere behind us."

"I don't know, Liz." Tim shook his head.

"Besides, even if he's waiting on the other side for us, it's a very busy and populated part of the gardens. There's nothing he can do with so many people around. He wouldn't dare pull out his gun."

"I guess we'll soon find out," Tim said. "When I decided to come to Cape Town, this isn't exactly what I had in mind."

Liz stopped and turned to face him. "I'm really glad you're here."

"Does this mean you'll finally go on a date with me?"

"Don't push your luck!"

Several minutes passed before they emerged into the sunlight of the Protea garden. Soon they were back in the main part of the park, and sure enough Tim could see crowds of people admiring the beauty and enjoying the tranquility. The man with the gun was nowhere in sight.

They headed past the picnickers and made their way towards the cycads.

"That's where we need to go," said Liz, nodding her head in the direction of a bench on a slope just above the cycads.

They climbed up some steps that jutted out of the narrow path and soon they were standing at a faded brown bench.

"I think the lion statues are down there just behind those thick green bushes."

Tim followed Liz along the slope towards the garden Liz was pointing to. His hands were in his pockets and his fingers glided across his cellphone that was bouncing around. *I need to make the call soon.*

———

Rafik struggled on to his feet, rubbing his head as he regained his focus. He looked around but they had gone.

"Dammit!" He kicked some pebbles into the river.

He couldn't believe they had gotten the better of him. He needed to find them before they left the gardens. He couldn't afford to encounter the wrath of the Fox. Failure was not an option.

He put his pistol into his jacket pocket and thought about where the best place to find them would be. He decided to head back to the main gardens.

———

Liz and Tim made their way through another patch of indigenous plants and then past a high rockery. Before Tim could even catch his breath they were going down the path towards what he assumed were the main gardens.

"It's down here somewhere."

Well that narrows it down, thought Tim. He was about to collapse. "Great!"

They paused as their path merged with a few other contour paths heading in various directions. Liz pointed to a sign that indicated which route to take to the statue garden. "Over there. This way. There are only about three or four lion statues, so it shouldn't be too difficult to spot."

"Why would your father come specially into the heart of these botanical gardens to hide a microchip in a statue? Surely it would have been easier just to hide it somewhere easily accessible? Like in a safe in his house or something?" Tim had been wondering this as they had made the convoluted journey to this spot.

"Anything is possible with my father," said Liz. "He would definitely do something like this. We always used to play these types of games when I was a child."

"So you're sure we're on the right track?"

"We have to be," said Liz as they walked down some steps and approached the shaded area surrounded by a group of tall trees. "It has to be here."

They made their way through a clump of rose bushes and suddenly found themselves in a circular clearing.

"Down there," she pointed towards the middle of the lawn where an array of statues was interspersed among the flowerbeds.

They ran to the middle of the lawn and stopped when they saw the first few statues. Liz gasped in horror.

"No! It can't be."

"These aren't lions, are they?" Tim was puzzled. "They look like leopards to me."

"They are leopards," Liz said quietly. "But they are supposed to be lions. This is the lion statue garden. The sign even said that we were heading towards the lion statue garden. I've never seen leopard statues here before."

CHAPTER 40

Rafik grinned when he spotted Liz and her companion walking across the lawn to towards the busy visitors center. *How stupid can they be walking in the middle of an open field?* He clutched the gun in his pocket excitedly.

He waited for a few other people to head on to the lawn and stuck to the side path parallel to the lawn. He ducked in the shadows of the towering trees without risk of being spotted.

A group of uniformed school kids on an official outing ran onto the lawn. *Damn! Don't lose them now.* Rafik walked faster toward the visitors center. More kids appeared on the lawn. He could barely make out Liz, but was still able to keep them in his eyesight.

"Would you mind taking a picture of us, young man?"

Rafik whirled around to see three elderly people smiling eagerly at him.

"I'm sorry?"

"Could you take a photo of me with my husband and my sister who is visiting us from Kent?"

"I'm not good at photographs."

"I'm sure you'll do just fine," said the old lady as she held out the camera. "Shouldn't take more than a few seconds."

Rafik glanced in the direction of the visitors center. He could still make out Liz. "Okay…"

"What a nice man."

After three snaps and big smiles all round, Rafik hurried down the path. He couldn't see them. He ignored the chattering kids and was almost at the entrance to the visitors center when he stopped.

Some of the schoolboys had broken away from the group and were playing with a soccer ball on the grass. One of the boys missed a kick and the ball went rolling towards the side path. A thin grey Schnauzer had meandered from the upper section of the gardens where dogs were allowed and was poking around in the *fynbos* next to the tree. The dog walked up to the ball, sniffed it, and then

103

lifted up its hind leg. As the Schnauzer began to urinate over the ball, one of the schoolboys rushed up to it amidst laughter and cheers.

"Get away from that!" the schoolboy shouted. "Stupid dog."

The dog looked up as the boy kicked the ball away. The boy was about to run off when he turned around again and stared at the dog.

"Bloody mutt," he said and gave the dog a sharp kick. The dog yelped as the boy kicked him again and again. "You shouldn't be in this section of the gardens anyway."

Rafik saw what had happened and froze the minute the dog started whining. His hairs stood on end and he felt his blood begin to boil. His hand clenched into a fist and he glared at the boy from his vantage point. Rafik knew he didn't need to be exposed by causing a scene now. But no matter how serious his mission, no matter how important it was that he didn't fail the Fox, there was one thing in life that Rafik could not tolerate. Rafik could not handle cruelty to animals, on any level. And especially when it came to the treatment of dogs.

You could throw Rafik into a deep hole and bury him alive. You could throw him off a moving train. You could throw him into a fire. None of that would bother him. He wouldn't flinch. He would get on with it. He would bounce back. He was a survivor. But being cruel to a helpless dog just meters in front of him was like ripping open his chest and cutting into the very fibers of his soul.

Rafik charged towards the boy. He had turned and was walking back to his friends when he felt a heavy thump and went tumbling over. Rafik had jumped on the schoolboy and they both rolled towards the bottom level of the garden.

"Now who's the piece of shit?" Rafik spat.

The schoolboy tried to speak but couldn't. He stared at Rafik wide-eyed as the tears began to slide down his face.

"It was pissing on my ball," he eventually squeaked.

"Why don't you kick this instead?" Rafik pulled out his gun, standing over the child now.

The boy tried to edge back away from the weapon glinting in the sunlight.

"Please," he said.

"Fuck you," said Rafik. "It's just a dog that was minding its own business."

"I'm sorry."

"What the fuck did you do that for?"

"I said I was sorry."

"Sorry is just not good enough, you fucking worthless piece of shit."

Rafik lunged towards the boy and kicked his leg. The cloud of rage still shrouded him and he hadn't noticed the gathering crowd.

"He's got a gun!" an American voice shouted. Cameras were snapping away amidst the gasps of the people now standing around.

"Someone stop him!"

"Someone call the police!"

The crowd of onlookers was growing every second.

"What's going on?" a man with a British accent asked.

"Not quite sure," said another. "Looks like that guy's threatening that kid with a gun."

Rafik was oblivious of the crowd and waved the gun again towards the schoolboy. "This will teach you to kick a dog!"

"Please!" The schoolboy was hysterical. "I said I was sorry. Please don't hurt me."

"Here come the police," someone called.

This awoke Rafik. There in the distance chugging along at its fastest pace were some Kirstenbosch security guards seated on one of the garden's mini-cart cars.

"Consider this your lucky day," Rafik said to the boy. "And if I ever see you again doing something like you did, you better beware."

Rafik tried to go through the crowd.

"Stop him!" A security guard had jumped off the cart and was sprinting toward the crowd. "Don't let him get away!"

Rafik tried to get past some Chinese women standing in front of him. One of them put out her foot and Rafik tripped over it. His gun flew through the air and landed in a flowerbed.

The crowd broke out into applause as the garden guards raced toward Rafik.

One of the guards pointed a gun at Rafik while the other one collected Rafik's gun from the soil.

"Keep your arms where I can see them," one of the guards said.

Rafik raised his arms. He saw that one of the officers was talking into a two-way radio. There were probably more security officials on their way.

The crying schoolboy was being consoled by several people at the side of the lawn while his shocked schoolmates looked on. As far as school outings go, this was not an ordinary occurrence, Rafik thought wryly.

The guards edged closer to Rafik, their guns not wavering in their steadfast grips.

"No funny business," the one guard said. "Don't make things worse for yourself."

Stupid fucking botanical security guards. Why don't you get a real job?

"I'm co-operating, I'm co-operating."

"Do you have any other weapons on you?"

"No."

"Check him anyway," a guard ordered.

The guard was now face to face with Rafik. He tried to avoid Rafik's cold stare and patted him down.

"Don't move or I'll shoot," said the other guard.

The guard felt around Rafik's legs and upper pockets but couldn't feel any weapons there. He began to move his hands towards Rafik's chest and jacket.

Rafik grabbed the guard's arm and whirled him around. The guard was now facing the crowd, his throat was gripped tightly behind Rafik's arm.

"He's got the guard's gun!" someone screamed.

Rafik was pointing his pistol into the temple of the guard.

"You fucked with the wrong person today," Rafik hissed in his ear.

"Don't hurt me," the guard pleaded. "I'm just doing my job."

"If anyone tries any funny business with me, I will shoot this man!" Rafik shouted. "And if you think I'm joking, just try me."

The crowd remained silent.

"Do you fucking understand me? Nobody try anything, and I'll let this guy live."

Nobody moved.

"Call your personnel and tell them you don't need more back-up and that the situation has been sorted out," Rafik said to the other guard.

"I don't think anyone else knows—"

"Do it," Rafik interrupted. "Do it now. Don't fuck with me."

The pale-faced guard froze momentarily.

"Do you want your friend here to die?"

"No."

"Then contact the fucking idiots you work with and tell them you don't need backup and that the situation is under control."

The guard nodded and spoke into his receiver.

"Drop your weapon now," a voice suddenly manifested from behind Rafik. A gun rammed into his back.

"Fuck it," Rafik muttered.

"Let the guard go," the voice ordered. "Now."

Rafik took a look at the growing crowd and the other security guards who were staring at him brazenly. He realized that he wouldn't be able to make a run for it.

"Drop your weapon," the voice ordered. It was firm and commanding.

Rafik sighed and lowered the pistol to the ground.

CHAPTER 41

The policeman swung open the back door of his patrol car and another two guards flung Rafik into the vehicle and slammed the door shut behind him.

"Let this be a lesson to you!" the one said.

Rafik didn't say anything. He surveyed his surroundings. A small barred window was the only way he could view the outside and it was too small for him to crawl through, even if he were to break the bars. His only way out would be the door behind him. He had to make a plan and he had to make it fast.

Two policemen got into the front seats while the other two walked on to their other vehicle parked in front of it.

"Hey, I'm still holding these handcuffs," the one policeman turned to the driver of Rafik's patrol car. "Do you want them still?"

"*Nee*, it's fine, he's not going anywhere. We got him!"

"No worries. See you at the station."

The policemen drove off. Rafik's driver started their engine and soon the car was moving.

"Wow, what a busy morning. And now this."

"I'm starving. Should we take him directly to the station?"

"Or we can stop at the shop and I can quickly get some chicken burgers or something?"

"Okay, I'll watch the car."

"He's not getting out of there anyway."

"Nope, he's not!"

Rafik had been charged formally twice in the past. Once for theft and once for criminal harassment and intent to do grievous bodily harm to his brother's girlfriend's sister. Although he firmly denied the latter charge, he knew that he would have hurt her very badly if his brother and the girlfriend hadn't come home half an hour earlier.

It was not as if Rafik generally tried to hurt people just for the sake of it. In

107

this instance, the girl deserved what was coming for her. In the weeks building up to the incident, the girl had taunted Rafik at every opportunity. She had a degree in Social Science and had no problem in constantly reminding Rafik how stupid and uneducated he was. Rafik tried to ignore the barrage of words that continued to come his way but on the day in question, she had managed to get under his skin leading him into a fit of rage. He had come to visit his brother at the girlfriend's home not knowing they had gone to the latest showing of *The Hunger Games*.

The sister had opened the door, given Rafik a dirty look, and then plunged into a foray of demeaning and condescending words that made an impact on the usually emotionless Rafik. He had pushed her inside and had slammed the door behind him.

"Don't push me! Who do you think you are?" she had yelled.

Rafik consequently pushed her some more and when she spat at him he gave her a solid jab on her left cheek. She went flying into the wall and he was about to punch her again when his brother and girlfriend arrived home. They had inadvertently prevented her from probably being beaten to death.

Rafik had no regrets. But charges were laid against him and the charges stuck. Despite the fact he had killed many people during his life, he had never been caught, and so the event with the sister remained as his worst act officially. Unofficially, his record portrayed a completely different story.

Peering through the barred window as the police car slowed and then parked, he saw they had stopped in a busy parking lot outside a mall. *Are you kidding me?* He had to take advantage of this.

He heard the front doors swing open as the officers exited the vehicle and walked past the window. They were chatting to each other almost as if they had forgotten there was a prisoner in the car.

"The burgers are usually quite good here," said the one officer.

"I suppose, but I think I'm in a chicken kind of mood."

"I'm gonna stick to my regular."

"I'll go for the chicken shwarma. And a cream soda!"

Their conversation was interrupted by Rafik's groaning.

"Did you hear that?"

"It's coming from inside the car."

They ran to the window and tried to both peer in at the same time. The moaning intensified as Rafik lay on his stomach and looked like he was about to burst into tears.

"Help me!" Rafik cried. "Help me, please!"

"Hey, sit up." The guard tapped on the window.

"I can't. My stomach."

"Hold on there," the guard said to his colleague. "He could be pretending."

"Looks like he really might be in pain."

"I'm so sore," Rafik groaned. "Excruciating!"

"Might be his appendix, who knows?"

The guard slid the bolt and unlocked the heavy padlock. The other guard aimed his gun in the direction of the door as it swung open. Rafik was on his stomach on the floor, writhing and groaning.

"Help me. Help me, please."

"Let's just get him to the station and they can call a doctor there."

"I don't want him dying on us."

"*Ja*. We don't need that type of paperwork."

Rafik rolled over onto his back. "It really hurts here in my stomach."

Both policemen edged forward, the gun still pointed at Rafik.

"I need to go to a bathroom urgently."

"I don't know."

"Please," Rafik said. "You can keep the gun right against me if you want. I won't do anything stupid."

"He's looking quite yellow."

"Okay, get up," the policeman instructed. "And definitely no messing around."

The one helped him to his feet while the other made sure Rafik knew the gun wasn't going away, then headed towards the public bathrooms.

Rafik leaned over the toilet and stared at the stagnant water below him. The stench hovering around the cubicle was enough to make anyone vomit. The guards were standing right next to him. He let out another groan and stuck his face deeper down the toilet.

"We don't actually need to watch this," the one policeman said.

They waited on the other side.

Inside the cubicle, Rafik lifted his head slightly and turned to glance behind him. He could see that the door was almost closed but he couldn't see the policemen from his vantage point. He could still hear them though.

He made another groaning sound, but now had moved his face away from the toilet. His attention was focused on the window just above the toilet. He wasn't sure he would be able to get through it but he was running out of options.

He gave another loud groan and faked a vomiting sound.

"Easy tiger," one of the policemen said.

Rafik pulled the window frame. The first of the four nails was easy to take out. So was the second nail. The third nail was slightly more problematic; it was rusted and not budging. Rafik made a few more vomiting sounds, while yanking at the nail before finally releasing it. He didn't even bother with the fourth nail and let the window swing around on its hinges.

Rafik gave out one last loud groan before he thrust himself through the tiny space in the wall. The groaning drowned out the sound of his body dragging itself through the frame, and seconds later he found himself on the cold pavement outside the building.

Rafik sprinted towards where they had parked their vehicle. He knew they would pursue him by foot before returning to their car. And that would give him time to jumpstart it. Another reason why it made sense to head back to where he was least likely expected to go was that by stealing the car he would be preventing the policemen from broadcasting his escape on their airwaves. He didn't need the entire police force of Cape Town to pursue him. He didn't need that at all. Especially today. The Fox was counting on him. *I'm certainly not going to let him down.* Rafik shuddered at the thought.

CHAPTER 42

Liz and Tim rushed towards the busy visitors center at Kirstenbosch. They quickly made their way through the gift shop towards the exit to the parking lot.

"I can't believe this," Liz said again as she squeezed past a large woman looking at a postcard rack. "I can't believe there were no lions there. There always used to be lions."

"I'm sorry." Tim looked behind them again just to make sure their pursuer had not found them. "Where to now?"

"Well, I'm stumped as to what the clue could mean. I'm not sure what else my father could have been talking about."

"I'm sure you'll figure it out."

Liz went pale. "I can't believe I forgot."

"Forgot what?"

Liz had reached for her cellphone, and it was now against her ear as she muttered, "Answer the phone, answer your damn phone."

Tim stared at her. "Liz, what's going on?"

They had arrived at Liz's car and jumped in. Liz ended the call and pushed the call button again. But the result was the same. "Why isn't she answering her phone? This is so unlike her."

"Who are you trying to get hold of?"

"I'll explain now," said Liz. "Maybe I should try the landline."

Liz kicked the engine into gear and dialed another number. She pressed the phone against her ear for several rings. But nobody was answering. Liz pushed the red button to end the call.

Tim looked through the rear view mirror. After being sure no one had followed them to Liz's car, he looked at Liz again as she drove out of Kirstenbosch back towards the suburb of Rondebosch.

Michelle Sloane lay sprawled across the cold tiles of the floor. She groaned as she tried to lift her body up, but to no avail. She lifted her left arm and let out a huge cry as an excruciating pain shot through it. *I hope it's not broken. Not today of all days.*

Michelle slowly tried to stand up and felt a sharp shooting pain radiate around her left hip and down into her thigh. There was no way she would be able to stand up, let alone walk. She was still near the kitchen area and was not visible to anyone standing at her front door. She hoped someone would eventually come in.

She looked at her watch. It was almost ten o'clock and she remembered that Agnes, one of the kids, normally came home this time of the day. It was her task to feed the rabbits, and being a border at Harmony Haven meant that every kid who stayed there had to honor their commitments. Michelle couldn't recall when last Agnes had missed a rabbit feed. *I've got three minutes to haul myself near the front door or entrance hall. Three minutes.*

Michelle wiggled her body and tried to move herself with just one arm. She shuffled her body over another few tiles. Her body was aching all over. *I've got to do this. If Agnes doesn't know I'm here I might have to wait all day.*

Michelle thought of Eric Simms and wondered how he would react if she missed the meeting. Agnes was her only hope. She doubted Liz would realize she had never left the house.

CHAPTER 43

Rafik took the corner at a vicious pace. The vehicle swayed heavily from side to side and almost veered over the edge of the road. He was thrust against the door as he turned, but was able to regain his composure just as he steered the car away from a nearby tree. He focused on the road ahead and continued to rev the engine. He didn't need to look in his rearview mirror to see that another police car was chasing him. Those bastards must have used their walkie-talkies. Rafik grimaced as he heard the wailing of the sirens.

Just let me get out of here. I'm not going to succumb to those pricks.

Rafik had been the target of one or two high-speed police chases in his time. Not often, but there were instances where he had thought his luck was about to run out. Yet, here he was again, a survivor, fleeing for his life from people who had no interest in really hearing his story, people who would be happy to chuck him in a dirty prison cell where they could let him rot for the rest of his life.

Rafik was not going to let them take him prisoner. Not if he had anything to do with it. He had considered taking the money he had saved from some of his big jobs and going to start a new life in another country, somewhere near the sea of course, but he had decided to work in Cape Town for a while longer and finish off some high-paying projects, including his latest work for the Fox. While now trying to escape the blue lights, Rafik decided that perhaps this was a wake-up call to finally make the move. He would give it a few more months, and then would start packing his bags. A new city, a new country, and new opportunities would be just the thing his subdued life was craving.

Damn cops! The sirens were getting louder. Rafik stamped on the accelerator as fast as he could.

Mike had stormed out of Professor Greene's house in a fit of rage. In addition to facing the possibility of being kept away from his family for even longer, there was the added stress of knowing he had let potential killers escape from right in front of him. *They just vanished,* he thought. *But I won't let them get the better of me.*

Mike had taken two of the photographs of Professor Greene he had seen on the mantelpiece and was grateful that while waiting in his car he had had the opportunity to take some pictures on his cellphone of the girl and guy he now believed were also linked to the murder of the security guard at UCT. While looking around the professor's house, Mike had discovered newspaper articles and other documents that gave him names for two of his three suspects—Professor Harry Greene and his daughter, Elizabeth Greene.

Mike had promptly gone back to his base where he had issued the "wanted" posters and faxed them off to various police stations. Now he was back in Rondebosch busy putting up the posters on lampposts scattered among the houses and trees. The local neighborhood was always the best place to start one's search, and Mike knew that the chances of others in the area knowing his suspects would be high.

Enjoying the fresh air and the greenery, Mike had left his car near Professor Greene's house and had walked around the area. Now, at least nine streets later, Mike attached yet another poster to a pole and stopped to watch some squirrels nibbling on fallen acorns.

———

Eight years ago, Liz's boyfriend had ended their three-year relationship, claiming he did not love her. The sudden shock caused Liz to sink into a major depression. She broke off all contact with her friends and family. She stopped exercising and she stopped eating. Soon, Liz looked like an anorexic. She spent her days half asleep on the couch and vegetated in front of her TV.

One crisp autumn morning, Liz got dressed and drove her car to the cable car station and bought a ticket to go up Table Mountain. Liz looked through the glass windows of the cable car as it moved upwards in the belief that the ride would be her last one ever.

When she arrived at the summit, she walked with the group to the main area. There were groups of tourists and visitors on top of the mountain, many of them eagerly snapping their cameras. Liz was not one of them. She moved through the crowd and soon found herself away from the chatter. She walked along a quieter path where she saw a flat ledge in the distance and, like a programmed robot, headed quickly towards it.

The magnificent view of the city and its surrounds went unnoticed. Instead, Liz's thoughts remained ones of desperation and isolation. All she knew was that she was high up and that leaping off the ledge would take her out of her misery. Instantly. And the mess she was in would be over.

She looked around to make sure no one else was there or watching her. The paths were deserted. All the visitors were in the main area. Liz made her way to the edge of the slope. She surveyed the views in front of her. She held her hand in the air as the Southeaster pummeled it. She knew she just had to end everything. It was as if a dark cloud surrounded her and there was no way of seeing the light.

My problems are about to end, Liz thought. *Soon my troubles will all be over and I'll be in a better place.*

Liz took a deep breath. She was determined that her final view of her life on Earth would be the city bowl of Cape Town and its surrounds. What Liz didn't know was that her actions were being watched by a lady a few inches away. The lady had been climbing up from a steep contour path and as she got to the summit had seen Liz walk beyond the sign that said, "Do not walk beyond this point".

The lady had yelled at Liz that she shouldn't be walking there but Liz didn't hear the sound of anyone or anything. She was like a zombie marching to her death. The lady had yelled again but still there was no reaction from Liz.

In a matter of seconds the woman had ditched her rucksack and was charging towards Liz.

"Stop!" the woman yelled.

Liz thought she heard something but didn't let the distant sound bother her.

Goodbye.

"Don't do it!" the voice shouted.

Liz took another breath and leapt into the air. But she didn't fall straight down as she expected to. Something was pulling on her jersey that was wrapped tightly around her waist. Half her body was dangling over the ledge. She gasped and turned her head to see a hand gripping her clothing.

"Let me go!" Liz screamed.

"You can't do this!"

"I can do what I like. It's my life."

"I won't let you!"

"You don't even know me!"

"Whatever's going on with you, it's not worth ending your life over."

"You don't know that…" Liz couldn't see anything now through the tears.

"I know that things are never as bad as they seem," said the woman. She reached for Liz's other hand.

"He left me. Out of the blue," Liz sobbed.

"He's not worth it anyway," said the woman. She was pulling Liz up over the ledge now.

"What am I going to do?"

"You'll do what everyone does," said the woman. "You'll start over. Live your life."

Liz was on the level again and she looked at the woman but didn't say anything. It suddenly hit her what a deep pit she had been in and what she had almost just done. She tried to open her mouth but the words wouldn't come out. Through the tears, she eventually managed to muster two words: "Thank you."

Michelle Sloane had been her savior that day. Now Liz and Tim stood outside Michelle's front door pushing the doorbell button. A lawnmower from one of the nearby houses began to throttle and its loudness pierced through the air and reverberated the area.

"Michelle!" Liz shouted. "Are you here? It's Liz." Liz pushed the doorbell button again. She and Tim waited in silence for a few more minutes.

"Maybe she's not home?" said Tim.

"She should be here," said Liz. "She was waiting for me."

"Maybe she changed her plans?"

"No. Not today," said Liz. "She would never do that. She needed me for something very important."

Liz banged on the door again. "Michelle? Are you home?"

"Liz, there's clearly no one here," said Tim.

As they were walking towards her car, Tim said, "Oh shit," freezing on the spot. Running up the street towards them was a man waving a gun.

"Stop where you are!" he shouted.

Liz and Tim bolted down the street, not daring to even glance behind them.

"Someone else chasing us with a gun… Liz, what's going on?" Tim gasped.

CHAPTER 44

"He's gaining on us," Tim said, glancing over his shoulder and almost running into a thorn bush overlapping a wall.

"Keep going," said Liz. "I know these roads, we can lose him somewhere."

"Stop!" the man yelled behind them. "Stop right there!"

Liz and Tim kept running. Soon the pavement ended and they charged across a busy road, cars heading in both directions. There was a flurry of hooting horns and screeching tires as they leapt across the lanes.

"Are you fucking mad?" a truck driver yelled through his open window.

But Tim and Liz had already disappeared into a thicket of trees serving as the border for the next suburb they had just crossed into.

Horns could still be heard in the distance as Mike Bonnington sprinted across the street.

"Fuck you!" a driver yelled.

Mike waved his hand apologetically as he jumped into the thicket and left the traffic behind him. Once he had clambered through an army of bushes, Bonnington found himself at a quiet intersection. He cursed. There was no sign of Elizabeth and her friend. He wondered which way they might have gone. He had three choices—left, right, or straight. He looked at the road going to the left. It was fairly open with not too many buildings. His instinct and extensive training told him they wouldn't have gone that route. Not many buildings and structures to hide in. So that left two other possible flight paths. Straight down or the road to the right.

He thought for a few more seconds and then asked himself which path he would have taken. Definitely the path to the right. He crossed the quiet road and headed down the path. There was some mud in his pathway and a huge footprint was embedded in it. He recognized it as that of a running shoe and excitedly recalled that the man he was pursuing was wearing a pair of Nike Air Pegasus. He had also done some running in his time. Bonnington started running in the direction of his targets. He had no doubt he would find them soon.

Two minutes later, Mike was on the outskirts of the neighborhood. This part was desolate and away from the bustle of the many popular restaurants and shops. The industrial area that Mike was making his way through comprised several factories and warehouses with trucks and tractors sporadically parked on the sides of the roads and pavements. With each footstep he began to leave the comfort of suburbia behind him.

A few men wearing blue overalls and yellow builders' hats appeared on the corner, laughing among each other.

"I'm looking for a man and a woman, possibly mid to late thirties. The guy is wearing jeans and running shoes. They might have looked like they were in a hurry. You seen them?"

They shook their heads at the same time.

Mike tossed his head in frustration. He was not prepared to give up. He needed this. His career depended on it. His sanity depended on it. He needed to get back to his old life in the US, and apprehending these apparent criminals would be just the ticket he needed to get him home.

Just then, he thought he saw something move out of the corner of his eye. He turned towards the entrance of an adjacent building and ran to its front door. He pulled the handle but it was locked. And then he saw it, a bit of blue disappearing round the corner. *He was wearing a blue cap.* It had to be them.

Mike sprinted in that direction. He felt for his gun and tightened his grip on it. He dashed to the end of the street and leaned against the building. Cocking the pistol, he tiptoed around the corner. One foot carefully stepping in front of the next. There in the distance he saw some blue sticking out from next to a huge container. *Gotcha!* he thought, and tiptoed a few more steps towards the side of the container. *They think they can't be seen!*

A few more steps and Mike jumped out, aiming his gun in front of him.

"Game's over, bitch!"

CHAPTER 45

The squalor and decay outside caused American President Daniel Rafferty to shake his head in sadness. He stared out the window of the presidential limousine as his convoy headed out of the Khayelitsha township where he had just visited one of the local schools. The convoy made its way towards the N2 Highway in the direction of his hotel district. Street kids in the distance were huddling over a small tin barrel that contained a fire. They wore torn t-shirts and shorts. Rafferty couldn't see a jersey on any of them. They stared ahead as the convoy drove down the road whose sidewalk they inhabited. They couldn't have been older than ten or eleven.

Rafferty stared at them as the limousine glided past. Even though they couldn't see through the dark bulletproof windows, they all turned to face the convoy and began waving madly, sporting toothless grins and expressions of delight. The president smiled as the car moved on, leaving the street kids to go back to their fire in the distance.

It was Rafferty's first visit to South Africa and he was determined to seek to improve trade and investment with the country, and to take some of the interest away from South Africa's two growing trading partners, India and China. His desire to come to South Africa turned into an enormous planning operation run by the Department of International Relations and Cooperation (Dirco) and the United States Embassy in South Africa.

It is estimated that Bill Clinton's presidential trip to six African countries in 1998 cost the United States government at least forty-two point seven million dollars. Barack Obama's visit to South Africa, and two other African countries, in 2013 was described as one of the largest security operations of his presidency and purportedly cost almost one hundred million dollars.

No one believed that the amount could be topped, yet President Dan Rafferty's trip to South Africa and two other countries on the continent exceeded that amount by at least another twenty million dollars, costing in total almost one hundred and twenty million. All in the name of security.

The entourage that was delivered by United States military cargo planes brought at least sixty-five vehicles, including fifteen parade limousines and seven trucks loaded with layers of bulletproof glass to cover the windows of the hotels where the first family was staying. A specialized communications vehicle for secure telephone and video connections and two trucks to scramble radio frequencies around the presidential motorcade were also flown to South Africa. There was even a special ambulance set up to deal with any possible biological or chemical contaminants.

Hundreds of secret service agents were brought in for Rafferty's visit and utilized for the security and transportation operations. Fighter jets to man the airspace over the president twenty-four hours a day, a special navy aircraft carrier complete with a fully staffed medical trauma center, and various US Marine Chinook helicopters, as well as several other newly developed helicopters were also standard accompaniments on what the United States and global media had described as the "Rafferty Expedition".

As they headed towards suburbia, Rafferty could see Table Mountain getting clearer. Fifteen minutes later and the convoy drove through what seemed like another world. In the space of a few minutes they had left the poverty-stricken neighborhood for luxurious mansions and high security walls all around.

What a contrast, Rafferty thought. *Two completely different worlds in the space of one city.*

A phone ringing in the front part of the limo cut into the president's thoughts. One of his aides turned to him.

"We seem to be a few minutes ahead of schedule, Mr President. We've been informed that the hotel just needs a few more minutes before we can drive into their premises."

"I would have thought everything was taken care of already," said Rafferty.

"Just a minor security glitch."

"Security glitch? Should I be concerned?"

"No, Mr President. It seems that a Labrador ran through the hotel lobby and, well, shall I say caused some damage to the main carpets."

"My security detail let a dog in?"

"Well, not exactly, sir. It seems the dog was already inside the building before they did their initial sweep. It belongs to one of the cleaners."

"Well, well." Rafferty grinned. "Just as well I'm a dog lover."

"Yes, sir!"

"Speaking of dogs, are we going to go visit the grave of that famous Great Dane?"

"I'm sorry, sir?"

"That famous dog, the one that joined the navy and served his country."

"A dog joined the navy and served its country, sir?"

"Yes, it's buried in Simonstown, near one of the South African naval bases. 'Just Nuisance', I think they called him."

"Unfortunately a visit there has not been scheduled for this trip, Mr President."

"Well why am I not surprised!" Rafferty sighed.

The Fox looked at his watch and drummed his fingers on his desk. He did not expect to hear from Wahied, but he was sure that by now Wahied would have found the briefcase that had been left at the house for Wahied's stopover. It was not so much the briefcase that the Fox wanted Wahied to have but rather the white A4 envelope that lay inside the briefcase, and more importantly the numerous sheets of special stickers inside. The stickers for the water bottles that Wahied had in his truck. The Fox smiled. The devil was always in the detail.

CHAPTER 46

It was Tim's idea to leave his baseball cap to slow down their pursuer. They had then fled northwards where they could find a busy area to get lost among tourists and shoppers. They sprinted down several desolate roads stacked with equally desolate buildings and a few minutes later Liz stopped. "I can't do this," she said as she tried to catch her breath.

"Just keep going." Tim looked over his shoulder. There was no one in sight.

"I need some water."

"I'm sure we'll get to a shop or something soon."

"I don't think I can wait."

Tim stared at Liz. She had become quite pale and was obviously out of breath. Tim was not the most religious of people but at that moment he prayed Liz would not suddenly faint and leave him to fend against that madman who was chasing them with a gun. It was a brief prayer but a prayer nonetheless!

"Come on, Liz, I'm sure we'll get water soon. See those buildings down there? Must be some shops or something."

They started in the direction of what seemed like a busier area still on the outskirts of the quiet neighborhood.

———

Bonnington charged down the street, the warm sun lighting up the path ahead of him. He cursed the man and woman he was chasing, as well as his bad luck in being relegated to meager assignments in a place so far away from home. A place so far away from his family. This time there would be no turning back. He'd sort out this problem if it was the last thing he ever did. He wanted his old job back. He wanted his old life back. And this time nothing was going to stop him. Not some amateurs who seemed intent on being elusive. They couldn't run forever. Just like a buck on the run from a hungry cheetah, they would have to stop eventually. Even if it was just for a minute to catch their breath. He would be there for that. He would make sure of it. There was no room for second chances.

The sun momentarily disappeared behind a looming cloud but Mike didn't even notice nor care. He was trained to act in the light of day or the dark of night. The busy tourist area he now found himself in seemed crammed with hundreds of shoppers and food lovers. It was the perfect place for someone to hide in, the perfect place for those amateurs to seek refuge in. Mike slowed down and stopped by a bench near a bus stop. He gave a half smile to no one in particular. The man and woman he was chasing might think they would be lost amongst the crowds, but they had to show their faces eventually.

———

Liz and Tim raced down another quiet side road. As they sprinted to the bottom they stopped.

"Cul-de-sac." Tim was horrified.

"Let's go in there. I really need some water."

Tim looked up to where Liz was pointing. A rusted metal sign was dangling off a piece of wood outside the building in front of them. "The Flying Pig Bar & Grill Extraordinaire," Tim mumbled. "I don't know... Maybe we should keep going? I feel like we're still in the middle of nowhere."

"He might be waiting for us at the end of the road. We don't seem to have much of a choice right now."

"Okay, okay, let's go in then." Tim waved his hands as he spoke. Either way he knew he would not be able to get rid of the nauseating feeling in the pit of his belly.

CHAPTER 47

A car crept up behind Theunis Botha and revved past him, causing water from a roadside puddle to splash up at the jogger as the car roared into the distance.

"Damn!" Botha lamented but continued his jog anyway. It was his day off and he wasn't going to let some muddy water get the better of him.

Botha ran along the Rondebosch pavement, admiring the trees lining the road. He took a left and paced steadily towards the park, a popular place for both the suburb's many students and residents.

He wore dark blue tracksuit pants with a single red line down on each leg. Despite being off duty, he still wore a standard South African Police Services grey t-shirt which had SAPS emblazoned across it, coupled with the distinctive and recognizable police badge logo of the SAPS.

He approached the sandy trail barely visible through the growing grass in the park and smiled politely at a couple strolling across the lawn. In the distance, someone seemed to be waving at him. He jogged nearer and saw a thin man in tattered clothes jumping up and down. He was one of the beggars who often frequented the park.

"*Meneer, meneer*," the beggar was calling.

"I've got no money today." Botha shrugged but tried not to slow down.

"No, man, I want you to see this." The beggar was pointing to one of the park's large plastic bins behind him.

"No time today," Botha puffed.

"It's urgent, man! Come look."

Botha shook his head.

"Please, bossie, I think it's a bomb."

At the word "bomb" Botha stopped. "What?"

"*Kom.*" The beggar motioned again for him to come near the bin.

Botha walked to the bin and gazed inside it. Sure enough the beggar was right. Wedged between some dirty cardboard and the leftovers of somebody's *slap* fish and chips meal was a metallic device surrounded by different color

124

THE MIND OF GOD

wires. The wires wound through three silver canisters that had been welded together with large strands of brown masking tape. All the canisters were covered with large sharp nails. A small orange light at the bottom of the middle canister continued to flash as Botha peered into the bin, his face getting redder with each passing second. Although Botha had not had much involvement with the study and working of bombs, he knew enough to know this had to be the work of a professional and that he needed to call someone. Fast. He wiped the strands of sweat that were trickling down his forehead and dialed the number of his station commander. "We've got a problem; get the bomb squad here now."

The station commander was currently halfway through his late morning muffin when he received the call and dropped his snack in shock. Within minutes, a barrage of armored vehicles and flashing blue lights was speeding to the park in Rondebosch.

He then dialed the Chief of Police, someone whom he had met personally a few times but someone with whom he would rather not have had the pleasure of speaking with.

"It seems that a bomb has been found in the vicinity of the park in Rondebosch and that the bomb appears to be live."

"Who's on the way?"

"Bomb disposal squad, more police, fire trucks, and I believe that the press are already there."

"I'll bet they are," growled the police chief.

"And obviously the place will be crawling with secret service agents."

"Where's Rafferty now?"

"I'm not sure. They've probably whisked him off before he even arrived."

"He's probably sipping a tumbler of Chivas at his hotel," said the chief. "How long until we know where we stand with the explosive?"

"We still don't know how big a bomb it is, and its nature and severity. It's obvious that the president was a target."

"But why didn't intelligence pick this up?"

"I'm not sure. We're still trying to ascertain all the facts."

"The American Presidency travels with this apparently highly sophisticated and trained entourage, and it takes a hungry beggar to alert the authorities?"

"Yes, Chief!"

"Okay, keep me posted."

"Yes, sir."

The police chief crumpled another piece of paper off his yellow desk pad and aimed it at the small basketball net perched above a bin in the corner of his stuffy windowless office. He didn't remember seeing the park on the president's itinerary. He really doubted that given the President Rafferty's tight schedule he would bother going to a suburban park when there was so much else to see and do. Why would someone plant a bomb if it was not guaranteed the president would be there? And if the president wasn't a target then who was? And why?

———

The bar was dimly lit and stank of a mixture of alcohol, smoke, cherry tobacco, and damp wood. Pictures of pirate ships adorned the musty corridor that led to the vomit-stained bathrooms. The bar counter towered over the thin stools that rocked against the counter wall.

"Please don't hurt me," a voice whimpered in the passage around the corner from the toilets.

"That will teach you to fuck with me," a deep voice growled.

A thump echoed throughout the establishment followed by several punching sounds and then a moan. Liz and Tim stared at each other in horror.

"What was that?" Tim whispered.

"I don't know."

"Well, I don't think we should stick around to find out. Let's get out of here."

They both tiptoed down the passage in the direction from which they had originally come.

They stepped cautiously down another passage, even dimmer than the first one they had entered.

"I sure as hell hope there is an exit here," said Liz.

Seconds later they reached the end of another passage.

"A dead end," Tim was able to let out a horrified whisper. "We have to go back the way we came."

Liz nodded, unable to speak. They had no choice but to turn around and head back to where the horrible sounds had been coming from.

They got to the corridors where they had heard the whimpering. But now they were just greeted with an eerie silence.

"This way," Tim whispered.

They turned right and all they could hear was the reverberating thud of their footsteps no matter how softly they tried to walk.

They were almost at the end when a door at the side of the corridor was thrust open. Liz and Tim ran straight into a wall of three burly men who stared back at them in equal surprise.

"What have we here?" The words were muffled behind the man's long gray beard. All three men had sleeveless jackets revealing an array of tattoos on their arms.

"Um, sorry, I think we might be in the wrong place," Tim said.

"You're definitely in the wrong place," another beard snarled.

"We'll just be on our way then," Liz tried to edge past them but they were blocking the passage.

"I don't think so." The third man gave out a long whistle as he looked Liz up and down. "We don't often get pretty girls inside here."

Liz could feel her heart skipping several beats.

126

"We mean no trouble," said Tim. "Just looking for the exit."

"Through here." The man pointed to the door they had just walked out from. He motioned for Liz and Tim to go through.

Liz hesitated. So did Tim. They glanced at each other but didn't move. It certainly didn't look like an exit door.

"I said, through here," the man growled.

Before they had time to think, the other two men began to push Liz and Tim through the open doorway. Liz winced as she tried to break free from the icy grip on both her shoulders.

"Hey, leave us alone," said Tim.

"Or what?" the man said and laughed. "What are you going to do about it?"

The others roared with laughter as Tim and Liz found themselves in the middle of another bar area. Tim was pushed onto the floor. He went flying across the dirty tiles and landed with a thud.

"Leave him alone!" Liz screamed, trying to break free from the grimy arms that were holding her back.

The men ignored her and continued to hone in on their prey. A baseball bat appeared out of nowhere and seemed to find its grip in the hands of the burliest of the beards. They were circling Tim, like vultures ready to dive into their helpless feast.

CHAPTER 48

Jon Macray was forced to awake from his slumber by the ringing phone. *Jesus, my head hurts.* He tried to sit up but the pain was unbearable so he lay down again. He stared at the phone on his bedside table. It was still ringing.

Who the fuck is that? What time is it?

He stared at the tiny alarm clock next to a towering reading lamp. It was almost lunchtime and a memory of the night before flashed through Jon's mind. His friend's bachelor party, some wild sexy strippers, and a whole lot of booze.

The phone continued to ring. Jon sighed. *Dammit!* He stretched his arm out, managed to grab the phone, and put it to his ear.

"Hello."

"Jon, we've been trying to get hold of you."

"What's going on?"

"Possible bomb at the Rondebosch Park. Get there asap."

Jon sat up. His head was pounding. "I'll be there now."

Minutes later after popping some aspirins in his mouth Jon was in his car speeding to the park. *The day after my big night out I get a fucking bomb.*

He really needed to get back to sleep. *Hope it's just a hoax.* But these days one could never be sure, especially with the President of the United States currently on a visit to the Mother City.

An old lady in a Toyota Camry changed lanes without indicating and Jon narrowly missed her vehicle.

"Fuck it!" He pushed the horn several times but the lady chugged along in front of him as if she hadn't even heard the hooter. "The elderly really need to go for regular driving tests," he mumbled.

He hooted again. The cars were speeding furiously in the next lane; there was no way he could change lanes. The Camry continued to chug along at its leisurely pace.

"In breaking news we can announce that a bomb has just been found in a rubbish bin in the park in the suburb of Rondebosch"

The Fox turned the volume up on the remote and watched the news announcer reveal that police had cordoned off the area and members of the public were advised to keep away from the vicinity. No one had yet claimed responsibility for the device that was still live and could explode at any time.

The broadcast then switched to a reporter on the scene.

"The bomb squad is apparently on its way and no doubt will be here in the next few minutes. The place is already crawling with police and fire personnel. It's still not clear how the bomb was discovered but it would seem a vagrant was rummaging through the bins and then pointed the device out to a policeman who was patrolling the park."

The Fox reached for a beer shandy and sat back, his eyes glued to the screen.

The television was replaying the same scene of police cars speeding up to the vicinity and police cordoning off the area with yellow tape. Footage of several people being pushed away from the tape was repeated.

"Speculation is mounting if this bomb is linked to the American President's visit or if it is just a coincidence."

"Don't they know that there's no such thing as coincidence?" The Fox couldn't help but smile.

The channel then switched to the news studio where a terrorism expert was being interviewed. The expert wasn't surprised at news of the bomb as there was always this sort of trouble that followed the President of the United States wherever he went in the world. It was only a matter of time before one of these terrorist attacks slipped through the net. It was impossible to avoid this, the expert maintained.

The interviewer nodded as the so-called expert continued to say how the USA brought these types of vigilante actions on itself and that it still needed to change its foreign policy—and drastically, especially in the Middle East.

"I don't know how much longer counter terrorism and intelligence officials can stave off the storm," the expert said. "At some point one of these fanatics will be successful with their endeavors and 9/11 will ultimately look like a picnic in comparison."

"But why a bomb here today?" the anchor asked. "The president wasn't even on site."

"It's about symbolism," the expert explained slowly. "It's a message to the world and to Rafferty himself."

The Fox smiled some more as he gulped down the shandy. *What on Earth will they think of next?*

CHAPTER 49

"Stand back, stand back!" A burly police officer pushed the crowd even further back as he unfolded special yellow tape that he used to cordon off the area.

Several police and law enforcement officers had now appeared on the scene. Sirens of more police vans wailed in the distance. The flashing lights of a fire engine also greeted the frantic crowd.

Other than the scattered officials the taped area was clear. A man in a suit and dark glasses stood near the fire truck. He spoke into the loudspeaker.

"We are going to have to ask everybody to go back even further." He pointed down the road. "Even further away from where the tape is."

The crowd took a few steps back.

"Way back!" the man said. "We're cordoning off a larger area. For your own safety."

"Keep those crowds away." A blond unshaven man leapt out a car. "We don't know what we dealing with yet."

"Yes, sir."

———

Jon Macray, now dressed in faded blue jeans, a Freshly Ground t-shirt, and worn sneakers, reached for a small metallic case from the back of his vehicle and headed towards the cordoned off area.

"It's in there?"

"Yes, sir, that's where the device is located."

Macray walked quickly and stopped a meter or two away from the dustbin.

"Let's do this," he said to no one in particular.

The crowd watched in silence. Nobody moved except the bomb disposal expert who by now was standing right next to the bin. He gave a quick glance to the most senior of the police on the scene and then peered inside.

Jesus! Are those nails stuck to the canister? Definitely the work of a professional. "I want you to check all the bins in all the streets in this vicinity," Macray yelled.

As a specialist in counter-terrorism activities, Macray knew that terrorists often planned a second bomb to go off near the place of the first. The strategy was simple: Get as many law enforcement personnel to come to the scene of the crime and suddenly they all become casualties when a second bomb hidden nearby explodes. Macray was not taking any chances. Nails stuck to the canisters indicated that whoever assembled and planted the bomb meant business. Macray was not prepared to allow a catastrophe to unfold. "Not on my watch," he muttered as he shoved a pair of white plastic gloves over his large hands.

A sniffer dog whined in the distance.

"Everybody back!"

The group of officers who had been keeping guard was glad to take a few steps further away from the device. Macray took a deep breath and then, clutching a small screwdriver, put his hands into the dustbin. He maneuvered the screwdriver through the section where the orange light continued to flash. To the untrained eye, it would have seemed Macray was mad to stick a screwdriver into a live bomb, but all that he was doing was familiarizing himself with what type of bomb he was dealing with and how it had been set up. As he tinkered with the canisters, his objective was clear. He needed to see if a timer or countdown device had been attached to any of the parts. And seconds later he found one. A tiny digital clock was dangling underneath the middle canister. Its bright red numerals were constantly changing. As Macray stared at the bomb the clock clicked on to ten.

"We've got ten minutes!" Macray shouted. He beckoned to two officers nearby. They edged forward, hesitantly.

"Okay." Macray spoke very slowly. "This is how it's going to work. I need to disconnect this bomb. I can only do a proper job if I have full view of this entire explosive device. On the count of three we are going to lift the bomb at exactly the same time and very very slowly we are going to lower it to the ground."

The officers nodded in unison.

"It's very important that we lower the device at the same time," Macray continued gravely. "Do you understand me? If the device is placed unevenly on the ground it might be triggered prematurely."

The officers nodded again.

"Okay, here goes. One... two... three!"

The men gripped their fingers around the bottom of the wedged canisters that formed the heavy bomb and slowly placed it on the tar. As one of the officers turned to walk away a few beeps emanated from the middle canister.

"Don't fucking move," Macray hissed. "There seems to be a motion detector on this device. This means that even the soft sound of your footsteps on the tar will be enough to trigger the device prematurely."

The officer nodded. He stood frozen, his eyes fixated on Macray and the device.

"Eight minutes," Macray said. He moved his hand slowly to the ground and carefully laid the screwdriver down. Then he reached into the metallic toolbox and brought out a pair of pliers. He gripped the red handle and edged his hand towards the largest clump of wires that were wedged between the canisters.

His hand trembled slightly but no one would have noticed. They always trembled when he danced with death but here he was, after all these years, still standing. He hovered the pliers over the large clump of wires and lifted them slightly to create a small gap. Then he sifted the pliers through some more wires into the gap. Underneath was another smaller group of wires clumped together with double-sided masking tape.

Macray wedged the pliers over the middle of the second group of wires. He hesitated as he saw the digits turn. Four minutes. The world around him faded into oblivion as a blanket of heavy concentration encapsulated him. It was just him and the device. If he had the pliers on the right wires, then he would be the hero of the day. If he was about to cut the wrong wires, well, he wouldn't be there to face the music anyway.

He held the pliers over the wires but didn't try to cut anything. Three minutes. *Come on, you can do it! You can fucking do this!* Macray took a deep breath and edged the sharp bits of the plier right over the wires. Then he closed the pliers over them and clenched until the wires snipped.

He exhaled as the wires were cut and the ticking clock stopped instantly.

"Got it!" Macray yelled to everyone but no one in particular. "This bomb is no longer active."

The security personnel, officers, and press broke into applause.

Macray reached for the clock part of the bomb and lifted it. He turned it over so he could examine underneath it.

"Well, I'll be damned," he said.

CHAPTER 50

Liz gasped as one of the men raised the baseball bat above Tim's head. The rest of the men were laughing and cheering their comrade on. The laughter must have attracted attention as another door at the other end of the bar creaked open.

A man emerged from a dingy back office amidst a haze of cigarette smoke. He was tall, had black greased spiky hair, and wore long brown snakeskin boots tight around his calves. He glared at a waiter who scurried past, hoping to avoid his gaze.

"Yeeoow," he exclaimed in a high-pitched voice, a voice that instantly catapulted Liz to another time of her life.

Liz stared at the man in the snakeskin boots. She blinked and stared again. Was she dreaming? She didn't think so. She would have recognized that high pitch anywhere. It had been many years since she had seen him. She couldn't remember if it was fifteen or twenty. As the years went by they had merged into one and it was difficult to pinpoint exactly when they had last seen each other. Either way, it seemed like a lifetime ago. A world far away from the grim reality of the present moment.

The man with the snake boots glared at everyone who dared to look and took a few steps towards the bar.

"Don't hurt me," Tim whimpered. Two of the men held his arms in a tight grip behind his back. The other watched over them—baseball bat still in hand.

"What do we have here?" said the man in snakeskin boots.

"We found him hovering around the corridors."

"Oh really?"

"Yes, in the section that is clearly marked 'Private'. Looked very suspicious if you ask us. I think he was spying on us."

"Spying on us?" The man with the snakeskin boots went pale, then blood red, his eyes remaining fixed on their prisoner.

"Don't hurt me," Tim said again. "Please don't hurt me!"

133

"Yeeoow!" The man with the snakeskin boots twitched his head and shoulders in one movement. "You see these knuckles? You know how many people's faces have met them?"

Liz could see his fists were decorated with rings in several colors containing various emblems and signs. They would certainly pack a power punch. Possibly even a deadly one.

The man in snakeskin boots edged even closer, snarling. He raised his hand into the air ready to swing it into Tim's face.

"Calvin?" Liz spluttered from her corner of the room.

The room was suddenly silent. The fist of the man in the snakeskin boots stopped and his icy gaze turned into one of puzzlement. He whirled around and glared in Liz's direction. "What did you just say?"

"Calvin, is that really you?"

He was stepping slowly towards Liz.

Liz could see his face more clearly as he approached. "Calvin Deacon! It is you!"

The beard holding Liz released his grip on her as the man walking towards them gave him an instructing nod. He peered down at Liz. "And who do we have here?"

"Calvin!" Liz was now smiling. "You don't recognize me? Even after all these years."

For a moment the room was silent again.

"Yeeoow! No fucking way!" A smile began to spread across his face. "Elizabeth Greene? From high school?"

"The one and only!"

Before Liz could utter another word she found herself in the midst of a tight hug.

"It's been what, twenty years?" Calvin was now beaming like a five-year-old child who had just been given his first bicycle.

"Something like that!"

"Unfuckingbelievable! Where has time gone?"

"It has been a long time," Liz acknowledged.

"Wow, those were some great times back then." Calvin's eyes were gleaming. "Bruce Springsteen was right. They really were glory days!"

"It's good to see you."

"I had a crush on her in high school," Calvin explained to his audience.

The men nodded approvingly.

"And him?" Calvin pointed his thumb in Tim's direction.

"He's okay. He's with me."

"With you, or *with* you?"

Liz just smiled and then her expression changed.

"I'm afraid we're in a bit of trouble."

"Trouble? Not Liz Greene!"

"It's serious," said Liz.

"Come to my office," said Calvin, gesturing for the men to let Tim go. "Yeeoow! Sorry about that. They mean you no harm."

"I'm sure they don't," said Tim as he clambered back onto his feet and quickly stepped away from the beards and the baseball bat.

"You can't be too careful these days," said Calvin.

"No, I guess you can't." Tim was brushing the dust off his pants.

They headed through another door into a small backroom.

"What brings you here?" said Calvin, who was still beaming from ear to ear.

"Other than a wrong turn?" said Liz.

Calvin roared with laughter. "Yeeooow! And here I thought that you had regrets about not dating me and wanted to make amends."

"Very funny," said Liz. "You certainly haven't lost your sense of humor."

The office was tiny and cramped. Liz and Tim sat on two tattered chairs facing a small metal desk. Calvin walked behind the desk and sat on a matching metal chair.

"A drink, anyone?" Calvin reached for the phone at the end of his desk.

"Just some water," said Liz as she took off her jersey and draped it over the back of her chair. Tim nodded in agreement.

Calvin spoke into his receiver and ordered waters for them and a double scotch for himself.

CHAPTER 51

After much strenuous wriggling and painfully maneuvering her body towards the front of the house, Michelle finally made her way to the entrance hall. She looked up at the clock hanging on the entrance wall. Twenty minutes had passed and still no one had come into the house. There was no sign of Agnes or anyone for that matter. And she couldn't get near the landline phone even if she tried. She cursed her misfortune that the day had brought her so far.

Another agonizing few minutes passed when Michelle heard a fumbling on the other side of the door. *Somebody's here. Thank goodness!* She stared up in eager anticipation as Agnes entered the house.

Michelle had not moved herself as close to the front door as she would have liked. She was lying to the side of the room, right next to a walnut cabinet with bright red figurines perched on it. The dark carpet she lay on camouflaged her quite well, given that she was wearing dark clothes.

To Michelle's shock, Agnes didn't even glance her way. She closed the door behind her and headed towards the side passage just to the left of the front door.

"Agnes!" Michelle yelled. "Here! Help!"

But Agnes continued walking. As she turned down the corridor Michelle saw to her horror that she had a large pair of headphones covering her ears and was humming a tune.

"Agnes!" Michelle yelled again.

And in an instant Agnes had disappeared down the passage completely oblivious of Michelle lying on the carpet.

"Agnes!" Michelle screamed. "Help me!"

But there was no response, and Michelle was left to stare at the ceiling in anguish. *She's got to come back that way. Maybe she'll see me then.*

Michelle didn't want to risk it and thought about how she could get Agnes to see her. *The figurines! Of course!* She reached for the cloth that the figurines were perched on at the top of the cabinet and pulled the cloth towards her.

One of the figurines fell off the cloth but landed further back on the cabinet, out of Michelle's reach.

She continued to pull the cloth. It was almost at the end and she gave it one last yank and the figurines were lifted. One of them fell backwards like the other one had, but the last one toppled off the table.

She caught it as it fell off the cabinet and clutched it. Now she had to make sure she could see Agnes when she walked back to the entrance hall.

"Agnes! Can you hear me?"

But she was still met with no response. The minutes ticked by but for Michelle they seemed like hours. Several long minutes later Agnes appeared again.

"I'm here!" Michelle yelled as she threw the figurine at Agnes trying to catch her attention. "Help me!"

But Agnes continued her walk out of the house singing to the music that was streaming into her ears. She slammed the front door behind her as she stepped outside, oblivious of the fact that Michelle was lying sprawled across the side of the entrance hall floor.

"Agnes," Michelle screamed. She realized the futility of it all and punched her fist onto the cold stone tiles as the tears began to fall. *Why couldn't she just look down? Why is this happening to me today?*

She wondered if Agnes would come back in but doubted it. She stared at the front door for the next ten minutes just in case, but there was no sign of Agnes returning or of anyone else entering the house.

"Is there anyone there? Can anybody hear me?" She finally admitted defeat. It was going to be a very long day.

Michelle attempted to push herself forward towards the front door. She leaned on her elbows and lunged herself forward. She was able to heave her body a few meters. She groaned in agony and spent the next few minutes dealing with the pain shooting into her thigh. Then she lunged herself forward on her elbow again and repeated the process several times, each time taking a while to recover from the severe pain.

About an hour later Michelle had slumped herself on the floor area right in front of the entrance. Anyone walking into the house again would literally step on her if they didn't see her first. Michelle didn't know when anyone would next be returning to the house. She looked up at the clock and the tears started to come down again. And this time they didn't stop.

CHAPTER 52

"If you've just tuned in, we have breaking news from Cape Town, South Africa, where President Rafferty is on an official visit."

The Fox chewed ferociously on some candied peanuts.

The television screen shifted from the studio to a reporter speaking into the camera excitedly. Behind him were several parked police vehicles and fire trucks, the bright lights on top of each vehicle still flashing.

"Thanks, Jim. Yes, I'm speaking to you live from a park in the leafy suburb of Rondebosch in Cape Town where a bomb was discovered a bit earlier. And I can tell you that in the last few minutes the explosive device has been dismantled, Jim."

"Dismantled? You're saying it's no longer a threat?"

"That is correct. I am told that the device has been taken apart but it now seems that the whole thing was a hoax."

"A hoax?"

"I repeat, I have been informed that although the bomb was made with real parts, it was not actually connected to explode, but looked real enough to warrant all this attention."

"What on earth is going on here?"

"Looks like someone might have been playing a practical joke."

"You're kidding?"

"We are just waiting to get some official comment and we'll keep you updated as soon as we know exactly what has just happened."

The Fox broke into laughter. *Perfect,* he thought. *Everything is going according to plan.*

CHAPTER 53

"There's a problem with the fish."

"What did you say?"

"I said, there's a problem with the fish."

Sol Arendse scratched his forehead furiously; something he always did when he was uptight.

"What type of problem?" He was almost afraid to ask.

"It's off. Plain and simple." The voice of the obnoxious caterer boomed through the receiver that was firmly pressed against Sol's ear.

"Off?" he almost choked. "What do you mean, it's off?"

"I mean that what with the recent electricity load shedding, the fridge stopped working, and the fish started to acquire its own unusual aroma. I don't think it's fit for human consumption, or any consumption for that matter."

Sol was fuming. It had been a stressful and busy year for him so far. An expensive knee operation, followed by an even more expensive protracted and ugly divorce had left him highly strung and short tempered. He'd just about had it with Mrs Bun, supposedly one of the best caterers in the business.

"And why is this suddenly my problem?" he barked into the receiver. "I'm not interested in the minute-to-minute occurrences in your kitchen."

"Well, what do you want me to do?" Mrs Bun asked haughtily.

"Sort it out."

"It's going to cost you more than I originally quoted."

"What?" Sol was fuming.

"Are you deaf? I said it's obviously going to cost you more. The menu might have to be changed slightly. We might have to use kabeljou if we don't have enough yellowtail."

"Jesus."

"I will not allow my name to be compromised," said Mrs Bun. "I'm the best in the business and if the yellowtail is off, I will use kabeljou, and your

139

company will pay for it. Simple as that. This is after all going to be served to the President of the United States."

Sol sighed. The forthcoming arrival of the President of the United States was coming out of his ears. The president this. The president that. The president here. The president there. He was sick of it. He wondered just how far away he was from a nervous breakdown.

"Just sort it all out, Mrs Bun."

CHAPTER 54

"So what brings you to my neck of the woods?" Calvin downed his double scotch.

"It's, er… complicated," Liz tried to muster a smile.

"Complicated? Yeeeeeooow! It always is!" Calvin began to hum the tune of Billy Joel's "She's Always a Woman to Me".

"So much happening at once," said Liz.

"Well, if there's anything I can do," said Calvin, "and I mean anything, just ask."

"Tintin," Tim pointed to the handcrafted statue balanced on the corner of the table. "Nice."

"I'm a fan." Liz watched as Calvin shot Tim another disapproving nod, as if to say how dare you even talk to me. Tim shrank into his seat.

"Actually, we might need a lift somewhere," said Liz.

"Anywhere," said Calvin. "How about your place?"

"Rhodes Memorial." Liz ignored Calvin's question.

"That's near enough!" said Calvin.

"It's where we need to be." Liz smiled. "I'll explain later."

"Yeeeeooow! That sounds intriguing," said Calvin. "But unfortunately I won't be joining you there. Got an important meeting in twenty minutes."

"Do you mind if we go now then?" said Liz.

"We'll have to take a car," said Calvin, glaring at Tim again. "Won't fit the three of us on my Harley. On condition that you give me your number and we have a proper catch up some other time."

"Sure." Despite what he did for a living, Liz knew Calvin would never harm her.

"I'll be back in twenty," Calvin called to no one in particular and stood up. "And tell the Reaper to wait for me. I haven't forgotten about the meeting."

"Okay," a deep male voice said from one of the other rooms.

Calvin led them down another dimly lit corridor and pushed open a door at the end of it. It opened to a small enclosed parking lot. In front of them was a Bentley. It was light blue and looked like one of the original models.

"It's a vintage piece," Calvin said, grinning. "Goes at a fair pace but I take good care of her."

Calvin opened the front door for Liz and gestured at Tim to sit in the back. Soon they were heading in the direction of Rhodes Memorial. The Bentley glided its way through several side roads until they hit a busier street and then an intersection. In front of them the rows of cars stood still.

"Gridlock," said Tim.

"What's with all this traffic?" Liz asked as her heart began to sink.

"Yeeeeooooow!" Calvin screeched the car to a halt. "I forgot there'd be traffic at this time of day."

"What's going on?"

"They've blocked up the roads and set up some security points around these suburbs and on the M3."

"Why?"

"Because of that fake bomb that was planted in Rondebosch earlier."

"A fake bomb?"

"Sickos." Calvin shrugged. "Probably some stupid attention seeker. Yeeeeooooow!"

"I had no idea."

"Anyways I'm going to turn around and head back." Calvin shrugged at Liz. "I can't be late for my meeting. Big business deal!"

"It's okay," said Liz. "We're quite near the highway anyway. If there's a traffic jam we'll be able to literally walk across the M3."

"Exactly!" Calvin beamed. "That's my girl!"

"Thanks for the ride, Calvin. I really appreciate it."

"Yeeeeooooow! Don't forget about our catch up!"

Tim and Liz got out of the Bentley.

"Thank you," said Tim. "Great to meet you."

Calvin glared at Tim.

"This way," Liz showed Tim. "The part of the M3 that's near Rhodes Memorial is just down there."

She waved at Calvin as he turned the car around and then continued to make her way with Tim up the road.

Liz and Tim stuck to the sides of the roads and hoped they would not be noticed among the crowds. They were now on Main Road and merged themselves among the shoppers and businesspeople engrossed in their own activities.

After an uphill climb they were soon on the side of the M3 highway. Sure enough, the lanes were congested with stationery traffic.

"Look, there's a roadblock down there," Liz said. "Let's walk further down a bit and then cross."

Tim nodded. They needed to keep far away as possible from any police.

CHAPTER 55

It had been another long night on the streets of Cape Town for young Nkosi. Most nights were the same—long, cold, and hard. Never sleeping in the same place for two nights, Nkosi would move around between the murky alleyways, the open spaces of the city gardens, and the vast emptiness of the open parking lots. There were times when Nkosi stayed in the safe confines of shelters but, generally, and in the summers especially, Nkosi preferred to sleep on the soft grassy patches nestled between sandy flowerbeds in local parks. In the winters, he would usually spend the night on some flattened cardboard boxes in the welcome shelter of unused office building doorways.

With his father having died of HIV/Aids when Nkosi was just two, and his mother a victim in her own surreal world of a crystal meth, Nkosi was forced to leave home at an early age to fend for himself.

On this particular morning, Nkosi walked along slowly, in no rush to get anywhere. His thin legs knocked against each other, as his bare feet, which had been hardened over time, remained oblivious of the sharp pebbles scattered in his path. He wore a large red T-shirt with the words "Habonim Dror" across it in black letters that he had picked up at one of the shelters. He stared at all the people walking by, as he did every day, looking for the unsuspecting tourists with expensive cameras to grab or shiny necklaces to rip off their necks. When it was more of the locals walking up and down the gardens, Nkosi would normally go up to them and beg for some money. But today there weren't that many people about. No tourist groups in sight yet, and the handful of locals he'd already approached for a few rand had refused to give him anything. Nkosi sighed and leaned against the trunk of a towering oak, seeking some temporary shade from the strengthening sunlight. Amidst the chirping of birds, Nkosi thought he heard a voice talking to him.

"Hey kid," the stranger hissed. "What's your name?"

Nkosi looked up. It wasn't often that people stopped to ask him his name. In fact, he didn't think anybody had ever just stopped him and asked him who

143

he was. He stared at the stranger cautiously. He could see some gray hair peeping out from behind his hat. The man was grasping a long walking stick and wore an oversized pair of sunglasses. *What difference does it make if he knows my name,* he thought. *It's not as if it's a secret.*

"Nkosi," he said.

"How would you like to make some extra money, Nkosi?"

"How much?"

"I'll give you a hundred and fifty rand now, and if you do what I say, I'll give you another hundred and fifty."

"What do you need done?" asked Nkosi, his eyes wide.

The stranger nodded towards a bench on the side of the path, and they walked over to it and sat down. Looking around to make sure no one else was in earshot, the stranger started whispering. After a few minutes of instructions and the occasional nod by Nkosi, Nkosi was handed three fifty-rand notes that he shoved into his pocket.

"And remember, Nkosi, if you say I told you to do this or that I gave you money, I'll deny it. And you won't get the rest of the money then either."

Nkosi nodded again.

"Don't mess with me, Nkosi, or this will be a day you'll regret for a very long time," said the stranger. "Don't fuck this up."

"You can count on me," said Nkosi as he stood up and glanced at the stranger one more time before heading down the path.

———

Miles Oakley was doing his usual foot patrol of the parking lot levels of the Cape Town International Convention Centre. He saw the street kid in the distance and immediately proceeded towards him.

"Hey, kid!" he called. "Can I help you?"

"Actually, can you help me?" said a voice behind Miles.

Miles turned around to see a man leaning on a walking stick, a white sunhat and large sunglasses covering most of his face.

"Sorry?' said Miles.

"Could you help me?" said the stranger. "I seem to be lost."

"Sure," said Miles, forgetting momentarily about the street kid who had just disappeared into the parking lot. "Where do you need to be?"

The stranger was holding an unfolded map of the City of Cape Town and pointed to an area on it. "I was trying to get to this restaurant here," he said. "I'm told they have great jazz."

"They sure do," Miles agreed.

"According to the map, I should be here, but I seem to still find myself at the Convention Centre."

"It's an easy mistake," Miles explained. "The jazz restaurant you are looking for is quite near. You just need to go back to the central entrance, and then go left."

"You mean here?" the stranger pointed to the map.

Meanwhile, as planned, Nkosi made his way into the main parking lot and headed towards a section of cars at the side of the huge garage area marked "Reserved Parking Only".

Nkosi looked around and crouched down, softly moving from one parked car to the next. He stared at each number plate until he came to the car he had been told to go to. And sure enough, here it was. A blue 4x4 with the number plate "Cape Sol WP".

Nkosi reached into his pocket for the sharp stone he had picked up in the gardens. He clutched it and breathed deeply. Then he swung his arm back and with full force smashed the stone against the driver's window.

The glass shattered but there were remnants in the window frame. As the stone broke the glass, the car's alarm started to blare. Nkosi smashed the glass that was still left in the frame. This time the last bits crumbled onto the tarred floor. His work done, Nkosi sprinted to the other side of the garage and hid behind a parked truck.

Seconds later a security guard raced past the truck, heading towards what would probably seem like a random car theft attempt to him. Once the patrol officer was out of sight, Nkosi slipped out of the garage entrance and into the sunlight.

Several more people had run into the parking lot and a group of curious bystanders were gathering around the section where the break-in had occurred. By this time, Nkosi was already walking away from the Convention Centre in the direction of the gardens where he had first received his instructions. He had just earned his extra hundred and fifty rand.

CHAPTER 56

Nestled high among the trees on the slopes of Table Mountain is Rhodes Memorial. It is a national monument dedicated to Cecil John Rhodes, a former Prime Minister of what was once known as the Cape Colony. The monument can be found on the eastern slopes of Devil's Peak on a portion of land Rhodes specifically set aside to preserve the beauty and grandeur of the mountain. The memorial itself was designed by Sir Francis Macey and Sir Herbert Baker, and was built on the site where Rhodes would apparently often sit in deep contemplation of matters affecting his life.

Liz and Tim entered the mountainous estate through the large wrought-iron gates just off the M3. After a strenuous walk up the long steep road, they found themselves in an empty parking lot near the memorial. A soft breeze blew through the surrounding pine forests. A squirrel darted in front of them before disappearing into a thicket of greenery.

A group of weary students lazed on the grass beside the parking lot, sipping coffee from their metal flasks and enjoying the latest gossip. Beyond the parking lot was another smaller, busier parking lot on a higher slope to which Liz headed.

Tim followed her. A lady with a bright yellow and orange jacket eyed them suspiciously.

"Careful, that person's watching us," Tim whispered. "Do you think she recognizes us?"

"It's okay, she's just an informal car guard."

"Car guard?"

"Yes, they've sprung up everywhere. Some 'guards' are homeless and unemployed, while others are migrants from other African countries who escaped the problems of their birthplaces. They find various parking lots and then spend their time watching over the vehicles in the hope that the drivers when returning to their cars will give them some money."

"And do they?"

"Sometimes."

"And if they don't?"

"It just depends. I know they're trying to make a living but sometimes these guards can have real attitude. A friend of mine once returned to her car to find that someone had smashed the front passenger window and stolen the radio. The guard still had the cheek to ask for money!"

Tim laughed. "Did she pay?"

"No ways."

The guard nodded at them as they walked to the end of the parking lot.

"Welcome to Rhodes Memorial," Liz said and smiled. "Let's check out the memorial."

"I need to go to the restroom first."

"It's there," Liz pointed. "I'll wait here for you."

Tim walked to the gent's bathroom, closing the door behind him. He bolted it so that the "occupied" sign would light up on the other side. He sat on top of the toilet seat, holding his head, trying to calm his breathing. It had been quite a day so far and he really wasn't coping.

He reached into his pocket and pulled out his cellphone. He stared at it for several minutes and let out a long sigh. Then he dialed the number he had been trying to call all morning. He pressed the phone against his ear and waited a few seconds for the connection and the number to be reached. He held on for a few more minutes as he listened to the ringing on the other side. But the phone continued to ring and didn't go to voicemail.

"Damn!" Tim muttered as he hung up. *I'll have to try again later.* He stared at the phone in his hands and tried to ignore the fact that they were trembling. He stuffed the phone back into his pants pocket and headed outside.

CHAPTER 57

The driver of the Citroen switched off the engine and stepped out the car. He was wearing a black suit jacket and jeans. He walked to the front door of the house and rang the doorbell. A few minutes went by and still no one came to the door. He looked at his watch. The delivery note stipulated that someone would be there to receive the package.

"Hello, anybody home?" He banged on the door now. "Hello?"

Suddenly something leapt into the air and let out a shriek as it landed in front of him.

"Whoa!" he took a step back in fright and then breathed a huge sigh of relief to see that it was just a cat. "Damn cat," he muttered as he brushed the ginger tabby aside and continued to walk down the path. He hated cats. He found them callous and without personality. Give him a dog any day.

The house seemed locked and the windows at the back were tightly shut.

"Hello?" he shouted again. "Anybody home?"

The driver cursed. He was sick of wasting his time with deliveries for people who never bothered to make sure there would be someone at the house to accept them. It happened so often with his bloody job. If someone was going to order a gift for someone else they should always ensure there would be no hitches regarding the actual delivery. He looked at the package in his hands. It was wrapped with red paper with white circles all over it. It felt soft like a folded tie. *Who wears ties these days anyway?*

He reversed out of the driveway and sped off.

Rafik waited for the man to leave and then emerged from behind the bushes he had been hiding in. He walked to the large wooden garage door at the top of the driveway. A lot of these houses had superior alarm systems but more often than not the garage doors were not armed. Rafik had found this out on several occasions. He didn't know why garage doors were often excluded from these top security systems but he wasn't complaining. Especially on a driveway that was not closed off at the bottom by large wrought-iron gates, which had become a popular feature of suburbs over the years.

Rafik had abandoned the police car a few blocks back. It was good enough to escape in, but he knew that with the satellite tracking system in it, as well as the obvious number plate, it would just be a matter of time before he was caught again. He had jumped over some garden walls, run across a small field, and then run up some leafy suburban avenues before heading down this road and on to the driveway of this particular house.

Rafik knelt down on the bricks to pick the padlock on the garage door.

———

Marcel le Beauf was sipping a glass of Chardonnay on a pristine beach in the Seychelles. He was sprawled on a deck chair and was sleepily gazing ahead at the waves that were lapping gently onto the sand. He had just requested one of the waiters to please bring an umbrella to set up near him. Shade was urgently needed! It was already day three of his much-needed holiday, and Marcel had been soaking it all up as best as he could.

He marveled at the views around him, particularly two young women clad in yellow and red bikinis respectively who were playing beach bats a mere fifty meters away. *This is paradise*, he thought. *What more does a man want?* As he watched the sexy beach bat players go back and forth, one of them gave the ball a huge wallop and it landed right next to Marcel's deck chair. He leaned over to grab it as one of the ladies came running towards him.

"Sorry about that," she said and smiled.

"Not a problem at all," Marcel said in his broken English as he handed her the ball.

"Thanks." Before he could begin the small talk he saved for sexy women, the lady had already run back to her friend. Seconds later they were hitting the ball back and forth again.

So quick! Maybe I'll go up to them later and get a conversation going.

Marcel's relaxation was jolted by the ringing of his cellphone. He reached beneath the towels in his beach bag to find his mobile. *Who the hell is phoning me now?* Marcel was in real estate and had given instructions to everyone back at the office not to call him unless it was extremely urgent. And even then, they shouldn't call him unless the problem was unsolvable. Normally, Marcel thought, problems were solvable.

He stared curiously at the ringing phone. It was from a private number so definitely not from his office. He hesitated, sighed, and then pushed the green button.

"Good day. Mr Le Beauf?"

"Yes, this is he."

"Good day to you, sir, I am phoning you from eKapa Security Systems." The voice on the other end of the line was firm and gruff.

"Yes?"

"Well, sir, we just wanted to do a check up with you that everything is in order."

"In order? Why shouldn't everything be in order?" Le Beauf was almost shouting into the receiver. In the near distance one of the sexy beach bat players bent down to retrieve the ball off the sand.

"Sir, where about are you at the moment?"

"I'm in the Seychelles having a much-needed break."

"So you're not in Newlands then?" The voice suddenly seemed alarmed.

"No, I'm not anywhere in Cape Town. I just told you I'm in the Seychelles. What's going on?"

"Sir, our vehicle tracking devices indicate that your BMW motor vehicle, the one you instructed us to implement our anti-hijacking system in, our systems show that your BMW is currently driving through Newlands."

"Newlands?" Le Beauf was now beyond calm. The ladies with the beach bats both stopped their game and briefly turned around after they heard Le Beauf shout. "What the hell is it doing in Newlands?"

"We don't know, sir. We are calling you because you informed our company previously that you would be away. We just needed to confirm that you are indeed away."

"I am clearly away!" Le Beauf roared. "Someone has unlawfully taken my car from my house."

"We're sending out a squad car now to pursue it. We'll contact the local police as well. It shouldn't be hard to find. Our tracking devices are very sophisticated."

"Just get my damn car back!" Le Beauf shouted.

"We'll keep you updated, sir."

Le Beauf clicked off the receiver in disgust. Another bottle of Chardonnay was urgently needed.

CHAPTER 58

Sol had been preparing for President Rafferty's visit for months, and his duties had increased in scope and focus. From the food to the hospitality to the dignitaries and the accompanying security, Sol's task as head coordinator, chief liaison with the presidential entourage, and chief supervisor was a mammoth one. Despite all the stresses, Sol was able to juggle his various duties immaculately and it was these qualities that inspired confidence in his employers. If there was one person who could get the job done and coordinate a banquet that was playing host to the President of the United States, it was Sol Arendse.

Sol, however, like every other person on the planet, was only human. It is a known fact that no one can be in two different places at exactly the same time. Being the hectic morning that it had been, just like every day for Sol recently, Sol had not yet had his morning cup of coffee. He decided it would be a good time to take a quick break and arrange a cup of strong caffeine. At twelve fifty pm, just as he was about to tell his personal assistant Ursula to organize his beverage, his phone rang.

It never ever stops, Sol thought as he pulled out his cellphone from the front pocket of his shirt. "Sol speaking, hello."

"Er, Mr Arendse, I'm phoning from the parking lot."

"The parking lot?"

"My name is Miles. I monitor the security in the parking lot."

"What's the problem, Miles?"

"Er, sir, just to confirm that you drive a blue 4x4 car with number plate 'Cape Sol WP'?"

"Yes, that's my car..."

"Um, unfortunately someone seems to have broken into your car."

"What?"

"Your front window has been smashed, and your alarm is still going off."

"Christ! When did this happen?" Sol's face was reddening rapidly.

"In the last few minutes."

"Did you catch anyone?"

"Sir, it's preferable that you come down to the parking lot. We can sort out everything when you get here."

Sol shoved the phone in his pocket and headed for the elevator.

"Ursula, my car's been broken into!" he said as he stalked past his personal assistant. "If anyone needs me, I'm currently unavailable. You hear me?"

"It's one thing after the next," Sol muttered to himself. He was hoping the insurance would cover the broken window, but it had been so long since he'd signed up for the policy he couldn't remember what they covered any more.

Sol hurried out of the elevator into the parking lot. Several people had gathered around his car. He shook his head sullenly as he pushed through the curious bystanders. Sure enough, the driver's window had been smashed and bits of broken glass were scattered on the ground.

"Did you have any valuables that might have been visible?" asked the security guard as Sol approached the car.

"No." Sol shook his head. "There was nothing of value in the car. I never leave anything lying around in it anyway."

"Okay," said Miles as he scribbled away into his notebook. "Just getting the facts together for my report."

"I wonder why someone smashed the windows if there was nothing to steal," said Sol.

"It looks like the bugger was going to steal the actual car," said Miles. "Luckily your car alarm was working!"

"Lucky my ass," fumed Sol as he reached into his pocket for his cellphone. He pushed speed-dial and held the receiver to his ear.

"Ursula, cancel my appointments for the next hour or hour and a half. I've got to take my damn car in now to get new windows fitted."

What with everything else happening he now had to worry about this too. Insurance better pay out for this, he thought as he climbed into the vehicle.

"I'll let you know if we're able to trace the perpetrator," said Miles. "I'm going to order a screening of the cctv camera footage."

"Whatever," Sol grumbled as he switched on the ignition and revved the engine before speeding out towards the exit, leaving the handful of onlookers to cough in the dust.

CHAPTER 59

Eric Simms spent the morning on Table Mountain and even found the time to devour a delicious curry chicken pasta salad. Not being one to indulge in alcohol often, he decided to try a local lager and thoroughly enjoyed it. He then made his way to the cable car and headed down the mountain.

Forty-five minutes later, Eric was waiting at the coffee house as arranged with Michelle Sloane. He glanced at his Rolex. He had a few minutes to spare until the scheduled meeting. With the aftertastes of lunch still circulating, he decided to round it all off with a fresh espresso.

Thirty-five minutes later, he had finished his coffee and, as he stared around at the chic artwork displayed on the walls, he began to drum his fingers on the table. Michelle was half an hour late and he wasn't used to being messed around. He glanced at his watch for the umpteenth time in the last ten minutes and then looked around, but there was no one whom he recognized from the preliminary Skype conversations that had taken place. *This is unbelievable. How can she not be here?*

He sighed. He didn't enjoy waiting around and he never tolerated people being late. He believed unpunctuality to be improper and the height of rudeness.

I'll give her ten more minutes and if she doesn't show then I'm outta here.

He had traveled so far for this meeting. It seemed like a worthy cause and he was happy to consider putting his money into it, but this waiting around was unacceptable. He wondered when he would ever be in Cape Town again. His thoughts shifted briefly to his next interview scheduled in Malawi two days later. He certainly would be more inclined to invest his energy into the other candidates' projects.

He glanced at his watch again.

Five more minutes. Then it's bye-bye to Michelle and her orphanage.

When Eric Simms was an apprentice coming into the business world, he had worked as a junior in a big international company. It was his first exposure to the corporate world and, being wet behind the ears, he had a lot to learn. One morning, after three weeks on the job, he left his house a few minutes later than usual and as a result got caught up in obscene traffic. He was subsequently at least half an hour late.

He remembered apologizing profusely to his superior, explaining that he was never normally late, and that morning had been beyond his control. Traffic happens to everyone, he tried to explain to his glaring employer. His boss was not interested in excuses. The rest of the company managed to be here on time, he told Eric.

After listening to Eric plead that he was a victim of circumstance and that it would never happen again, the employer fired Eric on the spot. He explained to Eric that being late was disrespectful to the company, to the staff, and to the clients. Their company could not tolerate such actions. Eric was given twenty minutes to pack up his desk.

His first lesson in the corporate world had been a bruising but valuable one. Eric was never late for anything in his life again.

"Everything okay, mister?" A waitress scuttled past.

Eric Simms nodded and she disappeared into the kitchen. Another five minutes went by and the fingers continued to tap on the table. *She better be here soon.*

No one was late for a meeting with Eric Simms. No one dared.

I can't understand it. She confirmed she would be here. This is probably a big deal for her.

He looked at the second hand chug along the golden perimeter of his watch.

"You sure you okay, you look kinda glum!" The waitress was walking past again, now with a tray of homemade chocolate mousse desserts.

"Just the check," said Eric.

"Sure, be back in a minute."

His time was so precious. *That's it. I guess it's bye-bye to Michelle then.* He paid for his coffee and stormed out of the coffee house.

CHAPTER 60

Rhodes Memorial is built of Cape granite quarried on Table Mountain and is supposedly modeled on the memorial after the Greek temple at Segesta, although in reality its design is closer to the temple of Pergamon. A lengthy staircase with forty-nine steps, one for each year of Rhodes's life, leads from a semi-circular terrace up to a rectangular U-shaped monument formed of pillars. Granite walls garnish the stairs on which statues of eight life-size bronze lions keep a watchful eye over Cape Town. A sculpture of Rhodes can also be found at the memorial as well as a statue of Energy, at the bottom of the steps, which is identical to the statue in Kensington Palace Gardens in London.

Liz and Tim made their way down the steps towards the famous statues. Liz ran down the steps to the furthest lion statue. Tim followed her, brushing his way past a group of Chinese tourists who were staring at their cameras as they snapped away.

"My dad would bring me here when I was a kid," Liz said. "This was the statue that he let me 'ride'."

Liz frowned and slowly walked around the lion, staring at it intensely. She brushed over the claws with her hands. The truth was she didn't know exactly what to look for or where, but all she could do was follow her instinct. This memorial now seemed the most logical place to find the microchip, given the words in the rhyme. *In the clutches of the strong lion, a wafer will quench your thirst.*

She crouched at the foot of the lion to see if there was any hollow panel underneath it, a place where her father might have been able to hide something. There was nothing of the sort. The statue was solid.

"We need to examine the rest of the lions," she said.

Twenty minutes later they had still found nothing.

"There's one lion left," Liz pointed down the stairs to a statue in the corner that they had not yet searched.

"Okay, let's check it out," said Tim.

Liz methodically began her search by exploring the open mouth and sharp teeth that they had deduced to be the most logical place for the placing of a microchip.

"It feels empty," Liz said.

"Let me try," said Tim and placed his fingers in the lion's mouth. "I can't find anything either."

A group of tourists emerged at the top of the stairs pointing excitedly at the surroundings amidst the clicks of their cameras and cellphones.

"I can't believe this." Liz sat on the ledge with her back leaning against the side of the lion. "I don't know what to do."

It had been one of the longest drives for Wahied Madat, but as he approached the city of Cape Town, he knew that he was almost at his destination. Soon enough, he had made his way through the busy roads to the Convention Centre.

At exactly one pm, Wahied pulled the truck to a halt as he arrived at the delivery section at the other side of the Convention Centre. A large billboard stated: "Stop. Security Checkpoint Ahead". He stopped just in front of the security barrier in front of the sign as a uniformed guard emerged.

"Can I help you?" came the standard comment when vehicles presented themselves at the delivery section.

"I've got a delivery," said Wahied.

"Wait here, please," said the guard as he fetched a brown clip file.

Wahied drummed his fingers on the steering wheel.

"Any ID on you?" asked the guard.

"Sure," said Wahied, reaching for the glove compartment.

"Hold on, please," said the guard and proceeded to turn through the various pages on his clipboard.

Wahied scratched his head. It had been such a long journey with risky stops. But he was here now, finally. That's what counted. His work was almost done. His heart was pounding. He silently prayed that everything would go smoothly. He couldn't afford for his efforts to come undone at this stage. Not after all the hard work and planning.

All he could do was hope that everything was in place for his arrival. He'd dare not even begin to think about the consequences if it wasn't.

Tim was convinced that they had embarked on another wild goose chase. He had gone with her to the bank because Liz had been so sure that her father's clue had intended for her to go there. He had even argued with the officials there in order to help Liz get access to the elite banking division. Then there were no lion statues at Kirstenbosch. Instead they had to flee the gardens from some armed madman. He and Liz had then rushed off to her friend's house only to find that the friend wasn't there. Before they could do anything, someone else was chasing them with a gun. Then they met those thugs in the bar. And they were at Rhodes Memorial because Liz had been convinced the lions in the clue referred to this monument.

Come on! Tim thought. *No one in their right mind would stick a piece of a valuable scientific experiment in the open like this. Surely not?*

"It must be here," Liz continued to run her hand along the teeth of the first lion again. "The words of the clue make sense. If it wasn't the bank or Kirstenbosch, then it has to be here. My father always used to bring me here when I was a child."

"But where exactly would he have hidden a microchip so no one else would have spotted it?"

"It's got to be in a relatively hidden spot."

Relatively hidden? "What do you mean?"

"I mean in the mouth or tucked under the tail or something. A place where a kid playing or a tourist taking a photo would not come across it."

A needle in a bloody haystack. "Clearly there's nothing here, Liz," said Tim, trying to hide his irritation.

"But this was one of my favorite spots," said Liz. "The lions are here. Why else would my father have deliberately mentioned them in his message?"

"We might be on the wrong track again," said Tim.

"It has to be here. There are no other options I can think of that involve lions."

"What if whatever we are looking for is not by the lions themselves, but maybe just somewhere nearby?" said Tim.

"We can try that statue over there," said Liz, pointing to the statue of Cecil Rhodes on his horse, Energy.

CHAPTER 61

Mike could not believe that his suspects had disappeared yet again. He had continued his hunt as he made his way on foot in and out of the maze of streets. After no sign of them anywhere he traced his steps back to his car near Professor Greene's house and drove slowly towards the highway where he encountered the traffic jam as a result of the roadblock. Mike had spoken to one of the police officials and had shown him the "wanted" poster. The officer had remembered recently seeing two of the three people on the poster crossing the highway and pointed towards Rhodes Memorial.

Now, standing in the upper far corner at Rhodes Memorial, Mike had an overview of the Memorial and after a quick scan of the crowds, he was able to spot Liz and the guy on the bottom steps.

"Bingo! Mother-fuckers aren't going anywhere now."

Mike stared incredulously at Liz. *What the fuck is going on here?* The girl was taking her hand and rubbing it along the lion's head and mouth. She said something to her companion, and then she was kneeling down gliding her hand over the lion's paws. She repeated these movements three times. They then walked over to another lion on the other side.

"They seem to be looking for something?" he mumbled. "Whatever it is, I'll bet it's linked to the campus murder."

Some light rain began to descend over Rhodes Memorial. Bonnington looked up at the sky. It had been sunny just a few minutes ago but more clouds were gathering. He wasn't surprised. He had become used to the unpredictability and variety of Cape Town's weather patterns. A busload of British tourists had just made their way down the steps and as the rain began to fall, most of the group huddled on the top part of the steps that was under shelter.

You think they'd be used to the rain, Mike mused as the crowds shuffled past him. With each passing second and each new raindrop, the gathering on the stairs became bigger and bigger until Mike involuntarily found himself squashed in the corner.

He cursed silently as his view of Liz and her friend became obscured. He stood on his tiptoes but it was no use. And whatever partial views he had left of the bottom steps were now obscured by a myriad of colorful umbrellas.

Dammit!

There was nothing else he could do but wait for the crowds to move. He consoled himself with the fact there was no way the runaways would be able to get near the exit either. And being at the top he was positioned nearer the exit anyway. Once the crowd dispersed, Mike would have a clear view of Liz and her friend once more.

Not for the first time that day, Mike began to wait.

———

"Let's just get out of here," Tim said.

"Okay, give me a minute." Liz walked to the ladies' toilet.

Once Liz had closed the door, Tim stepped through a gate into a little garden adjoining the tearoom. He looked around to make sure no one else was around. The garden was quiet. He was about to push the redial button on his phone when a waiter walking past noticed him and stepped into the garden.

"Can I get you anything, sir?"

Tim shook his head and waited until the waiter was out of sight. Then he made the call. He was met once more with an incessant ringing sound. The ringing suddenly stopped and there was a muffled silence on the other end.

"Hello?"

But all Tim could hear was a muffled background noise. It wasn't clear if someone had actually answered the call or if there was just a poor signal.

"Hello?" Tim spoke slightly louder. "Can you hear me? Anyone there?"

Tim had turned his back away from the garden entrance as he tried to focus on his call.

"Tim?" Liz appeared from behind some shrubbery at the garden gate.

Shit! Tim clicked off the call as he heard Liz trample through the flowers. He shoved the phone into his pocket but in his rush he missed his pocket hole and the phone fell to the ground. Liz stared at the phone on the ground. It was still lit up from the call.

"What's going on?"

"Nothing—why?"

"It's just that you keep acting suspicious."

"Suspicious?"

"Who were you on the phone to?"

"What makes you think I was on the phone?"

Liz pointed to the phone on the ground.

"It just fell." Tim wondered if Liz could see how sheepish he felt. "Relax, Liz. I'm not the enemy here."

"But what's with the phone?"

"Liz, I don't know what you're talking about."

"I don't know what I would do if you've been leaking this to the press, or if

159

you are writing an article about all this."

"Liz, I promise you that everything you've discussed with me has stayed with me. What can I do to make you believe that I'm telling the truth?"

"What the hell's going on with you?" Liz shouted. "I can see that you were using your phone. Why are you lying about it?"

"Please, just hear me out."

"So you can tell me how conniving you've been? How you've gone behind my back revealing information about the black box and my father when I specifically told you that no one could know at this stage. No press, no magazines, no radio, no nothing!"

Liz's face was blood red, and Tim wondered whether it would be safer to actually take a few steps back from her. He had learned early on in life that it was generally a futile exercise to argue with an angry woman. He stared at her, hoping her rage would subside soon. He couldn't believe the sudden outburst. *One moment she's relatively calm and the next moment she's almost manic.*

"Are you quite finished?" he said to her softly.

"What?"

"I need you to calm down before I can tell you what is going on."

"You need me to be calm? Which means I probably won't like what you are going to say. Which means I'm actually not interested in hearing your petty excuses."

"Liz, please."

"Screw you!" Liz shouted. "Go back on the plane and go back to where you came from."

"Please, let me explain."

Liz turned away and began heading down the path without him.

"Where you going?"

"Away from you."

CHAPTER 62

"Liz, wait, you can't just go away on your own."

"You've been sneaking around behind my back!" Liz snapped. She had stopped and turned around to glare at Tim again.

"I haven't," said Tim.

"I'm not an idiot. I know you've been talking to someone. I trusted you, Tim. Do you know how much it took for me to trust you? Do you?"

"You can trust me."

"A lot. It took a lot for me to trust you. And you go and betray me. Just like that."

"Please listen to me. I haven't betrayed you. Please."

"Was it another journalist who you keep making these calls to? Or your editor? Or some major newspaper in the States?"

"No," Tim spoke softly. "It's none of those. It's not what you think."

"The hell it isn't." Before Tim could say another word Liz had stormed off again. Tim walked fast behind her trying to keep up.

"Men, you're all the same. I can't believe I was so stupid to let you in on what's going on. Now the black box is going to be all over the *New York Times*."

"Liz, please just calm down and listen to me."

Liz kicked a nearby stone. It went flying into a tree branch and then dropped onto the bricks. "I'm perfectly calm," she said. "Now leave me alone."

"Please, Liz."

"Not interested. You had a chance and you blew it."

"Liz, you're obviously very stressed about everything that's happened but please don't take it out on me."

"You think I'm stressed?" Liz shouted. "What gives you that idea?"

Before Tim could answer her, she shot off down the path, like a runner determined to win the hundred-meter final. The sandy path was not a formal

161

path as such, but wound its way along the side of the tearoom, the Memorial and then the remaining trees and shrubbery. By the time Tim realized that Liz had finished arguing with him, she was out of sight.

Liz sprinted down the steep hill. She found herself under a thicket of trees. A squirrel appeared in front of her holding an acorn. It stared wide-eyed before darting back behind a tree.

Liz jumped over some small logs scattered over the path. There were many logs further ahead along with a clutter of pinecones. She narrowly avoided a tree trunk on the sandy path and continued her descent. The path became steeper and more slippery.

The sound of Tim's voice carried through the air but Liz didn't bother to turn around or stop. She hastily climbed over some rocks, not noticing they had become wet from the rain earlier. As Liz climbed down another rock, she momentarily lost her footing and slipped. Seconds later, she was in a deep narrow ditch off the side of the main path. The long leafy branches of two pine trees towered over her, completely shielding the ditch from any views from the path.

Liz tried to get to her feet and felt a sharp shooting pain penetrate her left leg. She winced as she looked down. Blood was oozing from her knee.

Tim dashed down the slope but Liz was nowhere in sight.

"Liz!" he shouted.

He ran further down the path and stepped into a muddy puddle, the dirty water splashing high in the air.

"Liz, where are you?"

Tim continued his descent and found himself skidding in the sand. His skid was broken by a cluster of rocks which signaled that the stony area of the path had begun. He continued down the path at a slower pace.

A loud noise erupted towards the top of the hill. Tim whirled around to see a flock of birds scurry into the sky. *My nerves!* He peered up the path and, after the birds had disappeared, he thought he saw some other movement. There was definitely someone walking down. He scrunched up his eyes as he stared into the distance.

He was about to shout Liz's name again when the distant figure stopped and seemed to look around. His heart began pounding wildly when he realized that the figure was not Liz, nor was it some tourist admiring the views. It was definitely one of the men who had been chasing them with a gun.

Tim turned around and charged down the path again. Liz had told him that there were pathways from Rhodes Memorial that led to the University of Cape Town. He hoped he was on that path. Maybe Liz would be waiting for him there? It would be easier to hide from their attacker on a campus. He had to get off this track fast.

As he ran, Tim reached for his cellphone and quickly dialed the number for Liz, looking up every few seconds just to make sure he wouldn't stumble over anything. But her number rang for a few seconds and then went to voicemail. Tim dialed the number again but was met with the same response.

He ran for several more minutes without even daring to stop and look behind him, nodding with approval as he saw the first shapes of some buildings in the distance. *That's got to be UCT.* He stepped on some pinecones and almost lost his footing, then steadied himself. Soon the momentum was with him again as he rapidly continued downwards.

Five more minutes of running, and Tim came across some people sitting on a ledge. There were three of them, one guy and two girls, and they were drinking from silver flasks. *Students. I'm almost there.*

"Hey," Tim said to one of the men. "Did you see a lady, blond hair, tight jeans run past here in the last few minutes?"

"No man. Sorry!"

"How long until I get to the campus from here?"

"It's just down there," he pointed.

Tim darted past without thanking them and ignored their frowns. Seconds later he was on the top part of the upper campus of the University of Cape Town.

Rafik had decided to lie low for a while and catch his breath from the morning's grueling events. He knew there was a chance the car theft had been discovered. On the other hand, it was also probable that no one knew the car he was driving had just been stolen from the owner's garage. He didn't necessarily want to chance it though. And he desperately needed a cup of something hot. He pulled in to the parking garage of a busy shopping center nearby and drove the car all the way down to the basement parking level, where he steered the vehicle into a bay tucked behind a pillar in the far corner.

He exited the vehicle and proceeded to the elevators on the other side. Soon he was in the heart of the shopping complex and found a restaurant where he ordered his Chai latte. While sipping on the drink, he pondered his fate. The Fox would certainly not be pleased to hear that he had lost his targets.

CHAPTER 63

When Sol Arendse made his way down the passage toward the elevator that would take him to the parking lot at the Convention Centre, he was observed by Sindy, who had had left her office on the floor above to make sure that Sol would leave.

She watched him head into the elevator and once the doors closed she went closer to look at the lights above it. The elevator went down and the red numbers above it changed from second level to first level to ground, and then to parking level one. Once the light went on at parking level one, Sindy knew Sol was going to his car.

She looked at her watch, breathed a sigh of relief, and walked back towards his office, where she waited in the passage outside his reception room.

Wahied revved his engine as he waited to be let in. The guard finished filling in the required paperwork and then picked up some type of receiver and spoke into it.

"Get me Sol Arendse's office."

There were a few beeps and chimes while the guard was placed on hold until the call was transferred.

"Sol Arendse's office." It was a woman's voice.

"Mr Arendse, please."

"Mr Arendse is unavailable for the next few hours. Can I perhaps help you? I'm Mr Arendse's PA."

"Ursula, I'm phoning from the delivery gate. It's about the presidential visit. A delivery pertaining to the dinner has just arrived. I normally need Mr Arendse's clearance. Can you confirm that this delivery is scheduled?"

"Um, which is it then? Food or beverage?"

"Which is it?" the guard repeated to Wahied. "Food or beverage?"

"Beverage," said Wahied. "Bottled water to be precise."

"It's bottled water," the guard repeated into the phone.

"Hmm, water, water, water," Wahied could hear Ursula say, and imagined her perusing a delivery form in front of her to find his name.

———

At exactly one pm, while the guard was speaking to Ursula, Sindy exited the elevator and walked towards the delivery entrance where Wahied's truck was standing. Waiting for her outside the elevator were two presidential security officials with accompanying identity tags. With barely an acknowledging nod, they fell in line behind her as they all strolled to the entrance.

"We'll take it from here," said Sindy.

The guard looked up from his clipboard.

"We've been expecting this delivery," Sindy told him.

Two men appeared behind Sindy. They were dressed in black pants and blue shirts with the accompanying security identity tags. The guard stared at the tags. The words were quite clear—USA Presidential Security. Sindy knew he would have seen several of these uniformed officials over the last few weeks as they laid the final preparations for the president's visit.

"Um, Ursula don't worry," said the guard. "Some of those American security detail are here and someone else from the Convention Centre. They say they've been expecting this delivery."

———

Wahied drove through the security gate and into the delivery section of the Centre. This cul-de-sac had been sealed off from other Convention Centre activities and reserved specifically for matters relating to the presidential banquet.

He nodded to Sindy as he walked around to unlock the back doors of the truck. Wahied, Sindy, and the uniformed guards jumped in the cargo hold.

There were several boxes and crates that covered most of the floor area. They were all sealed.

"All of these?" asked Sindy.

"Yes," said Wahied.

"Do you have the envelope?"

"Yes." Wahied's eyes were gleaming.

"Follow me," Sindy nodded approvingly and made her way towards a doorway that exposed a long corridor. The guards and Wahied began lifting the boxes and crates out of the truck and started moving them in Sindy's direction.

The sign on the storage room said: "Authorized Personnel Only". Sindy took out a small disk from her pocket and swiped it against the scanner on the wall. There was a brief buzzing sound and the door opened.

"Everything needs to go in here," she said.

CHAPTER 64

While the sun is generally known to give light and heat that facilitates life on Earth, it can also have a more ominous effect by causing enormous eruptions of hot gas. These eruptions are known as solar storms and transmit billions of tons of matter traveling at millions of kilometers an hour in our direction. The shock waves created from solar storms cause electrons to create radio waves that eventually penetrate the Earth's atmosphere.

Recent research by scientists at Trinity College Dublin, University College London, and the University of Hawaii, published online in *Nature Physics*, showed for the first time a direct link between solar storms, shock waves, and solar radio bursts. Solar radio bursts can cause damaging effects on many of the technologies we rely on in our everyday lives, such as mobile phone connection and GPS devices.

Unaware that a solar storm had just unleashed itself and rendered all mobile devices temporarily useless over the entire Western Cape and beyond, Tim made his way to University Avenue on UCT's main campus and tried to phone Liz again.

That's strange. There doesn't seem to be any signal.

He looked around for someone to help him.

"Cellphone working?" he asked a petite girl jogging past him.

The girl shook her head and continued with her jog.

"Hey, do you know where the phones are?" Tim called after her.

She ignored him and ran out of his line of vision. Tim continued along the road. A group of students appeared out of a nearby building marked, "Engineering".

"Are your cellphones perhaps working?" Tim asked them.

"Sorry, dude, there's no signal."

"Are you sure?"

"Just tried." A girl in a loose red sweater and tight blue jeans waved her phone in the air. "Nothing. Looks like the network is down."

"Are there any public phone boxes?"

The girl in the loose red jersey turned around. "Try down there," she pointed.

Tim dashed in the direction she had pointed, still not sure where he was actually going.

"Money for the poor..." A skinny man with long white hair and beard sat on the pavement with his legs outstretched. He held a battered can, which he was waving up and down.

Tim shook his head and tried to walk past but the man raised his legs as Tim moved forward and stopped him in his tracks. He had wedged himself between a large green dustbin and a wall so people walking down the pavement had no choice but
to cross his path.

"Money for the poor?"

"Sorry, I got no change."

"Well, how about a note then?"

"Um, I can't right now."

"Please, sir. I need anything I can get."

"Look, I'm in quite a rush."

"Ah, the rush of life."

"No, I'm looking for someone."

"Aren't we all..."

"Look, let me get past please." Tim tried to walk around the man and stepped off the pavement into the road.

"We're all doomed," the man said.

"What?"

"We're all doomed!"

"What are you talking about?"

The man looked around to make sure no one else was there. "It's time," he whispered, "the end of the world is nigh."

"Nigh?"

"The world is going to end and where will you be when it happens?"

"Oh bugger off." Tim was now on the other side of the beggar and continued walking.

"Where will you be?" the man called after him. "It's the end of the world. Who is going to save you?"

The man's banter soon faded as Tim turned the corner. *Bloody creep.* But his words did not leave Tim's mind. *It's the end of the world. Who is going to save you?*

He climbed up a flight of stairs and found himself on the famous Jameson plaza. This area of the campus was very busy and what looked like many students and academics were chatting and socializing with each other.

Tim was frantic. He needed to make a phone call and he needed to find Liz. There was a large party going on and Tim had walked right into it.

A few drunk well-built guys stumbled past Tim. They could barely stand straight. Tim looked at the vests they were all wearing, which showed they were members of the UCT varsity rugby team, the Ikeys. They reeked of sweat and beer.

"Do any of you have a phone I could borrow?" Tim asked.

The players just laughed at Tim and stumbled onwards. He needed a phone fast and hopefully someone belonging to a different cellphone network would have signal.

A scantily clad female appeared wearing a pink bikini.

"Let's dance!" She took Tim's hand and smiled at him as she jiggled a few steps to the blaring music coming from massive black speakers on either side of the plaza.

"I'm actually in a rush," said Tim. "Do you know if the cellphone signal is back?"

"Cellphone signal? Dance with me baby!"

Tim shrugged her arms off his body and edged away.

"Party pooper!" She shuffled off to the next group of students.

CHAPTER 65

It had been an agonizing few days in the buildup. Now Wahied had finally done what he had set out to do and it was just the formality of waiting for events to unfold on their own. As he drove away from the Convention Centre, Wahied decided he would take it slow over the next few days as he made his way home.

For Wahied, there had never been any doubt about his involvement. Right from the start when Sindy had tested the waters to hear about his beliefs and ambitions, he'd never given it a second thought. When he learned eventually of what Sindy was a part of he knew in an instant that he wanted to be part of it too. It was a cause he believed in, and for which he was prepared to sacrifice himself. Not that he believed it would come to that. The plans that had been put in place were so well scripted, there was little chance of his life being on the line. If all the parties stuck to their roles, then the production would be a resounding success. *Standing ovations all round,* he mused.

He didn't know who exactly was behind the grand plan but he did know there were several actors who would each in their own way contribute to the successful turning of the wheels of history. The plan was ingenious. His face broke into a wry smile.

He turned the steering wheel and pushed the volume up on the radio. A song had just ended and the DJ was discussing the presidential visit. Authorities were still trying to work out why a fake bomb was left in Rondebosch. There were currently no suspects at this time. In addition to the roads that had been closed in the vicinity of the fake bomb, roads near the CBD had also been closed off due to President Rafferty's forthcoming address. "We'll keep you updated but it's advisable to use alternative routes," said the announcer.

Wahied was proud his older sister had invited him to be part of something so noble and worthwhile. He had underestimated the extent of her confidence in him. So when the day came when she took him under her wing for this project, he'd been delighted, realizing she did value him. And it made him burst with pride.

And as predicted, everything had been so meticulous and had run so smoothly. So there was just no chance of their mission being unsuccessful. Wahied had learned that the art of patience and endurance was a tough one to master, but once it was embraced, it could lead to great things.

CHAPTER 66

Tim veered off the campus road and walked into a hall that was equally full of partygoers and just as loud as the speakers blaring outside. *Looks like I've hit campus mardi gras!* He shifted through the dancing crowds and found himself in a smaller adjoining room that was being used as a bar area. Some students stood behind a row of desks that had been propped up with a variety of local beers and wines. Several large metallic ice drums were spread out over the weary wooden flooring.

"Can I get you a drink?" A curly-haired brunette was reaching for a wine glass.

"Um, no, thanks." Tim tried to be polite.

"It's an award winning Chenin Blanc. You can have a free sample."

"I'm good, thanks."

But the girl either didn't hear Tim's second refusal because of the music, or she simply was not prepared to take no for an answer. She reached for the bottle of wine and filled up a quarter of the glass.

"I said I don't want anything to drink!" Tim found himself raising his voice in anger, but he couldn't stop looking at the girl and the glass that she was now offering him.

"I've already poured it," she said and smiled. "Come on, you might even enjoy it. And then you can decide whether you want more or not."

"I really can't," said Tim. His eyes were transfixed on Chenin Blanc.

"It's really delicious," said the girl. She was swirling the glass now and Tim could see the wine splashing gently against the inside of the glass. Despite the stuffiness and stench of the body odor in the small room, the distinctive scent of the wine was still able to waft in Tim's direction and hover momentarily under his nostrils. It was a sweet smell that instantly took Tim back to feelings and memories he thought he would never revisit.

The girl smiled at him, her arm still thrust out. "Take it," she said.

Tim's body felt heavy but he put his hand forward and clenched his fingers around the glass. He gripped it tightly and moved the glass out of her hands. He took a deep sniff and closed his eyes as the aroma streamed through his body.

"Smells good?"

"Smells very good," said Tim. His eyes were still closed.

"Wait until you taste it!"

Just one sip, Tim thought. *It's only a sample. It's not like I'm having a whole glass.*

Still holding the glass of Chenin Blanc, Tim reached into his pocket with his other hand and glanced at his phone. *I really need to make that call now.* But there was still no cellphone reception.

"Do you by any chance have signal on your phone?"

"Sorry?" The girl leaned forward and motioned to her ear as three students with clown noses and wigs stumbled past them, singing at the top of their voices.

"Do you have any signal on your cellphone? I've got no reception."

The girl picked up a small phone behind a six-pack of beer.

"Nope, sorry. I haven't had signal for a while. My friends too. I think there must be something wrong with the networks."

Tim nodded. The aroma was now more intense than ever.

Just one quarter of a glass of wine isn't going to kill anyone.

Tim stared at the wine and took a deep breath. Then he lifted the glass slowly to his lips and let the scent linger before he took his first sip. He closed his eyes again and let the wine swirl softly around his mouth. A few seconds later he swallowed. The wine raced down his throat and into his stomach, causing a warmth to envelop his entire being, like a glowing fire raging deep inside of him. Tim took another sip and then another one. His sample of wine had come to an end.

"How much for the whole bottle?" Tim was reaching for his wallet.

"It's fine." The girl grinned and handed Tim the bottle. "Just take it!"

Tim took a few swigs from the bottle as he walked. He saw an exit in the distance and headed back outside.

CHAPTER 67

Liz managed to sit herself up and lean against the thick wall of leaves that had cushioned the blow from her fall. Her knee was grazed and bloody. She winced slightly and straightened it out. The graze was in the same spot where she had cut her knee on another occasion and her mind was jolted to that day. She had been eight years old.

When Liz was a kid she used to run down the long road in her neighborhood with two other girls she had known from school. They would run to a meadow that was at the bottom of their road. Several large trees towered over a shallow stream and the girls liked to play there. One sunny day, Liz and the others had made their way to the meadow and were chasing each other through the high grass.

The girls had arrived at a tall tree and to their delight they had spotted a rusty ladder lying nearby. One of the elder girls, an overweight ten-year-old, Amy, dragged the ladder towards the tree, and Liz and the other girl, Lucy, helped put it upright against the branches. They decided that it would be fun to climb the tree as high as possible, and view the entire meadow from a lofty height.

"You should go first," Amy instructed Liz. As any eight-year-old would do, Liz followed the instruction of the elder girl.

She climbed the rusty ladder while the other two tried to hold it as firmly as they could from the ground. She proceeded to the top, rung after rung, and soon was at the top of the ladder.

"Now climb onto that nearest branch," she was instructed.

It was daunting to take that final step off the top rung onto the nearest branch, as there was a substantial gap between the ladder and the bark, so Liz hesitated.

"Come on, don't be a sissy," Amy called from down below.

After a few moments of deliberation, Liz managed to grab the branch and hoisted herself onto it, leaving the ladder to fall to the ground beneath her.

"Hey, it almost knocked us!" Amy yelled. Lucy, not one for speaking much, just looked up at Liz.

"Sorry," said Liz. "At least I'm up though. Who's coming up next?"

"I've changed my mind," said Amy. "I'm not coming up."

"Oh. So, Lucy, you're coming up, right?"

"No, she's not."

"What? You made me come up by myself?"

"Have fun," Amy sneered and started walking towards the stream. "Coming, Lucy?"

Liz was almost in tears. "Where are you going?"

"Away from you, dumbass."

"How am I going to get down from here?"

Amy continued to walk away.

"Don't leave me up here." Liz's voice was a whine now. "Please put the ladder back. I can't get down without it."

But the girls just walked away. Lucy stopped momentarily and glanced behind her.

"Lucy, please!"

She stared blankly and then followed Amy.

"Don't leave me up here, please." The tears were streaming down Liz's face. "Come back, don't leave me up here."

The girls had disappeared out of sight and Liz was left clutching to the branch.

"Help me!" Liz screamed. "I want to come down. Help me!"

But the meadow was quiet that afternoon and the area where the trees were was deserted. No matter how long or loudly Liz screamed, no one else was there to hear her. Liz cried continuously for the next hour and a half until there were no more tears to cry. She was shaking and her body was beginning to ache, as it felt the discomfort of the hard cold bark. Her hands were scratched from clinging so tightly to the wood and she had scraped the top of her knee. Blood from the gash started trickling down her leg.

The sun began to set and darkness eventually cloaked her as the minutes turned to hours. The moon and stars made their way out into the night sky and it was the strength of the full moon that lit up the meadow now. Liz continued to scream in the dark but there was no one near enough to hear her pleas. Several more hours passed by and the cold, hungry, tired eight-year-old girl clung to the branch with all her might.

She didn't know what else she could do and was on the verge of despair. And then she saw the flicker of a flashlight. At first she thought she was seeing things because the light disappeared. But seconds later it reappeared and she began to shout.

"Help me! Help! Over here!"

The flashlight went out again and then it reappeared, and this time it seemed to be getting closer to Liz.

"Over here!" Liz shouted. "Please help me, I'm high up in a tree."

The light remained constant. It became bolder and brighter, and seconds later she could make out the silhouette of someone holding a torch at the bottom of the tree.

Liz had never forgotten the next four words she heard. "Liz, is that you?"

She looked down and this time tears of joy streamed down her face as she heard her father's voice.

"Dad, I'm up here."

"Good grief, your mum and I have been so worried."

"I can't get down," Liz cried.

"Hold on, I'm coming up."

Professor Greene had seen the ladder and leaned it against the tree, climbing up with the torch clenched between his teeth. When he got to the top he stopped, took the torch, and stretched it out to Liz.

"Take this." Liz took the torch and shone it on the professor so he could climb onto the branch next to her.

"I've been stuck here," Liz sobbed.

Professor Greene didn't say a word, and put his arms around his daughter. They hugged tightly.

"You're okay now," he said. "We've been so worried. We were searching everywhere for you. We were about to call the police."

"Thank you for finding me." Liz was still crying.

Professor Greene held the top of the ladder and instructed Liz to climb down slowly. He would wait on the branch until she was on the ground again. Soon Liz was down and the professor climbed down the ladder too.

"My precious baby," Professor Greene had said to his daughter. "I love you so much."

CHAPTER 68

Tim stumbled out of Jameson Hall on UCT's upper campus and moved himself down the plaza before he collapsed into the bushes in one of the small gardens interspersed among the buildings. Now, hours later, his head was swirling. He rolled around in the soil and stared at the trees towering above him. They were swinging and he could have sworn they were hissing at him too. He tried to reach for a branch but could not move his body off the ground. He tried again to cling to a clump of leaves but failed. The leaves became very blurry and Tim tried to say something out loud but only managed an inaudible mumble.

He tried to sit up and then fell back into the flowerbed he had found himself in. His stared at the red, yellow and white roses surrounding him.

"Back off!" he yelled. "Back the fuck off."

He stumbled on to his feet and this time managed to cling to one of the branches nearby. He held onto it like a drowning man clinging to a lifejacket.

Where the hell am I? What's going on?

A clump of trees and a cold breeze greeted him. There were all sorts of flowers popping out of the grass. A squirrel pecking on an acorn stopped momentarily to satisfy its curiosity. It stared at Tim before scurrying off.

"Wait!" Tim shouted. "Come back."

He took a shaky step forward and another one but almost tumbled over. He swaggered along and the world in front of him suddenly seemed very unstable.

What are all those lights? Am I seeing lights?

His vision was blurred and his head was spinning, like he was on the big wheel at the local fair. He took another step and found himself clinging onto a cold rail that appeared at the side of the lawn.

He couldn't remember when he had last felt so bilious. In fact, he couldn't remember much at all.

Where am I?

176

He edged forward shakily in a sideways movement with both of his hands trying to grasp the rail. He knew if he let go he would fall down properly and he wasn't sure if he would be able to get up again.

He heard loud noises that seemed to be right next to him but he couldn't see anyone or anything else other than the misty haze of bright lights.

What the hell is going on here?

The ground around him began to swell once more and Tim lost his grip. He fell and rolled down the lawn, crunching one flowerbed after the next.

He thumped his way over several bushes before landing in a shallow part of a muddy pond at the foot of the garden. Two ducks angrily flew off as Tim's head and chest hit the water.

The cold water brought welcome relief as he lifted his head up and choked. Water spluttered out of his mouth but he was happy about it. He was now more awake, and out of his drunken stupor.

Tim was exhausted. His body felt weak and his bones ached. He'd been catapulted into a grim state of anguish. As the rest of his memories came flooding back, he gasped in horror. Rhodes Memorial, Liz storming off, and then fleeing his attacker and arriving at UCT. And then there had been the wine.

Tim realized that he had consumed a great deal of booze. Not that that made a difference. He knew that one sip or swig was just as lethal as downing a whole bottle. And he had plunged right back into the dark pit to which he had so desperately tried to avoid returning for years.

The alcohol had been a step backwards. He knew that; there was no point in harping on it. What's done was done. He couldn't believe he had actually broken his sober run. He had been trying to phone his sponsor all morning but with no luck of getting hold of him. And he hadn't been able to explain the truth to Liz. That's what pained him even more.

He rubbed his pounding head. He had to focus on getting his strength back and being able to push himself forward. He shuddered. He was on the brink of a dark place and he could plunge himself deeper into an abyss if he took the wrong steps. If it wasn't too late already.

He reached for his cellphone and stared at it. *No signal.* And then he remembered the phone blackout. With no cellphone signal, there was no way he would reach his sponsor now.

Dammit. I hope Liz is okay.

Tim tried to stand up but this time his legs wouldn't help him up at all. His legs felt heavy, as if they were welded into the ground beneath him. Although his body swayed, he was at least able to sit up, and steadied himself slightly.

And then he felt the pounding of his head. It throbbed like someone was gonging a large bell right next to his ear. And all he wanted to do was to run as far away as possible and cover his ears until the ringing stopped. But the noise continued and he groaned in agony.

Please stop!

The landscape whirled around him and he was reminded of how he used to feel when going on rides at the fun fair as a kid. The difference was that everything was simple back then. He didn't have the weight of the world crushing down on him like he had now.

Tim lay on the grass cursing the sunlight that was now peeping through the trees and into his eyes. More specifically, he cursed the fact that he had danced with alcohol again, and then his thoughts moved back to Liz. It was all enough for the tears to start falling down his muddy cheeks.

CHAPTER 69

After eventually managing to climb out of the ditch, Liz emerged from the thicket of leaves and headed back up to Rhodes Memorial. Maybe she had been too harsh on Tim? Maybe he wasn't revealing anything to his editors? It was not as if she'd told him too much about the black box anyway. Not that she even knew much herself about it at the moment. In fact, she still didn't know what exactly had been happening to her that day at all.

There was no sign of Tim. Liz sighed. She tried to call him on his cellphone but his phone seemed dead. She tried her father's number again. *Please let him answer.* But his number was not working either. *What's going on here?* She stared at her phone, and then noticed that the signal beacon indicated there was currently no cellphone reception.

Liz walked to the Memorial steps and frantically scanned her surroundings. But the man she had stormed away from was nowhere in sight. *Come on, Tim, where are you?* There were fewer tourists around the Memorial than when they had first arrived so it wasn't as if she had missed him in a crowd.

She turned around and headed towards the tearoom, walking through it towards the adjoining garden. *No sign of him anywhere. That's strange; he wouldn't have gone far.* Liz smiled as she suddenly remembered Tim's bad sense of direction. *No, he couldn't have gone far at all. And it's not like he knows Cape Town.*

Liz noticed a policeman walking in the distance. She quickly took another cobbled path around the side of the tearoom and avoided the law enforcer who was now heading in the opposite direction. Before her, two boys, probably in their teens, were throwing a rugby ball to each other. One of them was wearing a Stormers cap.

"Howzit," Liz greeted him. "I'll give you fifty rand for your cap."

"Sure, I suppose!" The teenager took off the cap, straightened out his hair with his grubby hand and gave the cap to Liz.

"Thanks!" Liz pulled the peak as far over her face as it would go, and scurried off towards the bathrooms and back part of the tearoom's kitchen.

The policeman appeared in the distance again, so Liz headed around another corner into a smaller area scattered with a few tables and chairs. She moved towards the far side where there was an exit towards the main tearoom. Hopefully the policeman would not go back that way.

An overweight bald man with dark black reading glasses was lounging at one of the tables, immersed in the contents of his newspaper. It was one of at least seven major daily newspapers available in Cape Town, and was still the traditional newspaper size. He folded over one of the pages and turned it to read the other side.

Liz looked up, and to her dismay the figure of the uniformed policeman emerged from the other side. Liz yanked the cap further over her face and pulled out a chair at the overweight bald man's table.

He looked up from his paper, eyebrows raised.

"I just need to tie my shoelace," Liz explained. "Sorry to intrude."

"Oh, no problem." The man shifted his attention back to his broadsheet.

Liz stared at the newspaper as the man turned another page.

"You finished with that section?" She pointed to a section of the newspaper lying on the table.

"Yip." The man didn't even look up.

The policeman was almost upon them. Liz grabbed the newspaper, leaned back in her chair and held the pages up high, pretending to be focused on an article ironically about the demise of traditional newspapers and the rise of online content.

Liz clenched her teeth as the policeman headed towards their table. She desperately hoped the ground would swallow her up, or she would wake up and find the day's events to have been one horrible dream, a nightmare she could laugh off. But she knew she wasn't going to become invisible. The events of the day were real.

The policeman was meters away from the table now and continued to walk towards them. Liz desperately clutched the newspaper with both hands. The policeman stopped just before them. He was looking up at the wall, and then turned down another side path. Liz looked up at the wall. There was a sign with an arrow indicating the way back to the toilets. Liz exhaled slowly. Although adrenalin was pumping heavily throughout her body, she could not move. She felt paralyzed.

She turned the page and stared at it mindlessly. It would be better to stay at the table and wait for the policeman to do his business and then, once he had left, she would give it another few minutes before leaving.

A large full-color advert suddenly caught her eye. Liz's heart began to beat even faster. Before Liz could gather her thoughts a waiter appeared.

"Coffee for you, miss?"

"No, thank you."

"And you, sir, would you like a refill."

"No, thanks." The man looked up, stared disapprovingly at Liz, and then continued his read.

Liz ignored his look, her eyes transfixed on the page.

Am I going mad?

She read the advert again.

It makes sense now. It makes so much sense.

The spread was for a steel company that was advertizing a social upliftment project with which it had been involved.

Liz had heard of this company before, which said a lot, as she never usually remembered details of businesses like that. *I think I know exactly what it refers to now. This has to be it. How could I not have seen this before?* Liz's face broke into a smile as she stared at the advert. It was not just for any steel company, but a specific one that Liz had not given a moment's thought until this point. The company name was emblazoned across the advert in bold red letters. *Lion Steel.*

CHAPTER 70

The slope had become very slippery and Mike almost went flying as he chased the man down the path, leaving Rhodes Memorial behind him.

"Stop!" he yelled, but the person had now become a distant speck. *Mother fucker.* Mike could see UCT's upper campus in the distance. *I didn't see the girl with him. Maybe she was ahead of him.* He paced down the incline, carefully maintaining his balance with each step.

He passed some students lazing on the rocks. He nodded at them as he rushed past. Mike noticed the sweatshirt on one of the students. In big letters across the shirt's front were three words that instantly made Mike wish he was back home—Boston Red Sox. *What I would do to be out of this damn place.*

He thought about how things used to be for him in the CIA and brooded over his situation now. He missed his family. *I'm going to call them again later. But I need to find those bastards first so I can at least tell everyone I'll be home soon.*

He was out of breath and his chest felt tight once he reached upper campus. *Bloody asthma.* He pulled out his pump and inhaled as he surveyed his surroundings. It was early that same day when he had been on campus, witnessing Professor Greene hauling the dead staff worker along the road. It seemed like a long time ago! Now he was back, and although he always marveled at how pretty the campus was and how amazing its views were, he just wanted out.

How the hell had he landed up in Cape Town of all places? *So fucking far away from home.* As is often the case in life, things had not gone according to plan and had spiraled out of control. In fact, he had no control at all. He had tried to help his brother-in-law and all he got was a kick in the pants.

"You've gotta believe me, Mike."

"Why should I?"

"Because I'm family."

"Sometimes that's not good enough."

"Just trust me."

And that's exactly what Mike had done. He had put his complete faith in the man. The information he had received from Troy became the building blocks for a crucial stakeout operation for some of the special undercover intelligence divisions. The targets were a group of suspected illegal diamond traffickers linked to an international criminal group the CIA had been observing in California of all places.

A good friend of Troy's happened to be a member of this criminal grouping and had bragged to Troy about the money he was about to make through these illegal diamonds. Troy had mentioned it in passing to Mike at a family barbecue a few days later. The CIA had known about the illicit diamond smuggling, but had been unsuccessful with their informants for that specific project. Their main informant, the one with all the street cred, had disappeared. According to his wife, he had left his apartment one night to buy cigarettes from the local store and was never seen again. The agents in the intelligence community suspected the worst, and the operation was put on hold immediately.

The information that Troy revealed to Mike at the barbecue confirmed that the diamond smugglers were preparing to offload a huge shipment. Troy would have had no way of knowing certain aspects of the operation unless he had heard it from someone involved in the process. After further fishing for facts, Mike concluded that the agency needed to act on this information.

He called a meeting with his superiors. The facts seemed to tie in with their prior research. They prepared arduously for the stakeout, investing a great deal of time, money, and resources into the operation. But there must have been a tip-off, the source of which was never discovered. When D-day finally arrived for the shipment to be offloaded, the intelligence officials and law enforcers brought in for the sting operation were met with a shootout. And no diamonds were found. It had all been a decoy for the real diamond offload. The high-caliber weapons the gang used were enough to result in the loss of one of Mike's colleagues, and several injuries.

Although Mike was not to blame as such for his colleague's death, he took the whole thing quite personally. He became unproductive and uncooperative, and his superiors, still smarting from the ordeal, did not hesitate in sending Mike off to Cape Town, where he would do mundane tasks relating to CIA business. As far as they were concerned, the sooner he was off active duty the better.

While Mike tried to have a positive outlook on life, even when the odds were always stacked against him, it had been a terrible year. He had tried to hold his head high when he was given his marching orders to Cape Town. The odds were definitely stacked against him now that he had lost his suspects. And that meant that the odds of an imminent departure home were stacked against him too.

CHAPTER 71

The overweight bald man left the table while Liz decided to stay there for a few more minutes. She couldn't afford the risk of having a close encounter with the hovering policeman. She stared at the newspaper advert again; she couldn't believe it. The emblem for Lion Steel was a sketched outline of the shape of a lion's head. She was sure that she knew the connection.

She drummed her fingers as the waiter appeared again to clear the table. Liz smiled at him and stood up. She walked towards the exit and into the parking lot. She could walk down the road that wound itself through the estate, the one she had walked up with Tim. But that might be too visible. She certainly didn't want to attract any unwarranted attention, especially with her face plastered on "wanted" posters. And who knew how many of those signs had already been posted in the Western Cape?

Liz decided that it made the most sense to trudge through the greenery that formed a vast area between the road and the M3 stretching across the other side of the bottom of the estate. She glanced behind her as she walked out of the parking lot. Just the car guard in the distance. No sign of any police.

Her knee was still stinging but Liz was determined not to let it get the better of her. She trekked down through the field, and every now and again stopped behind a tree to make sure she wasn't being followed or that no one was lying in wait.

She eventually reached the bottom of the estate and quickly made her way through the large open gates through which she and Tim had entered earlier. Turning left into a small parking lot on the outskirts of the university, she looked around. A short brunette with a red jersey wrapped around her waist was getting into her car.

"Which direction you going?" Liz asked.

"Wynberg," the girl said.

"I'm going to Rondebosch," said Liz. "Could I get a lift? Even if it's just somewhere nearby."

"Sure, hop in."

CHAPTER 72

The roadblock on the M3 was affecting traffic heading towards the city but did not affect the route Liz's driver took heading in the direction of the Southern Suburbs. Fifteen minutes later, Liz was at her father's house where she headed straight to the lounge. She trudged over the bits of broken glass that remained scattered on the floor.

"Time for nuts!"

Liz startled as the familiar sounds of her father's parrot shrieked through the room. "Hello, Alex," Liz said and smiled.

"Time for nuts! Time for nuts!"

Liz stepped forward, tripping over something hard. She went sprawling on to the carpet and saw the tattered green suitcase she had just fallen over. *Where the hell did that come from?* She stared nervously at the suitcase as she got back onto her feet. She didn't remember seeing it there earlier that day. In fact, she was sure the suitcase had definitely not been there during her earlier visit.

Instinctively, she took a step back. She yelped as something hard poked into her back.

"Don't move," a voice spoke into her ear. "Don't move or I'll shoot."

"Okay," Liz gasped. *I can't believe what's been happening to me.*

"Put your hands up slowly where I can see them."

Liz obeyed and immediately raised her arms.

"Very good. Now take a few steps towards that couch in front of you."

Liz nodded as she slowly walked forward. She was trembling in every part of her body. "What do you want?" she whispered.

"I should be asking you that question," the man said. "You didn't even knock or ring the bell. You just came into someone else's house."

"It's my father's house!" Liz protested.

"Turn around very slowly," said the voice. "And remember that my gun is loaded."

Liz turned around to face her captor. He seemed a similar age to her father, and also had a beard that was turning gray. His eyes didn't look harsh like her pursuers from earlier.

"What do you want?" Liz asked, feeling more in control now.

"Whose house did you say this was?"

"My father's."

"Your father has a name?"

"Harry. Professor Harry Greene."

"And you are?"

"I'm his daughter... Elizabeth."

The man stared at her closely but kept his gun aimed at her.

"Well, Elizabeth, how do I know you're telling the truth?"

"Why would I lie?"

"Well, I don't know. But so much is going on how do I know that I can trust you?"

So much is going on? "I really am his daughter."

She noticed some of the framed photographs on the small brown and gold antique table near the door. "Look," she pointed. "Look at those pictures over there. You can see I'm in some of them with my father."

"Don't you dare move," the man warned.

He glanced at the table and began to move towards it. He lifted up the largest frame and eyed the photograph. Harry Greene was standing with his arms around a lady. They were both grinning. The photograph looked like it had been taken on Blaauwberg Beach. A famous shot of Table Mountain and the sea that graced many postcards and books. The man looked at the photo and then looked at Liz. He did this twice and then he lowered his gun.

"When I last saw you, you were just a little girl!" The man's eyes were glistening.

"What?" Liz wasn't quite sure how to react.

The man put the photograph and his gun on the table. Then he extended his hand to Liz. "I'm Eric Macmanus," he said. "An old friend of your father."

"I'm sorry about your father," said Macmanus. He and Liz were sitting next to each other on the couch in the lounge. Liz's eyes welled up, and Macmanus decided it would be better not to dwell on that. "And I believe the microchip is missing?"

"How do you know about the microchip?" Liz said.

"Word gets around in my circles," said Macmanus. "What's more important is that we urgently have to find it."

"What's so special about it anyway?"

"Your father never told you?"

"We didn't discuss much in recent months," said Liz.

"It's imperative we find it. A lot is at stake here. I believe there is some cryptic clue your father left you?"

"Yes. In the clutches of the strong lion a wafer will quench your thirst."

"And you thought you deciphered it?"

"Yes, I've exhausted all avenues since the clue was made known to me, but I've found nothing."

"And you're all out of ideas?"

"Well, I was—until earlier!"

"What do you mean?"

"I came back here because something dawned on me that I hadn't thought of before."

"Time for nuts! Time for nuts!"

Professor Macmanus looked up in surprise. He had not expected the parrot to speak. Alex hopped around in his cage from one perch to the next. A little bell hanging from the top of the cage chimed as Alex moved.

"I saw an advert for a company called Lion Steel," Liz began to explain. "And I think that is what my father must have been referring to in his clue."

"So you've worked it out?"

"My friend Tim and I have been searching various lion clues around Cape Town," said Liz.

"Ah, your gentleman friend... And where's he now?"

"I'm not sure." Liz looked crestfallen. "Anyway, every time the result has been the same—no microchip. We were going from one lion to the next but with nothing to show for it."

"And now you think we should go to Lion Steel?" said Macmanus. "It's near here?"

"It's not a place. It's a company."

"So the company probably has a place?"

"Yes, but no."

"I'm really not following you!"

"Yes, the company has a place, probably several, I'm sure. But that's not where we need to go."

"It's not?"

"No, I'm not interested in the office or warehouse or shop of Lion Steel. I'm interested in a product that has been made by Lion Steel. Something very specific."

"Sounds intriguing."

"I can't believe that I didn't get it sooner," said Liz. "If I'm right it's the most obvious clue in the world. And the most genius at the same time! I think it has been here all along," Liz said, beaming.

"Maybe buried deep in the sand behind the back yard or something?"

"No, I believe it's in this house. In fact, I think the microchip has been here under my nose!"

"Well, where is it then?"

She looked at Macmanus. "We're about to find out!"

CHAPTER 73

Liz approached Alex's cage. It was dangling from a heavy chain attached to a small rusty clasp fixed to the ceiling. The cage was quite large by anyone's standards. Professor Greene had always wanted Alex to be as comfortable as possible, and the cage itself was clean and neat.

Too neat, Liz thought as she edged closer to the enclosure. There were several strips curving down from the top of the cage. The strips formed a wall ensuring Alex was secure. The gaps were wide enough to stick one's hand in sideways but not wide enough for the parrot to fly out. Liz tapped on one of the curves. It was very hard.

"'In the clutches of the strong lion a wafer will quench your thirst'," Liz said. "As I thought, this cage is made out of steel."

Liz leaned forward to see what had been scratched into the steel on the bottom outer rim of the cage. It was the letterhead for the company that had manufactured Alex's cage. Liz smiled at what her eyes now rested on. She was looking at the company emblem—an outline of a lion's face. Next to the logo two words were prominently displayed: "Lion Steel!"

"Good grief!" Macmanus gasped.

"I thought I recognized the logo when I spotted it while at Rhodes Memorial."

Her fingers reached for the door at the front of the dangling cage, and opened it.

"It's not even locked," Macmanus said. "Surely if Harry has hidden the microchip there, he would have at least locked the cage door?"

"When it comes to my father, I've learned to expect the unexpected."

Liz's hand was now in the cage and she reached for the little red plastic container that kept the parrot's seeds. She took it out of the cage and threw the seeds onto the floor.

"It's empty." Macmanus stared at the container in Liz's hands.

"Things are never as they seem." She tapped the bottom of the container.

There was a slight echo every time she tapped it.

"You see, it's hollow. I'm willing to bet the chip is somehow tucked inside this container." Liz held it up to the light. She couldn't see a shadow of any object that could have been hidden in the container.

There was a sudden bang and the two of them jumped.

"The window." Macmanus pointed behind them to the far corner. "The wind must have blown the window shut."

Their eyes scrutinized the room and they returned their attention to the container.

"It's got to be here." Liz was adamant. "It makes sense now."

"Perhaps there is something else in the clue you've overlooked?"

"I don't think so."

They stared into the cage as Alex squawked back at them.

"'In the clutches of the strong lion a wafer will quench your thirst'," Macmanus repeated.

"I think we need to shift our emphasis to 'thirst'," said Liz.

She stuck her hand back in the cage and took out a dark blue plastic container of water. There was a little mirror attached to it. She threw out the water and held it up.

"There's nothing there," said Macmanus.

"You're right," she said. "There is nothing in the water container. Which makes sense. Why would a microchip be placed in a container which keeps water?"

"It wouldn't."

"Exactly. Which means it has to be stored amid something dry."

There were two other small containers, one in the left corner of the cage and one in the right corner. Liz reached out to the one in the left corner and threw out the birdseed. She glided her fingers along the edge hoping to find a lump or something uneven to indicate the microchip might have been stuck inside. Nothing.

Liz then stuck her hand back inside the cage again and reached for the container in the far right corner. It was slightly smaller than the other container and full of sunflower seeds. Again Liz chucked out the seeds. The bottom of the container was empty.

"I'm sorry," said Macmanus. "I guess it's back to the drawing board!"

"I'm telling you it's here. It has to be. That's where the rhyme points towards."

"But you can see for yourself there's nothing there."

Just like with the other container, Liz glided her fingers along the bottom of the container to see if there were any lumps or levers of any kind to indicate a disguised microchip. But the container was smooth.

"Why would my father have steered us to this?"

"We don't know that he did."

"I think it's still in here." Liz was still staring at the container in her hands.

Her eyes shifted back to the water container. *He mentioned "quench your thirst". It must be a reference to water.* She held up the empty water container again in the light.

There was definitely something unusual about the water container. She hadn't noticed it before, but now that she was studying it closely, the bottom of it seemed far too high.

"A false bottom! I think this could be it." Liz's body trembled as her fingers glided over the circumference of the container. She took in a deep breath and exhaled. "I think we've found it."

As Liz's fingers slid around the bottom of the water container she found that the bottom was becoming looser. She continued to turn it and the more she twisted it, the looser it became.

"Do you see this?" Liz said excitedly.

"I see it!" Macmanus beamed.

Liz had now twisted the bottom off completely to form two separate plastic containers.

"This must be it!" she said. "It must be!"

She grasped the top of the new container and her eyes gleamed as she twisted its lid. Seconds later, the lid was off, and Liz and Macmanus peered into the container. There, entrenched in a bed of sponge, lay a small microchip.

CHAPTER 74

The Fox prided himself on leaving no stone unturned when it came to his work. He had invested so much time, money, and energy into acquiring the black box that he had exhausted all possible avenues. When he first learned of the black box, he had been intrigued. After reading more about it, he had become fascinated with it. But after learning how Professor Greene had taken the black box one step further thanks to the groundbreaking ability of the special microchip, the Fox had been obsessed.

He knew then that he wanted to get the black box for himself. He desperately needed to get it and he decided he would do whatever it took. He already had two potential buyers for the black box, one from Russia and the other from China. He hadn't decided yet on price or to whom he would sell it. He already had a lot of money thanks to the dubious activities he had immersed himself in over the years. But the price for the black box complete with microchip would surely catapult him onto the list of the top twenty richest people in the world. There was no doubt about that.

And that was if he went ahead and sold it. He still wasn't completely sure he was even going to go ahead with the sale. He could do so much with the black box. *Money versus power*, he thought. Or was it money and power? Either way his life would never be the same again.

Sitting in his study, he marveled at the thought of the wonderful future that lay ahead for him. He just needed the girl to find the microchip and everything would fall into place. Known as the Fox, he prided himself on being witty, intelligent, opportunity-seeking, and one step ahead of the rest.

Bugging various rooms in Professor Greene's house as well as the professor's telephone lines had enabled the Fox to keep abreast of all the professor's research and developments. The Fox had been a part of it for every step of the way.

And as he opened another beer, he grinned like an excited boy at his high school prom. The conversation he could now hear between Greene's daughter and the professor from the USA delighted him. Especially the fact that they had now just found the microchip.

———

"All this time and it was here all along," said Macmanus. "Right in front of you."

"Right in front of me."

"In the parrot's cage! What a place to hide it!"

"No one would have ever thought to look there," Liz said. "That's my dad for you!"

"I would never have thought to look there! Well done, Liz."

"So what happens now?"

"I'll keep the microchip safe," Macmanus said, holding out his hand. "We cannot afford to lose it, especially now that we have it."

"I still don't know why it's so important," said Liz.

"I think it might be better for you if I provide some explanation as to what this is all about."

"You think we're safe here for now?"

"I think you are safer here than on the streets."

Liz nodded and collapsed on the couch. Her body felt weak. She hadn't realized just how tired she was. "I'm listening!"

"I'm not quite sure where to begin," said Macmanus.

"I don't know much," said Liz. "Just that my father was involved in a huge scientific experiment about a black box and obviously a microchip. Not sure what type of research he was doing. Just that it seemed very important and occupied most of his time."

"Have you heard of Robert Jahn?" Macmanus asked.

"No."

"He was a well-known scientist who created quite a stir several decades ago at Princeton University." Macmanus tugged on his beard as he spoke. "He was one of the first modern scientists to take the notion of paranormal phenomena seriously.

"Professor Jahn was a strong believer in using modern technology to further his scientific research," he said. "He used whatever technology was available to him at the time to pursue his goals. He could, one might say, be the person who created what is now known as the black box.

"Professor Jahn used something which resembled a small black box to further his experiments and research. The box itself is covered in metal and is slightly bigger than two cigarette boxes placed together. The box churns out an endless flow of random numbers."

"Random numbers?"

"Yes. In scientific terms, the box is also known as a Random Event Generator, or Random Number Generator. The black box uses computer technology to generate two numbers—a one and a zero—in an entirely random sequence, almost like an electronic coin flipper.

"If one examines the outline of ones and zeros, or in simple terms heads or tails, then the pattern can be printed out as a graph. According to the laws of chance, the generator should toss out an equal number of ones and zeros, and this would be represented by a nearly flat line on the graph. Any movement from this equal number would lead to a rising curve in the graph.

"Professor Jahn wanted to determine whether the power of human thought could have any influence on the outcome of the usual readings on the machine. He got random strangers to focus their minds with intensity on his black box. The professor wanted to see if it was possible that the machine could flip more heads than tails, even if at the time this very notion might have seemed ridiculous."

"And what were the results?"

"The results were so amazing that Professor Jahn decided to perform many more of these experiments. The results were the same as before. Each time ordinary people proved that their minds had influenced the black box, causing considerable changes on the graph. Ordinary people were in fact guiding the machine to produce unequal numbers of heads or tails. These results were inexplicable and totally contrary to the known laws of science!"

"That's amazing."

"Many years ago I was at a science convention in Washington where I met a man by the name of Roger Nelson." Macmanus was now speaking very fast. Dr Nelson, also an academic at Princeton University, had been fascinated with Professor Jahn's experiments and decided to investigate them even further.

"One day, Dr Nelson took the black box to a group meditation. Sure enough, the black box responded to the intentions of the group and the graph fluctuated accordingly. Nelson then took the black box to several more group meditations and the result was the same each time. The collective group seemed to influence the patterns of numbers on the box.

"Taking advantage of modern technology such as the Internet, Dr Nelson set up several black boxes across the world, and hooked them all up to his computer in his Princeton laboratory."

"You mean to say there's more than one black box?" said Liz.

"Actually, there are at least sixty-five black boxes spread across the globe!"

"Then why the fuss over the one my father was busy with?"

"I'll get there," said Macmanus. "Anyway, we called our new network of black boxes around the world the EGG project. It literally means 'ElectroGaiaGram' which is a play on the word 'electroencephalogram' and is similar to the EEG technology used to record brain waves. We call the black box and software at each host location around the world an egg. The software that collects and archives all the data, via the Internet, onto the Princeton server can be seen to be the basket. Our more formal public name is the Global Consciousness Project. And I'm the acting head. And your father was in charge of the South African chapter."

"I didn't know," said Liz.

"Our theory is that the collection of random data from the black boxes will become non-random during global events," said Macmanus. "We predict departures from expectation when there is a widespread, profound sharing of mental and emotional responses.

"For the computer-based data collection we use black box devices that are an electronic equivalent of high-speed coin-flippers. They work in measurements of white noise similar to the random static between radio stations. The voltage level of the noise, which varies unpredictably above and below an average level, is, as I mentioned, turned into ones and zeros, which we can count as if they were heads and tails. These electronic random sources make a steady stream of unpredictable binary events, or bits. We record a type of a trial from each black box in the entire network, once every second. The trial consists of two hundred bits and its value is recorded by counting the ones. We expect that this count will be about one hundred because there is a fifty-fifty chance for a bit to be one or zero."

"It sounds quite complicated," said Liz.

"Not at all," Macmanus smiled. "Anyway, data from the black boxes were constantly running through Dr Nelson's computer, twenty-four hours a day. Generally the line on the graph on his computer remained flat. But then on September 6, 1997, something astonishing happened. The graph suddenly shot upwards, recording a huge shift in the number sequence as the machines all over the world started reflecting large deviations from the norm."

"What was so special about September 6, 1997?" Liz asked.

Macmanus edged closer to Liz and answered her very slowly. "It was the day of Princess Diana's funeral."

CHAPTER 75

The Fox picked up his phone and dialed Rafik's number, but the ramifications of the Solar Storm were still apparent. He debated whether to use his landline to call Rafik. He could still block the number. But then he realized Rafik's number was a cellphone, so it still wouldn't connect as there was no signal.

Being a fox, he always had a back-up plan in place. He hadn't used this option in ages, but he knew it would still work. It was the only other way he could communicate with Rafik, and he knew Rafik would get the message.

Good old-fashioned beepers. While most people he knew of just used cellphones to conduct their business, the Fox knew of several people who still liked to be contacted via their beepers that they clipped onto their belts. And now with cellphone signals non-existent, the Fox was grateful he had insisted that Rafik always carry a pager with him. Although Rafik would not be able to get hold of him, he could at least always be able to contact Rafik. But that was fine. The Fox would continue to give his instructions as necessary.

The Fox dialed the pager service number from his landline. He held his breath to see if there would be a connection. There was, and he heaved a sigh of relief. He followed the automatic voice prompts and entered the code for the pager for Rafik. Seconds later he recorded his message: "Chip at father's house. Go now".

"But that's preposterous," said Liz. "You're basically saying that because lots of people on a global level were deeply upset by what had happened to Princess Diana, that their sad thoughts—no matter where in the world these people were—their sad thoughts somehow caused the number sequences on the black box to change?"

"That's exactly what I am saying."

"But how can the thoughts of people have any effect on any black box? Thoughts are thoughts. They shouldn't have any influence on physical numbers or graphs generated by something tangible like your black box."

"The world is changing," Macmanus said. "Science is changing. As that old saying goes, the future is not what it used to be!'"

"Maybe the numbers that shifted like that on the black box had absolutely nothing to do with Princess Diana," Liz said. "Maybe you're just trying to find reasons for something that doesn't exist."

Macmanus tried to hide his surprise at Liz's outburst. *I know she is Harry Greene's daughter, but she is so skeptical.*

"It's not just me," said Macmanus. "There are several top scientists who examined the results of the black box during Princess Diana's funeral, and who continued with the research afterwards.

"After Diana was killed but before the funeral proceedings had been finalized, Dr Nelson and his team decided to examine whether there would be any movements or deviations from the black box during the funeral itself.

"At the time there were predictions that at least two million people would try to be present at the processions and ceremonies, and that over two billion people would watch live coverage of the event on their TV screens. Because this was a sad time for people all over the world, Dr Nelson realized the funeral would certainly create a shared consciousness experience with a huge emotional impact for many, many people.

"The theory was that the worldwide sharing of grief would create a so-called consciousness field whose resonance or coherence might affect the black box."

Liz shifted on the couch. Macmanus noticed her uneasiness but continued to talk. "Various colleagues were invited by Dr Nelson to record the data coming from the black box, beginning on the Friday night before the funeral, and continuing throughout the events on the Saturday, and even for several hours afterwards.

"Obviously, the aim of the experiment was that a standard measure of coherence within the data would correlate with global public attention to the events, and particularly with the level of shared emotional engagement.

"Dr Nelson believed it could be very possible that there would be a major effect on the black box during the ceremonies, but in order to have a formal assessment, there needed to be the specification of a precise analytical expectation.

"As the order of the funeral events became known, Dr Nelson and some of his colleagues decided to make use of the funeral schedule that had been posted on the CNN website on September 4, 1997. The schedule basically divided all the public funeral proceedings into four main components.

"The first component on the funeral schedule was on the Saturday morning of September 6 at eight minutes past nine when the coffin left Kensington Palace in London. The next event that was significant in terms of attracting public interest was at ten forty-five when the royal standard at Buckingham Palace was replaced by the Union Jack at half-mast. The funeral service itself began at eleven at Westminster Abbey. At noon, the service came to an end with a one-minute silence. The coffin was then moved to Althorp, and arrived there at three pm. These well-defined components of the funeral became the focus of Dr Nelson's experiment, as they were attended by many people locally, and seen by many more thanks to TV coverage all over the world.

"Sure enough, the data which was captured in twelve independent recordings at various locations in America and Europe had important results. The results showed an anomalous global effect which would occur by chance probably only once in at least one hundred repetitions in this type of experiment.

"What is also amazing is that the most striking deviation on the graph was during the data segment corresponding with the invocation and recitation of the Lord's Prayer. This is when people's emotions were at their highest. This confirmed the prediction based on the potential of this tragic and unexpected occasion to produce emotional engagement and resonance."

"Is this for real?" Liz asked.

"Absolutely," said Macmanus. "In fact, these results were consistent with previous FieldREG studies pertaining to the black box and consciousness. The results supported provisional interpretations which suggested that groups of people, especially when they are attuned and engaged in a common theme, they may produce something like a consciousness field that brings about a small but statistically identifiable bias in a nominally random sequence.

"Basically, the grief and shock of Diana's death led to an overwhelming reaction that catapulted it as the main media topic for several days. The funeral ceremonies occupied all the major TV channels and thus the attention of an unprecedented number of people. As I have said, this focus of emotion might be expected to produce a widespread resonance of effect. And it did! These deviations on the graph are nothing short of amazing. What happened here can only be described as a truly global effect of consciousness, almost like a global mind's inchoate thoughts. Some would even go far enough to call it the Mind of God."

CHAPTER 76

Liz listened carefully to the words pouring furiously out of Macmanus, who remained unaware of just how fast he was talking.

"For centuries, humans have wondered whether we're all inter-connected, whether there's something that links us all even though we're unaware of it," Macmanus said. "The sages have said so. Religion says so. But there has been nothing concrete. We wanted to know, could we get scientific evidence of this on paper? Could Earth provide some type of holistic response to what happens to the living beings on this planet? Would we be able to uncover evidence of a global mind?

"And so, the Global Consciousness Project was born. The GCP is an international grouping of scientists who came together for this black box experiment that still continues today.

"There are many dates where events have occurred in recent years which have greatly affected the outcome of our experiments. But there is still one day that stands out where the results were phenomenal," said Macmanus as he paused for dramatic effect. "The events on September 11, 2001 became emblematic for the Global Consciousness Project because it was such a large and tragic event—"

"Are you saying that the black box experiment was affected on 9/11?" Liz interrupted.

"What happened on 9/11 was just the type of catastrophe the Global Consciousness Project would expect to create a strong emotion-related global consciousness because of the devastating effect it had on people around the world," said Macmanus. "In order to explore the possibility of global consciousness, some members of the GCP decided to analyze the events of 9/11 using data from the global EGG network. Independent exploratory analyses were also done.

"The formal global consciousness test prediction made by the GCP specified a time period over which it was thought that any PK-based global consciousness effects would be seen in the data produced by thirty-seven of the then-thirty-eight global black boxes actively running in the network that fateful day. The specified time period began ten minutes before the first plane crashed into the North Tower of the World Trade Center and ended four hours after that, so that the timeframe over which the global consciousness hypothesis would be formally tested ran from eight thirty-five am to twelve forty-five pm Eastern Daylight Time. This time period covers all the terrorist events and adds about two and a half hours of their aftermath."

"Okay," said Liz. "I think I'm still following you."

"For this particular test prediction analysis," Macmanus continued, "we used our standard procedure of working the data using Chi-square values cumulatively combined over time to represent a measure of the overall deviation, or departure, from the expected level of random behavior among the network of black boxes.

"Normally, based on the inherently unpredictable nature of a truly random number generator, we would expect the behavior of the global black boxes to be completely different from each other, with their deviation from chance expectation at exactly zero."

"Sorry, Professor, but now you are losing me in all this," said Liz. "If you can try and keep it simple. I don't have my father's scientific mind!"

"I'll try my best," Macmanus said and smiled. "It seems that when world events occur that greatly affect us, the network of these global black boxes tends to move away from randomness and the results they produce on the computer's graphs show anomalous patterns in the data that are beyond chance expectation."

"So you are saying that normally the black boxes churn out random results but on 9/11 the boxes churned out results that were not random at all? In other words they were more ordered or structured?"

"Research shows that on September 7, 8 and 9, there were only random fluctuations in the network," Macmanus said. "But, on September 11, 12 and even 13, the data was anything but random. In fact, the data streaming out of the black boxes was highly structured, coherent and linear, all of which are things we would rarely, if at all, expect to see in purely random data for long periods of time. This trend was so strong it lasted for two days after the attack.

"The graphs in the research display distinct signs that the data following the attacks was clearly removed from chance expectation and were extreme in nature. This is seen in stark contrast with the random data in the days prior to September 11. It turns out that this powerful and lingering trend, which lasts about fifty-one hours in total, is so statistically unlikely to occur in purely random data that we would only see a trend just like it occurring by chance alone once every two thousand three hundred days!

"Other independent studies remain consistent with this finding. This gives support to the likelihood that the result is no fluke at all and that it might represent some indirect indication of a strong 'movement' within the global black box network by some external source.

Liz had gone slightly pale but remained silent as she tried to absorb

Macmanus's words.

"On that fateful day, as you know, of the four airplanes that were hijacked on 9/11, only three of them actually hit their intended targets," said Macmanus. "The fourth plane, United Airlines Flight 93 out of Boston, instead crashed in a field in western Pennsylvania between seven minutes past ten and ten thirty EDT.

"We know that the failure of this plane to reach its target was due to the heroic sacrifice by a brave group of passengers, who had apparently tried to take down the terrorists on the plane and foil the hijacking, albeit at great risk to themselves.

"We wanted to explore the bravery of these passengers. The researchers thought that, since an intense physical struggle was likely to have taken place, as well as the great panic that may have erupted among the other passengers as a result of it, the event would be emotionally gripping enough to have had a notable effect on the global black box network.

"The research showed the data line coming from the boxes fluctuated and zigzagged greatly. This might have been due to the panic, confusion, and fear that presumably erupted aboard Flight 93. The graphs clearly show a strong deviation in the latter part of the time period, which, in some meaningful way, could be a 'signature' of the struggle."

"So," said Liz, "are you saying that the numbers churned out by the black box, when looking at the time period when there would have been that struggle between the terrorists and the hijackers on board Flight 93, are you saying that the numbers were higher than they should have been?"

"Yes, that's exactly what I am saying," said Macmanus. "For those six minutes at the time of the struggle, the fluctuations in the data were extremely high. It is almost as if an invisible force or presence reacted on a high emotional level to the events that were unfolding, causing the sequences emitted from the black box to spike."

CHAPTER 77

Macmanus watched Liz as he continued with his explanation. "All the findings from the GCP data seem collectively to provide some indication of small but statistically measurable randomness deviation irregularities present within the data recorded by the global network of random number generators on that horrifying day."

"There must be some logical explanation for why the numbers from the black box reacted the way they did," said Liz. "Maybe these irregular reactions have something to do with the general environment at the time?"

"Hardly—" said Macmanus.

"Well, I don't buy it." Liz interrupted him. "Surely you can't ignore environmental conditions. What about power surges and electrical disruptions around cities as a result of the events on September 11? How about the fact that there could have been increased electromagnetic interference as a result of increased use of radios, TVs, and cellphones? Maybe this could have affected the black box?"

"Good point," said Macmanus. *She is her father's daughter after all!* "But if power surges and electrical disruptions were the cause of the radical shift in the numbers generated by the black box, then it should be the logical explanation if there was only a black box in New York City. But there were black boxes throughout the world, and they all reacted in the same way. How can you explain that?"

Liz was silent.

"Another important point to consider is that some of the black boxes started reacting several hours *before* the actual attacks began in Washington and New York," Macmanus spoke slowly. "Also, the black box itself is designed in such a way that it blocks out any electromagnetic interference, so despite the possible increase at the time of radios, TVs and phones, your theory just doesn't hold any water!

"Also," said Macmanus, "another scientist at the Institute for Noetic

Sciences, Dean Radin, did a study of the natural changes in electromagnetism due to power usage and the study showed that there was actually no difference between day and night use of power around 9/11. So, the notion that the 9/11 anomalies on the black box were the result of the environmental conditions on that day are unfounded!"

"Maybe there are other explanations to explain the movement coming from the black box on 9/11?" Liz said.

"Like what?" said Macmanus.

"I don't know. What if the stats themselves are wrong? Wasn't it Mark Twain who said there are lies, damned lies, and statistics?"

Macmanus broke into a huge grin. "I can't believe you're quoting Mark Twain at a time like this! In any event, our statistical analyses are very reliable and credible, so I don't think you can just say that the stats are wrong."

"Well, maybe they are," said Liz.

"Several independent researchers have produced the same results by analyzing the same data. A study by Brian Williams examined whether the results could have been produced by inflating the stats of purely random data to make it look like it was non-random and uncharacteristic, but really wasn't. Also, the same statistical trends occurred across time ranges from second-by-second to fifteen-minute block periods, and there is no indication at all that these stats are artificial.

"So the only sound explanation then," Macmanus continued, "is that we detected the psi 'signature' of a developing global consciousness which was shared by the minds of people all over the world as they focused in horror on the terrorist attacks and responded in a similar emotional way. This somehow had the ability to momentarily and powerfully disrupt the natural behavior of random physical systems around the world.

"The global consciousness effects that have been seen in the global black box network have characteristics which have similar effects to PK or 'mind over matter' effects, and indicate that the two might have a common foundation. This is clear from the fact that the 9/11 results from the black box network reveal that the black boxes from all over the world were affected, even those which were so far away from the source of the main events.

"The results coming from the black boxes all showed the severe and widespread emotional response to the attacks, and this is consistent with a growing indication of a possible correlation between PK effects and emotional expression.

"As I said to you, one of the most intriguing aspects of all," said Macmanus, "is that the response of the black box network seemed to begin several hours before the attacks commenced. This is consistent with the evidence for retroactive, in other words 'backwards acting in time', PK effects on the black box data.

"Thus, the early morning changes that appeared on the black box before the actual attacks began on 9/11 might reflect some sort of anticipatory, emotion-related PK response to the tragic events by a supposed global consciousness, a type of global premonition. This is also similar, and might

THE MIND OF GOD

even be linked to, all the various subjective reports of premonitions relating to
the ensuing tragedy and chaos of 9/11 that occurred in the days and hours
before the attacks on the Twin Towers."

"Premonitions about 9/11?" Liz said in disbelief. "Assuming that what
you say is true, then what does all this mean for humankind?"

"Well, there is still a great deal we don't understand when it comes to
global consciousness, but the effects of the black box results for 9/11 have
given us several clues about its nature. What's as important as any of the
scientific evidence is the importance of the meaning. The bottom line is that if
a global consciousness does exist and if it was formed among all of us that
fateful morning, then it appears to have been greatly moved by the events on
September 11.

"The results show the depression and fear that gripped the world, and
which hovered around New York City for weeks after the attacks. Several
studies on depression have confirmed this. It seems then that the global
consciousness mind was itself wounded by the terror attacks. If global
consciousness and PK effects are indeed linked, then the results from the black
box network on 9/11 may also show that the power of a collective, emotion-
related PK effect is stronger than we ever imagined."

"Wow," said Liz.

"The results of the GCP experiments and its ramifications for humankind
is profound," Macmanus continued. "Just as the biosphere is made up of all
the organisms on Earth and their interactions, Pierre Teilhard de Chardin,
who was a French philosopher and Jesuit priest, maintained that there is a so-
called noosephere which is composed of all the interacting minds on Earth.
Noosephere refers to a transhuman consciousness emerging from our
interactions to become a guiding intelligence for the Earth. It sits parallel to
the biosphere and atmosphere.

"We can say that human beings are basically looking at the next stage of
our evolution. Evolution as we know it begins with particles that combine to
form atoms and then molecules and eventually complicated molecules. These
then become the building blocks for life from which smaller and then larger
animals emerge. Eventually you get humans—self-aware animals. The natural
development isn't over yet. We are in the throes of witnessing the next and
final stage of evolution, one where we become a new organ of consciousness
for the Earth, evolving into something analogous to the cerebral cortex in
humans. In order for the human race to survive, we have to engage in
conscious evolution to decide what the future will be."

CHAPTER 78

Rafik found himself treading back in the garden at the house of the crazy man he had shot into the sea. He'd received the beeper message from the Fox and had promptly proceeded back to Rondebosch. He wondered what the Fox had thought about how things had gone awry that morning. Rafik realized this was his last chance to get the damn microchip. *Salvation.*

He peered through the window and saw two people in the lounge. The girl he had been chasing was listening intently to an older man Rafik hadn't seen before. There was no one else in the room. Rafik decided it would be better to apprehend them from the door inside the house. He crept back towards the front garden and opened the front door.

"This is mind-blowing!" said Liz. "But I still don't get it. If there are black boxes in various locations around the world, then what is so special about my father's black box?"

Macmanus was about to answer Liz when he saw a shadow at the door. He instantly stopped talking as the gun-wielding figure entered the room. Macmanus stared in horror at the man with the scar across his face and one white eyebrow.

"Nobody move," the man said. "Now give me that damn microchip."

"Get away from us," said Liz.

"Give me the microchip."

"You mean this?" Macmanus held the chip into the air. "Come and get it, tough guy."

The scarred man stepped slowly towards Macmanus. "Give it to me now."

Macmanus waited until the intruder was further away from Liz. Then he threw the microchip into the air. "Take it, Liz!" he shouted. "And get out of here."

Their attacker was caught off guard as the microchip soared through the air. In a split second Macmanus had leapt onto his assailant and knocked him to the ground.

"Run, Liz!"

The microchip fell to the ground near Liz's feet. Macmanus was still wrestling on the floor with the thug.

"Go, Liz, he wants the microchip."

Liz hesitated.

"Forget about me, he's not interested in me."

––––––

Liz grabbed the microchip, gave one last look at Macmanus and charged out of the room. As she headed to the front door, she grabbed some keys hanging on a wooden rack.

The street was deserted. Liz leapt into her father's car and sped off down the road.

Liz was soon on the M3 highway. She glanced in her rearview mirror and her heart skipped an extra beat when she saw a Mazda heading towards her. She slammed her foot onto the accelerator and her father's car lunged forward. As she changed lanes to overtake a slow bus, she gasped in horror as her engine made several spitting sounds and began to chug to a grinding halt. Liz swiftly maneuvered the car on to the side of the road before the engine went dead.

She charged out of the car and looked down the road. The Mazda was close enough for Liz to see a big smile on the driver's face. Liz turned and ran along the side of the road away from her pursuer. Another car drove past.

"Help me!" Liz waved frantically at the motorist as he drove past, leaving Liz coughing in a splutter of smoke. Liz didn't blame him. She wouldn't have stopped either.

Liz ran on to the green embankment that stretched parallel to the highway. In the distance was Newlands forest. Liz knew that if she could just get there she might be able to lose her attacker.

––––––

Rafik saw her run higher and edged his Mazda closer to the side of the road. The road further down turned off into a clump of trees. If he were being chased it would be the perfect place to try to reach. Rafik watched Liz sprint along the greenery towards the trees at the side of the highway. She disappeared behind a clump of bushes. He revved and turned the vehicle off the highway, leaving the passing cars behind him.

The Mazda screeched into a small deserted parking lot. He leapt out of his car and dashed towards the greenery. As he ran, he reached for his pistol in his pocket and to his dismay realized that in his haste he had left it on the front seat. He fumbled in his other pocket and was relieved to find his trusty knife. *It will have to do.* The girl arrived at the end of the thicket and found herself in the parking lot just as he got there.

"You're not going anywhere now." Rafik waved the knife at her. "Now give me what I want."

The girl looked desperately around but they were alone.

"There's no way out. Give me that damn microchip."

They were standing in the open parking lot now and Liz realized that she had nowhere to run to, even though there was a busy highway on the other side of the trees.

"I don't want to make a scene," the man said. "Just give it to me and I'll be on my way."

Liz stared at her assailant but didn't respond.

He stepped closer to her and grabbed her arm. He held the knife against her neck and began to drag her towards his car.

"We can do this the easy way or the difficult way," he said. "What's it going to be?"

"Get away from me!"

The man punched her in the cheek. Liz fell backwards onto the ground near the Mazda. He was so close now that Liz could smell his sweat. He raised his arm again and leaned over her.

CHAPTER 79

There was a loud noise as several motorbikes roared their way into the parking lot. The motorcyclists were all kitted out in dark jeans and black leather jackets. They wore sunglasses, grinning as they appeared on the scene. Some of them waved while others just swung their baseball bats in the air. One of them almost fell off his bike.

"What the hell?" said Liz. She had rolled further away from her assailant, who looked just as shocked by the sudden infiltration of motorbikes.

"You left your jersey behind," Calvin Deacon waved it in the air from his Harley that was in the middle of all the other Harleys.

"What?" Liz looked up.

"Yeoooww! Your jersey. You left it in my bar!"

"And you came all the way to tell me that? How did you find me anyway?"

"We can find anyone," Calvin yelled above the noise. "It looks like an expensive jersey. Didn't think you would want to lose it."

Liz stared at the jersey dangling from Calvin's hands. *He actually tracked me down to give me my jersey back? How the hell did he find me?*

A flabby motorcyclist with a long grey beard and a red bandana tied on top of his head was holding a greasy baseball bat and swung it at her attacker as he rode past him.

———

Rafik saw it coming and just managed to step out of the way in time, causing the bat to swing into nothingness, and almost causing the driver to lose his balance and fall over. The driver steadied the bike and turned it around. The other bike riders were also driving around Rafik, and soon they had formed a circle around Rafik. Three of the drivers stopped their bikes near Liz.

Rafik was still armed with his knife, and lunged it in the air towards each biker who edged near him.

"Come try me!" Rafik shouted. "I'll take this knife and push it right through you, you miserable pieces of shit."

The bikers laughed but didn't move. They were waiting for Rafik to choose one of them for his target and then they would surround him even closer and take him down.

"In case you're not that good at math, there are nine of us and, hold on, only one of you!" The man with the baseball bat grinned, while his fellow riders continued to laugh.

"I don't care if there are twenty of you thugs!" Rafik shouted. "I'll kill each and every one of you with my bare hands."

"The guy also seems to be a comedian," one of the bikers said.

"What's the girl got to do with you? Why don't you mind your own fucking business?"

"Why don't you mind your own fucking business?" One of the bikers mimicked Rafik. "Hey guys maybe we should mind our own fucking business?"

"I'm so scared right now I think I'm going to piss in my pants," another biker cooed from behind his cigarette smoke.

Rafik ducked a swinging baseball bat as a bike swerved past him. This time his duck was unsuccessful and the bat made contact with his hand, the one holding his knife. He doubled up and instantly dropped his weapon in agony. The knife was promptly ridden over by the third motorbike.

Meanwhile, the other riders had driven towards a shell-shocked Liz.

"Hey, what happened to your leg?" Calvin pointed to where Liz's pants were torn above her knee.

"I fell."

"Looks like we got here just in time!"

"I don't know what to say," said Liz.

"You're welcome!" Calvin laughed. He switched off his engine, climbed off the bike and took a few steps towards her attacker. "Yeeeooow! What do we have here, gentlemen?"

The rest of the motorcyclists had now formed a complete circle around Calvin and her attacker. There was no way that anyone could have penetrated their enclosure. The scarred assailant stared at the men who were all laughing and cheering their leader on. Then he stared back into the cold eyes of the man in the snakeskin boots.

"It's a silent one!" Calvin cackled again.

The scarred man was standing still but his eyes were carefully following his captor's every step. "Fuck you!" he spat.

"Did you hear that, boys?"

The motorcyclists waved their fists in the air and grunted in unison. When all the shouts had died down, Liz watched Calvin stepped forward so that he was now very much in the attacker's space. Calvin leaned in and glared into his eyes.

"Yeeoow! Anything else to say? What's your name then?"

He glared back, then said, "Rafik, you fucker."

208

"It seems, boys, that Rafik doesn't have anything else to say. Or maybe he's just…" Calvin paused for dramatic effect as if he were in the middle of a Shakespearian monologue. The crowd waited in anticipation for some further pearls from their leader. "Maybe he's just a scared, cowardly miserable excuse for a human being?"

The motorcyclists punched their fists into the air again and grunted approvingly.

"Fuck you, who the hell do you think you are?" Rafik had his fists clenched too and was watching the man's every step.

Calvin remained silent for a few seconds and the only sound emanating from the group was the soft buzzing of some of the stationery motorcycle engines. Suddenly, Liz saw his arm shoot out and ram Rafik in the lower stomach. Before Rafik could react, Calvin had thrown another punch, this time making contact with Rafik's jaw. Rafik doubled up in pain as another fist came towards him. He moved out of the way and stuck his foot out as he moved. Calvin went tumbling onto the gravel.

One of the bikers nearby threw Calvin a silver chain that had been hanging around his neck. It was chunky and adorned with sharp emblems and spiky trinkets. Calvin had already leapt up and thrust the chain towards Rafik's face. Rafik ducked and Calvin swung the chain again. This time he was too fast for Rafik and much more accurate than his first swing. The chain collided with Rafik's face.

Rafik fell onto his knees and wiped the blood gushing under his eye.

"It hurts, does it?" Calvin towered over Rafik. "Ah, poor thing."

"Fuck you," Rafik wiped more blood away. "Fuck all of you."

Calvin towered over Rafik and grinned down on his victim like a lion about to devour his kill. "Now, now, why would you want to harm someone as sweet and innocent as my dear friend, Elizabeth?"

Rafik glared at his captor and tried to lunge himself at Calvin. It was a futile attempt and Rafik suddenly found himself sprawled on the ground.

"Fuck you," Rafik spat. "You don't know who you're dealing with!"

Calvin lifted a leg and crushed it down on Rafik's knee.

"No," said Calvin as he leaned down to face Rafik. "You don't know who you're dealing with."

———

Rafik spat on his captor. *Take that, you fucking piece of shit.* The man in the snakeskin boots stepped back. It took him a moment to realize he had been spat on, and he clenched his fist and buried it into Rafik's stomach. Rafik groaned as contact was made.

"Nobody, but nobody, spits in my face," he hissed.

Rafik's stomach was in such pain he couldn't even respond. Before he could try to take a breath, he felt the man's clenched fist pummel his face. He groaned as contact was made. In addition to having a strong punch, the man's fist was full of heavy rings that connected with Rafik's chin like nothing he had ever experienced. And Rafik had experienced a lot in his life.

The man in the snakeskin boots gave another hysterical roar of laughter and rammed his heel onto Rafik's chest. The heel was sharp and tore into Rafik's flesh. He yanked Rafik off the ground and threw another punch to Rafik's face. This was followed by another punch to the stomach. Rafik's eyes were watering and he couldn't see much beyond the blood. *Thump!* And then Rafik's world cascaded into darkness.

CHAPTER 80

"You okay?" said Calvin.

"A bit shaken up but I'll be okay."

"Need anything else? A lift somewhere perhaps?"

Liz looked at her phone. There was still no signal.

"There's been a blackout," Calvin explained. "No cellphones working anywhere!"

Liz thought about Tim. She hoped he was okay. The only other place where she would have some chance of making contact with him would be his friend's house in Clifton. It was the only other person Tim knew in Cape Town, and he had said that he wanted to see him during his stay. She didn't have many alternatives. She couldn't go back to her father's house with the microchip. And if they were watching her father's house they might be watching her apartment too. Who knew just exactly which places in her life had been watched over the last few months? No one would be watching Tim's friend's place. It suddenly made perfect sense.

Liz reached into the pocket of the jersey Calvin had given back to her. Inside was a scrunched up piece of paper that Tim had handed to her earlier that morning. She stared at Tim's scribbles. *Hank Cooper.* And the address in Clifton.

"Actually, I might need a ride."

"Anywhere. Just name it."

Two minutes later, Liz was sitting behind Calvin on his Harley. A few of the motorcyclists had stayed in the parking lot with Rafik, while the rest had decided to ride with their leader. The entourage made its way on to the M3 highway.

"A lot more roads have been closed because of the presidential visit," Calvin shouted above the throttling. "It's caused another major gridlock."

And with that Calvin veered the bike to the side of the road and the others followed suit. They sped along the side of the highway adjacent to Newlands forest and when they saw some more traffic beacons blocking the side they weaved back in and out of the regular lanes, whizzing past the stagnant cars and disgruntled drivers.

"Hold on tight!"

Liz clutched the bike as it soared into the air and landed with a thump before speeding up a hill.

Ever since Calvin had gone for a spin with his father on his father's motorbike at the age of five, he had been hooked. There had been something about clinging onto the bike and roaring into the breeze that had got his adrenaline soaring. He had held tightly onto his father's jacket that day, especially when they climbed over hills and skidded near the local river. It was his earliest memory of his childhood that he carried with him into his adult life. It had been the start of many exciting motorbike trips that Calvin would share with his father for several years until he turned seventeen, the year his father was gunned down by a notorious gangster who was owed a large debt by Calvin's father. It was the day he lost his innocence, became a cold adult, and embarked on a path of violence and destruction. His mother could not control the violence her son unleashed, and the tight-knit family they once were fell apart and crumbled into the mayhem.

When his mother shacked up with an old acquaintance of his father's twelve months later, Calvin decided to leave home. He didn't complete the last few months of school and instead went back to his love—motorbikes. He joined the staff of a motorcycle repair shop and spent his days amid the grease and grime of fixing other people's bikes. His nights he would spend getting pissed out of his mind and causing brawls in local bars. Not only did he build up a reputation of being a motorbike expert, but he also became known as a ruthless fighter.

At the age of nineteen, he killed his first victim in a bar fight. The person he killed was a hefty giant who was feared by most people. Calvin suddenly earned immeasurable respect and, as news of his conquest spread in underground circles, his reputation grew, and his name became a living legend among the lower belly of the society he inhabited.

Calvin and his troop were now speeding between the cars on Nelson Mandela Boulevard as they headed towards the Atlantic Seaboard. He stared into his rearview mirror. He couldn't see Liz properly through the helmet he had given her, but she was clutching his waist tightly. Calvin grinned in the breeze. *What an unfuckingbelievable day!*

CHAPTER 81

Tim had finally managed to stumble out of the garden on UCT's upper campus. His head was still sore but the pain manageable. He had meandered back on to University Avenue where he soon found a taxi and ordered the driver to take him to Clifton. Now they had arrived at their destination.

Tim paid the driver and watched the vehicle chug along the tarred road into the distance. He turned to face the polished natural stone brick building that looked squeaky-clean. Tim could smell the sea and gladly inhaled the fresh air around him. A large green buzzer was embedded in the wall just below the bold number of the building. Tim pushed the button and waited for a response.

Two cyclists sped past him and a few seconds later a Jaguar drove by. Frustrated, Tim pushed the buzzer again. This time he made sure he pushed it firmly and held his finger down for several seconds.

"Can I help you?" A voice came through the hidden speaker that seemed to be near the buzzer.

"Yes, I'm here to see Hank Cooper."

There was a pause and a few seconds later the door in front of Tim whirred open. The building itself was built like a fortress, and boasted the tightest automated security features. After being buzzed through the front doors, a guest entering the premises would walk down another short wide passage in a greenhouse-type atmosphere, with plants and shrubbery ordaining the ceramic tiles.

At the end of the passage, next to a luscious water feature, would be another set of strong glass doors with another buzzer to press. These doors led to the reception area where a guest would have to sign in with security. After this stage, the guest would have to talk into another intercom and the doors could then only be opened by the person the guest was visiting from that person's intercom control system in their home.

Tim was soon in the reception area. An elderly man sat behind a desk looking up at Tim expectantly. His gray hair was combed sideways along the top of his head. The sound of a CD of Richard Clayderman at the piano filtered through the area. Tim could not take his eyes off the massive fish tank behind the man's desk.

"Amazing, isn't it?" The elderly man nodded behind him.

Tim smiled tightly.

"Sign in here, please," the man handed Tim a clipboard with a typed piece of paper stuck tightly to it.

"But I already told you who I was coming to see. Hank Cooper."

"That was just the verification stage. You'll need to go through all the other procedures."

"I just want to go to my friend's apartment."

"Our residents insist on these stringent measures."

The old man reminded him of a great uncle he used to have, only this man was even more annoying. He signed the book, put the name of whom he was visiting and the apartment number.

Several minutes later and the old man had directed Tim to another foyer. An elevator door was situated at the end of the foyer. There was no elevator button, just another large buzzer with numbers next to it. Tim pushed the buzzer and then the digits for Hank's apartment. He waited a few seconds until a voice came through.

"Tim? Is that really you?"

"You better believe it!"

"Come in, you old dog!"

Tim entered the elevator and pushed the button to the penthouse suite on the top floor. Standing in the elevator reminded him of how much he hated being in confined spaces. For a supposedly modern building with top security and technology it felt as if the elevator rose very slowly.

Unlike the passages and corridors in the foyer that led to the elevator, the elevator itself had no glass or windows. Just four albeit luxurious-looking velvet walls with one huge mirror fixed to the back of it. Tim stared at himself and then turned to watch the numbers change with each floor that the elevator went through. After what seemed like an eternity, the elevator stopped at the top floor.

The doors opened and the front door to the penthouse suite appeared. A huge pot plant with long leaves almost covered the large steel door next to it. Tim hesitated and then found another buzzer hidden behind the pot plant. He couldn't remember when he had had to endure so many buzzers and security settings. Even my apartment block in New York isn't nearly as intense as this, he thought.

He pushed the button and there was an instant click as the door swung open.

CHAPTER 82

It had been many years since Hank had last seen Tim. The two of them had shared a dorm room in college for one year before Hank had left for grad school at the University of Texas in Austin. Although Hank was a few years older, they had hit it off and become instant buddies. They had some good times with their fraternity house and many memories to laugh about. But as with many friendships formed during one's higher education years, the changing of the seasons and the inevitable progression of time saw the two of them lose touch.

And then a few weeks previously, Hank had received an email from Tim. *Out of the blue!* Tim had tracked him down on Facebook and wanted to get in touch again. Hank had smiled as he read Tim's message, and for a few moments was briefly transported back to their carefree college days, a time where the world seemed like a different place and the biggest problems were whether the girls they liked would agree to go out with them.

Everything was so simple back then, Hank lamented. There were times when nostalgia gripped him so fiercely it didn't let go. Sure, Hank realized that with time memory always portrayed the past in a better light than it might have been in reality. But just the very connection with someone from that bygone era was enough to bring a lump to Hank's throat. He could not understand why he felt so overwhelmed, but his whole college era was suddenly swept towards him, like one giant wave rushing from his past into his future.

After reading Tim's message, Hank instantly replied saying how great it was to hear from his old college buddy again and how Tim should definitely get in touch when he came to Cape Town. Hank wouldn't take no for an answer. He knew how tight a schedule these trips often followed but he insisted that Tim at least come see his home and catch up with a few drinks and a few laughs.

Tim entered the apartment and found himself staring at a man with curly reddish hair sitting in a wheelchair. He was wearing a woolen polar neck jersey, and a checked blanket lay spread over his legs.

"Tim, I can't believe it's you! In South Africa of all places!"

"It's good to see you, Hank!" Tim smiled.

The apartment was warm and luxurious. Fine crystal and porcelain ornaments graced the solid side counter that stretched across the lounge. A sturdy oak table stood in the center of the room, a vase of colorful flowers perched in the middle of it.

"Welcome to my humble abode," said Hank.

The new orphanage was going to be a large well-built facility with plenty of comfortable rooms and a large secure garden for the children to run in. The project that Michelle envisaged also entailed building an additional wing with twenty-four hour nursing staff and medical facilities. The center would be the first of its kind for any orphanage in South Africa and Michelle was proud to be part of it.

It had taken her two years to get the momentum going and approval of the building plans in place. But any project as big as this needed major funding, and donors to ensure not only its success but the project's survival. Michelle had approached hundreds of potential donors, locally and abroad, and had been met with rejection after rejection. Given the global recession, rising unemployment, and the constant doom and gloom in the markets, it was not surprising that major players who would ordinarily have donated to such a cause were refusing to give Michelle their money.

And then on one dismally cold Cape Town afternoon three months previously, Michelle received a phone call that, despite all her efforts, she was not expecting at all.

"Please hold the line for Eric Simms," a lady in a deep southern American accent told Michelle when she answered the phone.

A few seconds later Michelle was speaking to the man who could potentially be the project lifesaver.

"Michelle?"

"Yes?"

"I like your project idea about the orphanage for kids with Aids."

"What?"

"The Aids orphanage, it sounds like a great idea."

"Who is this?" Michelle wanted to pinch herself.

"Eric Simms at your service, ma' am. I would love to invest in your project."

"I can't believe this. How did you hear about the project? I don't think I've spoken to you before?"

"No, ma'am, I heard about it from a friend of a friend and was able to get your contact details."

"I don't know what to say?"

"I must first just say that it's not a foregone conclusion that I'll be giving you my money."

"Oh?"

"There are two other projects who want my money and I need to meet with all three groups before I make my decision. They're all good causes but unfortunately I can only choose one of them."

"When do you want to meet with me?"

"I'll be in touch over the next few weeks. Probably hope to meet some time over the next few months."

Before Michelle could ask more questions, Eric Simms had ended the call, but Michelle's excitement and hope had remained. Liz had promised Michelle that she would help her plan her presentation for Eric Simms and even help deliver the pitch. She had after all won awards for public speaking when she was at school. Michelle knew that Liz would be the crucial factor in a potent delivery that would ensure victory came their way.

Yet those feelings of imminent success that had begun to govern Michelle's life for several weeks heading towards that crucial meeting had rapidly deteriorated in the space of a day, as Michelle lay on her entrance hall floor, desperately waiting for someone to walk in, or for Liz to make contact.

CHAPTER 83

The exclusive and affluent suburb of Clifton is located on Cape Town's Atlantic seaboard in between Bantry Bay and Camps Bay. Many of Clifton's homes and apartments lie on high cliffs, allowing for magnificent views of the Atlantic Ocean. Clifton boasts four beautiful beaches that attract holidaymakers and locals in their droves. Home to Millionaires' Row, the suburb is popular, chic, and luxurious.

According to the Cape Town Tourism official website, Clifton is known as Cape Town's St Tropez. It has been described as the French Riviera of South Africa. A visit to Wikipedia's website will point out that Clifton was previously rated as one of the Top Ten Beaches by the Discovery Travel Channel. *Forbes* magazine has also previously listed Clifton in its Top 10 Topless Beaches in the World.

A group of Harley Davidsons now throttled through the windy road stretching through Clifton, and formed a single neat line outside Hank's apartment complex. Calvin mounted his Harley onto the small pavement. "Is this the right address?" He turned to Liz who had climbed off the motorbike and was handing him her helmet.

"It's the right place," Liz said. "Thank you, Calvin, I don't know what I would have done without you today."

"Yeeeeooow! Don't mention it."

Liz began to walk towards the intercom on the outside wall.

"You sure you'll be safe here?" Calvin said.

"Yes, it's fine. I'm just going to hang low for a while."

"I know all about hanging low," Calvin said and winked.

"Goodbye, Calvin."

"Stay in touch!"

Calvin was grinning like a toddler who had just been given a triple chocolate ice cream cone. He revved his engine and thrust his bike into the air so that it rested momentarily on the back wheel alone.

"Let's go ladies! Yeeeeeooooow!"
Liz pushed the intercom button and waited for someone to answer.

CHAPTER 84

"They were some good times," said Hank.

"That they were," Tim said. He kicked his feet up and the La-Z-Boy chair instantly reclined.

"Can I get you a scotch?"

Tim felt a cold shiver run through him at the very mention of the word. Hank had already wheeled himself to the granite counter top where several bottles were perched. Hank reached for a crystal tumbler.

"Um, maybe just some water please." Tim took his gaze off the counter of temptation.

"Water?" Hank looked up incredulously.

"With ice and lemon!"

"That's not the Tim I remember."

It had been sports day in his final year of high school. Tim had been preparing for the hundred-meter sprint for months, so he had dedicated himself to a strict routine of running every day and getting fit. Being one who always enjoyed a tasty burger and milkshake with his friends, Tim had to make some sacrifices, and managed to get by without any junk food for those few months. As grueling as it was, Tim became disciplined and allowed the upcoming race to be the major focus in his life. Even his girlfriend at the time, Lisa Fernandez, took second fiddle, and grudgingly accepted that for those few months Tim's running would come first.

And so when the big day finally arrived, Tim woke up that morning ready for battle. He was in a positive mindset and ready to take on his competitors, as well as set a new record for the hundred-meter race. And when he arrived at the high school sports grounds, his confidence grew even further. He was the man of the moment, ready to earn his champion title.

The runners lined themselves up at the beginning of the track and waited for the starter gun to be fired. Tim ran like he had never run before and after a few power strides took the lead. As the runners approached the finish line, it was neck and neck between Tim and another worthy competitor, his friend from algebra class, Max Moody. But Tim managed to edge himself forward and in the end was the first one to cross the finish line.

The spectators all leapt into the air and applauded Tim. He received a medal not only for winning the race but for breaking the record that had stood for the past one hundred and seventeen years. Tim was on a natural high as adrenalin pumped through him. His classmates, teachers, and family all congratulated him, telling him how he had made their school and district proud.

That night, Tim, Lisa, and a bunch of friends had gone out to celebrate at a friend's party. He didn't need the discipline and the diet any more. And as he was now an athletic champion, he had the boldness and belief that that day had changed his life. He had tasted victory and it was so sweet. That day did change Tim's life, but it wasn't from winning the race and breaking a long-standing record. That night Tim had his first drink.

Tim had been battling alcohol since then. What started as a casual love of whisky often restricted to social nights out led to Tim drinking more and more. When he found himself often staying home and drinking alone, Tim realized he had crossed a threshold. He didn't do anything about it, though, and soon his whole life revolved around when he would have his next drink. Whisky became his drink of choice at breakfast; it became his substitute to mid-morning tea. Whisky became his lunch and dinner and everything in between.

Each day went by and Tim would immerse himself more in drink. He stopped socializing, stopped calling his family, and soon was abandoning his work assignments. After missing several crucial deadlines, his editor gave him his marching orders. Unemployed, Tim fell into the abyss.

It was only several months later when Tim's family was alerted to his true state of affairs. Tim's brother had come to visit again but, unlike the previous occasions, decided to force open the door to Tim's house to see what was wrong. He found Tim passed out on the carpet in his lounge, with the television blaring in the background.

Tim was taken to hospital, put on a drip, and remained under strict medical supervision. A few days later he was admitted to a local rehab clinic and stayed there for six months. The clinic helped Tim get back on his feet, but since then Tim's life had been a precarious tightrope as it hovered over temptation and the world of alcohol.

"I... I don't think it would be a good idea," said Tim now to Hank. He could still feel soft pounding in his head. "Not today."

Hank didn't push the issue. "One water with ice and lemon coming up."

The old buddies spent the next twenty minutes catching up and reminiscing about their exploits in their younger days.

"Where has the time gone?" said Tim. "Sometimes those days seem like a different world. Other times they seem like yesterday."

"I guess that's what happens when you get older," Hank acknowledged. "We're not spring chickens any more, you know."

A buzzer on the wall near the hallway went off, interrupting their conversation.

"Looks like we have a visitor," said Hank.

CHAPTER 85

President Rafferty drummed his fingers as he sat at his desk in the lounge of his hotel suite. He stared at the speech in front of him, but his mind was elsewhere. It had been a long trip with two other whirlwind stops before this visit, and he needed to have a good night's sleep. It wasn't easy being president of the most powerful country in the world and he had been averaging three hours' sleep for the last few months. It was bound to catch up with him sometime, and he had a feeling that time was now.

He cast his eyes back on the typed pages and reread the first two paragraphs. Despite being president, he hated giving speeches. He had never enjoyed public speaking. His disdain for it began in high school when he had to debate the concept of "To travel hopefully is better than to arrive" in front of the entire school at weekly assembly. And although he made an excellent argument and delivered his points extremely well—as he always tended to do—the butterflies would fly around the inside of his stomach and not let up until the minute he left the stage. He used to feel physically sick before opening his mouth, but while in the moment of speech, he found his adrenalin would take over and carry him through his arguments to a successful conclusion, like a giant wave that glides a surfer along the shaky waters to the shore.

A sudden knock on the door caused the president to break from his reflections.

"Come in," he said and looked up expectantly as his Chief of Staff entered the room.

"Good evening, Mr President."

"Hello John, any suspects yet?"

"No suspects yet, Mr President, but our intelligence officials are giving it their all, both here and back home."

"Okay, so for us we'll carry on as usual."

"That's why I'm here, Mr President. We don't think you should be in Cape

Town any longer."

"John, I've got this speech and banquet dinner in a few hours. I can't leave now!"

"We don't believe you are safe here, sir."

"Are you kidding me? Have you checked the hundreds of personnel that make up my security detail? Have you forgotten I have bodyguards, too numerous to count, who accompany me everywhere—and I mean everywhere?"

"Yes, Mr President, but after today's events there is a chance something else might happen, and we don't think it is worth it for you to hang around!"

"What information do you have that I'm not aware of?" Rafferty had pushed his chair back and walked to the crystal bottle of cognac that was on a side table in the lounge suite.

"There's no further information since we last briefed you, but we believe that today's explosive device was a warning."

"John, we have bomb squad experts as part of our entourage here. We have metal detection machines, lasers, x-ray equipment, and sniffer dogs. Did you hear me say sniffer dogs? So how on earth do you think a bomb would be able to get through our immaculate security channels that we have set up? Even my mother wouldn't be able to get her way through to the banquet hall tonight, and you know that is saying a lot."

CHAPTER 86

Sindy parked her car and headed to the emergency stairs. She could have taken the lift but she never did. Climbing countless levels of stairs on a daily basis was just part of her regular routine, and she tried to stay as fit as she could. Even if she felt tired or like she was about to catch a cold, she would still ignore the elevator and plough up the stairs. Sindy was always up to the challenge.

And after the day she had had, it was no different. She needed to get to her apartment and sort out some things. And she needed to make some decisions. Fast.

Sindy opened the front door and entered her apartment. She threw her keys onto the ornate entrance table and headed straight for the kitchen. She was dead thirsty and downed a vast amount of cold purified fridge water. She was about to go to her bedroom when she heard voices. They were muffled and coming from the lounge. Her husband was obviously home. She was slightly surprised, as she had not seen his car in the parking lot. Or maybe she had just missed it.

She edged closer to the lounge and leaned towards it, her ear almost merging with the wood. She recognized her husband's voice but did not know the other voices. She could hardly hear what they were saying but was intrigued. Who was there? It's not like her husband usually had visitors, especially at this time of the day. In fact, he never had visitors at all.

Sindy's husband had become a recluse over the last ten years—ever since the accident. He had become withdrawn, and the socializing was left to her and her alone. He just wasn't interested.

Sindy didn't blame him, but she had her life to live and wasn't going into isolation just because he wanted her to. She had maintained her independence but the reality was that she and her husband had drifted, and she didn't have much extra time to put into building the relationship up again. Not with her heavy workload and the noble cause that consumed her.

Sindy edged closer to the door. She could hear the voices inside talking softly. She hesitated for a brief second and then pushed it open.

"Darling, you're home!" Hank smiled and wheeled towards her.

He held out his arms as Sindy leaned down and kissed him. "How was your day, my love?"

"Busy as usual!" she said and smiled.

"Darling, I would like you to meet an old college friend of mine, Tim Fletcher. Tim, this is my wife, Sindy."

"Nice to meet you, Tim," said Sindy. "What brings you to this part of the world?"

"A woman!" Hank grinned. "And there she is. Her name is Liz!" Liz had just re-entered the room after a visit to the guest toilet.

"Only kidding," said Tim. "I'm here on business, a special assignment."

"He's a journo," said Hank. "Always was the good writer."

Sindy smiled politely. "You're a long way from home," she said.

"Your city's growing on me," said Tim.

"Nice that you came to visit Hank."

"Well, I'd planned on looking him up in Cape Town anyway, and I thought now would be as a good a time as any."

"And you?" Sindy shot an enquiring look at Liz.

"It's okay." Hank eyed Tim and then Liz. "You can trust my wife. I trust her with my life."

Tim hesitated. "Well, actually we're on the run. People with guns are chasing us. I urgently needed a place to hide."

"What?" Sindy's eyes widened in shock.

"Liz is in grave danger. I lost her earlier and wasn't able to contact her again. But she knew to meet me here."

"Grave danger? What's going on?"

"It's a long story," said Tim.

"I'm all ears…" Sindy reached for the jug of iced lemon water that Hank had prepared for Tim. She glanced at the metallic silver round face clock ticking away on the wall. *Just a few minutes. Then I really need to get going.*

They filled her in on the events of the morning.

"Maybe we should call the police?" Hank ventured. "Once Liz and Tim explain everything, the cops will see that this whole thing has been one big misunderstanding."

"I'm sure it's something we can sort out ourselves," said Sindy. "No need to get the police involved."

Liz nodded. "No police right now."

"Let's go over some of the main issues," said Sindy. "You have some science thing which has been stolen and Liz's dad was shot dead?"

"Baby, some delicacy please," Hank said softly as he noticed Liz's eyes welling up.

"And some guy has been chasing you halfway round the city?"

"Something like that," said Tim. "He might have seen us enter this building."

"Well, there's no way anyone can penetrate the security here," said Hank.

"Yes, but he is probably waiting for us outside the building," said Liz. "He knows we have to leave here eventually."

"Why exactly are you being chased?" Sindy probed.

"We might have something he wants." Sindy watched as Liz fingered the pocket of her pants.

"What are you talking about?"

"It's okay, love," said Hank. "We don't need to know all the details. It looks like they've been through a lot."

"So how exactly are we going to get them out of here?" Sindy tried to conceal her irritation. She didn't need these extra hassles, especially not on this day. She started moving away to the bedroom.

"I need some time to think." Tim was pacing up and down the living area. "What options do we have?"

I'll give you some options, Sindy thought. *Wrong place, wrong time, buddy.*

"I think maybe we should stay here for a few more hours until we figure things out," she heard Liz say. "It's too dangerous to go back to my father's house or my apartment."

"Absolutely," said Hank. "You're safe here and you guys are most welcome to stay however long you like."

Sindy walked back into the room and slammed the door behind her. They all gasped as Sindy pulled out a .45 pistol and aimed it at them.

"Sindy?" Hank was frowning deeply. "You've got a gun pointed at us? At me?"

"I'm sorry it has to be like this."

"What's going on? What are you doing?"

"I hoped it would never get to this, but it has." Sindy's icy stare was trained on her prisoners.

"What's going on? I'm your husband."

"I really am sorry."

"You've got a gun to my head and you're sorry? We're married for Christ's sake. Have you lost your mind?"

"Shut up. Just shut up. I need to think." Sindy waved the gun at Liz and Tim and then pointed it back at Hank again.

"Who are you working for? What do you want with us?" Tim said.

"I said shut up." Sindy took a step forward and thrust the edge of the pistol against the side of Tim's head. "What's it going to be, college boy?"

Tim was trembling but remained silent.

"If you cooperate with me, I'll let you live."

"And if we don't?" Hank asked.

"I'll shoot you." Sindy spoke slowly as her cold eyes met Hank's.

"You wouldn't."

"Watch me."

"I'm your husband. I can't believe this is happening. What's gotten into you?"

"Nothing's gotten into me!" Sindy snapped. "And nothing you say is going to change anything. So just cut your crap and stop asking me all these questions."

"I won't. I need to know what's going on. What happened to the lady I married? The one who I called my wife? The one who loved me?"

Sindy laughed. "I've enjoyed the last few years, but you flatter yourself. I've never loved you. Not the way you loved me."

Hank's face reddened.

"It's not worth it, Hank," said Tim quietly. "She's obviously not the person you thought she was."

"Just shut up!" Sindy shouted. "All of you just shut up. I need to gather my thoughts."

"I can't believe you would do something like this," said Hank. "You're my wife."

"Well, consider this the equivalent of filing for divorce."

"Why are you acting like this?" said Hank.

"It's none of your fucking business. Now shut up."

"My own wife..." Hank looked at Tim and Liz. "You live with someone for so long and you think you know them."

"Don't wind me up, Hank, not now."

"Screw you."

"What?"

"Screw you. I loved you."

Sindy glared at Hank. She gave his wheelchair a firm side kick. The wheelchair fell back onto one wheel, and spun around for a few seconds, before toppling over completely.

"You pathetic piece of shit!" Sindy shouted. "What have you ever done for me?"

"You won't get away with this. Surely you realize that?"

"Oh, on the contrary, I will get away with this. I already have gotten away with this."

"There's no chance you'll get out of all this," said Liz.

Sindy walked over to Liz and slapped her across her cheek. Liz stepped back aghast, blood trickling down from her nose.

"Don't speak to me unless I ask you to. Hank won't be shot immediately. I guess I can give him that much, but you and your friend, I will shoot you right now without any hesitation. Do you understand me?"

"Yes, I understand you," said Liz. "Loud and clear."

"Don't hurt them," cried Hank from the floor. "They shouldn't be involved in whatever you're doing. Please don't hurt them."

CHAPTER 87

When Professor Greene had faced Rafik Jaffer on his boat, he had thought his life was about to end. But at the time when the first bullet fired by Rafik was released from his pistol, the boat knocked against a rock. The boat swayed and Professor Greene toppled over into the water a split second before the trigger went off. In situations of life and death, one split second can make all the difference.

As he had catapulted off the boat, Professor Greene felt himself submerged in the icy depths of the ocean. He swam deeper and deeper away from his captor, then stared up at the bottom of the boat in the distance. There had been a hail of bullets that penetrated the water, all of them narrowly whizzing past him. He swam towards the surface in the direction opposite to which the boat was travelling but remained underwater.

With a few brisk strokes, he edged himself further away. Seconds later, he pushed himself up to the water's edge and emerged, gasping for air. He took a few deep breaths and ducked under again.

After what seemed like an eternity under the water, the professor stuck his head out among the ripples of the ocean surface. In the distance, Rafik's boat was heading in the other direction. Professor Greene sighed in relief as he treaded the water.

He looked around him. There was nothing or no one in sight. Just him and the vast ocean. He slowly started to swim back to near where he had fallen off the boat. Maybe he could find the rocks, or whatever it was the boat had knocked into. He could hold onto it and rest. Someone was bound to come by soon. A speedboat, a private yacht, or even a fishing trawler. Cape Town had such a busy harbor, and there were several mini harbors along the coastline too.

A few more strokes, and he found himself in the area where he'd been knocked into the sea. There were no rocks anywhere near him. Just the relatively calm waters of the ocean. Surely this was where the rock had been?

He hadn't swum that far away? He turned and swam a few more meters. Still nothing.

Ten minutes of treading water turned into twenty minutes, and then thirty minutes. Not a boat in sight. Not even the lifesavers' helicopter that would sometimes purvey the vast stretch of coast.

While the professor became more and more consumed with fatigue, he did not realize just how strong the deceptive currents were. He was being pulled further away from where the rock had been and lulled into a powerful current stream that not even the best swimmers would have liked to endure.

An hour later, he had almost passed out. Still treading water in the middle of the sea, there was not another person in sight. Not even a kayaker. Professor Greene tried to get his mind off the fact that he might not survive this ordeal. He wondered just how far from the shore he actually was. He hoped there were no sharks nearby, nor any other creatures that could emerge from the ocean bed to lure him to death.

He tried to think of more positive thoughts, and inevitably his thoughts turned to Liz. Had she by now realized that she had to find the microchip? And would she have the insight to discover where the microchip had been hidden? He inadvertently swallowed a large dose of salt water as a small wave swept against his face.

The ripples were becoming stronger and a tidal current snatched him into a pressure zone. *Liz, it's up to you now*, he thought. *Only you can keep it going.* He had always had faith in Liz, his precious daughter. He could see her now, her bright smile lighting up her entire face. He clung to the image as the current pulled him under the water once more. Deeper and deeper and deeper, until there was no room to breathe. And then like a lion spitting out a bone after it has chewed its meat, the professor's unconscious body was thrust to the ocean surface, floating further down the sea.

CHAPTER 88

Sindy ignored the sounds of Hank's desperate pleas. *He's not going anywhere, even if he tried!* She remained focused on Tim and Liz, and continued to point her pistol at them.

"Let's talk about this," said Tim.

"No more talking," Sindy growled. "Now both of you move."

Liz and Tim stepped slowly in the direction Sindy was pointing in. It was a small room located just off the lounge.

Holding a large coil of rope, Sindy eyed Tim and pointed at Liz. "Now tie her up."

He didn't move. Sindy clicked the gun and moved it closer to Tim's face.

"Okay, okay!" Tim picked up the rope and began to tie Liz's hands behind her.

"Hurry up!" Sindy waved the gun.

Tim trembled as he tried to tie a knot.

"And make it tight," Sindy said. "So tight I don't even care if you draw blood."

"It's okay," Liz said and winced.

"Shut up," said Sindy. "And her feet too."

Keeping the gun pointed on Tim, Sindy examined the knots. "Looks like we have quite the Boy Scout here," she mused.

Sindy walked to the counter top to fetch another piece of rope. She handed it to Tim. "Tie your legs up."

When Sindy was sure that they were firmly tied and that Tim couldn't walk, she retrieved another piece of rope. She pulled his hands behind his back and wrapped the rope around his arms. Tim groaned.

"Too sore for the pretty boy?" Sindy smirked.

"You'll never get away with this," Liz said. "Not in a million years."

"I will most certainly get away with it. In fact, I am getting away with it."

Sindy bent down and peered into Liz's face. "As you can see, there are three people in this room at the moment. Two of them are tied up. I wonder who the person about to walk out of here is? Oh, hold on, it's me!"

Sindy walked to the door and glanced at her two prisoners. She started to laugh. Then she closed the door behind her.

Sindy returned to the lounge where Hank was still writhing around like a fish that had been yanked out of the ocean and left helpless in despair.

"You've always been so weak," Sindy said. She began to wrap rope around Hank's hands.

"I loved you," Hank said.

"Spare me the emotions."

"What have you done with the others?"

"They're tied up in the spare room."

"Why did you bring them into this?"

"I had no choice. They're your stupid friends. I couldn't waste any more time than I already have. They're lucky I didn't put a bullet through their brains." Sindy waved her pistol and then aimed it straight at Hank. "I should put a bullet through you too."

"Sindy, please don't do this. I'm begging you."

"So long, Hank."

"Please, we can work this out."

But Sindy had gone into their bedroom and didn't look back at her quivering husband. She pulled out a large duffel bag from her walk-in closet and began shoving clothes into it. She glanced at the digital bedside clock that was on Hank's pedestal. *Good, I've lost some time, but I'll still be able to make my flight.*

CHAPTER 89

Sindy was almost finished packing when she heard a click behind her.

"You're not going anywhere."

Sindy whirled around to see the barrel of a gun rammed straight into her face. At the other end of the gun was none other than Hank.

What the hell?

"You really should make your knots tighter in future."

"I... you... you're standing?"

"I sure seem to be."

"You're standing? Jesus! You can walk?"

Hank broke into a guffaw of laughter and did a little tap dance, his gun not wavering at all. "I can walk and I can dance."

"You fucking bastard. You could walk all along?"

"Every single minute."

"You fucking piece of shit. You made my life such a misery with that fucking wheelchair and all along it was one big act?"

"Oh, my dear wife, would it really have changed anything?"

Sindy glared at Hank. "It might have."

"Don't lie. We both know it wouldn't have made any difference."

"You're pathetic!" Sindy shouted. "You fucking bastard."

"On the contrary, if anyone is pathetic, it's you. How could you just walk out and leave me like that? After all these years? You pulled a gun on me, tied me up and then left me for dead," Hank hissed. "Give me one good reason why I shouldn't shoot you right now."

Sindy couldn't think of any immediate reason. She viewed Hank with extreme contempt. *The bastard could walk all along.*

"Why would you pretend you couldn't walk? I don't get it."

Hank held his gun firmly in the direction of Sindy's chest.

"It was a good way of not being bothered. I could carry on with my main business dealings without any hint of suspicion."

"Business dealings? Suspicion of what? What on earth could you possibly be doing that you would be worried about getting attention?"

Hank laughed again but didn't answer her.

"If anything, you always wanted more attention for your sorry miserable existence." Sindy was fuming.

Hank continued to laugh.

———

When he was in his early twenties, soon after finishing college, Hank acquired a disease which attacked his muscles. As a result of the sickness, he lost the use of his legs, and was told by several doctors and specialists that he would unfortunately never be able to walk again. Hank did not take kindly to the news, and despite the severity of the diagnosis, was determined not to spend the rest of his life confined to a wheelchair.

Every morning, he would lift himself out of his wheelchair and attempt to do various exercises. He started with simple things such as ten push-ups a day. For someone not able to use his legs, the push-ups were grueling, and it took a long time before Hank could complete ten of them. He eventually mastered them and then gradually built on his exercise routine just using his upper body.

After his daily upper body exercise routine was in place and he was able to keep fairly fit, Hank would spend another hour each day meditating. He would gather his thoughts and allow himself to sink deeply into a meditative state. Once he became in tune with his inner being, Hank used the process of visualization and the law of attraction, of which he was a firm believer, to help heal his disease.

As part of his ritual, he would visualize himself doing all sorts of activities using his legs. He would see himself running along the contour path on Sea Point's beachfront. He would see himself hiking up Lion's Head, and he would see himself cycling past the Twelve Apostles. He kept on with these visualizations and sunk his thoughts deep into each experience as if his body was actually there.

And with this persistent routine of exercise, meditation and visualization, two years later, Hank was able to use his legs again. He had proved wrong all the doctors and specialists who had treated him and told him he would never be able to walk again. He had achieved what people in medical circles had thought to be unthinkable. He had triumphed, and for himself had proved the powerful truth that is known as the law of attraction. He had shown that the mind is an all-conquering place and if one desperately wants something, miracles can be performed.

Hank decided it would be better not to tell anyone that he had use of his legs again. Given his chosen work activities and the need to work anonymously, it suited him for his family and friends to think of him as the poor soul who was wheelchair-bound. He did not want to attract any more attention than necessary and, particularly when it came to his wife, he could not reveal his achievement.

Sindy had stopped swearing now and was trying to come to terms with the fact that Hank could actually walk. It was not something she had ever seen coming. And now she was staring down the barrel of his gun. *Why didn't I just tie his legs anyway?*

"Let's give us another try." Sindy slowly stretched out her right leg to rub it against Hank's but he stepped to the side and caught her foot.

"Don't try anything stupid," Hank said.

Hank took a deep look into her eyes. For a few moments they were both silent.

"You're as shallow as you always were. Even when we met and I thought I was in love with you. How the tables have turned." Hank now lowered the gun slightly and aimed it at Sindy's chest. "I must admit that you played your role very well with regards to tonight." Hank's eyes gleamed as his gun remained firmly focused on Sindy.

"Tonight?" Sindy spoke slowly. "What are you talking about?"

"Rafferty's banquet. And the part you've played."

Sindy stumbled backwards onto the bed. *How would he know that?* "I don't know what you are talking about."

Hank laughed. "Then why have you gone so pale?"

"I'm not."

"I'm sure everything will go according to plan. Thanks in part of course to your involvement."

"What are you going on about?"

"Oh, come on. Have you not worked it out yet? Do I really need to spell out the obvious?"

It can't be. It just can't...

"Your orders were clear and the project is almost over. All for a good cause, right?"

"You're the Fox?" Sindy did not want to utter the words that she knew would confirm a shocking ugly truth for her.

"You better believe it." Hank was laughing hysterically.

"It can't be."

"Oh, but it is, my dear dear Sindy."

"All this time? But how... ?"

"I've been playing you as I needed to do." Hank was grinning. "You were just one of the many pawns in my game."

"I can't believe it." It wasn't often that Sindy struggled to find words. "How could I not have known? We've been together for so long. We live together, dammit."

"You didn't know because I didn't want you to know. Isn't this fairly obvious?"

"But you? How could you be the Fox? Why would you hide yourself from me when you knew I was doing work for you anyway?"

"That's the way I wanted it. No inter-connectedness."

"But we were fighting for the same cause."

"No," said Hank. "We weren't fighting for the same cause. Mine is a much higher purpose than just terrorism."

"I'm not a terrorist!" Sindy spat.

"Let me guess, freedom fighter?" Hank said. "Don't be ridiculous. You're so narrowly focused. You always were."

"Fuck you, Hank."

"And since I don't need your services any longer, and since you've never really cared or shown compassion for anyone in a wheelchair, I might as well just shoot you now."

"You bastard. You'll always be a hapless cripple to me."

"And you'll always be the terrorist lady who worked for one of the greatest masterminds of our time and didn't know it." Hank pointed the gun at Sindy.

"You won't get away with this."

"If you could only see the expression on your face now!"

"So after everything I've done for you, you're just going to shoot me?"

"I don't see why not. You've done what I needed you to do. I'm really sorry, though, that you won't see how things unfold at the banquet."

"I'm sure you are." *How could I not have known he is the Fox?*

"You had your chance," Hank said and laughed. "And you blew it."

"It doesn't have to be over," said Sindy; her elbows were leaning back on the bed now. "It really doesn't have to be."

"It was over a long time ago. You said as much yourself."

"Well, I didn't know the real you, did I?"

"So suddenly you like what you see?"

"I can help you with your business pursuits. Now that I have seen the real you, don't you think that I can be an asset?"

"Why on earth would I think that?"

"We can make such a great team."

"I have no use for you, Sindy."

"Take a chance. I'll make it with your while."

"Goodbye, Sindy."

Before Hank could pull the trigger, Sindy launched herself off the bed and executed one of her trademark kicks, knocking the gun out of Hank's hand. The gun fell to the floor, and Sindy quickly gave another kick, knocking Hank to the ground. As he fell to the floor, his foot inadvertently knocked the gun and it went sliding far under the bed.

Before Hank could even gather his breath and stand up again, Sindy had grabbed her duffel bag and sprinted out the bedroom and then out of the apartment.

CHAPTER 90

The fresh ocean breeze gave Odwa Mckaiser a renewed sense of vigor as he continued to paddle furiously through the currents. As he lifted his oar, he focused on what it would feel like to win the Dusi canoe marathon. His daily kayaking in the sea was just part of his training. He had almost decided to sleep in that day, but his motivation had gotten the better of him. Now, he was glad he had not broken from his routine. It had been a strenuous two hours so far, and the strong tide was making his strokes more difficult. But twenty minutes earlier, he had kayaked near several dolphins that were edging in and out of the waves. Being so close to the dolphins was exhilarating, and Odwa was on the lookout to see if any more of these magnificent creatures were nearby as he headed towards the shore.

He moved his oar again through the water and the kayak suddenly tilted as it collided with something. Odwa regained his balance and stared ahead to see if he could spot what was floating in the sea. *Please let it not be a shark.* He leaned forward slightly and peered over. *Maybe it's just a seal?*

The current weakened momentarily, and a look of sheer horror spread across Odwa's face as he saw that it wasn't sea life he was looking at but a human. Odwa dived into the sea, not even noticing just how cold the water was. He turned the body over to see an elderly man with a beard. *Is he alive?* The man was not moving. Odwa grabbed onto the kayak with one hand and pulled it toward them. Then he nudged the body as close as he could to the kayak.

Odwa released his grip on the kayak so that he could use both hands to try to lift the body. He treaded the water as he hoisted the man upwards. He could only get the upper half of the man onto the kayak. He rested his arms briefly on the kayak and took another deep breath. Then he swum underneath the man's feet and now elevated the rest of him upwards, pushing him onto the kayak.

Odwa stared at the man on the kayak and his eyes widened as the person

237

he had just hauled out of the sea opened his eyes and looked at Odwa in equal surprise.

The floating body of Professor Greene had edged through the waves like an abandoned canoe. Every few seconds his body was briefly flung into the air where it would remain momentarily before plunging into the ocean once more.

Professor Greene was sprung into consciousness as he found himself being pushed out of the sea. He lay on the kayak and stared at the person looking at him from the sea. A wave enveloped him and, as he gasped, the water cascaded into his mouth causing him to splutter. He coughed as another wave crashed over him and the kayak rocked back and forth. He felt weak throughout his body as his mind replayed the events at sea. He remembered staring at the madman pointing the gun at him and then he remembered falling over the edge of the boat just as the thug was going to fire at him. He had miraculously dodged the bullets that had then littered the ocean. He had been treading water and did not know how long he had been in the sea. He had become exhausted and eventually he couldn't hold out for any longer. The next thing, he was being lifted into a kayak. He wondered just how much time had passed. And then the professor's thoughts shifted to Liz.

I've got to get him to shore fast, Odwa thought as he tugged the kayak in the direction of the shoreline. Odwa was kicking frantically now and urgently trying to push through the treacherous currents with one hand.

He saw some rocks in the distance and took solace in the fact this could only mean they were nearer to the shore than he thought. The tide was still trying to pull Odwa back into the ocean's depths, but he resisted with all his might. He was determined to navigate his cargo to the safety of the beach.

The kayak jolted suddenly. Odwa turned in alarm. It had knocked into the tip of a jutting rock, and a hole Odwa had repaired recently was instantly ripped open. Odwa reached for the man in his kayak and grabbed him as the kayak began to sink rapidly.

He pulled the bearded man next to him in a type of bear hug, making sure he was facing upwards. Then he glided him along while desperately pushing through the water with his other arm. Odwa gasped for air as a wave crashed against them. He could feel the sting of the salt on his lips. He was grateful they were approaching shallow water.

They were able to dodge some of the protruding rocks as he guided them towards the low waves of the beach. Before they even got out of the sea, they were able to stand in the sinking sand while the water still nudged against them. Odwa trudged nearer the beach and with each step tried to make sure that his companion was still conscious. Soon, they were on the sand.

They stumbled onto the ground together. Odwa was out of breath and fell backwards onto the sand. Every muscle in his body ached. He was sure he was dehydrated, and felt very fatigued. The sun shone brightly into his eyes and he lifted his arm to shield himself.

———

Professor Greene's head was swirling and he began coughing out salty seawater. He closed his eyes and groaned softly. The morning's events had taken their toll on him. Although he was alive to tell the tale, he was sapped of all his energy and didn't have the strength to crawl further up the beach. A wave reached his feet and then another one behind it reached his hips. A third wave covered his whole body, including his head. He spluttered some more and tried to sit up before collapsing back onto the sand.

"I must find Liz," he muttered. "The microchip."

As the waves continued to rise on the sand, Professor Greene felt the water envelop him. And then he passed out.

CHAPTER 91

Hank couldn't believe it. Rafik had stolen the black box for him as ordered. Then he had discovered that the chip was missing. Despite his further instructions to Rafik not to let the girl out of his sight, they had managed to get rid of their tail and the Fox had thought himself to be in a dire situation as the missing microchip eluded him. He had wondered if this whole mission had been in vain, and if he ever would be in possession of a fully functional black box.

And then the girl stumbled right into his life. The odds of that happening were just so bizarre, Hank had to pinch himself to make sure that this was really happening. He knew that Tim was coming, but he had been so busy he had lost sight of the actual dates Tim was going to be in Cape Town. He couldn't believe then that, out of all the girls Tim landed up with, it was the professor's daughter. And he couldn't believe that Tim had inadvertently brought her to his lair. *With the microchip!* Opportunity had literally knocked on his door and he had grabbed the situation with both hands.

Now, Hank walked into his study. A large bookcase stacked with books, both fiction and non-fiction, were on display. Hank reached for a brown book that was towards the end of the top shelf. He removed the spine to reveal a button he then pushed. There was a soft hissing sound as the entire bookcase slid forwards slightly, revealing a gap behind it. He sauntered through the gap and into his hidden study, where he loaded the black box and his computers into a secure steel case on wheels. He had a few discs and several memory sticks, which he shoved into the case too.

He looked around the small room that had been his workstation and operational center for so long. He was sure he had packed everything he needed. There would be no trace of his work once the police eventually showed up. By that stage, he would be long gone. It would be as if he had never been there, besides all his other personal possessions he had inevitably accumulated over the years. And his wheelchair! He smiled as he looked down at it. All those long hours he had to sit in it to keep up his charade. The sacrifices of living a lie!

He laughed out loud. In the end, it had been worth it after seeing Sindy's face. He wished he'd taken a photograph or two. But, as with many of life's priceless moments, that happened unpredictably; cameras were often not there or not ready to capture the event, and if they were ready they inevitably missed that crucial split second that makes up a moment.

Hank always knew that the time to depart his home in Cape Town would come. His plans were all in place. He had specifically kept his computer system mobile so that, when the time came, everything could be easily packed up and transported with him. It was a quick exit plan. Hank stuffed some loose pieces of paper into the back pocket of his pants, and after one more look around the room he was satisfied everything important had now been removed. *I just need to get the microchip now and I can be on my way.*

———

Tim's hands ached as he continued wiggling them around, trying to loosen the rope.

"I've got a slight gap in the rope over my right hand," Tim whispered.

"Good, keep trying," said Liz. "I can't move my hands or legs at all. And they're going numb."

"I'm sure I'll be able to get at least one hand out of this bind."

"You can do it," said Liz.

Tim grimaced as the hard rope wedged into his skin while he strained his wrists. He maneuvered his fingers and was able to find a small gap. There was definitely a slight loosening.

The door suddenly opened and Hank strolled in.

"What? You can walk?" Tim's mouth fell open. "Or are my eyes playing tricks on me?"

"You better believe it!" Hank said and grinned, evidently enjoying the shocked looks on the faces of his prisoners.

"How?" Tim demanded.

"Because no doctor could tell me I would never walk again," said Hank fiercely. "I will not live my life how someone tells me I can or can't do something. I do things on my terms, and I decided that I would walk again."

"Why the charade then?" Tim said.

"Ah, the mysteries of life." Hank chuckled. "Anyway as much as I would love to chat, it's not you I came in here to see."

Hank turned to Liz and sauntered towards her. "You have something I've been trying to lay my hands on for ages. I would say hand it over but that might be a bit difficult given the fact that your hands are tied."

"Well, untie me then," said Liz.

Hank was standing right in front of her now. "I don't think so," he said.

"Leave her alone," said Tim. He had managed to free one hand behind his back. "Liz doesn't have anything that you need."

"Ah, but she does," said Hank. His eyes were gleaming. "And it's fallen right into my lap."

Hank leaned closer to Liz and stuck his hand into the small pocket on the side of her jersey.

"Take your hands off me!" Liz yelled.

"Temper, temper." There was nothing in the pocket. He put his hand in the pocket on the other side of the jersey.

"Leave her alone, Hank," said Tim.

"What are you going to do about it, Tim? Wait, let me guess. Nothing! As usual." Hank turned back to Liz. "Well there's nothing in your jersey pockets, so it looks like I am going to have to venture downwards."

"Get away from me!" Liz shouted. "I don't know what it is you want from me."

"Lies, lies," Hank said. He reached down to Liz's jeans and pushed his hand deep into her pocket.

"Get away from her!" Tim yelled. His other hand was almost free now.

Hank pulled out a container from Liz's pocket. "Well, well, what have we here?"

"It's nothing!" Liz said furiously.

Hank ignored her and opened the container. He stared inside it and lifted out the microchip. Tim watched as Hank beamed at it, almost in a trance.

"Isn't it amazing, Liz, how an object so small holds so much power?"

"Please don't do this," Liz pleaded.

"What do you want it for anyway?" said Tim.

Hank just laughed and headed towards the door. "That's all folks!" he waved and slammed the door behind him.

In his excitement to be finally holding the microchip, Hank did not notice that the loose sheets of paper he had shoved into the back of his pants' pocket only moments earlier were now lying on the carpet in front of Liz and Tim.

Tim leapt up and ran to Liz.

"You're free!" Liz said.

"Let's hope we can still get the microchip back," said Tim as he pulled open the double knot that had bound Liz's legs together, and then untied her hands. He helped her to her feet. "You okay?"

"I'm okay..." She smiled.

"Let's keep our voices down," Tim whispered. "We need to take Hank by surprise."

"Hopefully he's still here," said Liz. She bent down and picked up the papers that had fallen out of Hank's pocket.

"What are those?" said Tim.

"Not sure..." Liz stared at the first page. "But we can worry about these later. Let's get that microchip."

They stood by the door and listened for any sounds on the other side. But they couldn't hear anything.

Liz nodded to Tim as if to say, *Let's take a chance.* Tim opened the door slowly and they peered around. The apartment was quiet.

They tiptoed towards the lounge. As they passed the main bedroom, Tim

THE MIND OF GOD

noticed a gun sticking out from under the bed. Tim grabbed it and gave Liz a nod. They headed to the lounge; it was clear the apartment was deserted.

"He must have just left," said Liz.

A throttling sound emerged from behind the windows. It was coming from above them and was getting louder with each passing second.

"Can you hear that?" said Tim.

But Liz was already dashing out of the front door.

CHAPTER 92

Professor Greene's weary sea-battered eyes opened again, this time on the beach with his open mouth full of sand. He tried to sit up but didn't have the strength. He spat out the sand from under his tongue and between his teeth. The sun's rays streamed onto his face and he closed his eyes gratefully that he was on firm ground again.

It had been yet another lucky escape for the professor, who seemed to equate his survival with that of a cat. He tried to move his body up the beach but was still too drained. In the distance he thought he saw a group of people running towards him. He lifted his head slightly and used his arm to shield his eyes as he peered at the moving picture that was becoming clearer now. Indeed, several people were shouting and waving their hands as they sprinted towards him.

Two muscular men, with bright red lifesaver caps, and several other men and women in swimming costumes had run to the spot where Professor Greene and the man who had saved him had landed up.

"Are you okay?"

The professor nodded as one of the men crouched down and stared into his face.

"Are you all right? Can you hear me?"

"I'm okay."

"What did you say? Can you hear me? Are you okay?"

They had all surrounded the professor now and were staring at him intently.

"Okay. I'm okay."

Another wave swept itself over the professor's legs.

"Let's get him away from the tide," the other lifesaver said.

At least eight pairs of hands gripped the professor and lifted him into the air before moving him several meters away from the water's edge and into the welcome shade of some unusually leafy palm trees further up the beach.

"Get him some water," someone said.

Seconds later, someone was holding a bottle at the professor's mouth as the water trickled inside. The professor sipped the water slowly and began to feel better with each sip.

Soon he could sit up. He could see people crowding around the man who had saved him. They were giving him water to drink too.

"Are you okay?" The man with the red lifesaver cap leaned down.

"Yes, I'm okay."

"These seas can be rough. What happened?"

"It's a long story…"

"You're lucky you got here in one piece. These tides can be vicious, and so can the sharks."

"That guy saved me," the professor murmured.

"What did you say?"

"That gentleman saved my life." The professor sipped some more water. "If he hadn't spotted me from his kayak I wouldn't be here right now."

"That's amazing," said someone in the crowd. "Wow."

The professor tried to stand and almost fell down again.

"Whoa, what you doing? Take it easy; your body has just been through so much. Just rest a bit."

The professor looked at his watch. The glass on the face had been smashed by some of the rocks and the watch was broken.

"I need to go," said the professor. "I've got urgent business to attend to."

"Just need the paramedic here to check you out. Then can we take you somewhere?"

"Yes!" The professor's mind was starting to swing back into action. "Yes, thank you, there is most definitely some place you can take me."

———

Hank had run out of his apartment and down the corridor. He opted to use the stairs in the emergency fire exit instead of the elevator. There were only a few flights of steps to the actual roof of the building and he leapt up two stairs at a time. A minute later, and he reached a large dirty cream-colored door. He pushed down the silver rail that stretched across it and forced the door open. He made sure it swung closed behind him and ran through a small tunnel before emerging onto the roof of his building, which was also the launch pad for his private helicopter.

He fumbled in his jacket pocket for his key and unlocked the large door in front of him. Once inside, he flipped some of the buttons above him and on the dashboard, and the helicopter engine began to throttle while the propellers started to swing around. As the propellers gained momentum, the helicopter began to shake even more. He glanced one more time at the apartment complex roof.

So long!

Hank smiled as he felt for the microchip now safely tucked in the inner zipped pocket of his jacket. He would not reunite it with the black box just yet.

A few seconds later the helicopter lifted off the ground, hovered over the launch pad as it swayed from side to side, and then charged up into the sky. Hank looked down at the roof of his complex as the helicopter surged higher and higher.

All the lights on the dashboard indicated that everything was in proper working order. Hank had serviced the chopper three weeks before. In fact, he made sure he gave it a full and proper inspection every two months. Just in case he had to use it suddenly like he was doing now. He liked to believe that he always had any contingency covered.

———

Liz and Tim stepped through the door leading to the outside area and saw the helicopter lift off in the distance. They raced towards it. Tim clutched the gun. *How the hell do you fire this thing?* He aimed it at the helicopter, closed his eyes, and pulled the trigger.

The helicopter swayed as Hank quickly veered it to the left.

Tim looked over the railings at the end of the deck and peered at the ocean below. He noticed a speedboat that was docked in a small private jetty. He climbed over the railing.

"Get yourself to safety!" he yelled to Liz as the helicopter began to lift itself higher.

"What?" Liz shouted. The throttling was deafening.

"Go help Michelle and get help," Tim shouted, gesturing for Liz to go back inside. "Take Hank's car."

"What are you doing?"

"I'm going to get the microchip for you."

"You'll lose him."

"Just get yourself to safety. I'll sort this out!" *Unfinished business.*

Tim fired another bullet at the helicopter but Hank had already moved the chopper away and there was no impact. Before Liz could say anything else, Tim had run down the outer flight of steps leading to the jetty and halfway down he jumped into the sea next to the boat. He quickly pulled himself onto the boat, pulled the starting cord, and the engine purred as he kicked it into gear. The boat went even faster than Tim had expected and he held onto the steering wheel while at the same time trying—literally—to stand up to the breeze and the heavy Southeaster wind that was now battering itself against anything in its path.

The sea was choppy. The boat moved slowly at first. Then, after navigating the strong currents, it kicked up a gear and sped into the distance. Tim stared ahead as he tried to navigate the currents. The Southeaster seemed to hold the boat in its clutches and no matter how Tim tried to turn the wheel he couldn't escape its might. It seemed as if the boat had come to a standstill although it was still travelling quite fast.

He steered left but the boat hardly turned. He tried to then veer to the right but again it was as if he were in the middle of two brick walls and was getting sucked along a narrow passage leading into the abyss.

Tim stared up at the helicopter. Despite their college friendship, Tim had always regarded Hank as a bully. Hank would often belittle Tim or pass negative comments. Tim had never been able to work out whether Hank's disparaging remarks had been to boost Hank's own ego or to deliberately put Tim down. Either way, he had reluctantly put up with it during their years of study in order to keep some semblance of friendship alive and also to keep the peace. Tim was not one to make enemies, and he had gone through his life deliberately avoiding any conflict that would make its way towards him.

And here he was. In a speedboat shooting bullets at a helicopter above him being piloted by none other than his old college buddy. Tim had wanted to catch up with Hank in Cape Town but he had no idea that it would be like this. And in that moment while the sea breeze pummeled icy drops into him, he knew that he would make sure Hank did not get the better of him in this situation. It had been a long time coming, but Tim would finally put Hank in his place. No one was above anybody else. Least of all a friend from college. Tim would get the microchip if it was the last thing he did. And Liz would be eternally grateful.

CHAPTER 93

Sindy was about to get into her car when she realized that she didn't have her passport with her. *How could I be so stupid?* She slammed the door shut and deliberated what to do.

It certainly was a risk heading towards Hank again. *He really is the Fox?* On the other hand, she would have to come back again at some point if she left now without her passport. And she wouldn't be surprised if in the meantime Hank changed their security access codes.

Sindy could hear the distant throttling of a helicopter kicking into gear.

Hank must be leaving here in his helicopter! Sindy smiled and waited a few more seconds. The throttling sounds were getting louder and louder as the helicopter got ready for lift-off. *Perfect!*

She turned and headed back to the underground parking entrance for residents only, leaping up the stairs.

She could handle those other idiots, but Hank had probably left them tied or locked up. He wasn't that stupid. Sindy contemplated everything that had been revealed to her. No, Hank wasn't stupid at all. All this time, and she had no idea that he was actually the Fox, nor that he was able to walk again. It was a surprise that he could even fly that damned helicopter. How could she have not picked up the truth?

Sindy got to the floor of her apartment and stopped cautiously outside the stairwell. The front door was wide open.

Arsenic has long been described as the "Poison of Kings" and the "King of Poisons". The tiniest drop is enough to cause maximum damage and destruction. Throughout history, this poison has led to numerous famous deaths. Many believe Napoleon Bonaparte, King George the Third of England and the nineteenth century political leader Simon Bolivar all lost their lives as a result of arsenic. The classic signs of severe arsenic poisoning include nausea, vomiting, low blood pressure, diarrhea, and then death.

Driving back towards the outskirts of Cape Town, Wahied turned the corner. His thoughts shifted to President Rafferty and all of his guests drinking their specially prepared bottled water at the looming banquet. There would certainly be bodies everywhere, including that of the most powerful man in the world. Wahied couldn't stop smiling.

———

Hank had seen the speedboat below and had not realized that it was someone trying to pursue him until the bullet whizzed past the chopper, missing his windscreen by a centimeter. He pulled the gearstick and the helicopter did a sideways maneuver before darting higher into the sky.

There's no way it could be Tim and Liz. Not so soon. I just left them all tied up.

The wind had died down and another few shots were fired from the boat below.

"Dammit!" Hank cursed.

Hank ducked and dived the helicopter as another volley of shots sounded. A bullet smashed into his side window. He steered the helicopter sideways again. The force of the air gushing through where the side window used to be was too much for the chopper to retain its equilibrium and it fell a few meters.

Hank pushed the chopper into autopilot and reached behind his seat for the compartment where he kept his spare gun. He pushed it through the smashed window and began firing back. He launched bullet after bullet, round after round, and soon he had struck the speedboat below.

Hank grinned. He had successfully caused some major holes in the boat.

He could make out Tim's figure in the boat now. "Say hi to the sharks for me!" Hank was laughing now as he steered the helicopter higher again.

But then the helicopter began to chug and splutter. Hank stared at the dashboard in horror. The bastard had struck his fuel tank. In a few seconds the helicopter began to sway and veer downwards. Hank zipped up his jacket, grabbed the metal case that contained the black box, and reached for his parachute. He swung open the helicopter door and jumped out. Seconds later, his helicopter crashed into the sea, causing a fiery red cloud to smoke its way into the sky.

The icy seawater enveloped Hank's body like a coiled python as his parachute glided him into the water. As he hit the ocean, he lost the grip of his gun, and the metallic case began to float away from him. He tried to ignore the cold pangs as he lunged himself towards the case. He couldn't let the black box go like this.

Another bullet hit the water and another one. Hank swam beneath some waves and opened up his mouth for air as he came momentarily to the surface. He saw the boat had stopped moving. It must have been fifty meters from him. As he gasped for air, he saw Tim standing on the boat still aiming his gun at him.

"You wouldn't really shoot me," Hank coughed. "You don't have it in you."

"Give me the microchip!" Tim shouted.

"Fuck you."

Tim clicked the gun and fired it. But nothing came out.

"Looks like you're out of ammo, old buddy!"

Tim dived into the water. Hank saw Tim approach through the swirling current and ducked to the left just as his Tim launched himself through the wave.

Hank kicked as fast as he could to propel him faster and move his entire body forward. But everyone has their limits, and the Fox knew that his limit was the ocean. He had always hated being in the water, from his very first swimming lesson as a child when his instructor had literally thrown him into the deep end of the pool. Hank could tread water for hours and he could swim far distances if he had to, but he could only do that with all his energy. He couldn't focus on anything else when he was in water but the water itself. And he knew if it came to fighting with someone in the sea, he couldn't rely on the outcome going his way.

———

Tim tried to see through the bobbing waves where Hank had gone. He spotted an arm gliding through the water and immediately dived in that direction. He swam with all his might and energy, and soon Hank was once again within his grasp.

With one large butterfly swoop, Tim landed on Hank's back.

"Give it up, Hank," Tim spluttered.

"Screw you."

Tim pushed Hank's head under the water and held it for a few seconds while Hank writhed like a guppy. Then he yanked Hank's head out of the water and shoved it under the water again. He was on top of Hank and mustered all his energy to pull out Hank's head once more before shoving it under the water.

"This will teach you!" Tim shouted. "Not the hero you've always liked to make out are you?"

Hank coughed up some more water as Tim yanked his head out of the water again.

"Please, Tim."

"How does it feel now, to be so helpless? To be on the receiving end for once in your fucking life?"

A strong current ploughed into Tim and he began losing his grip on Hank. Tim lunged forward again to grab Hank's neck but could not get a firm hold. He began to slide off completely but was able to hold onto both legs. Hank turned his head and took a swipe at Tim as Tim pulled both of them under the waves. He missed Tim's face by inches and Hank then threw a punch at Tim as they plunged deeper. His fist connected with Tim's chin but because of the strong currents, it was not a strong punch at all.

———

Both men shot up to the surface and gasped for air. Tim was still holding onto Hank. Another tidal current swelled around them and while ducking another punch Hank noticed that the metallic case with the black box had drifted a few more meters.

"My case," Hank pointed and gave a sturdy kick with his left leg into Tim's face. This time he made contact with Tim and Tim let go his grasp in agony.

Hank turned away and swam towards the metallic case, which was bobbing on the surface. He stretched his arm out and grabbed it. Then he reeled it in towards him.

He couldn't see Tim anywhere, and hoped he had been sucked in by the overwhelming tide. The speedboat was now sinking. *Must have been from my bullets.* Hank clung to the case and swam a few meters further. He could tread water for ages if he had to.

CHAPTER 94

Liz watched Tim jump over the railings and head towards the boat as Hank's helicopter roared into the sky. She turned around and charged back inside the building and slid down the stairs as fast as she could.

She desperately wanted to go help Tim get the microchip, but she had to trust him. She had to believe he would get the microchip back, somehow. *I don't know how a boat can pursue a helicopter anyway.* No one could have predicted they would walk right into the lion's lair, and that Hank was the one responsible for stealing the black box in the first place. And so Liz had to do something she had battled to do previously—put her trust in someone else and accept that Tim could help her.

Liz headed back into the apartment and began searching for where Hank kept his car keys. *Maybe in the bedroom?* She started walking towards the main bedroom but stopped suddenly. *Was that a creak?* She peered inside but the room was empty. *My nerves!* She walked into the room towards the dressing table on the far end.

She glanced into the nearby mirror and her mouth fell open in shock as she stared straight into the reflection of Hank's wife standing behind her.

Liz turned around but, before she could even try to run past Sindy, Sindy had leapt into the air and kicked Liz in the stomach. It was another neat roundhouse kick and landed firmly in the solar plexus. Liz doubled up in pain and fell to the floor. She lay there holding her stomach.

"Please just leave me alone," Liz said.

But Sindy had jumped in the air and, as she came down to land on Liz's writhing body, like a wrestler trying to score the winning point, Liz rolled out the way and Sindy thumped to the floor.

"Bitch!" Sindy shouted.

Liz grabbed a bedside lamp and smashed it onto Sindy's head. Liz charged towards the bedroom door. She had almost made it through when an arm grabbed her ankle and she tumbled over. She kicked out and yanked her leg away. Liz rolled away and found herself in front of the room she and Tim had been held captive in.

Sindy clambered to her feet and jumped on Liz again, this time landing right on her. Liz winced as Sindy's knees jutted into her lower back. She tried to wiggle away but Sindy was too strong for her and had now grabbed her throat from behind.

Liz edged sideways slightly and moved her hands up to try to loosen Sindy's grip on her. She was unsuccessful and choked for air as Sindy's grip tightened.

"You little piece of shit!" Sindy said. "You fucked with the wrong person today."

Liz mustered the last bit of strength she could find and turned her head towards one of Sindy's arms. She sunk her teeth into Sindy's arm like an angry pitbull. Sindy screamed in pain and let go her grip.

Liz was able to shake her off her back and rolled away again. As she turned, Sindy tried to lean forward again to grab her, and Liz was able to kick her in the face. Contact was made with Sindy's cheekbone and she yelped as Liz now stumbled to her feet.

Liz knew what she was looking for now. She had seen it earlier on the granite countertop next to a silver tissue box holder and a few loose pegs. She managed to get to the counter top before Sindy grabbed her again, this time reaching for her hair. She yanked her back with all her might and Liz whined in pain. As she fell back she was able to reach for the object that she had seen earlier. *Thank goodness I noticed it.* The memory games she used to play with her father when she was a child had held her in good stead.

Liz flicked open the small object she was clutching. It was a pocket can of mace. She sprayed it into Sindy's face and Sindy reeled back as the spray gushed into her eyes.

"What have you done, you bitch?" Sindy rubbed her eyes, trying to stand up at the same time.

Liz looked around. The only large object nearby was the crystal vase. *Such a nice vase. Oh well.* She lifted the vase and smashed it onto Sindy's head. Sindy fell down again and this time she didn't get up. Liz stared at her as the tears began to flow. She had survived yet another attack on her life that day. She leaned down to see if she could hear any breathing. She was relieved to hear that Sindy was alive. *Knocked out but still alive.*

Liz grabbed Sindy's arms and dragged her into the room in which she had been a prisoner. She locked the door from the outside, then breathed another sigh of relief. On the key ring was the Audi emblem. These must have a spare key for Hank's car. It couldn't be too difficult to find the Audi in the parking lot downstairs. Liz grabbed the bunch of keys, charged out of the apartment, and headed down the stairs.

CHAPTER 95

"It's over for you, Hank!" Tim shouted even though he couldn't see where Hank was.

"It's never over for me!" Hank yelled. "Never."

"What have you done this for anyway?" Tim shouted back. "Why the hell do you need Liz's father's experiment so much anyway?"

"I have my reasons."

The flames from the crashed helicopter had not gone unnoticed by two police patrol boats that were routinely touring the coast. Hank and Tim's verbal exchange was now drowned out as the police patrol boats roared towards them.

"Officers, please arrest that man!" Hank sounded hysterical. "He tried to kill me."

The officers looked suspiciously at the men floating in the water.

"Don't listen to him," Tim pleaded. "He's a criminal."

"We'll have to take you both in for questioning," the officer said, nodding towards the bullet holes.

Two officers leaned over the railing and helped hoist Hank onto the boat. The other officers kept their guns aimed at Hank. Another officer kept his weapon on Tim, who was now edging towards the speedboat.

Tim was then hoisted onto the other patrol boat. He gladly slumped onto the cushioned seat near the entrance to a small sheltered area. His body was aching from his fight with Hank but he knew that Hank would not give up. *It's not over yet!*

"He tried to kill me," Hank said and pointed at Tim.

"We'll sort it out at the station," one of the officers said gruffly. He glanced at the officer behind the wheel. "Let's go."

The police boats edged in closer towards the harbor jetty. In front of them the hustle and bustle of one of Cape Town's premier tourist attractions, the V&A Waterfront, beckoned.

The afternoon was rapidly approaching sundowner time and cocktail hour as the numerous restaurants, bars and cafés would be doing their best to lure customers to their establishments. The Waterfront would be packed with holidaymakers and locals alike. *The perfect place to get lost in the crowds,* Hank mused as the boat he was in came to a standstill.

Tim's boat pulled up behind them. The officers formed a circle around Hank and Tim as they headed towards the station house. Not wanting to cause unnecessary alarm among the tourists, the policemen kept their weapons in their holsters but remained ready for anything untoward from their new suspects.

"Officers, you need to arrest this man." Hank said. "He's responsible for this whole mess."

"We'll get to the bottom of it when we're in the station house," said one of the officers.

"We need to bring you in and get your statements and so on," another officer said and looked at Hank.

"Very well." Hank nodded. "But I'm the victim here."

Tim opened his mouth as if to protest but seemed to realize it was of no use.

Some crowds ahead had stopped to admire a mime artist posing as a statue. At first glance it looked like the artist was indeed a statue. There was no movement at all. More and more people were stopping to appreciate this spectacle and the path in front of them was now blocked.

The entourage came to a standstill as the policemen laughed at the mime. Tim turned to glare at Hank again. But with all the attention focused on the mime artist, Hank had disappeared.

———

As the Audi sped into the suburb of Rondebosch, Liz wondered what Macmanus had been doing during her ordeal. She needed to tell him that the Fox had taken the microchip but that Tim was in pursuit.

Macmanus was standing on the front lawn puffing away at his pipe and staring at the daffodils.

"Are you all right?" He looked surprised to see Liz.

"Quick, get in," Liz beckoned.

"Do you still have the microchip?"

Liz explained what had happened while she steered the car in the direction of Michelle's house. They would be safer there. Macmanus looked deep in thought and nodded gravely as Liz gave an account of the last few hours since she had fled.

"We didn't get to finish our conversation earlier about the microchip," said Liz. With all the stress, she had almost forgotten to ask the question again that had been puzzling her the most. "If there are all these black boxes around the world, why was my father's black box targeted? Why should anyone care specifically about his microchip?"

"Your father's black box is different to all the others," he said.

"How so?"

"Well, for starters, the other black boxes don't have any microchips."

"They don't?"

"Nope. Your father developed the microchip aspect himself."

"So what is so special about the microchip?"

Macmanus paused. "Well, it's still a work in progress but your father has taken a great leap forward in the world of quantum physics. Your father was working on another scientific experiment that was not specifically linked to what we were doing at the Global Consciousness Project," Macmanus explained. "Some time ago your father independently developed some very complicated algorithms that have changed the face of science completely."

"I thought the black box has changed the face of science completely," said Liz. "And now you're saying that in addition to this, my father worked on something else so groundbreaking?"

"Exactly! In a nutshell, without explaining to you all the actual scientific complexities, your father's experiment was able to tap into the future on a scale not seen by the black box experiments."

"What do you mean?"

"The algorithms revealed elements of being able to predict the future, although the experiment was not conclusive. Professor Greene then took his research one step further. He incorporated his research into a small microchip that he then fused with his black box—with our permission, of course.

"He wanted to mix the algorithms with the ordered effects of the black box. Whereas the black box with its transhuman tendencies and mass event predictions is shared by a global consciousness, your father believed that if he synergized his findings with the black box, it would then be able to reveal the exact date, time, and nature of events in the future."

"What?" Liz shook her head in disbelief. "Maybe you should be discussing this with Michael J Fox! It sounds like another *Back to the Future* movie to me."

"This is serious stuff." Macmanus looked grave.

"So what were the results after my father merged his microchip with the black box?"

"The results were startling." Macmanus was almost whispering now. "The microchip accurately predicted the exact fluctuations of Apple shares on Wall Street for one week after the prediction."

Liz felt a cold shiver run through her as she tried to absorb what she was hearing. As if the knowledge of the black box was not enough, she now had to try and come to grips with this new information about the microchip that could accurately predict the future.

"But shares always go up and down," Liz shrugged. "Maybe the prediction was just a lucky one?"

"It was an extremely accurate prediction," said Macmanus. "The exact date and amount were predicted. It's uncanny."

"Surely you can't be saying that you can predict the future based just on that?"

"Well, not just that. As with all our science, one needs to perform the experiment numerous times in order to see if the results are consistent."

"And did you do more experiments then?"

"Your father conducted several more stock exchange experiments with the microchip embedded in the black box. Some of the predictions were vague and inaccurate, but for the most part the results have been astonishing."

"So you're saying that you can basically take control of Wall Street?"

"I'm saying that if we can predict the exact time and amount of a rising share in the future, then why can't we expand beyond stocks? Surely we should be able to predict other things too? Who will win the Super Bowl next year? Who will find the cure for HIV/Aids and when will it be found? Will Iran really drop a nuclear bomb on Israel? The questions are endless. The course of humankind as we know it has changed forever."

"So that's why the microchip is in such demand," said Liz as the realization began to sink in. "If you know who is going to win the Super Bowl next year, then you can place your bets now and get great odds. If you know when HIV/Aids will be cured you can plan towards it. If you know that there will be a nuclear holocaust, you can take steps to prevent it. In the right hands, it can do great good for humanity. In the wrong hands, it could be manipulated by those wishing to make money, destroy lives or control the world and its destiny."

"Now that's the type of clever reasoning I'd expect from Harry Greene's daughter," Macmanus said and nodded approvingly. "I must iterate, though, that your father's experiment is a work in progress. The black box combined with the microchip has only predicted very short-term events. We can't currently prove anything further than a few months. There are predictions that it has made for the next few years, including startling revelations about life on Mars, but we need to wait for the years to pass so we can get to that point in the future to see if the predictions are correct."

"I still can't believe something like that is plausible though."

"You can adopt an ostrich mentality like so many other people on the planet, or you can embrace new science and possibility as part of man's journey towards our next stage of evolution, our inevitable noosephere."

"It's a lot to take in," Liz said quietly.

"We were going to meet in three weeks' time with the senior executive members of the GCP to discuss the implications of the microchip, and the way forward given your father's extraordinary breakthrough," said Macmanus. "We had suspected your father was being watched, and he knew he had to be cautious just in case. And luckily he took all those steps to hide the microchip. Although events have now just got out of hand."

Macmanus paused and then leaned closer to Liz as he stared into her eyes. "We better pray that your friend is able to get the microchip back."

CHAPTER 96

Liz parked on the driveway of Michelle Sloane's house and ran to the front door, knocking on it frantically.

"Michelle," she yelled, pushing the small button for the doorbell too. "Michelle. Are you here?"

"There's no car on the driveway." Macmanus appeared behind her.

"I've just had this bad feeling all day," Liz said. "I was supposed to be here this morning to help her with something very important."

Liz started walking around to the back of the house.

Macmanus followed her back to the driveway at the side of the house and headed straight for the garage door at the end of it. Liz realized that the door would probably be locked but she tried to pull it open anyway. But the door remained tightly closed. There were several tiny cracks in the wood on the door, and Liz leaned down and placed her right eye against a crack near the bottom. She squinted but it was no use. She couldn't see anything; it just wasn't big enough.

Liz scrutinized a few more cracks and as she looked through the last one, she thought her eye caught a blur of a car.

"Hold on, I think I see something."

Macmanus looked on with interest as Liz continued to try make out the blurred shape she was seeing on the other side of the garage door.

"I think I see her car. No wait, I'm sure it's her car. So she is here then," Liz said and ran to the front door. "Michelle, are you in here? Michelle?"

"Anybody home?" Macmanus yelled.

They stood and listened for a response as a passing truck roared past them.

"Michelle?"

"I'm in here." The sound of a soft voice emanated from the inside of the house.

"Michelle? Is that you?"

"I'm in here." The voice got slightly louder. "Help me, Liz. I'm inside the house."

Liz turned to Macmanus. "Did you hear that?"

"I did. Sounds like she needs help."

"Michelle? Are you okay? What's wrong?"

"Help me. I've fallen and can't get up off the floor."

"I'm here, don't worry. We'll sort this out."

"I can't move and the front door is locked."

Liz turned the handle on the door and leaned against it, trying to push it open. Her knee still ached from her fall at Rhodes Memorial, and her arm was still bruised and sore from her scuffle with Sindy. She tried to ram it with her shoulder and winced in pain as the door didn't budge.

Without a word, Macmanus walked over to the flowerbed and dragged a large log behind him as he trudged back to the front door. He picked it up and rammed it against the door. There was a loud crack as it connected to the door but the door remained steadfast. Macmanus took another deep breath and charged towards the door again. This time the log caused another crack in the door that was much louder than the first one.

"Wow, that's great," said Liz. "You're almost there!"

"Whew, I'm not as young as I used to be," said Macmanus. He let out a groan as he charged towards the door for a third time. There was a loud thump as he crashed through the door and landed onto the cold tiles staring right into the face of Michelle.

———

Michelle stared dumbstruck at the man who had just crashed through her front door and was now lying on the tiles face to face with her. He seemed as startled as she was, and was rubbing his head.

"Eric Macmanus at your service." He winked at her.

Before Michelle could say anything, Liz rushed in and was leaning over both of them.

"Are you okay?"

"I'm fine," Macmanus uttered.

"I was talking to Michelle! What's wrong?"

Michelle pointed to her leg. "I can't move it. I think it's broken."

"What happened?"

"I slipped down the stairs. Can you believe it? Of all the things to happen to me, I fall down the stairs on the day I'm supposed to be meeting Eric Simms."

They carried Michelle outside the house towards the chaise lounge on the stoop. The breeze brought some welcome relief to Michelle, sure that the fresh air would help her until they could get her to the hospital.

"Let me get you some water." Macmanus walked back inside to search for the kitchen.

"I still can't believe this day," said Michelle.

"It's not over yet, Michelle," Liz said determinedly. She began to explain the events of the last few hours to Michelle and finished as Macmanus came back outside.

"Here's some water."

Michelle gulped it down.

Liz sat down and immediately stood up again as the papers she had stuffed into her back pocket wedged against her. She hauled them out and sat down again. They were the papers that had fallen out of Hank's pocket when he had locked her and Tim in the room in his apartment. She had forgotten about them.

"What are those?" said Macmanus.

"I don't know," said Liz. "They fell out of Hank's pocket. I figured they must be important, otherwise why would he have been carrying them around?"

Liz scrutinized the details in front of her. It looked like a map of various corridors and rooms. She looked to see if there was a name or a place on it that she recognized but could not find anything among the detailed lines and shapes.

"I'm not sure what this is a map of," she said. "Looks like the inner workings of some building."

Macmanus peered over the document. "Conference rooms," he said, pointing to some small words that had been scribbled in various parts.

Liz lifted the page and looked at the second page behind it. It was a page that was filled with stickers. The stickers were oval in shape and consisted of writing that surrounded an emblem in the middle that resembled the White House.

Liz and Macmanus looked at each other in surprise and both repeated the words out loud at the same time: "*Office of the Presidency!*"

CHAPTER 97

After exploring as much of UCT's upper campus as he could, Mike wearily trudged up the hill all the way back to Rhodes Memorial and to the parking lot where he had left his car. He was sweating and out of breath. It had been hours and there had still been no sign of Liz and her male friend anywhere.

Mike slumped into the driver's seat and slammed the door behind him. He rested his arms over the steering wheel and buried his head into them.

How could I have let them get away? I was so close. So fucking close.

Mike closed his eyes and reflected on the day's events. He had to sort this out. He couldn't be away from his home and his family any longer.

A tapping on the glass interrupted his thoughts. He stared up quickly, his heart racing at the intrusive sound. A car guard was standing at the window, moving his hand in a backwards motion as if to tell Mike that there were no cars behind him and it was fine for him to reverse.

"Fuck off!" Mike waved the guard away. He watched the guard head off to an old lady walking towards a Mercedes.

Each time Mike had gotten close, and each time they had slipped away. Elusive like a tadpole that you think you've caught in your hand but each time you try and scoop it up it slips through your fingers. *So close yet so far.*

There had to be something that stood out for him. Some type of clue that could indicate where they would flee to. He had already covered the professor's house and the university campus. He had looked up Liz's address and sent the police to her apartment. They had told him there was no one there. They were keeping an officer outside the apartment block, and would inform Mike the minute the girl or her friend pitched up. But Mike knew she wouldn't go to her apartment. *She doesn't seem that stupid.*

Mike sighed as he continued to retrace his steps. And then it dawned on him that he had completely overlooked something. They had approached another house in Rondebosch before they fled from him again. Another house that was near Professor Greene's house. If they were trying to make contact

261

with someone there, chances were they might try again. Whether or not this theory would work, Mike decided to roll the dice one more time, like a gambler who puts his last chips on the table and prays that good luck and fortune will favor him.

Mike kicked the engine into gear, reversed out of the parking lot, and drove out of the mountainous estate.

———

After an unproductive interrogation, the station commander decided to release Tim, especially when it became clear that Hank was the one who they needed to find and bring into custody. Tim was exhausted and just wanted to get back to Liz. He walked slowly out of the police station and headed towards the bustling shopping precincts. As he went down a small flight of stairs, a tasty scent of barbeque wafted towards him. He hadn't realized just how hungry he was until now. He saw the restaurants in the distance and thought he would grab a quick burger before trying to get a cab back to Rondebosch.

As Tim turned a corner he felt something hard being rammed into his back.

"Don't move," a voice hissed in his ear. "Or I'll blow your fucking brains out."

"Hank?"

"For starters, keep your voice down. Now you're going to listen very carefully to what I tell you. Understand?"

The object was pressed even harder into Tim's back.

"Understood?"

"Yes."

"Which pocket is the microchip in?"

"Which pocket?" Tim repeated.

"Don't fucking play games with me, Tim."

"It's in my jacket pocket, the zipped one."

"You're going to slowly unzip it and then you are going to put your one hand in your pocket and take out the microchip."

Tim wondered if this was how his life was going to end. There was still so much he wanted to do. He certainly wasn't ready to die.

"Do I make myself clear?" Hank rammed Tim's back again.

"Yes," said Tim. "Crystal."

"You see that bench down there?"

Tim nodded.

"Let's go there where you'll be less noticeable. If you play another trick on me then it's game over for you."

Tim nodded again. His heart was pounding violently.

"Okay," said Hank. "Now we're going to walk very slowly towards it. I don't want you so much as looking at anyone or anything else."

Tim contemplated what his odds were if he made a run for it.

"Do you fucking understand me?" Hank barked.

"Yes, I understand you."

"One wrong move and you can kiss your miserable life goodbye. And I mean it. Don't think I'm joking with you."

"I understand," Tim said again. "I'll cooperate."

"Damn straight you will. Now let's go."

They walked along the paved path towards the bench in question. It was on the side of the path that streamed off from the main area and was not as busy. As they walked, a man and a lady holding hands walked casually in their direction.

"Stay cool," Hank whispered. "Don't fucking play me."

The couple sauntered past them and the lady gave them a smile and the man ventured a polite nod. If they had stopped and looked closely, they would have seen the fear in Tim's eyes. His heart froze as they walked past and sank when they disappeared into the distance. No one could help him now.

CHAPTER 98

"Office of the Presidency?" Michelle pointed to the stickers.

"That's what it says..." Liz was mystified.

A screeching noise came from the side of the stoop. Startled, they all whirled around to face the driveway. A thin kid on a skateboard whizzed past them.

"Goodness," said Liz. "My nerves!"

"Nkosi, come here," Michelle beckoned. "He was one of the first orphans who I helped. Like a son to me."

Nkosi gave them a polite smile and jumped off the skateboard.

"I want you to meet my good friend, Liz," said Michelle. "And her friend, Professor Eric Macmanus."

Nkosi shook their hands and then leaned down to tie his shoelace. As he bent over, something fell out of his pocket. Macmanus reached to the ground and picked it up. It was a hundred-rand note.

"You dropped this." He handed the money back to Nkosi.

"Nkosi, where did you get that?" Michelle asked firmly.

"It's mine!" Nkosi protested.

"Nkosi?"

"Okay, someone gave it to me."

"Someone gave you a hundred rand?"

"Yip."

"Just like that?"

"They asked me to do something for them. It's not a big deal." Nkosi began to skate towards the main part of the house.

"Nkosi, come back here; we're not finished discussing this."

Nkosi sighed. "It's really no biggie."

"When someone hands you one hundred rand it is a big deal to me," said Michelle.

"I was walking in the gardens in town. Some old guy offered me some money to do something for him."

"What guy? What did he ask you to do?"

Nkosi stared at the floor.

"Nkosi?"

"No one was hurt or anything. I didn't do anything wrong. It's nothing."

"Just tell me."

"But then you can't be cross with me. The man said that the insurance would sort it out and that I would only be causing a temporary inconvenience."

"Nkosi, what is going on?"

Liz and Macmanus watched in silence.

"This guy asked me to go down to the Convention Centre parking lot. There was a specific car I had to go to and break a window in it. That's all."

"That's all?"

"I didn't take anything from the car if that's what you are wondering." Nkosi was indignant. "I just had to smash the glass and run off."

"Are you saying some man in the street came up to you and offered you money so you could go smash someone's car window?"

Nkosi nodded. "I didn't hurt anyone or anything."

"And you were told to smash the car window and then run off?"

Nkosi nodded again.

"Without taking anything from the car?"

"Yes," said Nkosi. "I didn't take anything at all. The man said I was just to smash the window and run out of there."

"And you don't know whose car it was? Was there a logo or something on it?"

"Nope." Nkosi shrugged.

"Okay," Michelle said. "We can chat more later."

Nkosi nodded and sped off around the corner on his skateboard.

"It sounds very strange," said Liz.

"I'm afraid I don't know what's going on either," Macmanus confessed.

"Some guy out of the blue asks a street kid, someone he doesn't know, to go do something like this," said Liz. "It doesn't make any sense."

"It would be more understandable if the guy had asked Nkosi to take something specific from the car," said Macmanus.

"But just to smash the window and run?"

Liz stared at the presidential stickers in her hand. She then looked again at the other document, the map that contained various rooms and passages.

"It's a mystery indeed," said Michelle. "But it's probably something we'll never know the truth about."

Liz suddenly went pale. "Isn't the American President due to speak at the Convention Centre?"

Macmanus nodded. "Rafferty is giving a speech at some function there tonight."

"It's got to be linked," said Liz. "We were wondering what this map was of. It has to be of the Convention Centre."

"How can a car break-in be linked to a presidential banquet?" Macmanus scratched his cheek thoughtfully.

"They're connected. I can't explain it; I just know it."

"Well, what are you going to do then?" Macmanus said. "Run up to President Rafferty and say, *Excuse me, I think your life is at risk tonight. I've got no proof or anything but I just thought I would let you know?*"

"Well, what other explanation could there be?" said Liz.

"We just don't really know if this incident with Nkosi is even linked to the presidential visit."

"It must be linked. The whole incident sounds very suspect. And now we have documents that were in possession of a criminal that show passages in a convention center."

"Suspect, yes. A presidential assassination plot, hardly."

Liz suddenly remembered Tim telling her about the stranger he was chatting to on the plane, and how the man had told him to stay away from the places of business. She had completely forgotten about it until now. At first she had thought it was just someone engaging in strange banter, as it didn't make any sense at all. But now it seemed another vital piece to add to the puzzle.

"It's another reason pointing to something happening at the Convention Centre," Liz said after telling Macmanus and Michelle.

"It might be a bit of a stretch," said Macmanus.

"I can't just sit here. We've got to do something," said Liz.

"And even if there was some plot, don't you think the presidential security agents are up to protecting Rafferty? We're talking about bodyguards for the President of the United States here. You won't even get close to the guy. No one will get close."

"We have to try do something," said Liz.

"She's right, I'm afraid," said Michelle. "Nkosi would never make something like this up."

"Yes, but maybe this incident was about something else. You yourself told me how high crime is in this country."

"Hands up now!"

Liz, Michelle, and Professor Macmanus looked up in shock as a man appeared in the doorway. He'd come from the back part of the house.

"What's going on?" Liz gasped.

"Hands where I can see them!" A man stepped onto the stoop. "You!" he said to Macmanus. "Go sit next to them."

Liz was pale. *It's the same guy who was chasing Tim and me today.* "Who are you? What do you want with us?"

"You've got a lot of questions to answer, young lady." He had his pistol aimed at all of them, moving it slightly every now and again from side to side so they knew he could shoot any of them at any time.

"You won't get away with this," said Michelle. "The police often patrol this area."

"The police listen to me," said the man. He reached into his pocket and hauled out his badge card. "CIA. Special division."

Liz looked at the card incredulously. "CIA?" *What the hell is the CIA doing here in Cape Town?*

The man was about to put it in his pocket when Nkosi appeared again, this time holding a raspberry ice cream.

"Freeze," he said and dropped his ID, aiming the gun at the kid whose ice cream immediately fell to the floor.

Nkosi immediately scurried into the corner and wedged himself between Michelle and Liz.

"If you're CIA, why have you been chasing me?" Liz demanded.

"Why have you been running?"

"I didn't know that you were on the side of the law."

"It looks like your father murdered someone at UCT in the early hours of this morning," he said slowly. "And as you were last seen with him at his house, that makes you an accomplice."

"What?" Liz felt like a truck had just knocked into her. "Did you just say my father murdered someone?"

"Yes, I happened to be on the campus. I saw him drag the body."

"My father is not a murderer," Liz said. "He wouldn't harm a fly."

"Well, I know what I saw," said the man.

"There must be a suitable explanation," said Liz.

"And then he goes back to his house and then you go there, and suddenly when I go inside you've all gone."

"There's been a mistake," said Michelle. "Liz's father can't be responsible for such a crime. He just can't be."

"In any event, Liz was informed earlier that her father has been killed," Macmanus spoke slowly, conscious of the fact that a gun was being pointed at him by someone who looked like he was about to pull the trigger.

"Been killed?" said the man. "Who killed him?"

"Some gangster who has been chasing us around all day," Liz said. "We thought he was with you."

"I don't know any gangsters," he spat.

"So then who has been chasing her?" said Michelle.

"Beats me," said the man. "I'm not out to kill anyone. I just want answers. And justice."

"I think he was after my father's microchip," said Liz.

"What?"

Liz briefly explained about the black box and the microchip but the man remained expressionless as he listened.

"Don't fuck with me," he said. "You better be telling me the truth."

"I am telling you the truth," Liz pleaded. "I want answers too. This has been the worst day of my life."

———

The girl's story seemed authentic. Her version of the events of the day could be plausible. Mike's instincts told him that there was maybe more to it; that maybe her father was innocent. And if that was the case, then Mike had been chasing the wrong people all day. He needed to find the thug who had been chasing them too. He could care less about some scientific microchip. He just wanted to be on the soonest flight home.

"I'm just handing the young lady a tissue." The elderly man motioned to his pocket and waited for Mike to nod before he handed it to Liz, who promptly tried to wipe off the relentless onslaught of tears.

"What the hell is that?" Mike had noticed the map and the page of presidential stickers that were now lying by Liz's feet.

"It's a map of the Convention Centre."

"And those stickers? Those are the official emblems for the US Presidency." Mike's eyes remained transfixed on the documents as his face went crimson.

"I think we've got a huge problem on our hands," said Liz. "I think President Rafferty's life is in danger."

Still in the lounge of his secure hotel suite, Dan Rafferty brushed the curtain to the side and peered out the newly implanted bulletproof window overlooking the bay. In the distance, several ships were docked in the harbor and the waterfront itself was a hub of activity. He looked in awe at Table Mountain as he tried to consume its majestic splendor. What a place. He had traveled all over the world, although this was his first visit to Cape Town. And he loved it. Truth was, he was totally bowled over by the scenery. Pity he wouldn't have time to see the sights. He would definitely have to make a point of coming back. Perhaps when he retired? He smiled at even the thought of retirement.

His thoughts were interrupted by a soft knock at the door.

"Enter."

"Everything is on schedule, Mr President. We are just fine-tuning the last segment of the changes you requested for your speech."

"Good." Rafferty nodded. "And my meeting with our ambassador is still in forty-five minutes?"

"Yes, Mr President. From there we'll make our way to the banquet dinner."

"Thank you, John."

"Thank you, Mr President." The Chief of Staff closed the door behind him.

Rafferty returned his gaze to the panoramic view and his mind shifted to the fake bomb that had been discovered earlier that day. He still believed there was no realistic or credible threat to endanger him. All security channels were in place. How could they not be? He was after all the President of the United States of America! He had traveled many times with his entourage and he trusted them completely.

He was glad he had not canceled the rest of his Cape Town visit. What would it look like in the world's eyes if he had suddenly boarded Air Force One and headed for Washington just because of a hoax? Not good at all.

As the sun began to set, a cluster of clouds moved ominously over Table Mountain, causing the first part of the tablecloth to come into place. Rafferty was so deep in thought, he did not notice the sky darken.

———

Mike's gun was now back in his pocket. He reached for his cellphone. He could call whom he needed to directly to ensure the president did not go ahead with his banquet plans.

"Damn!" Mike swore. "Still no fucking cellphone reception."

"Why don't you try the landline?" Michelle pointed inside.

"The people I need to speak to won't answer calls from a random landline." Mike sighed. "I need to get to the Convention Centre immediately."

"And there's absolutely no one you can phone from the landline? Not even a call center or something?"

"No."

"And the police?"

"There's no guarantee that phoning the police will solve the problem speedily," said Mike. "We just don't know the intricacies of what's going on. Any actions now could endanger the president even more."

"I'm going with you," said Liz.

"No, you're not," said Mike. "Stay with your friend until an ambulance gets here."

"I'll be fine," said Michelle.

"I'll stay with her," Macmanus said.

"You won't be able to get through all the presidential security." Mike glared at Liz. "Some of his staff know me, and I've got clearance anyway."

"You've got nothing to lose with me coming," Liz insisted. "And if I stay here I might be putting my friends in danger. That killer is still after me."

Mike sighed and then gave a grudging nod. He had no strength or inclination to get into an argument with an already-emotional woman. "Let's go," he said.

Liz followed him off the stoop. She turned to wave to Macmanus and Michelle. "You sure you guys are okay here?"

"Of course we're okay," said Michelle.

Mike pointed to the Audi. "Yours?"

"Well, it's not quite mine, but I drove here in it."

"Throw me the key," said Mike. "It will get us there much faster than my hired car."

CHAPTER 99

"Give me the microchip now," Hank hissed.

Tim reached into his pocket and as he did so he caught their reflection in one of the large shop windows opposite the bench. As he fumbled for the plastic container, he noticed in the reflection that the object Hank was ramming into his back did not look like a gun at all. Tim stared at the window. It seemed that Hank was holding a stick. *He's been bluffing me! He's not carrying a gun.*

Tim clenched his fist in his pocket. He looked carefully at the reflection, and suddenly jerked his hand out and smashed it up behind him so that it collided with Hank's nose.

Tim didn't wait to see just how much or little he had hurt Hank. He charged off the bench and sprinted down the lane back towards the main path that led to the busy shopping district.

"Just give me that fucking microchip," Hank yelled after Tim.

"No way," Tim shouted back.

"Don't make me kill you!"

Tim had already cascaded down another flight of stairs and was now running through another restaurant district that stretched its way along the water's edge. He glanced over his shoulder to see Hank stumble a bit but then gain momentum again. He couldn't let him catch him.

Tim took a sharp turn and headed down another alleyway. He ran through another corridor that housed several shops and took another turn that led outside again.

A large crowd was making its way towards him. It looked like a tour group and judging by their accents it seemed they were from the Caribbean. He shifted closer to the group of tourists. As the group walked past Tim stepped out of the shadows and joined them. He pushed through some of the people until he was in the middle and less noticeable.

Tim looked behind them. He couldn't see Hank anywhere. He couldn't be totally sure but it seemed like he had lost him. He quickly deliberated whether to run inside the center or stay outside. He decided there was more chance of getting away if he stayed outdoors.

He sprinted ahead and found himself in the middle of a children's play area. Kids were running around with ice creams while parents hovered around making sure their children were safe. Tim headed past a clown on stilts. The clown was making balloon animals for a delighted group of kids who were tugging at his legs.

The loud bang of a balloon popping caused a nearby mother to scream and then grin sheepishly as Tim dashed past. He hastily turned another corner, colliding with a lady in a short brightly colored dress. They both tumbled to the ground. He recognized her instantly as the British music sensation Ellie Goulding. He had read about her in a magazine article on his flight.

Tim stared at her. "Ellie Goulding?"

"Yes," Ellie smiled.

"You okay?"

"I'm fine," said Ellie. "What's the rush?"

"What are you doing here?"

"A private fashion shoot for charity." Ellie pointed to a camera crew a few meters down.

Tim briefly considered whether it would be a good idea to ask her for some props to disguise himself. He thought he saw Hank in the distance and before Ellie could say anything further, he bolted off towards the big Ferris wheel ahead. He pushed to the front of the queue, much to the disdain of a young couple who were about to pay for their tickets.

The woman in the booth frowned at Tim but took his money anyway. Tim took his ticket and quickly made his way along the short maze formed by a coil of red rope, and entered the vacant compartment that now dangled before him.

"Expecting anyone else?" said the official as he took Tim's ticket.

"No." Tim shook his head.

The official slammed the door shut and seconds later the wheel started to move.

———

Hank navigated through the crowds. He cursed that he had lost sight of Tim. He surveyed his surroundings like a hungry vulture and headed down past the play area in the direction of the big wheel. Ahead of him some trapeze artists had hoisted one of them up into the air. As he gazed at the trapeze artists, his eyes shifted to the big wheel in front of him, and in particular to Tim getting into one of the carriages. In a fit of rage he pushed his way through the cheering crowd and ran towards the red ropes.

"You need a ticket first," the official pointed to the kiosk. "And you'll have to wait until the next ride. The wheel has already started to move."

"I'll pay later," Hank grumbled and shoved the official out of the way.

"Sir, you have to pay first."

"Bite me."

"Sir, come back. You cannot go there. The wheel is already in motion."

But Hank did not hear the pleading of the official nor did he really care. All he could see was Tim, and all he needed to get was the microchip. The wheel had started to move slowly and the doors for the carriages had all been tightly shut.

Hank waited for one to go past him and he jumped onto the outside of the compartment as it began to ascend. A woman was inside it with her two boys and her face went pale as Hank's figure was suddenly thrust against the glass. The boys pointed excitedly at the person holding on tightly to their moving carriage but within seconds Hank had edged past their window and had hoisted himself onto the top of the carriage. He crouched on the roof and balanced himself so as to not go tumbling to the ground.

The wheel continued to rotate. A few carriages above, Tim stared down in horror at Hank jumping onto the moving wheel and then maneuvering himself onto his compartment's roof. Hank looked up and his eyes gleamed when they met with Tim's. "I've got you now," he said.

The wheel turned further and now Hank's carriage was dangling higher than Tim's. Hank leapt down onto the carriage below him and in another instant onto the roof of the next carriage after that. Hank grinned menacingly, as he was now just one carriage away from Tim.

He leapt onto the roof of Tim's carriage and, lying across the roof, he tried the lever. It would not budge. Hank made a tight fist and punched the window. The glass cracked on impact but otherwise remained intact. Tim had backed away to the other end of the compartment.

Hank punched his fist at the glass again and this time caused the glass to smash.

He looked down. Several police officers had now cordoned off the area below the wheel and were pointing their guns at Tim's carriage. The screaming crowds were being pushed away and the wheel was being stopped periodically so that each carriage that got to the bottom could be urgently vacated.

But Tim and Hank were still high up. Their carriage came to a standstill as the officials tried to clear the carriage at the bottom of the wheel. Hank had managed to get through the door now and was climbing in when Tim charged at him.

Hank hurled his fist at Tim and Tim went sprawling into the far corner.

"Where is it?" Hank said.

"Fuck you, Hank." Tim was holding his chin.

"Where is the microchip?" Hank's words came out slowly.

The wheel began to move again and then stopped. Hank's hand was bleeding from the glass.

"The microchip is with me, and not with you," said Tim, standing up. "And that's what matters."

Hank glared at Tim and lunged towards him, this time with his other hand. Tim saw it coming and stepped out of the way just in time. It was Hank who now stumbled over into the far corner. Before he could get up, Tim landed a punch in Hank's face. And then another one.

"You think you can always get the better of me?" Tim shouted. "Well this time you didn't."

"Fuck you." Hank spat up some blood.

"You'll never get your hands on the microchip," Tim yelled. "It's over for you."

The wheel was moving again.

"And I've told you before," said Hank. "It's never over."

As the wheel stopped in midair, Tim lost his balance slightly. The next thing he knew, Hank had lunged into him and they both went down onto the floor rolling towards the glassless exit. Hank managed to rip off Tim's jacket, and pummeled his face and stomach. As the carriage began to descend again, Hank lost his grip on Tim and Tim rolled back into the corner of the compartment. Hank quickly unzipped the pocket of the jacket but there was nothing inside.

"Where is it?"

"You mean this?" Tim reached into his pants pocket and brought out the little plastic container. "Why do you want it so much anyway?" Tim dangled it in front of Hank.

"It's the future," Hank spluttered. "There's nothing else on this planet like it yet."

"So what are you going to do with it?"

"I don't know yet. But whatever I decide, the future belongs to me."

"Say goodbye!" Tim grinned and threw the container towards the opening.

"No!" Hank yelled as the container flew out of the compartment.

Tim moved out of the way as Hank charged after the container and leapt in the air to grab it. With the exception of one hand that was trying to hold onto the inner rail, most of Hank's body was out the compartment dangling in mid air. He caught the container with his other hand that was still bleeding profusely. His body thumped against the outside of the compartment.

"Got it," he gasped, turning to look at Tim.

The wheel clunked into gear again and began to move. The sudden jolt caused Hank to lose his grip of the inner rail. He stared wide-eyed at Tim as the momentum threw him out of the compartment and into the air. Seconds later he was lying in a pool of blood on the concrete below.

———

Tim stumbled to the seat in the carriage and slumped into the corner. This ordeal was finally over. He exhaled loudly. As the wheel descended, Tim stared at the crowds that had gathered. The area was swarming with police now. The medics would probably be there any minute too.

Tim's body ached and he could barely move his arms. He reached into the little coin pocket at the top of his jeans and pulled out the microchip. He held it up to the light and smiled. He was glad he had taken it out of the plastic container it had been kept in. A coin pocket had not been the best place to keep it in, but at least it had been kept safe from returning to Hank's grubby paws. *A silicone of wafer!*

Tim hoped Liz was okay; he couldn't wait to see the expression on her face when he handed the microchip back to her. His compartment arrived at the bottom of the wheel and Tim gladly welcomed the officials helping him onto firm ground.

CHAPTER 100

Mike drove into the underground parking lot at the Cape Town International Convention Centre and edged the Audi into one of the last available parking spaces. The CTICC had now been closed off to members of the public and only those on the guest list were being admitted through the booms. The official in charge of this latest roadblock was part of the visiting American security delegation. He recognized Mike and waved them through.

Liz leapt out of the car and Mike chased after her.

"Wait, there's a private entrance from the parking lot!" Mike yelled. "There'll be too many crowds at the regular entrances."

Liz stopped and looked to where Mike was pointing. She caught up with Mike again and a few minutes later they were inside one of the foyers of the CTICC.

Vast amounts of guests were queuing to get onto the escalators, so Liz and Mike headed for the emergency staircase. Again, there were crowds of people standing in the vicinity, as well as several armed guards and security officials.

Liz spotted a small area that housed four elevators. Luckily, there was hardly anyone standing on that side of the auditorium. "Down there." Liz nodded to Mike.

They rushed past a waitress holding a tray filled with champagne glasses and pushed the button on the wall marked "up".

The elevator chimed as it landed on the lobby floor and the doors slid open. Liz and Mike stepped in and were about to push the "close door" button when several more people stepped inside.

"Next floor, please," one of the men said and motioned for Liz to push the button.

The doors slid shut and the elevator began to ascend. Liz bit her lips. There would be two other stops before she got to the floor where the function was being held. She looked at Mike and then at her watch. She hoped there wouldn't be any problems with security. The elevator doors opened and three of the occupants got out. The doors began to close again when a grubby hand suddenly appeared and forced the doors to open. A group of laughing teenagers charged in. They were chattering excitingly and reeked of whisky.

"We're actually going up," a man in a green turban spoke from the back.

"Ah well, we'll come for the ride," one of them said.

"I don't think that the elevator will hold all of us." A small lady wedged next to Liz pointed to the sign above the floor buttons. "It says that the elevator can only take a maximum of ten people at one time."

"So what?" one of the teenagers sneered.

"Well, there are at least fifteen of us in here."

"We'll be fine. Who are you? My mother?"

The teenagers roared with laughter as the elevator continued throttling upwards. Liz wiped some sweat off her cheek. She and Mike were now wedged in the far back corner and would have to navigate through everyone when the elevator stopped on their floor.

The elevator began to slow down and started to shake.

———

The crowd rose and erupted into a chorus of clapping as President Rafferty headed for the podium.

"Thank you, thank you." He motioned the audience to sit. "It's not every day you get to speak in such a beautiful city like Cape Town. I can see why it has been referred to by many as God's Paradise." The audience clapped again and the president waved and smiled. "Indeed, the people of South Africa can be proud," said the president. "You are all a shining light of democracy."

The banquet room was packed. Chairs were tightly nestled together and there was not an empty one in sight. On the small makeshift stage, two large screens flanked either side of the podium. Behind the president was an array of South African and American flags. Secret Service personnel, as well as South African police members were scattered around the room, and also interspersed at various strategic points among the audience.

Tiny security cameras on the walls and ceiling blended in with the décor of the room and went unnoticed by the crowds. Unnoticed with the exception of one of the photographers who was seated in the third row. He stared anxiously at the walls and then shifted uneasily in his seat. He held his camera up and continued to snap away, just like the rest of the photographers in the room, who were all hoping their images of the president's speech would be the ones chosen by their editors to grace the front pages of their newspaper dailies, websites and magazines.

The photographer in the third row glanced nervously at his watch. Soon he would have the pictures for which he had flown into Cape Town this morning. He didn't really need the photos of the president speaking to the crowd. To him that was just mundane news. He was there specifically to capture images of something else relating to President Rafferty. Something that would really make people around the world take notice. His death.

The elevator grinded to an abrupt halt. The doors remained closed.

"What's going on?" someone enquired.

"Dunno."

There was a brief silence until the lights went off.

"Jesus."

"Looks like a power failure or something."

Motherfucking electricity, thought Mike. He hated elevators at the best of times.

The emergency lights flicked on. Although the lighting in the elevator was now a dim red glow, the occupants could all see each other.

"Not more load shedding," said the man with the turban. "I think the elevator might be stuck."

"Push the emergency button," Liz said from her corner.

I can't believe this is happening, thought Mike. *Of all the elevators, we had to choose this damn one.*

One of the teenagers pushed the emergency button. It released a shrill ringing.

"Switch the bloody thing off now," someone else shouted. "I'm sure someone would have heard it."

"I can't. Nothing happens when I push the button. It's been activated."

Liz took a deep breath and exhaled slowly. Mike looked up at the ceiling. *Maybe I could get through there?* They had to endure the ringing noise for the next few minutes when it finally stopped.

"It's stopped." One of the teenagers grinned.

"But why aren't we moving?"

Mike looked at his watch. It had been at least fifteen minutes since they had entered the elevator.

"I'm sure we'll start moving soon."

They stood in silence, staring at the doors in the hope that they would suddenly swing open or that the elevator would start moving again.

"Help, help!" Two of the teenagers began to pound their fists on the closed doors.

Suddenly, the elevator plunged downward and then came to a complete stop again.

"Careful!" Liz yelled. "Don't do that again. Do you want this thing to crash?"

The one teenager turned to glare at Liz. "What else do you suggest, lady?"

"Everybody calm down," Mike said. He then leaned closer to Liz and spoke softly. "I'm going to try my luck through the ceiling. Many elevators have a false ceiling. I should be able to theoretically stand on top of this elevator."

"What then?"

"I'll figure it out."

Before she could answer the emergency lights flickered and the elevator became dark.

CHAPTER 101

A few moments later the emergency lights in the elevator flickered on again. Before Mike could hoist himself towards the ceiling, the elevator chugged into motion once more and all its occupants heaved a collective sigh of relief.

"Let's get the fuck outta here," said Mike as the doors opened on their floor.

They exited the elevator and raced down the corridor towards some more escalators in the distance. Liz was in front with Mike slightly behind her. They leapt up, two steps at a time, until they arrived at the third floor, where they were greeted by a host of armed guards and men in suits, all with earpieces, weapons, and some even with bullet-proof vests.

Mike's chest was tight as he tried to catch his breath. He reached for his asthma pump from his jacket pocket and before he could even haul it out the armed guards had aimed their guns at them.

"Stop where you are!" barked a tall red-haired officer in front.

"I'm just—" Mike was about to explain that he was pulling out an asthma pump, not a weapon, when another guard started shouting.

"Keep your hands where we can see them!"

"It's not what you think," Mike said.

"Put your hands in the air. Now!"

"I'm CIA."

"This area has been cordoned off. Authorized personnel only."

"I am authorized," Mike spat. "Which part of CIA don't you fucking understand?"

"Let me see your access cards." A tall red haired officer stopped them.

"It's an emergency!" Liz said.

"Let me see your cards." Two of the officers were slowly moving towards them.

"Sure," said Mike as he fumbled through his pockets. A minute went by, and he couldn't find his ID card. Another minute. Then another minute.

Nothing. Mike rummaged through all his pockets and then came to a horrific realization. He had dropped his ID at Michelle's house.

———

As President Rafferty began his speech, Sol Arendse surveyed the room from a clear round window on one of the doors to the kitchen situated next to the stage. From his vantage point, he could see the entire room. He had already been through his checklist and everything was in order, from the carefully placed menus, to the shining chandeliers, and the delicate layout of the buffet table. The tables had been laid and the food was ready to be carried out to the buffet tables once the president had completed his speech. The silk serviettes, silver candlesticks and Protea vases had already been placed on the tables and the polished cutlery shone brightly alongside the crystal glasses. The waiters had been briefed several times about the pomp and ceremony behind serving dinner to a presidential delegation and were all clothed in pristine white shirts and black cotton pants.

Sol was so meticulous in his planning and so methodical in his execution that he rarely failed to ensure a smooth function. He beamed. That was after all why he had been designated to coordinate this fine function for the presidential visit. Sol stared at the crowd. Their gazes were focused on the podium where the president was waving his hands in the air and grinning broadly.

Sol was proud at how well everything had come together. So much food, he thought. He had lost a few hours because of the smashing of his car window, but once he returned after getting it fixed, everything had seemed to fall into place.

As Sol scrutinized the area, his warm glow turned into a look of horror. While all the food and cutlery had been laid out, it dawned on Sol that there were no drinks anywhere in the room. While alcohol and soft drinks could be ordered from the numerous waiters, there were supposed to be bottles of mineral water on all the tables.

And the president, Sol gasped! There was no water for the president. How embarrassing. Sol rushed back into the depths of the kitchen. Someone's head would roll for this. He couldn't believe it. What an oversight. How could he not have noticed this sooner? Everything else had been moved up from the storage rooms. Why not the water?

"Why is there no water on the tables?" Sol yelled. "Ernest, I'm going to *moer* you! Go get the water now. What will the president think? Esme and Riedewaan, go with him. Run!"

Sol wiped his brow as they raced off to get the water bottles. How could they not have brought in the water? He sighed. This certainly wasn't a job for the fainthearted!

———

"The president is in danger!" Mike snapped.

"What?" the officer asked incredulously. "We have the tightest security here.

There's no chance anything could have penetrated our system."

"Just let us go in. I have clearance. There's no time to lose."

"Well, it doesn't look like you have clearance," said the officer.

Mike tried to push past him but he held his arm.

"What is your name, officer?" Mike demanded.

"You can call me Mac."

"Mac, is Shadow working here tonight?"

Mac looked at Mike but didn't say anything. His look told Mike he was thinking, *He knows Shadow?*

"Where is Shadow? He can vouch that I'm part of the CIA."

Mac remained motionless.

"How would I have known that Shadow is even here?" said Mike. "How would I even know to use the guy's nickname, Shadow?"

"I don't know," said Mac. His weapon had lowered slightly.

"Very well, Mac. If something does happen to the president, would you really like to be the one cited for obstructing anything which could result in the prevention of a terror attack on the president occurring?"

Mac shifted uneasily. "I'm going to get hold of my supervisor," he declared. He turned away and spoke some words into a small microphone on his shirt collar.

"Make it quick," Liz pleaded. "Time's of the essence."

More guards approached while Mac waited for a response from whomever he had contacted. Liz and Mike were now completely surrounded.

"The guy I need clearance from is just in the middle of something," said Mac. "I've been told he will get back to me in the next ten or fifteen minutes."

"That's too long," said Mike as he inhaled his pump. His chest was still very tight.

"That's our only option," said Mac firmly. "If you want to get through then you'll just have to wait."

Mike looked at his watch. They really couldn't afford to wait for fifteen minutes. He didn't have time for red tape and bureaucracy at the best of times. He certainly didn't have time for it now. He thought back to his various training camps and intelligence seminars over the years. One of the rules that stood out in his mind was when you can't go through the normal channels and when all doors are seemingly closed, there is only one thing to do. Improvise.

"Make a run for it when you can," he leaned forward and whispered to Liz. "You'll be on your own, but I'll catch up with you later."

Liz nodded.

Mike turned to face Mac. "I can't wait any longer!" he shouted. "Let us in now or you'll be held accountable."

"I've already told you how it has to be," Mac said slowly.

"Well take this," Mike said and quickly swung his fist into Mac's jaw. Mac, despite all his own training in combat and VIP protection, did not react fast enough to the oncoming fist. In a situation like that, split seconds make all the difference, and Mac saw Mike's fist jam into his face a split second too late. He went flying to the ground while Mike turned and gave a flying karate kick to the two guards who had jumped forward trying to lure Mike to the ground.

The remaining officers leapt onto Mike and after a tussle they fell to the ground, hitting each other like angry school kids in a playground brawl. They rolled a few meters down as Mac resurfaced and along with the other guards ran after them.

———

In the furor Liz had been forgotten. Without even a glance again in their direction she sprinted past the entrance they had been guarding and ran along the winding passage that she hoped would lead her to the banquet room.

CHAPTER 102

Liz sprinted down the corridor without even a glance behind her. Soon she arrived at two large doors. A sign on the wall said "Banquet Wing" with a large arrow pointing in the direction beyond the doors. Liz pushed open the one door and rushed down the next passage, turned left into yet another corridor and then sprinted all the way down to one of the main doors to the banquet room. She knocked into another Secret Service agent patrolling the corridors. Mike was obviously still distracting the other guards, Liz thought. Otherwise this Secret Service agent would have been notified and ready for her.

"Can I help you?" asked the agent, who looked surprised at the sudden visitor.

"I'm looking for the banquet room."

"This is the back part." The agent nodded to the doors behind him. "The kitchens are there."

"Do they go through to the banquet room directly?"

"Yes, but you can't go in there. Are you staff?"

"No, but it's urgent."

"I don't know who let you in to this section but if you need to go to the banquet room you have to go in the proper way."

"I don't have time for this!" Liz said.

"Can I see your access card please?"

"It's an emergency, there's no time."

"Ma'am, I'm just following protocol."

"To hell with protocol," said Liz and kicked the agent in his groin. He clearly wasn't expecting it and doubled over in pain. Liz wasted no time barging through the doors into the kitchen.

"Take this bottled water to the pressie," Sol barked at a nearby waiter. The waters had all been brought up from the storeroom. "Okay, guys, let's start putting the bottled waters on those back tables near where we keeping the *koeksusters*."

The president had just made another good point about investing in Africa and paused as the crowd applauded again. They certainly were enjoying the speech, and why shouldn't they? He had the best speechwriting team the presidency had seen in decades.

Rafferty smiled gratefully at the waiter who appeared on the stage with a tray containing a bottle of mineral water and a crystal glass.

"I thought you were waiting until I dehydrate," he joked to the now very nervous waiter.

"Sorry, Mr President, sir, they only just realized they had forgotten to bring the water bottles through."

"You can take the glass back; I'll just drink from the bottle."

"Yes, Mr President."

The waiter scurried off while Rafferty placed the water bottle on the podium in front of him and continued to talk to his audience.

"I was starting to think that this might only be a cash bar!" he joked again as the crowd laughed. "Water under the bridge!"

The crowd broke into more laughter while the president slowly started to unscrew the lid. "This bottle is just like the budget proposals in congress," he said while the crowd waited for him to continue. "It's watertight!" The audience broke out into further guffaws of laughter. The president beamed at the crowds. He certainly was on a roll. He was known for his sense of humor, and had been excited to bring his gift of always being able to make a good pun to the White House. He put the lid onto the podium and lifted the open bottle of mineral water into the air.

"My case for investing in Africa is clear!" He held up the clear bottle to further laughter and applause. It was a standard five hundred-milliliter water bottle and the Madat Water emblem was emblazoned on the plastic. Another sticker had been placed onto the water bottle, just like the rest of the water bottles that had been stored in the storeroom. The sticker simply said "Approved" and the word appeared next to a stamp of the White House. It was a standard sticker used for the banquet meaning that the product, in this case the water, had been scrutinized and then approved by the Secret Service as being safe for consumption by the president or anyone in his delegation.

The agent recovered quickly from his blow and charged after Liz through the doors into the kitchen. The area was hot and steamy. Various chefs and staff wearing aprons and hats were cooking furiously and tossing ingredients into different pans and pots.

"Stop that woman!" the agent yelled. He had gained ground and was almost within reach of Liz.

Liz darted down another row of sinks and deliberately knocked a stack of plates behind her.

"We got a situation in the kitchen," he mouthed into an audio piece clasped onto his lapel.

"The president's in danger!" shouted Liz.

The agent leapt over the pieces of plates like a high jumper at the Olympics. "I repeat. Urgent back-up needed in kitchen. Target heading towards Potus."

CHAPTER 103

Liz charged towards the doors leading to the banquet room. She could hear the applause. As she got to the doors, they were already opening as other bodyguards and Secret Service agents responded to the initial call for help. Liz dodged a tackle by one of them and managed to get half of her body out of the doorway into the banquet room.

"Don't drink the water," she screamed towards the podium on the stage at the other end of the room. "Don't drink the water! It's poisoned."

Amidst the din that had broken out at the sight of a frantic lady running towards the president and being chased by security officials, Liz's words were muffled. It did not matter what she was saying. As she entered the room, the president's security detail immediately surrounded the stage where Dan Rafferty had been cracking a barrage of puns. One of the president's bodyguards leapt towards the president and pushed him onto the floor, knocking the bottle of water from his hands in the process. They came crashing down while some of the guests screamed.

Guests gasped at this unexpected turn of events. Almost instantaneously, the rest of the private presidential security detail posted throughout the room had their guns pulled out and were aimed at various strategic points around the room. A waitress, unaware of what had just happened, made her way through the kitchen doors to find a gun pointed towards her. She screamed, dropped her tray and charged back into the kitchen.

Liz was now surrounded by a wall of Secret Service officers and South African police, and found at least seven guns being aimed at her.

"One more move, and we'll shoot," one of the officers said.

Liz stared at the stage. The president had been rushed out the room, blanketed in his security entourage. On the stage, the podium lay on the floor. And next to it was a spilled bottle of water. Liz fell to her knees and the tears started streaming down. She had done it. President Dan Rafferty was safe. She couldn't believe it. It was only as she saw the president lifting the water bottle to his lips that she had realized the plan. On the pages she had taken from Hank, she had seen pictures of a water bottle and the Madat emblem. Her tears continued to blind her as she became oblivious of what was happening in front of her.

"Nobody drink any of the water," a voice boomed through the microphone that the president had been speaking through seconds ago. "I repeat, do not drink any of the water in this room."

Liz smiled through her tears as she heard the voice of Mike Bonnington sound through the loudspeakers. Seconds later Bonnington was at Liz's side. "There's been a misunderstanding," he told the guards. "She's not a threat at all, she just saved President Rafferty's life."

"That's true indeed," a senior official appeared next to Mike.

Mike turned to look. "Shadow."

The official nodded at Mike. "Lots of explaining to do."

Mike nodded.

"But it seems a job well done."

For the first time in a long time, Mike found himself smiling.

"Please come with us," another man in a dark suit appeared next to Liz.

"It's fine," Mike gave Liz a nod of encouragement. "I'll join you shortly."

President Rafferty rode a whirlwind of emotions as he was carried out by his security detail. There's always something, he thought. You can't expect to be the most powerful man in the world and that nothing will ever happen to you.

Of course he had enjoyed his presidency so far, despite the fact that the job was the most stressful thing he had ever had to endure. He didn't know what he was in for until he was in it. But that applied to everything in life.

Bloody terrorists.

When is this all going to end?

The good thing about travel is that it always offers one the chance to look outside the box. This trip had given the president plenty to think about, and he was looking forward to getting back home and to getting stuck into his work again. The trip had been a welcome breath of fresh air, and he felt invigorated.

Until the point where some screaming lady had barged through the doors from the kitchen and mayhem had broken out. *What was she shouting? And how the hell did she get past security?* The knowledge that his life had almost ended there and then did not sit very well with him.

Fifteen minutes passed while Liz sat at a shiny mahogany table trying to give answers to three members of the Secret Service who were furiously scribbling down every word.

A knock on the open door caused them to all look up and the agents leapt to attention as President Rafferty entered the room. Liz stood up too.

"Sit, please." The president motioned with his hands.

"Good evening, Mr President"

"Your name again?" President Rafferty stared at Liz with a grin on his face.

"It's Liz, sir, Elizabeth Greene."

"Well, Elizabeth Greene, looks like I owe you one!"

"It was nothing, sir."

"Oh, it was something. I'll bet my ranch on that!"

"Yes, sir."

"So you do this often?"

"Do what, sir?"

"Oh enough with the sirs!" The president was still smiling.

"Yes, sir!"

"Well, do you do this often?"

"Do what?"

"Save people's lives like you saved mine tonight."

"I try my best." Liz smiled. She was sitting on her hands, hoping the president wouldn't see them shake.

"Well, I don't know where I would be if it wasn't for you. Not here, I can tell you that much!"

"I had some help! We were just lucky we got to you in time once we figured out what was happening."

"And you made it past my security. You outshone and out-jumped some of my top guards! Ever considered playing American football?"

"No, sir."

"Well, you'll have to come over to the USA some time and try it out."

"I like rugby, sir."

"Rugby?"

"Yes, it's very big in this country, and women's rugby is on the rise."

"We've got a few women's football leagues back home that will cry out to have jumpers like you."

A lady and two other men entered the room. They all wore dark suits. The lady walked up to President Rafferty and whispered something in his ear. The president nodded.

"I'm afraid we have to go now," he said to Liz. "But I would like to continue this conversation another time."

"Yes, sir."

Rafferty headed for the door and turned to look at Liz just before he exited.

"Thank you." He smiled at her.

Liz smiled back and then he was gone.

CHAPTER 104

Liz had just finished explaining to her interlocutors about how they had realized that President Rafferty's life was in danger. She described seeing the blueprints that Hank had left behind, and Nkosi being approached with the strange instruction to break a specific car window without a need to actually steal anything.

"There's someone else who wants to have a word with you," said Mike, popping his head around the door.

Liz looked up. "Another CIA member?"

"No, someone more exciting than that."

A few more of the security detail entered the room. They were surrounding someone, and as they all entered they scattered themselves, some to the left and some to the right.

Mike stepped out of the way. Liz's face froze when her eyes fell on her father.

"Dad?" She leapt up. "Is that really you?"

"Liz, my dear dear Liz."

Liz stared in shock as her father walked towards her. He held out his arms and pulled her towards him for a tight hug.

"Dad?"

"My precious baby!" Neither of them let go.

"I thought... I thought you were dead." Liz was sobbing. "Those bastards told me they'd killed you."

"I'm not going to go that easily," the professor smiled. "Not without a fight anyway."

"I can't believe you're here. I just can't believe it. I'm so blessed."

"I think I'm the one who's blessed," said Professor Greene. "I'm probably the luckiest man on earth to you have you as my daughter."

Liz continued to cry. "I'm sorry how things got between us."

"Don't apologize, it was my fault. I should never have let things get so out of hand."

"But I should have made sure we patched things up too."

"Don't be so hard on yourself. In any event, it's in the past now. We're both here and we can look forward to the future."

"How did you get here? How did you get away from them?"

"Long story," said the professor. "I'll tell you everything but let's wait until I'm home!"

"Okay." Liz sniffed.

"And well done for finding the microchip." The professor beamed. "I never had any doubt. If anyone can solve anything it's you."

"The chip..." Liz said brushing away some more tears. "I had it. I had it but then it was taken from me."

"Lost! And found again!" Professor Greene winked.

"What?"

"We've got the microchip back again. All thanks to your friend Tim."

Liz looked at her father, stunned. Here he was, alive and well, and he had just told her that her efforts had not been in vain. The microchip had been retrieved? By Tim?

She suddenly felt sapped of any last bit of energy that had been miraculously carrying her through the day. The tears now gushed down and her knees felt weak. She opened her mouth but couldn't say another word.

The professor placed his hand on his daughter's shoulder. "It's not every day that someone saves the President of the USA from getting killed," said Professor Greene. "Let alone my own daughter!"

EPILOGUE

It was a quiet sunny afternoon in Rondebosch. In the lounge of his home, Professor Greene held the microchip to the light just to make sure again that it was intact.

"See," he said and smiled at the computer screen. "No damage at all."

"I'm still always amazed that something so small can do so much," Professor Macmanus marveled.

"Isn't that the truth!"

The professors were chatting on Skype. Macmanus was back in the comforts of his study at the Institute of Noetic Sciences. He watched Professor Greene hold the microchip. It glinted in the light. The bottom part of it was shiny and flat. The top of it was silver and had a slight black groove circling around the edges. It looked like a mere torchlight battery to someone who didn't know any better.

Professor Greene lifted the black box off the table and turned it upside down. There was a small hole visible exactly how the Fox would have first seen it after Rafik stole it from the UCT campus.

"Still a neat fit," the professor observed. He glided the microchip through his fingers and although the chip was cold in his hands he almost didn't want to let it go. Then he carefully inserted the chip into the empty hole. Once he heard a soft click, he took a small black lid lying on the table and covered the microchip. There was another soft click and the bottom of the black box was now completely black. It was even hard to tell where the hole had been.

"And I assume that all the data and algorithms are intact?" Macmanus asked.

"Nothing lost at all."

The sound of a long whistle permeated the room.

"Nice one, Alex." Professor Greene looked up in the direction of the large steel cage hanging in the corner of the room. "He has, shall we say, a bird's eye view to everything."

"To absolutely everything?" Macmanus winked.

"Just the important stuff!"

"Time for nuts! Time for nuts!" They watched the parrot slowly guzzle some seeds as its claws clung tightly to a strip of wood stretched across its cage.

"I must say I was quite alarmed when I heard about the break-in at UCT." Macmanus had become serious.

"Me too. But I had very strong contingencies in place. As you know, I tend to be over cautious. It's sometimes a bad thing but when it comes to our work, well, what can I say!"

"Indeed!"

"All's well that ends well though."

"For now, I suppose," said Macmanus. "Until the next big criminal or terrorist decides they want the black box and microchip."

"I don't think it will come to that. In any event, we are going to move our systems to another location, and are going to completely revamp the security structures. And need I mention I'm working on a few other contingencies, just in case!" This time it was Professor Greene who winked.

"At least I can report back to the others that the experiment continues without delay and that everything remains intact," said Macmanus.

"Yes. As far as we're concerned, it's business as usual."

"It's an exciting time for us and for science."

"We're on the cusp of changing the world." Professor Greene nodded. "Soon the black box will be much more specific with future predictions. It will be a major breakthrough for humanity."

"Hopefully a brighter future for all this world's inhabitants."

"We can only hope. One thing is certain is that whatever world we are heading towards, there's no turning back, for better or worse."

"Unless we work out and give substance to those time travel theories!"

The professors both laughed.

"Anyway, Eric, I best be off. Got some lamb chops on the fire that need my attention."

"I almost want to fly back to South Africa for those!" Macmanus grinned.

Professor Greene closed his screen and placed the black box on the side table before heading into the garden.

Liz was sitting on the patio chatting to Tim.

"Wow, these chops look terrific," said Tim.

"There's nothing like a South African braai," the professor said and grinned as he poured the entire bottle of barbeque marinade over the meat.

"I'll have to come back again so I can have more," Tim declared.

"Well, who knows if anyone will invite you?" Liz smiled.

"I got a hunch that I just might get that invitation."

"Get ready for some tasty tender *boerewors* as well." Professor Greene threw a string of traditional South African sausage onto the fire.

"Wow, how am I going to eat everything?"

"I'm sure you'll find space," said Liz.

"I'm sure I will!"

A loud chime emanated from inside.

"Doorbell," Liz said.

"Would you mind getting it?" said the Professor. "I can't leave the braai."

"Sure."

"Need some company?" Tim ventured.

"I think I'll be fine, it's just the front door."

"Suit yourself!" Tim stood up and offered to help the professor turn the meat.

Liz peered through the peephole of the front door. Outside, she could see five black X5 BMWs. They had blue lights on top that were flashing even though the engines of the cars had been switched off. A few uniformed guards leaned next to the end vehicle. One of them pulled out a cigarette and lit it.

Standing at Professor Greene's front door was a well-dressed lady. Liz couldn't make out the ID card that was clipped to her jacket, but it looked like Lindiwe Noxo, the Deputy President. An entourage from the South African government had come to pay Professor Greene a visit. Liz had a sick feeling in her stomach.

The doorbell rang again.

"Liz, are you going to answer the door?" Professor Greene called.

"Yes, sorry. I think it's the government possibly?"

"The government?" Professor Greene shouted from the fire. "Well, for goodness sake, let's find out what they want."

Liz turned the key and opened the door. "Hello?" she said to the lady.

"Is this the home of Professor Greene?"

"It is." Liz stared at the lady and the men hovering around the BMWs.

"I wish to chat to Professor Greene and to his daughter."

"I'm his daughter. What's this about?"

"Can we chat inside?" the lady asked.

"Oh sure, sorry, come in." Liz opened the door wide and beckoned for the lady to come in. "What about them?"

"They'll be fine where they are." The lady smiled.

"Come through." Liz led the lady through the lounge into the back garden. "Someone to see you."

Professor Greene looked up through the smoke. He blinked. "Tim, can you watch the meat? If it starts to burn, then please just lift it off and put on this plate here."

"After everything that's happened, I'm sure that lifting some sausage won't be a problem!" Tim grinned.

The professor asked the lady to have a seat in the lounge and Liz joined them.

"I'm here to speak to you about the night your scientific experiment was stolen from the University of Cape Town."

"Oh," said the professor. "Everything has been sorted out since then, although you won't believe everything that's happened since it all began."

"I'm sure it's a very interesting story and I'm glad it has all worked out."

"Yes, and I have my daughter here to thank. The situation might have ended very differently if it hadn't been for Liz's help and for her sound intuition."

"I'm sure!" said Lindiwe. "Anyway, the night that thug who worked for the terrorist broke into the science faculty, well, there was a security guard on duty whom it seems got caught in the crossfire."

The professor went red. "Yes?" He quivered but maintained a calm stare as he remembered how he had dragged the body of the security guard away from the area where the black box had been kept. *Just as well people can't read thoughts properly yet. Otherwise she might have had a pair of handcuffs in her hand for obstruction of justice and interfering with a crime scene.*

"While the security guard in question was doing his patrol, he must have spotted the burglar and that was when he got shot."

"Terrible," said the professor. "I hope he stays in jail for a very long time."

"I hope so too," said Liz.

"There were two shots. It seems that the guard died instantly after the first bullet. The second bullet was more precautionary. We think the thug was just making sure he couldn't be identified."

"Even though he was ultimately caught on the outskirts of Newlands forest," the professor said.

"The guard's name was Moses," Lindiwe said. "Moses Noxo."

"Your surname is Noxo too!" Liz exclaimed.

"Are you related?" Professor Greene asked.

"Yes, I am his great niece."

"We really are sorry for your loss."

"Thank you. He was a very good man. Very noble and dedicated to his job and his family. He leaves behind a strong legacy, and we'll all miss him."

"I'm glad I now know his name," said the professor. "He died trying to prevent our scientific equipment from being stolen from the faculty."

"Yes, indeed," said Lindiwe. "But I'm here to tell you that the South African government commends you on your breakthroughs and stands by your research."

"Thank you," said the professor.

"And we will be increasing our funding for science and technology when the next budgets are drawn up. You can be sure of that."

"Thank you." The professor smiled gratefully.

"Thank you, Professor Greene," said Lindiwe. "We're proud to have scientists of your caliber being at the forefront of global scientific developments."

Lindiwe turned to Liz. "And you, Elizabeth, on behalf of the South African government I would like to thank you for your heroic efforts in helping prevent the assassination of President Rafferty."

"We were just lucky everything worked out." Liz smiled.

The Deputy President stood up. "We'll be in touch. Now if you will excuse me, I have some urgent matters to attend to."

"Can I offer you some lunch first?"

"Some other time," the Deputy President said and smiled.

Professor Greene showed her out while Liz went to see how Tim was doing with the braai.

"Not a bad job," Liz peered over Tim's shoulder and looked at the meat.

"It's actually quite nice to relax around a fire," said Tim. "Always something therapeutic about the flames." He placed the braai tongs on a small fold out wooden table and edged closer to Liz. "Especially because things have been so crazy since I set foot in your country."

"Wrong place, wrong time?" Liz smiled.

"Hmm, maybe more like right place, right time." Tim's face had moved even closer to Liz's.

"Ah you're just saying that."

"A man needs adventure in his life!"

"Well, you certainly got one!"

"Maybe I should come back here again then!"

"Best you check that I'm actually here and not overseas myself," Liz said and chuckled. "Maybe we could meet up in London?"

"You're going to the UK?"

"Soon," said Liz. "Piers Morgan wants to interview me."

"Wow!" Tim was in awe. He gazed into her eyes. They were twinkling. The situation had been so tense that he had almost forgotten how beautiful her eyes were and how they lured him in and captivated him completely.

The breeze picked up and Tim pulled Liz right towards him. He stroked her hair and leaned in to kiss her. A quick, almost shy kiss at first. They looked at each other again and then he kissed her properly. They stood, oblivious of the world they were in, and lost themselves in each other's arms.

Liz had been trying to keep her guard up since this handsome clumsy man had entered her life, and despite all her efforts not to fall for him she was actually falling deep.

They stopped kissing and she stared into Tim's eyes. They didn't say anything and held each other. A bee buzzed in the distance and crickets chirped in a nearby bush. But Liz and Tim remained oblivious of the surrounding sounds and continued to be consumed by their moment.

I can't believe this is happening to me. Liz wanted to pinch herself. *Am I dreaming?*

"This feels right." Tim almost read her mind.

"I guess." *Yes, it feels right! It feels amazing!*

"Sorry to interrupt!"

Tim and Liz jumped. They turned to see Mike Bonnington, who looked unusually happy.

"The prof let me in," he pointed inside. "What's with all the sirens outside?"

"Government business!" Liz smiled.

"I'll bet! Never a dull moment around here!"

"What brings you here?"

"Just came to see how you all doing." Mike grinned. "And to say goodbye.

I'm flying home tonight."

"Well, you'll just have to join us for lunch first," said Liz.

"You bet! Smells awesome."

"Everything sorted out with the criminals?" Tim asked.

"Yip." Mike took a chair and placed it on the grass near the braai. "All the criminals involved have been taken care of, both relating the theft of the black box and the assassination attempt of President Rafferty."

"We understand that the poisoned water bottles would have been consumed by all the guests at the banquet too?" Tim said.

"Yes," said Mike. "That's what the Fox, or should I say Hank, was hoping for. He had been planning this terrorist event ever since it was announced that Rafferty would be visiting Cape Town."

"But why? What were his motives to destroy so many lives?" Liz offered them some garlic rolls, a popular starter snack at braais.

"He had his issues with American imperialism and interference in the Middle East," said Mike. "The usual stuff. But there was more to it as well. He wanted to plan this huge attack and he wanted the black box before it happened so he could see for himself if it would be predicted."

"He'd obviously been watching Liz's dad for a long time," said Tim.

"Yes, he had bugged Professor Greene's house and was therefore always in tune with the prof's latest research." Mike chewed on a piece of the garlic roll. "Hank was also very interested in having the box for himself. Sure, there would always be the temptation to sell it to the highest bidder, but it's not like he needed the money."

"He wanted to have power." Tim nodded. "I suppose those who know what the future holds can try and control it."

"Something like that," Mike said.

"You think you know people," said Tim. "Who would have thought that my college buddy would turn into a criminal mastermind terrorist?"

"Things are never as they seem."

"And the others who were involved?"

"Hank preferred to outsource. That was part of his modus operandi. He often used Rafik for various projects and he also hired Sindy, even though she had no idea she was actually married to the Fox himself!"

"And when the police got to Hank's apartment, Sindy was still locked up in the room I left her in," Liz said, feeling a great sense of satisfaction.

"The Fox planted the fake bomb in Rondebosch so attention would be diverted away from the Convention Centre when that crucial delivery was being made. The Fox had also instructed Sindy to hire her half-brother, Wahied, to bring the poisoned water. Obviously the fact that their family made bottled water was a no-brainer. And with printing technology as it is today, it was easy for Hank to forge the Presidential Seal stickers that were then put onto the Madat water bottles."

"It all seems to easy," said Liz. "How come intelligence didn't pick anything up?"

"He was that good," said Mike. "But you guys were even better!"

"At least it all worked out," said Liz.

"Hank even hired a professional photographer to take pictures of the bodies after Rafferty and the guests would have consumed the water," said Mike. "The aim was to show the world the images of death. It would have been a terrorist victory for sure."

"Anyone else involved?" Tim asked.

"Those were the main players," said Mike. "A few individuals were hired to help in the Convention Centre. Some other guy was also hired to get the street kid to break the car window, so that Sindy could take over proceedings at the exact time Wahied would deliver the water."

"Nkosi!" said Liz.

"Speaking of Nkosi, what happened with your friend?"

"Michelle's okay," said Liz. "They were able to get hold of Eric Simms as he was leaving his hotel. He understood the predicament Michelle had been in and was sympathetic to her cause. He actually called her last night to tell her he will fund her project, as it's a noble cause."

"Awesome!" said Mike.

Some fat from the *boerewors* fell into the fire, causing a surge of flames to leap up. Liz reached for the stainless steel metal jug on the table and flicked some water over the flames. They sat basking in the warm African sun and stared at the fire, all in deep reflection of the events of the last few days.

"Well that looks almost ready!" Professor Greene appeared. "Good job, everyone!"

"I'm thirsty. Anyone need anything from inside?" said Tim.

———

The others indicated that they didn't. Tim made his way inside to the lounge area. He looked at his watch. *Just in time for the news headlines!* He grabbed the remote.

"It's that time of the year again! If you've just joined us we're in the middle of an amazing live concert to celebrate the life of President Nelson Mandela," the commentator said. "This music spectacular is being televised live all around the world."

"It is indeed a coming together of many great artists to celebrate and commemorate South Africa's Madiba," the other commentator added. "We've just seen Bono give a short speech after U2 performed, and now South Africa's popular White Zulu himself, Johnny Clegg, back from his sold-out tour in France, is performing with his band as they sing 'Great Heart'. What a spectacle!"

Tim reached for one of the lemonade bottles in the ice bucket on the granite counter top. He screwed off the lid and headed back outside to Liz, Professor Greene and Mike.

As Tim went out, he did not notice that the black box on the side table had begun to move slightly. By the time he was in the garden, the black box was vibrating and buzzing frantically.

AUTHOR'S NOTES

The black box, or Random Event Generator, is real. There are approximately 65 of these devices scattered across the world; the exact locations of many of them remain secret.

The Global Consciousness Project is real. The GCP continues to break the boundaries of traditional science as it observes and analyzes data from the black boxes and their profound impact on and implications for humanity.

All events, information, and predictions relating to the black box in this novel are true. The only exception is the microchip, which is a work of fiction.

All the history, facts and research about the black box that appear in this novel come from the official GCP website: http://www.global-mind.org

The Institute of Noetic Sciences is real. It serves as the logistical home of the GCP, which is directed by Dr Roger Nelson from his home office in Princeton. The GCP is not a project of Princeton University.

ACKNOWLEDGMENTS

To my wife, Dana, for all her support, patience and encouragement. This book is dedicated to her.

To Jerry Cleaver, whose strategies and insights in his book *Immediate Fiction* helped me overcome my writer's block and change my approach to story writing.

To Guy Kawasaki and Shawn Welch, whose book *APE: Author, Publisher, Entrepreneur—How to Publish a Book* finally confirmed for me that the publishing revolution is indeed underway.

To my parents, Jack and Leonie, for encouraging me to write and to keep writing and reading since as far back as I can remember.

To my editor, Claire Strombeck of Strombeck Literary, for her sound input, editing and clarity.

And a special thank you to:

Dr Roger Nelson of the Global Consciousness Project, Jodi Ujimoto, David Ujimoto, Barbara Smith, Arthur Goldstuck, Jamie Murray, Henry Sudwarts, Shirley Sudwarts, Simon Hart, Hope Clark, Dan Blackman

Cover design by Ebook Launch

Ebook edition formatting by LK E-Book Formatting Service

Print edition formatting by By Your Side Self-Publishing

Author photograph by Jamie Murray

www.bevanfrank.com

ABOUT THE AUTHOR

Bevan Frank was born in Cape Town, South Africa. His love of writing and creating characters began in his early childhood where he wrote some short stories for his school library. Bevan has a BA degree in English and Political Studies as well as a postgraduate LLB degree, both from the University of Cape Town.

After qualifying as an attorney Bevan opted down the path of writing and editing. He has worked as a business magazine editor, journalist, writer, plain language practitioner and communications consultant. His articles have been published in numerous publications locally and globally.

Bevan currently works in corporate communications. He lives in London, England, with his wife and children. *The Mind of God* is his first novel.

Made in the USA
Columbia, SC
08 October 2018